ENO TIME
notes on the apocalypse

"G.A. Matiasz has created a charged, political, and very readable novel in End Time, jump-cutting P.O.V. from character to character, pulling the reader into the plot as each character, quick as a Polaroid, develops into a fascinating persona."

Factsheet Five

"This is not a happy vision of ourselves and the world we maintain. But it is an honest and compelling one. End Time, Notes On The Apocalypse is excellent speculative fiction. Full of heart and horror. Get it. Read it."

Pickles McGurck
Maximum Rock'n'Roll

"End Time ... is scarily realistic, fast paced, and detailed in vision. ... I don't know of any future fiction this chillingly real published since the debut of Gibson's Neuromancer. ... If Gibson preceded Matiasz, it must be admitted that Matiasz has topped him."

J.G. Eccarius
The Stake

"Matiasz constructs a fascinating and believable technoBaroque California in End Time. ... (He) has woven a zeitgeistish thread into the web of futurology. ... It's a compelling read once you get started. AK Press couldn't have sent a better book at the right time."

EdMar
The Lumpen Times

"This is, at the very least, the novel of the year. The characters really take you along with them. So realistic, it ought to give all sorts of saboteurs inspiration on possibilities for what can be done."

Irreverend David Crowbar
Editor, Popular Reality

"End Time is an engaging, thoroughly realistic novel that might very well frighten you into studying the political agenda of our leaders a bit more closely come November."

Pirate Writings

"Ackerman showed up, and Bennett - and some guy named G.A. Matiasz whose SF/Oakland-based early 21st-century thriller called End Time I'm currently in the middle of and finding not only highly professional but intelligent, a rare combination in fiction. It's fun reading, too!"

Bob Grumman
Small Press Review

"Although supposedly set in 2007, this intense new novel from a Maximum Rock'n'Roll columnist reads frighteningly real today."

Left Bank Distribution

"While dealing with future events that may not be, enough of the action takes place in a believable world to call this a 90's version of M. Gilliland's classic The Free. Over-all, well-written, near future science fiction novel brimming with believable characters in an all-too-familiar setting. Pick this one up and you probably won't be able to put it down 'til it's over!"

Dan
Profane Existence

"Do ya like subversion? How about nuclear terrorism? Good good, glad to see your priorities are set straight. End Time is packed full of goodies like this & much more. ... A highly entertaining & interesting read, with chapters that may soon be headlines."

Bruce Young
Cyber-Psycho's AOD

"Solidly-crafted thriller ... Provocative political discussion and 'what if's' raise the book's intellectual value without spoiling it as a good read."

TapRoot Reviews

"End Time: Notes On The Apocalypse is a very good book of future fiction, bordering on science fiction. ... (It's) a fun book to read ... Thick, chunky and tasty ... Well done, and well worth reading."

"Cookie" Mahoney
Gene Splice

"The plot is straight forward thriller-cum-cyberpunk ... (I)t's fast-paced and fun in the way only a fervent anarchist rant can be."

Q zine

"End Time presents as an apocalyptic future-fiction, but exhibits all the characteristics of a realistic psychological novel ... (Matiasz) extends current trends ingeniously to provide a context for characters winning their individual illuminations and liberations. ... (H)is novel (as Marge Piercy did for my 60's...) will bring the reader up to speed (or some approximation thereof) on contemporary anarchist ideas."

Iven Lourie
Inner Journeys

ENTER THE WORLD OF END TIME!

END TIME
Notes On The Apocalypse

G.A. MATIASZ

1994 · A.K. Press
Edinburgh · London · San Francisco

Front cover, back cover and spine built by John Yates at Stealworks.

END TIME
Notes on the Apocalypse

First printing January, 1994
Second printing September, 1996

Published by:

AK Press
P.O. Box 12766
Edinburgh, Scotland
EH8 9YE, Great Britain

AK Press
P.O. Box 40682
San Francisco, CA
94140-0682, USA

ISBN 1-873176-24-4

Library of Congress Catalogue Card Number: 93-74104

British Library Cataloguing in Publication Data
Matiasz, G. A.
    End Time: Notes on the Apocalypse
    I. Title
    823.914 [F]
    ISBN 1-873176-24-4

Printed in the United States of America

For the memory of my father and mother, who were always there for me. And, for 'Bump City.'

AUTHOR'S DISCLAIMER:
This is a work of fiction. Aside from the use of a few well known public personalities and current events to anchor down various parts of the plot, and except for Bob Barley, all of the characters and events in this book are fictional. They may be inspired by, but they are not identical representations of occurrences and people in real life. All are hybrids, composites and combinations. None are exact renditions. Just as the descriptions of southern Mexico are influenced by Spain from 1936 to 1939, and the portrait of the Bay Area in the 21st century is an extrapolation from that region in the 20th, so too are this book's characters and events informed by reality, but are not documentations of reality. Any author who claims that his or her characters, events, situations and settings are entirely fictional is lying through his or her teeth. All writing is based upon experience. It cannot be otherwise. In turn, those who insist on seeing particular individuals or events exactly portrayed in the people and occurrences detailed in this work have better imaginations than I do.

AUTHOR'S THANKS:
I wrote the first draft of this book long hand in four exhilarating months. I spent the next year and nine months rewriting it, an excruciating process even with word processing software and computers. Several people provided invaluable aid in editing, critiquing, and commenting on this work. I would like to thank Sharon Gregory, David Nestle, Karen Bennett, Karl Bates and Cathy Drake for their substantive help in making this book possible. I would also like to thank Tim Gonzales for his cover artwork and Kim Carlyle for her work on the book's maps. Thanks to Randall Cornish for his rock-steady friendship. Finally, thanks go to Bob Barley and the entire Chula Vista scene for showing me what is possible.

AUTHOR'S ACKNOWLEDGMENTS:
I have relied upon the literature of the Spanish 1936-39 Revolution in particular and the Spanish Anarchist experience in general to flesh out the Mixtecan and Mayapan Liberated Territories of southern Mexico in writing this novel. Gaston Leval ("Collectives in the Spanish Revolution"), Sam Dolgoff ("The Anarchist Collectives"), Murray Bookchin ("The Spanish Anarchists"), Burnett Bolton ("The Spanish Civil War"), and Ronald Fraser ("Blood of Spain") were invaluable in this regard. I have tried to acknowledge my other influences in the body of this work.

As for you, Daniel, keep secret the message and seal the book until the end time; many shall fall away and evil shall increase.

Daniel 12:4
The New American Bible

Ikkyu, the Zen master, was very clever even as a boy. His teacher had a precious teacup, a rare antique. Ikkyu happened to break this cup and was greatly perplexed. Hearing the footsteps of his teacher, he held the pieces of the cup behind him. When the master appeared, Ikkyu asked: "Why do people have to die?"

"This is natural," explained the older man. "Everything has to die and has just so long to live."

Ikkyu, producing the shattered cup, added: "It was time for your cup to die."

"Time To Die: 101 Zen Stories"
Zen Flesh, Zen Bones
Compiled by Paul Reps

But the day of the Lord will come as a thief in the night; in the which the heavens shall pass away with a great noise, and the elements shall melt with a great fervent heat, the earth also and the works that are therein shall be burned up.

II Peter 3:10
The Bible: King James Version

(may a lost god damballah, rest or save us...

"Black Dada Nihilismus"
The Dead Lecturer
LeRoi Jones

Contents

TO THE READER:
A variety of historical documents have been included throughout the story that follows for readers unfamiliar with the time. The experienced reader knowledgeable in the period may wish to pass over these portions of the work.

PERMISSION:
Excerpts from *The Amok World Almanac*, *'New Romantic' Historiography: A Survey* by Allen Meltzer, the BBC Special Report "Modern Counterinsurgency: The Weapons of War" with Nijal Thomas, "Musing on the Nature of Cybernetic CoEvolution" from Hamran Mossoud's *California Diaries*, and *None Dare Call It Betrayal* by Lieutenant-Colonel David Burns have been reprinted by permission of Electrostraca.

PALIMPSEST

Kate Parnell stopped crawling when she reached a three-way split in the air duct. The cramped, pitch black space reverberated with the rush of cool, sterile air from behind her. She leaned her sweaty right cheek against the duct's cold, invisible metal and closed her eyes. A deeper dark in the dark.

Hail Mary, full of grace...

The Stanford undergraduate senior reached into the backpack she had been pushing ahead of her for the flashlight. She should be praying to Gaia, the Mother Goddess Earth. Yet childhood ritual, permeated with incense and candle smoke, invariably resurfaced under stress. No headaches, and no depression, just the clean adrenaline from the clear danger of her blessed task. The flashlight's beam, once she flicked it on, momentarily blinded her, shining brightly against the muted blue duct metal. Kate had wormed her way into the bowels of Stanford University's new Experimental Biology Complex, where they created monsters. Biogenetic engineering. Gene splicing. Playing God. Whatever people called it, it meant taking Mother Earth's sublime life forms and changing them. Barbarously. Horribly. Dispassionately.

...The Lord is with you...

Next she pulled the bomb apparatus from her pack and took care to set it on the air duct's vibrating floor. Gene had purchased the CTX plastique from Sulawesi for Kate. Far more powerful than its Semtex H explosive cousin, it was now strung into a detonation frame. There were advantages to being the much doted upon daughter of America's fifteenth wealthiest man, Barry Parnell. Money had not been a problem. The switch that she unsnapped from a safety housing, when thrown, conducted the charge of a battery built into the apparatus, thus detonating the CTX. Soon, this abomination against Gaia, the Goddess, would be wiped off Her planet.

1

END TIME

...Blessed are you among women...

"This isn't working for me," Gene had said, after the third time he slept with her. He had been her section teaching assistant for her required World Civilizations course. She had waited until the History Department had given Gene the boot before inviting him to spend the night the first time. So, they had remained friends. She continued working with him in the Black and Red Bookstore, as well as the Stanford Anti-War Coalition, always keeping the door open, hoping against hope that he would want her again. The sparkling, blinding migraines started then. Kate had taken on the Coalition's riskiest direct actions, trying to hold Gene's attention and, miraculously, never getting caught. Trying to impress him with her militancy. The depression descended when Gene began seeing Serena. It had been all she could do to drag herself out of bed to take part in the brief actions he had asked her to join. His vibrant voice on the phone invariably, though only momentarily lifted the heavy gray pall that had enveloped her life. She had told him: "The CTX is for the Puertorriqueño underground."

...And blessed is the fruit of your womb, Jesus...

Kate's younger brother, Patrick, was the product of genetic manipulation. Doctors had removed the gene responsible for muscular dystrophy from her mother's egg, replacing it with a harmless place holder gene before fertilizing the egg with her father's sperm. She had been old enough for her parents to tell her what was going on, and young enough to confuse the procedure with grandmother Maureen's stories about changelings. After Pat's birth, her recurrent childhood nightmare in the cavernous Parnell Pennsylvania mansion involved watching her brother change before her eyes. His ears folding back into points, his canine teeth elongating, his fingernails sharpening... Of course, she had accepted the 1990's conspiracy theory that AIDS was a genetically engineered virus released, accidentally or on purpose, from some research laboratory. And at the depth of her depression, sometimes too weak and nauseated to get out of bed for days, Kate had seen things; artificial organisms creeping out from under the door, through the cracks between floor and walls, even floating in the air.

...Holy Mary, mother of God...

Satisfied that everything was ready, Kate snapped off the flashlight and welcomed the comforting dark. She closed her eyes, then pressed hot flesh against cold metal. She smiled, knowing that her deliverance was close at hand. The hammering depression shattered, the electric headaches dispelled once she had decided to eliminate Stanford's biogenetic labs. Her heart now raced from having broken into the guarded building undetected, through the ventilation system, as well as from the effort to get this far. Otherwise, she was at peace. In synch with

PALIMPSEST

the Goddess. Her troubled mind stilled. Pooled down into communion. Gaia.

...Pray for us sinners...

She had vowed to love, honor and protect the Mother visiting an Oregon Wicca on a Spring Equinox four years ago, long before knowing Gene. Surely he would recognize her heroism, after he read her letter. Pat, wherever her true brother was, would understand why she needed to do this. She reached for the switch, through the shuddering black...

...Now...

...And hit the toggle. White light. Intense. Pure. One.

***

Harold Nishimura knew that something was out of place as soon as he entered his room. He rented in a graduate student house leased by his good friend Gene, a Stanford graduate dropout. His door had a lock. But the flimsy, hollow, particle board barrier was a joke. He had stumbled into it more than once, intoxicated or simply clumsy, and the door had popped open. Popped the lock. Easily. And now, something was missing.

He carefully rested his briefcase on his orderly desk, next to his IBM clone, and pushed his chair into the middle of an equally orderly room before sitting. He minutely scanned his desk and the shelves around it. He did not have a photographic memory; just an excellent, systematic one. Little things were ever-so-slightly off position, as if moved and returned to their places in an effort to cover some search. He had it, after fifteen minutes. He checked a gap in his computer diskette library with the library log he kept in his bottom desk drawer. But he already knew what had occupied the space. Three bundled diskettes—numbers 330 through 332—were gone.

"That's not what they wanted," he said, under his breath. The gap in his library was too wide. Harold opened his briefcase, fished out another bundle of three diskettes—numbers 333 through 335—and tossed them on his desk.

The missing diskettes had contained his project done at the beginning of his second year as a doctoral student in Stanford's Mathematics Department; Harold's attempt to impress his academic liege lord, Professor Arthur Linscott. His original Hawking Transpositions. The very first instance of the Periodic Matrix. He had backups, of course. But those originals possessed bittersweet memories for him.

An accidental Grail he had let slip through his fingers.

He had come upon Stephen Hawking's half dozen equations over a year and a half ago. They were an unorthodox footnote to an end note in one of the late astrophysicist's more obscure treatises on the properties of matter approaching black hole singularities. He had transposed Hawking's esoteric mathematics into a long series of simpler differen-

3

END TIME

tial equations, which he had then converted into a computer simulation model using Stapledon 4.0's program analogs. Linscott had shrugged upon being presented with his graduate student's work, at the time. Then, Harold's professor had assigned him to install the Stapledon program into the Department's compunet, suggesting as well that he run some standard data bases through his simulation. Nishimura had plugged in a periodic table data base quantifying the properties of known elements. The Hawking Periodic Matrix had emerged as a consequence, initiating a profound transformation directly in elemental chemistry and indirectly throughout all of science.

Harold returned the library log to its drawer and tidied up after the thief. As he arranged things back into place, he visualized how the Periodic Matrix had first unfolded on the multimedia mainframe server's 40-inch HD CRT screen, when the periodic data hit his transpositions. It mapped out like a brightly colored, softly scintillating paper lantern chain. One that he might see at his uncle's San Francisco restaurant after a few too many beers. Two shimmering globes, strung together vertically, with a much smaller, third globe threaded two-thirds of the way up between them; the computer simulation's image of laced light turned, throwing off sparks. He picked up the diskettes from his briefcase once more.

Where conventional Periodic Tables sketched the known territory of matter and hinted, by extrapolation, that superheavy matter might exist; the Hawking Periodic Matrix precisely mapped matter and superheavy matter, as well as the fantastic realm of ultraheavy matter. It had stimulated Lawrence-Berkeley to forge stable superheavy elements 110 through 124, what were now termed the Hawking Island, using the latest in particle beam and accelerator technologies. Elements 122 through 124—Hawkium, Lobachevium, and Riemanium—were the extremely promising beginnings of a super actinide element series analogous to the transuranium elements. They were collectively called the Hawking Nexus, the powerful elemental node to the Hawking Island. The Matrix continued to change the world, even as Harold mulled over the ironies to his young life. The 24-year-old graduate student contemplated his two sets of diskettes, one stolen and one in hand. He leaned back in his chair, the chair balanced on its two back legs and his feet propped up against his desk.

Riemanium was now being hailed as a super plutonium. The Matrix complicated the debate over dark matter in astrophysics and super nucleons in subatomic physics; only two of its impacts in broader scientific circles. But matters were not so wonderful, closer to home.

Stanford owned his work. His Hawking Transpositions. Arthur Linscott appeared as sole author of the paper announcing Nishimura's transpositions to the scientific community, the same paper responsible

PALIMPSEST

for coining most of the Hawking nomenclature. Harold Nishimura's credit consisted of being listed first as one of Linscott's graduate assistants, and of a research footnote in Linscott's paper. To be sure, Harold could not own the original equations authored by Hawking. And while his transpositions had been exceptionally clean, he had used standard methodologies and had chosen a standard computer simulation program. He could not honestly claim true ownership of the work.

What his transpositions had done was to introduce a change in scientific notation. And changes in notation frequently ushered in revolutions. He considered all the world of change the zero had created. The changeover from hieroglyphics to an alphabet had liberated the written word, as that from Roman to Arabic numerals in Medieval Europe had unchained mathematics as a discipline. Similarly, the application of the eight tone musical scale to Medieval Europe's church music had permitted Western Europe's complex classical tradition to arise out of plainsong. Something as basic as an alphabet or a musical scale could not be copyrighted, patented or trademarked. The Matrix which emerged when Harold combined his Hawking Transpositions with the standard periodic data base had been an accident as well. But, it was Nishimura's accident. All he wanted was proper credit for his work. Co-authorship of the paper would have been enough.

"Be grateful for the credit I did give you," Linscott had warned him. Lawrence-Berkeley worked to produce large quantities of the Hawking Nexus elements for government and corporate research. Teams of experimenters stood poised at Riemanium, itching to cross the broad 40-element gulf of instability known as the TransHawking elements, to explore ultraheavy matter's bizarre realms. Harold was not at all grateful. He was angry instead, even as he could laugh at himself for expecting things to be any different. He had been incredibly naive in handing his work over to Linscott. So he had vowed to get even, in his own way. His computer metavirus, encoded on the three diskettes from his briefcase, was Nishimura's backhanded revenge. He flipped his bundled creation in his hands with a rueful smile, turning the plastic diskettes slowly, over and over.

He had worked out the mathematics for a universal translation between Apple/IBM, Microsoft, EvoStep, Gleishaltuung and Tanaka computer operating systems the summer before as a hobby, entirely independent of his graduate work. And he had opted to develop the super virus from it before marketing his universal translation as copyrightable software. His metavirus would penetrate any of the five standard operating systems, reproduce a cluster of four interactive subprograms, and carve out a concealed, autonomous operating system utilizing a mere one percent of the memory in any infected network, server mainframe, or suitably large individual computer. When Harold finally

5

perfected it, the super virus would steal information, transmit data, operate a CPU or modem, respond to a private password, obstruct host computer operations, and remain completely passive until he wanted to access it. Once Harold infected the Department's compunet, and Linscott's office and home PCs, Nishimura would be able to pirate Arthur Linscott's research even as the professor conducted it.

The Hawking Transpositions were history. The thief had wanted to steal his metavirus, without a doubt. Harold had told only two people about the metavirus, one of them Ralph, the cousin he had grown up with in LA who now resided in Seattle. The other one, Gene.

"Time to get the hell out of here," he said, out loud. He was remarkably calm as he pulled out a copy of the morning paper, dated Sunday, March 13, 2005, also from his briefcase. He opened it to the rental classifieds. The muffled sound of a distant explosion failed to distract him.

***

Gene was disappointed to find out from his Sulawesi fence what was on the diskettes he'd lifted from Nishimura's library. He hadn't found his house mate's log in the short time he'd been in Harold's room on a mission to steal the metavirus, and he didn't know how to operate the PC. Had he been computer literate, he would've confirmed the contents of the disks and made copies of the correct ones. But he disliked computers, so he'd grabbed at where he'd seen Harold stash the diskettes.

"Hawking Transpositions. High school stuff. Ain't worth a dime." This from his fence.

The Sulawesi middleman had copied the diskettes for Gene, who now carried the duplicates in an envelope as he strolled up the shady, tree lined walk to his current girlfriend's Palo Alto house, the originals in his leather jacket's inner pocket. With luck, he'd manage to sneak the originals back into his roommate's library before Harold noticed that they were missing. Gene had thought about placing blank substitutes in his house mate's computer disk library only after visiting his fence. Sun as thick as summer burned up the early spring day, the air smelling of heat and freshly mown lawns. A sprinkler stuttered rhythmically somewhere. In the distance to the east, a wing of B-52's cruised the scathing blue sky. Probably a training flight out of Mather near Sacramento, prepping for the real thing over southern Mexico. The door was not locked, and he removed his sunglasses upon entering the hall's gloom. Daylight sluiced in ahead.

"I'm working in the dining room," a woman's voice, Serena's, yelled above a low polyrhythmic thunder.

Serena's stage name was Stiletto Blue, and she'd been instrumental in defining the Raspie sound at the turn of the century. But she'd shaved off all of her black Rasputanic tangles two months before, when she'd started on her "new direction," generating Black Noise. Black

PALIMPSEST

Noise was a conscious response, her attempt to negate the musical travesty that Null had become. Serena also liked converting software programs into musical analogs as a hobby, for the sheer pleasure of listening to the results. She'd built her own equipment and developed her own software to that end. She sat on a high stool, bald and dressed in black, surrounded by an array of boards and consoles, all amidst a jumble of equipment, note pads, drums, guitars and fast food wrappers.

"It's a computer modeling program document, and a data base," she said after slotting the three disks into her 24-drive work deck. "Stapledon 4.0. I'll have it translated to Musik Alkemy in a sec."

They'd been lovers for only the past three months, and always at his place. Every square inch of Serena's house—floors, furniture, and fixtures—was covered with her music; heavily notated score sheets, cassette tapes and computer diskettes, hardware and software, and musical instruments. She'd even used the fast food wrappers to write down music and lyrics. Paths a shoe wide wandered around the junk piled everywhere. She offered him a joint of Kajan grass while the translation process blinked merrily. He lit it and coughed raucously with his first, good hit.

"Now, I take the translation and pour it into the Astral Frame," Serena commented, more to herself than to Gene.

Gene liked over-the-edge, but she was a step or two too far over that line for him. She'd developed her Frame as a "grand synthesis" of western, Chinese and Vedic, as well as ancient Egyptian and Mayan astrologies. Now she tried fitting everything, and most of all her music, into it. Their sex wasn't good enough for him to put up for long with drug-hazed ramblings about her "phenomenal" Astral Frame. He took another pungent hit. Since Leslie left to make her own way in the world—dependable, stable, conventional Leslie—he'd shared his bed with the likes of Stiletto Blue.

"That's weird," she said, and so he glanced over her shoulder.

Her main board's LCD splayed out two large blocks of dazzling, chameleon color; a small, colorful island positioned between them a third of the distance from the large block on the left. That island's colors melted, shifted, combined and split as he watched. A tiny, convoluted knot of shivering, iridescent hue extended out from the island toward the more distant color block. When he looked close enough, he discerned a hairline thread of shifting tint running from the large mass on the left through the island and its knot, to the big block far on the right.

"That node," she pointed to the eccentric knot, "That's where your 'center-of-being' plots when I map out your horoscope, Gene."

"Coincidence," Gene said, and handed her the joint, "Let's hear how it plays."

She copied the conversion onto one disk, then popped the disk into her sound system. She adjusted the equalizer levels and turned up the volume. First was the sound of bells, phasing in and out in long sinuous waves. Fuller than any bells Gene had ever heard. Deeper and darker than cathedral bells. Then came the clawed, rended sound of apocalypse. Implosion. The chime of crystal fracturing, chipping and falling concluded. Gene took another, long hit.

"Now, play it backwards, for the hidden messages."

PART ONE
PRIMING THE APOCALYPSE

ONE

Eduardo Sanchez Hernandez walked a dirt road 25 miles southwest of Dzitbalchén in Campeche State with the family's twelve goats and his dog, Guerre.

En una jaula de oro, pendiente de un balcón,
estaba una calandria llorando su prisión,
y luego un gorrioncito a su jaula se arrimó:
-Si tú te vas conmigo libre te saco yo.-

He sang to the dog who danced after the goats, nipping and barking those individualistic animals into a manageable herd.

Y luego la calandria al momento contestó:
-Si tú me sacas libre, contigo me voy yo.-
Y luego el gorrioncito a la juala se arrojó,
con alas, pies y pico los alambres quebró.
Y leugo la calandria al instante se fugó,
tomó los cuatro vientos, voló, voló, voló.

Eduardo was all of 12 years old in the predawn light. That light silhouetted the thick vined mass of an ancient Mayan step pyramid cut along the horizon, and smoked his footsteps as he took the goats out to graze. His family of three brothers, two sisters, father and mother, father's uncle and mother's mother, worked a small *ejido* and belonged to the Marti Cooperative. Folks considered his family well off in their village of Xlichécan, in that they had not starved or moved to the city before Liberation. The *ejido* provided them with subsistence corn and other vegetables as well as enough space to raise a few chickens. They owed their meager prosperity entirely to the goats. They owned eight of their goat herd outright, and the others they raised for the coop. They sold what they themselves did not use in the milk and cheese that their rebellious nanny goats produced. They took good care of

9

END TIME

their coop charges, and voluntarily tithed a percentage of their own goats' productivity toward maintaining the Marti Cooperative's rural lower-middle-class comforts. Whitewash on an ancient, decaying, low stone wall alongside the road bore the symbol:

Eduardo felt the sound more than he heard it. A thrumming in the air, in the primordial dark of the forest around him, in the very light of that breaking day. He felt as might the child of a New Kingdom Egyptian peasant, innocent of all blame when some jealous, monodeistic god brought the plague of locusts upon a pharaoh whose heart that god first had hardened. The boy ran back to his village, the dog snapping the goats into a gallop behind him. The plague of metal locusts, a cloud of US assault helicopters, rose above the rain forest to glint metal light on the sunrise.

The swarm swiftly passed Eduardo on waves of thunder, so that when he crested the final hill, hell erupted through the wooden and tin roofed huts of his village. His home. Lateral fireballs shredded trees, houses, animals and people indiscriminately in loud, long thumps that obscured any screams. Eduardo continued his mad dash toward his family's house. Surprisingly, so did the dog and goats. A helicopter wheeled and fired a short battery of sheriken missiles. They whisked in diamond formation to imbed into earth, trees, and flesh and bone before detonating.

Eduardo, Guerre and the goats all died relatively instantly.

TWO

The young man seated meditatively on the downtown Oakland warehouse rooftop had many names. Short dark hair, average in height, thin and wiry, with sharp tanned features; he looked ten years younger than his age. His eyes, closed now, were a chameleon hazel. He had an almost imperceptible cleft in his chin, and his smile, when he did, was broad. Black t-shirt, tightly pegged black jeans, and red high tops; he'd already stashed his tote bag earlier, locking it in a luggage locker in the downtown Oakland Greyhound station. He'd used two *nom de guerre* by 9 that morning.

He was Michael Baumann, Mike to his new lover Rosanne Casey, the weekend scheduling clerk for Security Pacific Services, whose fragrant bed he had left three hours before. During a long afterglow from lovemaking in her apartment over a month ago, Mike charmed Rosanne with feigned, friendly interest into talking about her work.

10

PRIMING THE APOCALYPSE

"Security Pacific handles some pretty big accounts," she snuggled into his warm embrace, "We're shipping the Piccoli gem collection for a museum show in San Francisco at the end of the month."

A quick eye and hand provided Mike with the Piccoli's exact schedule and route while picking up Rosanne often after work. He failed to note that Security Pacific management frequently coordinated several "high security" shipments into a single run, as a recent economy measure. A more in-depth probing of his lover might have revealed it. The Piccoli was to be just such a piggy-back run, the other client being UC Berkeley looking to "privatize" some of its operations. He regretted this hole in his knowledge all too soon.

He was also Peregrine, infamous second-story man, on the CB to his current employer after arriving at the warehouse that morning. Rossi Diamotti ran the operation. He'd started planning the theft two years before, bringing in Peregrine as a freelancer a year and a half ago to help track the gems. Now, Diamotti wanted a slam performance. Rossi had introduced Peregrine to the rest of his team six months before. The bearded Somali Vet weapons specialist Sidney. Austin Dread, the Afro-manic adrenaline freak/auto racer/pilot/computer wizard. And Peregrine's own personal nightmare Mako, a toothy six-foot-tall-five-foot-wide Hawaiian Samoan, profession assumed.

"I want the Piccoli, "Rossi said, eyes narrow and hard, "Whatever the cost."

Diamotti had earned his impressive fortune by questionable means; smuggling, protection, blackmail, scams of every sort. The stumpy bald-headed man was ugly in person and in business.

"No killing," Peregrine spoke up. Mako smirked, and his scarred, brown face was unpleasantly accented by white-white teeth. "I can plan things so that no one has to get killed. It won't come cheap."

"I said, whatever the cost," Rossi agreed, and so he had planned the operation.

Fifteenth century Borgia acquisitiveness represented the Piccoli's core collection, supplemented by Ghibelline, Medici and Sforza contributions. In all, it comprised forty-seven precious gems and over 300 semi-precious stones in expertly crafted silver and gold inlays. Antonio Benavito Piccoli managed to assemble it all into a private collection in 1930, under the auspices of Mussolini's fascist regime and personal friendship. Piccoli's death in 1956 in turn placed his gem collection under Italian government control. Rossi wanted this Italian national treasure for his own. What's more, he was willing to pay Peregrine's asking price, a solid million, for the job.

Peregrine opened his eyes and absorbed the random spread of clouds in rich blue sky before him. Absently, he toyed with a silver ring on his right hand, out of habit. The air smelled of heated asphalt and impend-

11

ing rain. The city spread dingy buildings and garish billboards all about him. Sounds of traffic drifted up to him. He unlimbered calmly, methodically, though not ritualistically. Then, he glanced at his watch. 9:18 a.m.

The operation had begun.

Peregrine had practiced the heist with the others so often that he could visualize it without effort. He pictured the Security Pacific armored car approaching the Highway 24 on ramp west after the scheduled "side pickup" from UC Berkeley; a brief detour in its route up from Oakland International across the bay bridge into the city with the Piccoli. Traffic was minimal. An armed guard rode shotgun with an armed driver, and two armed guards lounged in the back security cab. A nondescript Toyota mini-van drove behind the car at a modest distance, the driver not obviously following. The armored car trundled slowly down College to Claremont, then down Claremont to the freeway entrance at Martin. As the car geared down to take the ramp's incline, the mini-van hugged its tail, both easing past a massive, orange dressed highway worker with white-white teeth. Mako tossed several orange cones across the on ramp after the mini-van passed, then caught up to the van and jumped into its passenger seat. He then abruptly leaned out of his window upon a radioed signal, and fired a streamlined anti-tank rocket at the back of the armored car. Simultaneously, a high impact shell fired by Sidney, dressed as another highway worker further up the ramp, shattered through the car's bullet proof windshield.

Both glass-breaking shell and armor piercing rocket contained a selective neurological paralyzing agent, the organophosphorus based crowd control nerve gas known as PS gas. Both exploded as designed in the scenario he created in his mind. As the PS gas acted to strangle key nerves and muscles in the Security Pacific personnel, the car veered erratically off the road. The mini-van parked behind, and Austin and Mako, both now sporting gas masks, leaped out to run for the car. Sidney, similarly masked, ran down the on ramp. They rapidly molded pre-primed lumps of CTX plastic bonded explosive onto door lock and hinges, then efficiently detonated them to rip open the security compartment. With Sidney and Mako standing guard, Austin clambered into the car over the two sprawled security guards to scoop up everything in sight. All three jumped into the mini-van and sped off, or so Peregrine imagined it.

He had obtained the rocket and launcher, the PS gas and the CTX plastique from Sulawesi Outlaw Zone, purchasing them plus the team's contingency Ecureuil B-5 helicopter with Rossi's money. He'd managed to skim enough off of Diamotti by then to purchase a personal stash also from the Celebes; satellite-link "blue box," carton of four

PRIMING THE APOCALYPSE

Timpo grenades, short barrel PS riot gun and gas shells, small CTX slab, and expertly forged, computer perfect driver's license and social security card. All were now safely buried in the northern coastal range.

Peregrine stood and crossed the rooftop to the trap door left open into the warehouse's dark. He clambered down a metal ladder into the smell of grease and gasoline. His eyes adjusted to the gloom so that he placed the sixteen wheeler looming in the building's emptiness. He reached into the semi's cab, pulled out a portable radio/scanner, and set it on the engine hood. He dialed to DJ Elijah's pirate Oakland FM radio signal for a sample of African soklo music before switching to the police band scanner function. As police calls echoed in the dark space, Peregrine opened the back of the truck, pulled down a broad ramp, and unlocked the warehouse's alley entry door.

The robbery had a witness. The Highway Patrol responded rapidly. The mini-van, described down to the first four digits of its faked license plate, was now an all-points, along with the meager description of the three armed men. And, there had been a shooting. The shotgun guard had taken at least three bullets. He lived, but just barely.

9:47 a.m.

"Damn," Peregrine cursed aloud. His voice echoed back to him in recrimination.

Peregrine imagined what had happened. Sidney's shell shattered most of the windshield. The PC gas diffused, and so it only partially affected the guard. As the armored car careened off the road, the guard managed to open his door and stumble, or maybe to fall out, perhaps even to struggle with his gun. Mako then jumped from the parking mini-van and, with great pleasure, he shot the near helpless guard with a quick uzi burst. With great pleasure.

Peregrine fumed by the time the mini-van screeched into the warehouse alley and honked outside the door. 10:24 a.m. He turned on the winch and ducked out under the door when it was high enough.

"You fucking shot a guard!" Peregrine hissed at Austin.

"Shut the fuck up!" Sidney yelled from the passenger's seat, his dark, war wild eyes buried in his full beard.

"Don't want to hear it!" Austin growled.

Mako merely grinned from the back of the van. When the door opened, Austin lunged the van into the warehouse, up the ramp, and into the back of the semi. Peregrine folded his arms across his chest and narrowed his eyes. Austin scrambled from the van and leaped from the truck. He pulled up the ramp, pulled down the truck door, and then hopped into the cab, sweeping up the radio in the process. He started and gunned the semi's engine, then expertly backed the rig out of the warehouse.

"Shut the door and get in Peregrine," Austin snapped from the cab.

END TIME

Peregrine did both, reluctantly.

"You didn't have to shoot anybody," Peregrine snarled once inside the cab.

"Shut the fuck up," Austin engaged the forward gears, "You weren't there."

The truck eased onto a Highway 24 choked tight with cops.

11:16 a.m.

After turning onto 880 North, the police band revealed that, aside from the Piccoli gems, they'd heisted an unpleasant surprise. Two pounds of enriched riemanium, shipped from UC Berkeley's labs and experimental reactor, and destined for departure from Oakland Naval Base to San Diego under Department of Energy auspices. Enough bomb-grade riemanium to construct a high-intensity atomic weapon. It was the Security Pacific "side pick-up," also missing from the armored car, which Rossi's robbers now possessed.

12:32 p.m.

Peregrine heard of the guard's death under emergency surgery, just short of the Richmond/San Rafael Bridge, on the way to Diamotti's Marin safe house. Billboards taunted with messages of acceptance and easy sex in the purchase of liquor, tobacco or cars. Black, ugly power lines tangled up with wintering clouds. He gave Austin a venomous look, which the driver avoided by keeping his eyes to the road.

"Now, we're all accomplices to murder," Peregrine spat.

"Shut it," Austin gulped, "Or I'll shut it for you."

THREE

"Thanks for coming Bill," CHP Golden Gate Division Chief Darby Holbin welcomed SFPD Chief Williams Sliwa with a handshake, the last of his high powered guests to arrive for this emergency meeting.

"Hope we can cut this short," Sliwa said, "Darb, I've got a couple thousand anarchists and so called peace protesters turning an anti-war demonstration into riot on Market at this moment."

"I understand," Darby nodded, then glanced at his watch. 12:12 p.m. He turned to the roomful of individuals abuzz with personal conversation. "Everybody, deli is on the way. Maybe we should begin."

People slowly took seats around the table in the Patrol's north Oakland office conference room. Several metropolitan and freeway maps had been hastily pinned to walls and blackboards. The man actually responsible for calling this meeting, Edward Sumner, sat at Darby's left.

Edward was the FBI's West Coast Field Office Director, headquartered in San Jose. He was the national Director's on site oversight for all west coast FBI operations, at 38 the youngest of a council of eight brand new regional directors which the Director intended to use to rebridle the Bureau after the Heidelburg fiasco. They were defining

14

their positions as they went along. Two days before, Edward had held his first regional meeting for all of his field office directors. It had not gone smoothly, beginning with the resignation of Paul Chrisman as head of the San Francisco field office. The Oakland office director, Truman Marable, sat among the roomful of law enforcement agency heads. Sumner adjusted his tie and glanced around the table with faded blue eyes.

"Sergeant Copley, would you start?" Darby focused the meeting.

Allen Copley was a sergeant in the Oakland office which had first responded to the Security Pacific robbery call. He was squat, broad-shouldered, and ill-at-ease with all the brass in the conference room. He stood and cleared his throat.

"Well, I'm sure everyone is aware that a Security Pacific Service armored car was held up around 9:15 this morning, on the Claremont on ramp to Highway 24. One security guard has been shot and is presently in critical condition at Highland General. Two items of value were taken. The Piccoli gems are conservatively valued at 470 million dollars. The enriched riemanium is enough to produce an atomic bomb four to five times more powerful than the one detonated over Nagasaki. At present the criminals responsible seem to have, um, vanished."

"Be a little more specific, Sergeant," Darby hurumphed as low conversation started again around the table.

"Yes sir," Allen said, and passed around a prepared, xeroxed set of papers, "We have every available officer on the roads. Every law enforcement agency around the bay has been alerted. The car involved in the robbery has not yet been sighted. Nor have we found it abandoned anywhere. The plates are no doubt stolen, or forged. The robbery site is remarkably clean. What we do know is that whoever pulled this off was well-trained, well organized, possibly with access to inside Security Pacific information, and backed by considerable resources. Their armament is formidable..."

"Neural agents, plastic explosives, automatic weapons," Alameda County Sheriff Steven McCaffrey read from Allen's reports, "I'll say they're formidable. Real big money behind this."

"Exactly," Edward started to say. He was interrupted by the food's arrival, which necessitated a brief pause for the participants to prepare lunch. The Piccoli/riemanium theft was happening at an inopportune time. Edward was still in the throws of reviewing and reordering the priorities and operations of the field offices in the six states under his command. Matters of national security always took precedence, however, and it was a chance for him to meet and work with some of the locals in one of his larger jurisdictions. He had many long nights ahead of him putting matters together on top of this crisis. When things settled down once again around the table, Edward stood to command the floor.

"Perhaps I should introduce myself," Sumner glanced about the room, "I'm Edward Sumner, FBI West Coast Field Office Director. I'm partly responsible for why this meeting was called. As you're all aware, my position is new for the FBI. I am going to be dependent on the cooperation of your agencies and the good graces of your offices to aid the Bureau in investigating this theft."

"Italian government must be leaning hard on the State Department over the Piccoli," Chief Sliwa commented between bites of a meaty sandwich.

"The Italian government is the least of our worries at the moment." Edward said, glad for the lead-in. "The Director, the Attorney General, the NSC and the President are much more concerned with the riemanium theft."

He waited for the words to sink in.

"Gentlemen, we are once again at war in a not-so-distant country. American boys, and girls, are once more dying for freedom on a foreign soil. Needless to say, those who oppose our nation's involvement in southern Mexico would stop at little to sabotage our government's war effort, and endanger our national security. My superiors would like everyone here to take the idea quite seriously that what the thieves were after was not the Piccoli Collection, but the riemanium. We may be dealing with a case of domestic, anti-war terrorism."

His brief speech electrified those in attendance. Sliwa's jaw remained open, his sandwich unbitten. Rumsted Marsh, Marin County Sheriff, leaned on Sumner's words with obvious expectation, a posture mimicked by Darby Holbin, Edward's obvious yes-man at this meeting. Marable kept a serene poker face, while McCaffrey, clearly more skeptical than the rest, nevertheless frowned with the implications of Sumner's words.

"The organizational profile of Hardcore Autonomy, or Black Dada Nihilismus, or any of the other fringe anti-war groups hardly fits the MO for this robbery." This from Sliwa, once more enjoying his food.

"And what if one of these groups suddenly had access to money and training, say from an outside power?" Edward boldly laid out an assumption.

"What outside power?" Williams finished his sandwich with relish and set about building another. "The Russians are hip-deep in civil war, and when not fighting the Russians the Chinese are too busy with the Koreans, the Mongolians, the IndoChinese, and the Tibetans, not to mention their own students. Southern Mexico's insurgent Zapatistas are anarchists if they're anything. Cuba and Peru both appear to be steering clear of any support for these guerrillas."

PRIMING THE APOCALYPSE

"Appear to be..." Edward emphasized Sliwa's words. "And, in any case, it does not necessarily have to be an outside *national* power. There is evidence that a wealthy individual, perhaps a consortium of individuals might be involved in backing Mexican terrorists."

"Drug kingpins and cartels?" Rumsted asked. Edward flashed him a knowing look.

"Hell, anybody with the money can buy a Sulawesi package this advanced," Steven took the bull by the horns. "If we're going to make this meeting productive, we need to be systematic. We have three possibilities before us. The Security Pacific robbery was motivated by the Piccoli Collection, or by the riemanium, or by both. Whatever the case, I believe we need to involve the public in hunting down these thieves. The media are already broadcasting the gem theft. We need to keep a lid on the riemanium for as long as possible. But we also need to get the public's cooperation in tracing down the robbers."

As McCaffrey spoke, a CHP officer entered to briefly confer with Allen Copley.

"It's murder, as well," Allen interrupted, "The security guard just died."

FOUR

"Look," Burt Desmond ran after the attractive woman rapidly exiting the Cafe Vandee. Fleeing him. "I'm a reporter, not a rapist. All I need is a little bit of a story here. Something of human interest. This Security Pacific thing is hot, and you DO work for them."

"Sorry. No comment." Rosanne Casey avoided his eyes and flicked her purse at him as if trying to swat some pesky insect.

Burt jumped in front of her on the sidewalk and Rosanne jostled around him. She glanced around for a cop among the upscale boutiques, bistros and coffee shops, but could not find one in the heart of San Francisco's downtown business district.

All about them shoals of suits—execs and junior execs, businessmen and lawyers from around the Pacific Rim as well as from India, Africa and Europe—thronged the luncheon waters among corporate towers with Japanese, Taiwanese, Korean, Australian, European and American logos. Secretarial schools in bright colors also swam among the corporate reefs and kelp beds. This arm of the international corporate sea invariably found its cultures diluted with California casualness and eccentricity, yet squint up the eyes and it could be any major city in the developed world. A scraggly, long-haired and bearded man in greasy, tattered clothes mumbled to himself incoherently and wrapped himself in old newspapers in a nearby doorway. Creature from the black lagoon.

South somewhere, above the noise of cars, buses, pedestrians and street stand hawkers, but out of sight, she could hear something in progress, as if through shallow water. Massed voices shouted together, chanted slogans too distorted to understand, yet powerful enough to travel distance. Other sounds—loud bangs and pops, breaking glass, police sirens—accompanied the chanting. A plume of dark smoke rose from the direction of the tumult.

"Anti-war demo," Burt spoke up next to her, and she became aware of him again. Rosanne grimaced and headed off walking full tilt toward the Security Pacific offices. Security Pacific Services was a Pacific Rim operation. The media now besieged her downtown office building, which housed the Security Pacific corporate headquarters as well as its Bay Area offices.

"Come on, you at least have an opinion," Burt matched her pace and craned his head into her space, What's your take on the robbery? Corporate negligence? Inside job?"

"It's almost 1 o'clock." Rosanne growled and kept walking. "You're making me late for work."

"This will only take a minute," Burt pleaded, "I need an angle, something different on this story for my station. Come on, give me a break."

"I can't tell you anything," Rosanne was firm, "I've been forbidden by my boss to talk about the robbery. The Piccoli gems. The riemanium. Anything."

"There was riemanium in that armored car?" Burt blurted. "Bomb-grade riemanium was stolen?"

They stood now, stock-still, on a sidewalk fluid with pedestrians. Smoke from a burning downtown laced the early afternoon. Rosanne was pale. Fear in her eyes, she bolted from the reporter on a run. Burt knew he had a scoop. Once back at her desk, Rosanne tried calling her boyfriend, Mike, but his phone did not answer.

***

DL hammered another nail into the 2x4 with strong, sure blows. The wooden frame, intended eventually to be a room divider, was taking shape. Jack'o'Hearts, DL's co-worker on this project, carried in eight more lengths of board and dumped them onto the concrete first floor of their New Afrika Center in Oakland.

"That's the last of 'em," Jack'o'Hearts checked his callused hands for splinters. "Looks like we'll need to do another buy at the lumber yard to finish up."

"Gettin' low on cash," DL shook his head, "And we still ain't bought no dry wall."

"Maybe I can get my uncle to 'donate' some," Jack'o'Hearts picked up another hammer and scooped up a handful of nails, "He's a general contractor, down San Leandro."

The space they worked in had once been a warehouse with second story offices. Their diligent efforts, which now flavored the air with their sweat, had reduced the storehouse area considerably. The remainder was consigned to a Caribbean import/export business that intended to move in as soon as they put up the final wall. Jack'o'Hearts had set up the Center's speakers in the work area, and DJ Elijah's Liberation News Service on Liberation Station Afrika blared out over them.

"...Anti-war protesters and self-styled Hooligans continue to battle police along the eastern end of Market in downtown San Francisco's financial district. So far, the SFPD has managed to confine the street fighting to the area immediately around the Embarcadero peace rally.

"In other news, the Southern Poverty Law Center has filed a class action suit today against six midwest family planning clinics for sterilizing 484 welfare mothers under false pretenses after providing the women abortions. Sylvester Carmichael, who became Director of the SPLC after Victor Jackson was assassinated by the Aryan Revolutionary Movement two years ago, is scheduled to speak at a New Orleans press conference at 5..."

"How you think you'll go out?" Jack'o'Hearts asked, pounding in his own nail.

DL straightened up, wiped his forehead with the back of his left hand, and balanced his hammer over his fingers. His body did not show his prison conditioning, the muscles strong but unobtrusive. This, plus the fact that he was an inch shorter than average in height, and many people underestimated him in a fight. He looked upon the world through lively light brown eyes. His skin was dark brown, his hair was cut short and his smile was engaging despite a missing front tooth. A scar ran down his left cheek, reminder of a knife fight he had almost lost. DL had been born in Harlem, winding up in Oakland at five when his family moved to the west coast looking for work. Both mom and dad worked, so he had been raised by his black Cuban grandmother with a brother fifteen years older destined to die a soldier in Lebanon, and a sister six years older destined to marry up and disown her family of origin. Granny had taught him Spanish, a handy skill he had used often in dealing with the vatos on his turf. He wore construction boots, faded black jeans and white t-shirt; a striking symbol—black, green, and gold stars on a blood red background—silk-screened on the shirt's back.

END TIME

"When the Afrikan Lords be gangbangin', figured I'd go out with a bullet in the heart," DL smiled, "Pig bullet, bangin' bullet, it didn't matter. Now, with us doin' the Center, well, I don't know."

"Maybe we'll both die o' ol' age," Jack'o'Hearts laughed, doing a stooped over, arthritic caricature of an old man as he shambled over to pick up another 2x4, his voice changing from rich tenor to that of a toothless oldster.

"We should be so lucky," DL laughed along. He had never heard of Alprentice "Bunchy" Carter, Jeff Fort or the Black P. Stone Nation, the Young Lords Party or the Almighty Latin King Nation, and only recently had he learned of Fred Hampton. Ghosts walking the same road.

FIVE

Gregory Patrick Kovinski had made his polite exit from a half-million-strong peace march settled into a rally along the Embarcadero an hour and a half before. Just in time to escape the endless series of boring, PC speeches by spokespeople for everyone and everything in what was nebulously called "the progressive movement." Had he known that groups of black masked autonomists and anarchists, Hooligans all, would also get antsy, finally to spark thousands of other young people to take to the streets in direct action and riot, he might have hung around. As it was he had cleared the Golden Gate on his drive home when he heard of the demonstration's militant turn from public radio; the story after the Piccoli gem heist and before the Ukrainian cruise bombing of Moscow.

Clouds thickened for a storm. The ride was brisk in his classic 1968 Triumph Spitfire, Greg's summer rebuild. The air shredded with the smell of the bay on the way into San Rafael, shading into forest smells after he turned up Lucas Valley Road. Walled suburb alternated with mini-mall until the turn on County Road G18. His home town was some 11 miles north of Mill Valley as the crow flew, between wealthy hyper-suburban Marinwood and a more reclusive/exclusive Woodacre, directly north of Loma Alta mountain. The area had once been an Ohlone village, stumbled upon by Portola in 1771. It was named Alabaster later, for the white rock outcroppings on the mountain's north face. A collection of farm houses and a general store by 1850, it became a respectable, modest agricultural community by 1940, specializing in truck farming and poultry. In 1980, the agriculturally/vocationally oriented Alabaster State University, part of the CSU system, was established in the town, augmenting and replacing the already existing junior college. And California's governor proclaimed Alabaster a "model modern agricultural community" in the year 2000. As he wheeled onto Alabaster's Main Street at 1:20, Greg decided to check his campus mailbox at Merrick Cluster College, on Alabaster State

20

PRIMING THE APOCALYPSE

University, before going home.

He ran back down the campus post office steps. He jumped into his car, revved the engine violently, and squealed recklessly out of the parking lot. Thick white clouds, underbellied dark and portending rain, lumbered across the afternoon sky. Greg turned, tires screaming, out of the university grounds and back onto the streets of Alabaster. A large raven spread its wings and bounded up gently from a branch near the top of a thick needled pine ahead of Greg's race west along Main Street. She spread her black wings wide to cruise parallel to the roaring little car for a time, a cool black eye briefly taking in the Spitfire and its driver before the slightest tilt of wing spiraled the raven away on a search for food.

Dear Greg,

I'm deeply sorry to have to write you this letter, but this way I can get everything I want to say said. You're so good with arguments that I dreaded calling you on the phone to try and tell you. Greg, I'm in love with someone else. His name is Christopher, and I met him shortly after I started at Wellesley...

Greg took the turn east onto Foothill Scenic Drive at the split with San Geronimo Valley Drive as might a Grand Prix driver. He was in a state of terrible revelation, the visceral experience of apocalypse. Everything, every little clue in the past three months of his life had suddenly fallen into place in a wrenching, illuminating flash. A painful, razor-edged whole. The changed tone to her letters and phone calls after her first month as a junior transfer. The sudden hesitancy as to her summer commitments. The male voice which occasionally answered her house's phone. Her brief, aloof Christmas vacation home. The formal, almost stilted 21st birthday card she had sent him at the beginning of the month. Now it all made sense. He roared through the intersection with Sir Francis Drake Boulevard near Camp Arequipa, taking Foothill Scenic south along the coastal ranges as it generally paralleled the English pirate's road to the east.

Broad leafed and sharp needled brush and trees blended into walls of variegated green along both sides of the road. Greg took a long straight-away, pedal to the floor. During her holiday home, she had been almost too busy to see him, what with family, shopping, relatives, trips to the city, and the like. He had managed, with a good deal of effort, to have her alone for one night of her vacation's twenty, at his house with his father away on business. Their lovemaking had been strained and estranged, awkward and unsatisfying. Greg had been confused by her standoffishness and embarrassment. Tears now welled up into his eyes, a flood he held back, bitterly biting his lower lip.

...I know this will hurt you, but I can no longer hide my feelings. Since I moved to Boston, my perspective on things has changed pro-

END TIME

foundly. I still care for you deeply. But we were high school lovers, and ours was a high school relationship. My point of view has now broadened beyond Alabaster, and beyond the west coast. Christopher has been a crucial factor in my growth. He has widened my view of the world and allowed me to see how parochial my life was in Alabaster, and even in California. I still love you Greg. But I've come to realize that I love you as I would a brother. We grew up together, and our relationship came out of our familiarity. By contrast, my relationship with Christopher is a love based on true passion...

Greg reacted entirely from the gut on his mad ride. Wounded, in pain, he drove headlong to his personal space, a secluded, calm place where invariably he had gone during crises in his life in order to think things through and sort out his feelings. He lifted his foot off the accelerator in approaching the hairpin, then started accelerating again a third of the way through the turn, keyed into the g-force as the car held onto the edge of a spin-out. Once through it, he suddenly slammed on the brakes. Too late, he felt the Spitfire fishtail as his right front wheel, then rear wheel, ran over the large, gray object near the road's edge. Greg kept his head and quickly brought his car under control, momentarily jostled out of his raging emotions. He parked well onto the shoulder to catch his breath and dampen his adrenaline. He stepped out onto the gravel and crunched around, steadying his rampant breathing and shaking muscles.

Greg stood just under six feet tall, broad-shouldered in his brown leather flight jacket. He looked athletic, although he had not participated in organized sports since the swim and water polo teams his sophomore year of high school. His straight dark hair was cropped short, outlining broad Slavic features, high forehead and fiery green eyes. He ran a hand absently through his hair. Almost as an afterthought, he walked over to the object which had prompted the near accident.

It was a metal box. It was painted gray, with bright yellow lettering almost entirely covered by the road's grit and his tires' rubber. The box was about two and a half feet by one foot by two feet, well-machined with rounded edges not dented by impact with his car. It's form-fitted lid fastened to the base at each end of its length with sophisticated locks. The whole thing rested on its side not far from where he had hit it. Greg noticed the skid marks of paint on asphalt from an impact point, indicating that the box originally had struck the road at some speed before his own encounter with it. It was also surprisingly massive and, in hefting it, he confirmed that the side to the road had been scraped clean, revealing scratched stainless steel. Greg carried the heavy object to his car where he loaded it into his trunk, absently, vaguely thinking to salvage the well-made box for his workshop.

PRIMING THE APOCALYPSE

He restarted the engine and eased back onto the asphalt, spitting gravel. Once driving again, he moderated his speed. The road widened, and walled suburban tracts sprouted up on either side, in the solemn shadows of the mountains. He glimpsed the bay to the east, the northern Bay Area landscape checkered with strong sun through broken clouds. He passed two cars on a straightway. Once again, his anguish and anger boiled up.

He had never considered a corresponding junior transfer to follow her to the east coast. ASU's technical departments were rated quite high, more than sufficient for his education. He majored in electronic engineering and minored in biochemical engineering. What is more, he was a homeboy. Not born, but raised in Alabaster since three years old, he had lived close enough to The City to have experienced the metropolis in full. He did not like it that much. Nowhere near enough to move to the hyper sprawl of the east coast. He had joined the Sierra Club's John Muir Back Pack Society after Scouting, out of his love for wilderness, an interest that Janet had seemed to share. They had solemnly promised each other in September that this "temporary" separation would only strengthen their love, all the while planning their epic "Pacific Crest Trail" hike for the summer to come. It had taken her barely one month to abandon their five year relationship. Greg's sense of betrayal was acid.

...Greg, I still want us to be friends, if we can. You were a very important part of my life in Alabaster. I don't want to avoid you when I come back to visit. I hope we can both be adult about this. But, if you feel too hurt by what has happened to be my friend for a while, I will understand. I will always be here for you to talk to, so please do not feel that I've abandoned you. You will always be my dear friend.

Love
Janet

The incidence of suburbia increased as Greg approached Mount Tamalpais, clotting into guarded bedroom communities and hardening into the occasional telescanned mini-mall and yuppie professional center. Somewhere above Corte Madera, between Larkspur and Mill Valley, he recognized and turned onto a side street. He drove through a stratum of exclusive, expensive housing—secluded, terraced homes with acreage and views—until both street and urbanization ended in the State Park's fence. Greg parked and searched under the passenger's seat for a small, black leather pouch, which he pocketed in his jacket. The gated fire road was easy to enter by climbing over, once he put the hood up on his car. He took a side trail almost immediately, into the thickening forest, until all sight and most sound of the suburbs melted away behind him.

The brisk hike normally took over an hour. Greg made it in a little

23

END TIME

under 45 minutes, fueled by his emotional fury, and the once removed state in which it placed him. His meadow on the slopes of East Peak opened into a modest clearing of wind tossed grass. Once he located the old pine stump near its western edge the meadow revealed a panorama of urbanization given a kind of beauty by distance. The crisp winter air was remarkably clear of smog and haze. Mount Diablo bracketed the northern Bay Area in the east, and the far-off, purple edge of the Sierra Nevadas cut the horizon, at times merging with looming banks of dark thunderheads.

The meadow had been a refuge for Greg more than once since he had hiked upon it at twelve, a Boy Scout second class trying to come to terms with his parents' divorce. He had returned to the meadow's serenity at fourteen after his favorite uncle, Stephen, died of cancer, and again at sixteen when his best friend in high school, Toby Wallace, committed suicide by hanging himself in the boy's locker room at the school gym. The meadow's calm had afforded him the space to decide not to register for the draft when he turned 18 in high school, and he had sought its solitude at 19 to come to terms with Janet's decision to abort their unintended pregnancy. Now this peaceful enclosure served as the stage upon which he needed to thrash out Janet's unfaithfulness.

He had about two hours of daylight and a half hour of dusk left. Time at least to start. He sat cross-legged on the wide stump, and withdrew the small pouch. He removed a plastic film case, a small wooden and brass pipe, and a book of matches. He extracted a fragrant bud of sensimilla from the film case, crushed it into the pipe bowl with his thumb, and lit a match. He folded rich, spicy marijuana smoke into his lungs with a deep intake of breath. The high, like a soft furry bubble, rose up from his lungs, nuzzled into his brain, and ever-so-gently popped among the neural synapses there. The waning sunlight brothed up golden, accentuating the objects around him. Bird song and insect noise deepened into profundity. The smells of pine and sage undertoned the burning marijuana odor.

Greg imagined that he could project himself beyond the Sierra Nevadas now teething at storm clouds. Beyond the jagged Rockies, beyond the sluggish Mississippi, beyond the rolling Appalachians, to the grimy city of Boston. He reconstructed Janet's face in the air before him; her long black curls, her cool blue eyes, and her smiling mouth. He imagined he could see her, hovering disembodied outside her room's window. It was charred night in Boston, and she was not alone. Someone, a man was with her. Try as he might flitting outside her window in his imagination, Greg could not make out his face. But to his great agony, they were making love, savagely enjoying each other's bodies and laughing with their shared pleasure.

Two things occurred in what Greg would remember thereafter as a

PRIMING THE APOCALYPSE

single incident of synchronicity, an association forever welded together by THC resins. A great brown hawk took flight from a Douglas fir on the meadow's edge and soared down a straight line toward Greg. Its wicked, powerful talons outstretched, the bird of prey lightly touched them to the top of the human's head. With a flap of its broad wings it flew off, rising into the approaching sunset. He had not seen the hawk descend. As he gazed up watching the graceful bird arc away, and wondering what omen its touch had been, the racket began. It started off with an incomprehensible voice bellowing over a bullhorn. Greg always mistook the sound of gunfire for that of fireworks, and visa versa, so it sounded like the Chinese New Year had started up on the hillside below the meadow.

It did not take him long to realize that a full blown battle was under way, and nearby, replete with single-shot and automatic weaponry, not to mention the dull thuds of things exploding. Then he noticed white clouds, which he took to be tear gas, rising above the trees down to the east, accompanied by the distinctive sound of a helicopter taking off. Indeed, the throbbing rotary blade and tail of a chopper did eventually break the same line of trees amidst the whirling white clouds, but clearly it was in trouble. The helicopter pitched, yawed, shuddered and shook, seemed about to leap into the sky, only to suddenly crash back beneath the tree line in an ugly rending of metal. Percussive, fuel-fed explosions followed. A violent, greasy black smoke cloud punched into the air where the helicopter had been.

Greg stashed his paraphernalia and ran back full speed to his car, all thought of Janet momentarily expunged from his thoughts. He was flushed, sweating, and scratched up by the time he kicked over the engine to make the dash for home. Or tried to. Cops swarmed every street of the affluent foothill housing. He had to provide five separate roadblocks with his ID and an explanation about his presence in the area. The jumpy cops bristled with weapons, but they let him through without a hassle each time. They were not looking for him. And he was in no position, what with the contraband in his pocket, to harangue them about their "police state methods" or "governmental fascism." He relied on the radio during the ride home for information.

Apparently, an alert citizen clued in the police that the Piccoli robbers might be holed up in a house in this elite section of the Bay Area. Sure enough, when the Highway Patrol made their move, a gunfight erupted, culminating in the thieves' attempted escape by helicopter, evidently concealed on the grounds of the besieged house. The attempt had failed. The helicopter had been shot down. The Piccoli gems had been recovered intact. Most of the criminals were dead, killed in the helicopter's crash, though the cops were searching for a fifth, unidentified individual. The radio report mentioned something about stolen riemanium, but Greg did not catch all of it.

Halfway back to Alabaster, Janet once again seeped into his consciousness. By the time he rolled into the gravel driveway of his father's house, his home, he was once more in a terrible funk. He immediately dismissed the idea of buying a flight to Boston in order to beat the shit out of this Christopher, whoever he was. He also instantly shelved the wild notion of fabricating some lurid fiction involving Janet to send to the proper Wellesleyan administration in order to expel her from the college, and perhaps the east coast as well.

The house was dark, surrounded by wind and pines. Built as a one story farmhouse in the 1890's, the giddy prosperity of the 1920's added a second story and enlarged the basement, giving the whole a Victorian facade. Someone renovated the entire structure in 1954, and his father modernized parts of the house just before Rachel divorced him. Greg himself had converted the basement into a metal shop. As he slunk into the spacious, ultra-modern kitchen he saw the note from Dad:

Greg,

I'll be in New York until Tuesday. The Tullock Case again. Sorry I can't shop with you for a computer update on Sunday. I'm sure your choice will be fine. How about dinner Wednesday night?

Love

Andre

He creased the paper and left it on the counter. The maid was off after Thursday for the weekend. He scooped two precooked hamburger patties and a precooked mini-pizza from the freezer and fed them into the computerized microwave. The house's OXO message center in the downstairs den, alongside the Einstein DeskTop PC, registered calls for his dad, although a fax from Larry Reed was for Greg. The fax read: PARTY! Larry was his good friend from freshman year at ASU, Larry opting out with an AA last year to concentrate on business for a while. Greg applied the appropriate condiments and relishes, popped a Guiness from his father's reserve, and found the living room's TV for some mindless preoccupation while he ate. The evening news rattled on in the middle of a story about South Africa's third year of civil war initiated by a resurgent Boer white homeland movement.

Andre Kovinski was his work. Greg had long ago accepted this about his father. Andre was the stellar partner in the prominent San Francisco law firm Armstead, Burger, Kovinski, Raj, Soukharno and Stein. He was the Bay Area's brilliant criminal and corporate lawyer who never made the social pages, only the front pages, with splashy power-and-money cases, often internationally flavored. So wedded to his career was Greg's father that Rachel Kovinski (nee O'Brien), Greg's mother, had first left him to live with her parents in LA. Enrolling in UCLA, she had finally divorced Andre to gain her own life.

PRIMING THE APOCALYPSE

Greg had spent three summers, a month and a half each summer from his 12th through his 14th years, living with his mom in "HeLA." Her life with dad had been Andre's life. Rachel was pregnant at nineteen. In college, she had chosen to drop out to marry Andre and keep his family while Andre's father paid for his son to breeze through Harvard law school. They moved from west to east coast, and then back again after Greg's birth when Andre was offered a junior partnership in the above firm, minus Kovinski, immediately after graduation. He dictated the terms of their marriage through his career's success, which had been meteoric. In particular the demands of social decorum, high level corporate entertaining, and absolute propriety before the media, so essential to Andre's ever-advancing position, chafed upon the young couple. Rachel hated it, in truth. Greg's summers south in Smog City had been pretty much of a drag; no one he knew to play or hang out with when she was not home. But he had never regretted spending them with her. The TV fluttered images of a shopping mall mass murder spree from somewhere in Ohio.

He had tried to learn from his parent's divorce in his relationship with Janet. He had considered her the focus of his life, not a mere auxiliary. Few couples in high school, or at ASU, spent more time together. And now his love, his dearest love, had left him.

He drank another beer, guzzled the Guiness at the fridge, and opened a third to return with to the TV. The TV image startled him. It was a metal box. It was painted gray, with bright yellow lettering. It was in the trunk of his Spitfire, even as its image ghosted upon the TV screen.

"Scientists call riemanium 'super plutonium'," the newscaster said. "Critical mass, the amount that will spontaneously explode when brought together, must be considered by scientists when handling quantities in excess of a quarter of a pound. A half pound of riemanium will produce a Nagasaki-sized nuclear explosion."

Hardly breathing, Greg recovered the very massive object from the trunk and carried it, gingerly, into the basement. Two pounds of enriched, bomb-grade riemanium had disappeared from the Security Pacific armored car, along with the Piccoli gems, both presumably stolen by the Diamotti gang. He donned goggles and plastic gloves, then used a modest solvent to wipe off his impact with the object.

PROPERTY
UNITED STATES OF AMERICA
DEPARTMENT OF ENERGY
DANGER
RADIOACTIVE MATERIAL
WARNING
DO NOT OPEN

END TIME

The sign for radiation, a central circle with three accompanying triangles, was also stenciled next to the lettering. Greg fit the box into the vise of his computer guided laser lathe after a few brief moments of tipsy thought. The riemanium had not been recovered from Diamotti's safe house. He knew that the riemanium could not all be in one lump due to critical mass. Hence the necessity for some type of radiation-proof internal packing that would be safe if the outside casing was accidentally cracked. Intense, solar hot, green light threaded against one of the box's locks. He used the high-tech tool—a continuous wave, 60% efficient, gas dynamic laser—to make a living carving metal to spec for classic automobile engines, among them his own. Now he directed its clean, cutting, coherent light to the task of violation. The laser vaporized the lock's core under his manipulation. The beers hammered at him. Ozone, and his own sweat, drenched the air. The box's lid sighed open.

Ten sealed cylinders, resembling enlarged, stemless, metal CO_2 cartridges, rested in dense, form-fitting foam moldings inside lead and carbon lined steel case walls. Each cylinder bore a radiation mark, and recapitulated the warning on the box. The ghost of Hiroshima rested on his laser lathe counter. He pinched the bridge of his nose, slightly irritated by the basement's odors. He needed another beer.

SIX

Peregrine blended out of an arroyo on the outskirts of Corte Madera around 1:30 a.m. He was caked with dirt, coated with dust and sweat, and scratched bloody across most of his exposed skin. Transcending it all; he was alive.

He walked side streets and feigned a little too much to drink to make his way to the junker Toyota Celica hatchback parked unobtrusively in a 24-hour Safeway parking lot. He recovered the keys from a box welded near the engine. Then he collapsed among blankets and a sleeping bag in the back, entirely exhausted. He slept for two hours; one entire REM cycle.

Peregrine had insisted upon calling Rossi before crossing the Richmond/San Rafael Bridge.

"No fucking way," Austin shouted," The Boss don't want to be disturbed until we're ready for the approach."

"Now you shut the fuck up," Peregrine hissed, the CB already in hand as Austin negotiated the lunch traffic congestion. After explaining the riemanium situation to "the Boss," he concluded with the statement: "We're hotter than Muammar Qaddafi at a Bar Mitzvah." He was gratified to hear Rossi stammer:

"Dump that stuff. Find a back road and get rid of it."

Unfortunately, no one had managed to find the stolen riemanium before the thieves and the semi arrived at Diamotti's safe house in the

PRIMING THE APOCALYPSE

foothills of Mount Tamalpais with the Piccoli gems. They were still molten hot! The radio broadcast desperate appeals for public assistance to capture the robbers even as Austin parked the semi.

Peregrine could only guess how they'd been detected. Perhaps a neighbor, or a kid playing on the luxurious block, had seen the minivan when they'd let Sidney and Mako out the back. That's all he could figure.

No one stood watch. Rossi greedily forced open each security case to inspect his loot. The other members of the gang, except for Peregrine, hung about the short, ugly man like slavering dogs eager to fight over the scraps from Rossi's table. Peregrine was not sure of the whole sequence in hindsight. But it began while Rossi admired a jewel-encrusted, gaudy piece of gold smithed by Cellini.

"We didn't have to kill anyone," Peregrine fumed, "Sid had plenty of shells. He could have kept firing into the ground around that guard, until the gas finally got to him."

"Yeh," Sidney snorted, eyes fixed on the expensive bauble in Diamotti's hand, "Like we had all day."

"Listen buttfuck! You're getting on my nerves," Rossi put down the jewelry and leveled a threatening gaze at Peregrine, "You've just about outlived your usefulness to me. If you want your cut, and if you value your life, you'd better shut your trap."

"You listen up Diamotti," Peregrine snapped, "If a good friend of mine doesn't hear from me in 48 hours, a packet goes into the mail to the FBI with your name and every detail of this operation. You'll have to get out of the country, and how are you gonna enjoy your Piccoli gems when you're constantly looking over your shoulder for Interpol?"

"Don't you threaten me," Rossi yelled, but he knew it was a stalemate. He knew Peregrine's brother, and Peregrine's brother's lawyer had the packet of evidence. Still and all, Peregrine didn't bring up the murder again. He didn't have the time. Austin, who had drifted over to the plate glass window overlooking the northern Bay Area during their interchange, suddenly gurgled something incoherent.

"What the hell's wrong with you!" Rossi turned on him.

"Cops." Austin squeaked out. Sure enough, the late afternoon street crawled with them. Black-and-whites held a roadblock at the street entrance and fully three dozen uniformed CHP officers scuttled from cover to cover like cockroaches. Armed cockroaches.

"Goddamnit," Rossi snapped, Piccoli gem cases clutched in his arms, and eyes in a panic. "Austin, get some control. Let's get the chopper ready. Sidney, Mako, Peregrine; cover the front. I don't want any shooting until I give the order."

Rossi and Austin scooped up the gem cases and quickly stumbled out the back. A voice over a bullhorn boomed out a warning directed at

29

their house. Telling Mako not to shoot was like telling the hungry infant not to grab for the milk-loaded teat swinging in front of his face. Peregrine could detect the adrenaline rush and killing lust in Mako's twisted face. As soon as the police officer finished his announcement Mako bounded down the front door stairwell, leaned out the door, and hammered the cop dead with a single shot. The plate glass window exploded into angry shards with the first police volley. Peregrine hit the floor to crawl for the backyard. He'd reached the swinging dining room door when Rossi stuck his head through it, and shouted.

"Mako, Peregrine, Sid. Come on. We're getting the hell out of here."

Tear gas canisters crashed into the house at that point. They needed no further encouragement. They reached the kitchen's back door as Austin turned over the helicopter's engine. Ahead, in the middle of the landscaped acre of backyard, Diamotti and Austin had managed to knock down a temporary plywood shed from around the sleek Ecureuil B-5. Austin and Sidney had assembled the helicopter piece by piece in the last several months in case they'd needed to make a quick escape well ahead of pursuit. *Not* as a last second contingency under such tight circumstances. Now it waited for them, rotors pounding the air and flattening the grass. Roaring out their deaths.

Behind, the house shook under impact from bullets and tear gas canisters, walls shredding and brickwork shattering. Inside, the voice of Peregrine's hunch screamed: "Don't get on that helicopter! It'll be your death!" They crossed the yard in a line, strung out, ducking and crawling commando-style, even though they were not under direct fire. Peregrine kept to the end of the line. As they approached, Austin swung open the cargo door. Rossi waited, crouching, at the door, as Sidney and Mako clambered on board. Diamotti noticed Peregrine's hesitation and whipped out a gun.

"On board, fuckhead," he shouted above the deafening thunder, "We're all leaving the same way."

Peregrine did as he was told. Rossi followed on his ass, revolver at the ready.

"Hit it Austin," Rossi punched the pilot's shoulder. Austin reacted instantly. The helicopter leapt up several yards at once, throwing everybody else off balance, and giving Peregrine his chance. He dove from the chopper, hit the grass, and rolled. In rolling, he looked back and caught Rossi, Sidney and Mako leaning out the cargo door, their handguns blazing action, the chopper slowly rising. He continued his roll to the safety of several trees, bullets plowing up the ground around him. The helicopter came under fire from the cops in the street. As Diamotti's gang turned their attention once more to their escape, Peregrine made his break.

He ran for a far fence, not daring to look back. Feeling the itch of a

PRIMING THE APOCALYPSE

set of cross hairs between his shoulder blades. He hit the fence and vaulted over on adrenaline alone. Two red-eyed Dobermans ran for him howling in the new yard, from around a large fenced off flower garden. He tried keeping the garden between him and the maddened beasts in his frantic dash for another fence. He slammed on over the fence, and broke the tops to two boards in the process. The dogs hit the wood behind him, their jaws snapping bare inches from his butt. At the same instant, the helicopter crashed and exploded. Peregrine caught his breath in the concussive aftermath seated on the edge of a brush and tree choked arroyo. The dogs bayed wildly in the yard behind him.

He'd spent the next nine hours slowly, carefully making his way back to his car. Up Blithedale Ridge, across Warner Canyon, and along Crown Road; the fugitive had stumbled, expecting any moment to hear pursuit. Now, dredging himself up from his all-too-brief sleep, he took stock of his situation. He assumed the police were already looking for him, not having found him at the safe house. He'd intended to use his cut from the heist to secure his early retirement in Trieste or Rijeka on the Dalmatian coast of independent Slovenia. As it stood, he had a mere $220 to his name. Just enough to cover a few living expenses, with the rent paid on his Alabaster apartment. Seated in the front seat, he twisted his ring, deep in thought. One set of instincts told him to blow the area for a while, at least until things iced considerably. But he didn't have the money to split. So another packet of instincts prodded him to do another job to get some quick money; a second story job which would expose him to more unwanted police attention.

He started up the car with this dilemma in mind and drove within speed limits up Hwy. 101 to Alabaster and his apartment. He thought it strange that the radio news report still insisted that the riemanium had not been recovered. The gang safe house burndown story followed news of the funeral for another US journalist killed in the Peru/Bolivia war, ahead of the story about the disastrous ATF raid on the cannibalistic Transubstantiation cult compound outside of Butte, Montana. He was tempted to take the side road on which they'd tossed the case of riemanium in order to find it, as he was tempted to drive for his buried cache of Sulawesi contraband for the fake ID. But he didn't feel confident about finding the exact spot of either in the dark, so he remained on the highway until the Lucas Valley turnoff.

His third story apartment was off Main Street downtown, overlooking the favored youth hangouts. The Loop was for the town's teenagers, a circular street in the business district that surrounded a nicely landscaped Barbary Park around which they cruised in their cars. The Gondwana Cafe off the Loop was for the college set and their Bohemian pretensions. He checked his refrigerator once behind his locked door and cleaned it out of a beer and some leftover chicken.

31

END TIME

Then, he retired to the bathroom to remove his disguise.

Make-up, like lies, needed to be simple in order to be effective. If either were too complex or elaborate, there was the risk of tripping up on some inconsistency or forgotten detail. At least, that's how Peregrine understood it. He briefly showered, then applied strong cleansing compounds to his wet body in order to unbind the sophisticated make-up; a cream for his fake tan and a gel for his dark hair color, both of which washed away with another shower. As he toweled off, he demolished both chicken and beer. He decided to hang in until the end of February, and to do a few, as-safe-as-possible jobs to get the money to leave. He smoked a pipeful, then was ready for a troubled sleep, waking briefly for the rain.

SEVEN

"Honey. Mark. Someone's knocking at the door." Gwen shook her husband's shoulder, the two in bed. He woke with a groan. "Please, see who it is."

"What the hell time is it?" Marcus grumbled. He fumbled for both his glasses and the alarm clock. "Damn. It's one in the morning."

Again, the doorbell rang, followed by a long, steady knock. After several well-chosen curses, Marcus Dimapopulos hulked out of bed, stumbled about until he found his robe, and then trundled down the stairs. He felt all of his old wounds in the night chill. The door peephole revealed an old friend on the porch, Neal Emerson. Neal and Marcus had served together in the Marines in '65, Johnson's occupation of Santo Domingo in the Dominican Republic. Both credited their deployment to the Caribbean fresh out of Lejeune boot camp, not only for their friendship, but also for the lucky courses to their lives since. Had they gone to Nam, as had others they had known in the Corps, things likely would have been different.

They had each gone into similar lines of work after finishing up their respective tours of duty in the Mountain Warfare Training Center in Bridgeport, California; Marcus into private investigation and Neal into security services. Neal became the wealthy, playboy owner/president of Security Pacific Services, habitué of San Francisco's elite watering holes. Marcus settled down with a wife and a one-man South Bay detective agency known for its consistently outstanding work. They had remained friends, Neal the godfather of Mark and Gwen's two now-grown children. And Neal did look silly shivering on the porch, sheepish in his three-piece suit.

"Neal, what the hell are you doing out here at this godawful time of the morning?" Marcus bellowed as he opened the door. "Why didn't you call?"

"Sorry, Mark," Neal stepped into his friend's house, "Sorry, sorry, sorry. I did call, but I got transferred to your office answering machine.

32

PRIMING THE APOCALYPSE

Mark, I'm desperate. I need to ask you the biggest favor of my life. Name your price."

"Million bucks," Marcus was bemused, "Two million because it's after midnight."

"How do you spell that last name?" Neal theatrically reached into his jacket pocket for his checkbook.

"Later," the detective chuckled. He had solved a half dozen cases for Neal's company in the past, all of them when Security Pacific's best had reached dead-ends. "This IS about the heist this morning. Excuse me. Yesterday morning."

"Again, a thousand apologies," Neal's desperation haunted him just below his jocular performance, "Yes, it's the theft. The riemanium's still missing. I NEED your help. Immediately."

"And that means?" Mark cocked a mocking eyebrow.

"The next three hours of your life. Perhaps less." Neal laughed. Pleaded. "For which I'm also willing to pay you handsomely, even if you don't accept the case. $5,000 for your time."

"Excuse me, while I step into my office."

Dimapopulos actually stepped into his entry hall closet, one he had built to his own specifications. It was a walk-in with a reinforced door that locked from the inside. It had a back door into the kitchen, provided dressing mirrors with a line of last-minute clothing, and was wired with an emergency telephone and a terminal to the house's security computer. It also hid a small, defensive arsenal. He looked himself over once casually outfitted for business, an elderly man with the broad-boned build of an aging football half-back. He had been thinking of retirement lately. But he had been only partly successful in thinning out his cases to the easiest and most lucrative over the last year. Neal's cases were never easy. However, one last good one could secure that retirement. He excused himself to tiptoe to Gwen's bedside to whisper: "It's Neal. I'll be back for breakfast dear."

Neal eased out of Marcus's driveway in the solidly middle-class Santa Clara suburb, but turned south on 101. The silver haired president brought the gray haired PI up to date. As they sped along, mega-metro landscapes wrapped past the windows of the Rolls Sport. Caught between late night and early morning, the scenery was heavy on freeway light afterglowed by San Jose city lighting on a dense overcast. Marcus showed no reaction when Neal took an off ramp for a private airport, but flinched a bit when he parked at the jumpjet terminal. The detective hated flying. But while he could white knuckle a jumbo jet flight, as he had military transports, jumpjets were an entirely different matter.

Marcus had so far managed to keep his practice largely confined to the Bay Area, and to the ground, avoiding the terrors of a jump. His palms started to sweat as the two walked across the tarmac toward the small, streamlined VTOL turbojet, all bathed in yellow incandescence. He developed a noticeable tic in the left corner of his mouth when he ducked into the jumpjet's claustrophobic passenger cabin.

"I remember you don't like flying," Neal apologized, "But this really is the fastest way to get across the Bay. The only way to get you some sleep tonight. Hope you don't mind."

"Not at all," Marcus managed, after clearing his throat twice to avoid dry heaving.

He checked and double checked his webstrap, five times total. He kept his gaze out the window, concentrating on a night iced electric. Hardly breathing. Every muscle tensed when the jets whined up, like some maniac dentist's drill. Both heart and stomach leapt into his mouth, kept down only by clenched teeth, when the jumpjet slammed him into his seat with sudden acceleration. Fingernails bit into palms, and he struggled not to hyperventilate. The flight from the outskirts of San Jose to a smooth landing in a north Richmond industrial park took ten minutes. It lasted hours for Marcus, even as the rush of urban lighting outside the window panicked him with the feeling he rode a deadly, out-of-control roller coaster. A fetid wind off the bay cooled his wet face when he and Neal stepped down from the jet to walk to a waiting Mercedes.

"There's a common thread here," Neal related as he negotiated urban wasteland for a bridge-bound 580 on ramp, "The guy who escaped the Mill Valley burn-down, his description fits the description of Rosanne's missing boyfriend. I want to hire you to find him. He must have the riemanium."

"And this Rosanne Casey is your weekend scheduler," Marcus fumbled for his pocket notebook, still trying to steady his heartbeat with controlled breathing, "I can drop by tomorrow...I mean today, and talk to her."

"No," Neal seemed irritated, "I mean, not to bother. I intervened in the local office and fired her, um, yesterday."

"That was dumb," Marcus used the nub of his eraser to scratch out the note, "You said yourself that the police don't suspect her of providing her boyfriend with inside information. Do you?"

"No, the police don't think she gave this Michael any information deliberately," Neal admitted, "I guess I don't either."

"So, why did you fire her?" the detective continued probing.

"I...I guess I just don't want to reward stupidity," Neal averted his eyes to the road. "One way or another, he used her to gain access to company information."

"Too bad," Marcus hunched into his sheepskin jacket, "Folks learn the most from their stupid mistakes."

34

PRIMING THE APOCALYPSE

"I've got enough problems," Neal ignored his friend's implications, "I don't need to deal with someone else's stupid mistakes. Now I've got to pin down who INSIDE leaked the riemanium theft to the media."

Marcus did not buy it, but he did not continue pushing either. They had crossed San Pablo Bay, the lights of San Quentin greeting them reflected as well off the sullen, oily, black water. One of the bridge's last buttresses flourished a lurid, fluorescent, spray-painted piece of graffiti:

for Black dada Nihilismus. Neal dialed up connections on his cellular. Within minutes, they raced down 101 under police escort, which accompanied them through Mill Valley, and into the luxury suburbs of its foothills. Neal made small talk, inquiring about Gwen and the children, retirement, and mutual friends long-time-not-seen. The sight of over a dozen police cars brought them back to the subject.

"Captain Sampson," Neal announced, approaching a tall, weary-eyed man, graying at the temples, but still form fitting his CHP uniform, "This is Detective Marcus Dimapopulos. He's employed by Security Pacific to look into the riemanium theft. Please, help him in any way you can. Mark, I'll be nosing around myself. When you're ready, I'll take you home."

"I've heard of you," the Captain extended his hand to shake as Neal retreated into the night. Police radios squawked and spat static. "Big case, ten years ago. The Benson kidnapping, Berkeley, '97. You do class work. The name's Brian Sampson."

Brian conducted Marcus past the road blocks, the yellow police tape, and the semi splashed with fevered red, blue, yellow and white police car lights.

"The mini-van is in the truck," Sampson gestured absently at it, "The house and the gang had already attracted attention from the neighbors. Five guys going in and out for the past six months, perhaps as many as four of them living here on a somewhat regular basis. The truck in this neighborhood was a red flag. Guy down the block matched the police description of three of the gang and called. Four guys got out of the semi and one, Diamotti, the gang leader, was already here."

The house was in ruins. Bullet holes, cracked plaster and fragged bricks twisted the entrance stairwell. Neatly stacked evidence, all tagged and categorized, marked off the living room floor beneath the non-existent picture window.

"This is the stuff left in the house. Groceries, newspapers, personal

35

effects, bills, scraps of paper. We're still going over the place for finger-prints and other clues for the lab. Reconstructing this robbery is going to take time. If you want to look at anything, there are extra plastic gloves in the kitchen."

Brian then showed Marcus the back yard. A grizzly scene. The twist-ed, burned helicopter wreckage occupied the yard's center, still whis-pering smoke and smelling of fuel and fried insulation. Four body bags, each filled, waited in a row next to the crumpled fuselage.

"There wasn't any problem identifying any of these," the Captain leaned down to snag open the first bag, "Each has an arm-long record. Rossi Calvino Diamotti, aka Sylvatore, Chicago, twenty years ago. The ringleader. He's got Mob connections, but he was an independent on this coast. Ran his own operation and tithed to the 'big boys' back east, for special services. Next, Tyrone Austin Johnson, also known as 'Dread.' He did the transport and hacking. Started his record as an LA Crip. Applied his Army training after the second Gulf War to work for the New York Black Family syndicate. Sidney Thomas Franklin here handled the gang's munitions; one of those Somali Vets who didn't get enough of that war. Did mercenary work in Angola, South Africa and Peru. Also wanted in Illinois for 'questioning' in the death of his wife and his best friend. Finally, Bill 'Mako' Young. Last employer; the Hawaiian Mafia. One of their hit men, responsible for perhaps as many as twenty-two island murders. The advantages of Diamotti's mob connections."

"And the fifth suspect?" Marcus asked, poking his notebook with the point of his pencil.

"All we have definitely is a set of fingerprints," Brian said, "The FBI is cross-checking. But so far, nothing. We've got vague descriptions from the neighbors. Apparently, he's the one who didn't live here. Diamotti's phone book has six public telephone listings in the north Marin area, each noted with a day, time and the name Peregrine. From all the other evidence, this fifth suspect was the gang's procurer."

"Rosanne Casey's Michael Baumann?" the detective ventured.

"Neal told you," Sampson grew more weary by the minute and pulled a folded xerox from his pocket, "We've done a police composite sketch based on her description. I'll get you a better copy. She was as helpful as she could be. She does not appear involved, but I have no doubt he used his relationship with Rosanne to gain access to inside information on the Security Pacific run."

"You've talked to her then?"

"Yesterday afternoon, just before she got off work. Nice girl. 31. X-ray tech/nursing student at UCSF. Her Security Pacific job was only part-time."

"It's not even that, anymore," Marcus commented.

PRIMING THE APOCALYPSE

"I know. Neal fired her. She seems genuinely distressed about all of this. She says her 'Mike' is innocent."

"Now, for the 64-Dollar-Question..."

"There's no trace of the riemanium. Anywhere." Brian grimly shook his head. "Not in the van, not in the house, not in the helicopter. Not anywhere. The Piccoli collection is safe and sound at HQ. But just like this Peregrine, the riemanium's vanished into thin air. Now, our missing suspect could have gotten away any number of ways. But few with that riemanium. Case and all, it weighs over sixty pounds."

"But you go along with Neal's theory that if this Peregrine, or Mike, or whoever is found, the riemanium will be also?" the detective asked.

"There's a number of possibilities actually. They might have dumped the riemanium once it got too hot for them, and no one's found it yet. Perhaps they stashed it somewhere, intending to return for it. There might've been two different gangs involved in this robbery. Or maybe they had a buyer, and its already been delivered and paid for. Then again, maybe Peregrine drove away with the riemanium in a car between the time the neighbor called and we arrived here. We can't be sure that didn't happen. Its one of the more plausible scenarios. In any case, the fifth suspect is the only living witness to what happened. Accomplice to the guard's murder as well. We may not find the riemanium when we track him down. But, we'll be a step closer."

"True enough," Marcus said, "By the way, can I get a copy of your investigation so far? I'm particularly interested in getting hold of Rosanne Casey. I'm sure Neal Emerson would authorize it."

"Not a problem. Stop by my office on Monday." Sampson handed the detective his card. "Anything else you'd like to know?"

"Plenty. But for now, I'll just poke around on my own for a while."

"Be my guest," Brian waved a hand, "Told you about the gloves. I'll be around for the rest of the night."

Marcus contributed to the police investigation by digging up three more clues. He noticed right off the condition of the lawn to one side of the crashed helicopter. Besides excavating the bullets to match the dead men's guns, he also found a shirt button which did not match any of those worn by the corpses. Second, he called Rossi's list of six public phone numbers for Peregrine, and surprisingly for two-thirty in the morning, five answered. Not so surprising as all five were in late night cafes or clubs which featured "alternative music" on the nights Peregrine was scheduled in Diamotti's phone book. Three were in Alabaster, one was in Marinwood, and the other was in Fairfax.

"If the final number is in or around Alabaster, that's a logical place to start looking for this Peregrine," Marcus smiled at Brian over a paper cup of coffee.

And finally, the detective tracked Peregrine's flight from the house.

END TIME

"He climbed, actually jumped the first fence there," Marcus pointed out the section to the Captain, "You can't see it clearly on the safe house side, but you can see where he landed in this yard."

The owner of the transgressed yard held his Dobermans at bay and looked bewildered.

"He hit the second fence here. He probably used the canyon on the other side to escape the area. Now, if we could have those broken off fence boards there, on the other side.

Brian snapped his fingers, and a CHP officer jumped.

"There," Marcus held the board pieces up with pride, "Fabric, thread, blood, probably some skin cells."

"You've certainly earned your pay tonight, which I assume is better than mine," Sampson whistled, depositing the fence ends into an evidence zip-lock, "No indication that he was carrying anything as heavy as a case of riemanium."

"None," Marcus rubbed his tired eyes, "And every indication that this Peregrine had a falling out with the rest of the gang. Literally had to run for his life. 'Course, your boys would have gotten all of this. Eventually."

"Eventually," the Captain conceded, "Now, what's up?"

"I'm going home," Marcus grinned with satisfaction, "It'll be dawn in another couple of hours. I need my sleep, but I'll pick up that report Monday morning."

"Stop in for a talk, while you're at it," Brian said.

Neal sprawled, fast asleep, across the front seat of his car.

"I'll take the case," Marcus said as the corporate president drove away from the rich, gutted house. "Minimum, if I find Peregrine, it'll cost you $250,000; $50,000 up front. They find him tomorrow, that's all you lose. $100,000 if you want me off the case for any reason, and $150,000 if somewhere along the way the police get him, helped by my work. I'll be consulting closely with Captain Sampson. I'll tell you at $150,000 if there's going to be an overrun. Also I'll need a powerful portable computer and communications setup. I'll submit a formal contract Monday. Deal?"

"Agreed," Neal yawned.

"And Neal, no more one-in-the-morning visits. I'll get an answering service and a beeper, but I decide what's an emergency. You know my business hours. One more thing. We drive back to my house. No jump-jet."

They recrossed the Richmond-San Rafael bridge, and it started to rain.

EIGHT

Excerpted from
"Nations and People of Earth,"

PRIMING THE APOCALYPSE

The Amok World Almanac
and Book of Weird Facts
2010
(Electrostraca #: A/GR-010-367-582-2376)

The Celebes/Sulawesi Outlaw Zone is a collection of islands in Indonesia, east of Borneo; a sub-archipelago of about 73,000 square miles now populated by perhaps two million hardened international criminals. Until 1999 Celebes/Sulawesi was an integral part of Indonesia, inhabited by some ten million Malays, Indians, Chinese and indigenous peoples engaged principally in agriculture, fishing and forestry. Islam and Hinduism became forces with the rise of religious fundamentalism worldwide in the 1990's, and when the 1998 Third World economic collapse hit Indonesia, cutting earnings from exports in half, Moslem and Hindu separatists launched well organized insurrections across Celebes/Sulawesi by the fall. An aged, senile President-For-Life Suharto and his corrupt, nepotistic regime resorted to a counterinsurgency campaign some of the critics of which have called East Timor Cubed. This strategy of indiscriminate mass genocide and rapid population relocations left the Celebes virtually depopulated by the end of 1999. Then the old general surprised the international community by creating the Sulawesi Development Corporation and offering up the sub-archipelago as the world's largest prison colony.

What is more surprising is that the United States, United Kingdom, United Europe, and the remnants of the Commonwealth of Independent States, among many other nations large and small, quickly signed contracts with the Development Corporation. Incorrigible criminals were given a choice; life in prison without parole, perhaps the death penalty if it applied, or the slim chance of survival after being randomly parachuted into the Celebes. The entire island collection, in turn, was surrounded by state-of-the-art security; submarines, floating and aerial monitoring devices, as well as manned boat and air patrols armed to the teeth.

It is not clear how voluntary many of the prisoner drops over Sulawesi were in actuality. The penal colony's natural environment started, and remained brutally savage. Those who managed to survive rapidly formed competing, highly militarized, territorially based gangs, with a sprinkling of super survivalist solos in their midst. What was not anticipated was that, in forcing hundreds and then thousands of superbly criminal minds to survive together against a purposefully hardened natural world, not to mention each other, the Celebes prison colony might go beyond mere survival to take up their old occupations, with a vengeance.

Sulawesi became an outlaw zone; a high tech, high energy nexus practicing maximum black market economies. Conventional contra-band—drugs, weapons, high value stolen goods—were incidental to the stolen technologies, purloined scientific discoveries, hot software, and black market data bases which flowed in and out of the Celebes. Not a few surprises were beginning to emerge, what with the formation of Celebes Research and Development by an uneasy coalition of Sulawesi gangs two years after Suharto's death in 2003. And the military junta that took power after the death of Indonesia's President-For-Life was entirely too terrified to take any action against the outlaw zone in their nation's midst.

Of course, the Sulawesi gangs are cosmopolitan enough to keep the Indonesian government monetarily well greased. The US government, in spearheading the drive to replace a now laughable Development Corporation security with UN forces, does not expect such an action to have much affect on the outlaw zone. So the Pentagon plans for more forceful contingencies. In the meantime, the Sulawesi gangs continue their subtle incorporation of the Indonesian banking system into their financial laundering schemes. And, in the meantime, a number of nations still continue to routinely drop their criminals over the Celebes. It is rumored that Sulawesi took a strong interest in the bomb-grade riemanium stolen by anti-war activists in the U.S. San Francisco Bay Area in 2007...

CELEBES/SULAWESI PENAL COLONY

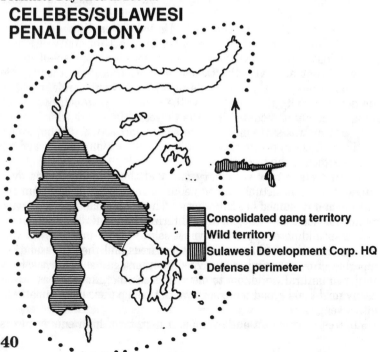

Consolidated gang territory
Wild territory
Sulawesi Development Corp. HQ
Defense perimeter

PART TWO
BABYLON BY THE BAY

NINE

Excerpted from the Introduction to
'New Romantic' Historiography: 2001-2004: A Survey
by Allen Meltzer
Published 2005 by University of California Press
(Electrostraca #: SH/H-005-995-384-4581)

THE "NEW ROMANTIC" MOVEMENT

The project of history, circa 1972, was mundane at best; limited to the task of determining what constitutes an historical event, historical cause-and-effect, historical fact and evidence, and like questions. Having long abandoned the nineteenth century labor of trying to determine patterns or cycles of development in the historical record, historians at the end of the twentieth century felt increasingly adrift. The pace, scope and magnitude of seemingly inchoate change all around the globe after 1972 was the basis for the historians' unease, which built until the publication in January, 2002 of Jerome Stachniw's monograph, "An Interstitial Approach to Post-Soviet Histories," breached the levees of a conventional historiography already at flood levels.

A number of scholars and academics devoted to the Muse Cleo began a scramble for new vocabularies, paradigms, and models to adequately explain the apparently escalating chaos in world events; what many increasingly described as a world interregnum. This broad tendency in the discipline of history was immediately and derisively termed the New Romantic movement by its critics which, like most epithets, became the loose movement's humorous, unofficial moniker. Historians unwilling to stand pat with micro-history and cleometrics, and unwilling to try fitting events and dynamics procrustean-style into "outworn"

41

historical theories and categories, in fact used several options to challenge historiographic orthodoxy. Existing historical models and methodologies, such as Marxism, were radically overhauled in order to describe and analyze new conditions, as San Liu accomplishes with her CyberMarxist series of histories and as is the case with the "World War Three" interpretation of Jawarah Chandler Krishnamurti. Inherently transhistoric or nonhistoric concepts were adapted to historical reality as Ngobo Nyere does to create "secular millennarianism." Or an entirely original system for describing and analyzing historical events and dynamics was attempted, as is the case with Stachniw's interstitial history and Bartlebee's cyberhistory.

In point of fact, most New Romantic historians do all three. This new interest in historical patterns, stages and cycles—albeit from unusual, often ingenious perspectives—has enjoyed a prodigious publishing record in the last three years, and as a consequence, individual pieces in the wealth of histories written through 2004 are sometimes difficult to precisely categorize. The call for a change in the researching and writing of history, this challenge to conventional historiography championed by the discipline's New Romantics, has yet to have any substantial impact on the History Establishment. Nor has one or another of this new movement's historical interpretations yet inherited the international revolutionary mantle of Marxism. Such ambitions depend solely, and ultimately upon how history plays out in the next two or three decades; the exact force which brought the movement into being in the first place.

In the interim, this volume's collection of essays attempts a critical survey of the New Romantic historians, offering an appreciative but, in the end non-believing appraisal of this wide ranging movement to date. History has been reinvigorated by the debates introduced from New Romantic challenges to orthodoxy, and this survey purposefully avoids the movement's more self-revelatory sentiments, such as those expressed in this quote from San Liu's introduction to *History Loops*, Bartlebee's three volume history of the 1998 Third World economic collapse:

We [members of the European Delgado Circle] felt like aboriginals—Amerindians from the Great Plains, Africans from the veldt, or Asiatics from the steppes—who had grown up in one very small corner of our world. After the collapse of our civilization's greatest enemy, we had naively come to expect that all of the world was becoming the same; green, peaceful, and accepting of the enlightened stewardship of our people. Then, upon climbing a nearby hill, we realize that, in fact, most of the world around us is in flames. A few areas have so far avoided the avaricious fires, and select areas such as our own are actually verdant; this greenery due to waters stolen from the rest of the grassland around us. Our people, far from husbanding the world, actually contribute to the scorched earth we now witness, all the while remaining secure in our rich, artificial oasis.[1.]

In contrast, this collection of historians emphasizes the dry, academic discussion of assumptions underlying historiographic methodologies and structures. A strong effort is made to describe and present excerpts from the often highly theoretical manifestos of the better known New Romantic historians, not only in relation to each other as intellectual history, but also as social history against the background of the vast social upheavals worldwide that they attempt to describe and interpret. For while much is made of the "audacity" and "originality" of New Romantic historical interpretations, in turn considered "flamboyant" and "dishonest" by their critics, what is often overlooked is the global context that gave rise to this tendency in the project of history to begin with; an historical context that influenced how individual New Romantic historians chose to question established historiography.

The focus of this work is historiography, the writing of history. How and why the writing of history changed from the end of the twentieth century to the beginning of the twenty-first cannot be understood, however, without a knowledge of historical events over the past thirty years. And while frequently it is difficult to objectively summarize events so close in time, contrary to the New Romantic spirit it is possible to describe them in conventional terms without doing them much damage. Indeed, the historically steeped World-System School of sociological analysis (Amin, Arrighi, Frank, Wallerstein, et. al.) has produced a credible description of world dynamics, without the *sturm und drang* reveled in by New Romantic historians. The summary of the historical context to New Romantic historiography that follows draws upon World-System insights, while insisting that the last thirty years can demonstrate an overarching theme; that being the growing obsolescence of the nation-state in world-system dynamics.

HISTORICAL CONTEXT TO "NEW ROMANTIC" MOVEMENT

A) WORLD SYSTEM, 1972: By 1972, the capitalist world-system comprised a fully developed, industrialized, prosperous capitalist core of nations dominated by the United States, and including western Europe and Japan; a developing, industrializing, struggling semi-periphery of nations in eastern Europe, the former Soviet Union, South Korea, Taiwan, etc.; and an undeveloped, imperialized, destitute periphery of nations over the rest of the world. What was termed the socialist world, or bloc, actually straddled semi-periphery and periphery, which by 1972 had become the fracture line for the socialist camp's Sino/Soviet split. In no way did the socialist bloc stand outside of the capitalist world-economy. The structure of the nation-state and the

END TIME

national economy, so instrumental in the capitalist core's affluence, the semi-periphery's development, and the periphery's aspirations, was already demonstrating limits.

B) BEGINNINGS OF REGIONAL CAPITALIST CONSOLIDATION: The United Kingdom, Ireland and Denmark joined the European Economic Community in 1973, insuring that eventually a supranational entity, a "United States of Europe," would emerge to create a Common Market out of formerly warring nations. The knitting together of western Europe into a federal community inspired the supersession of the nation-state in a wave of regional capitalist consolidation across north America, eastern Europe, and Asia. The United States, Canada and Mexico signed a North American Free Trade agreement in 1992, later called the Continental Trade agreement, the same year western Europe's Economic Community dropped most internal trade and customs barriers. Both north American and European consolidation continued through the 1990's, despite the protectionist turn to the former and the initial failures of Maastricht in the latter.

C) BEGINNINGS OF THIRD WORLD COLLAPSE: The United States withdrew from Vietnam in 1975 and thereafter matched the cry of "Two, Three, Many Vietnams" with the reality of two, three, many civil wars. The US, USSR and PRC initiated the disintegration of the nation-state in the Third World periphery by pitting one Third World country against another (Iraq and Iran), sponsoring guerrillas and contras in their opponent's client states (Afghanistan, Angola, Mozambique and Nicaragua), and promoting brush war, civil war and virulent factionalism (Lebanon, Kampuchea, and Ethiopia) through their "superpower" struggles. In truth, the nation-state was no longer a sufficient instrument either to pull a poor Third World country into successful industrialization and economic development, just as it no longer guaranteed a core country's continued economic prosperity and well being.

D) COLLAPSE OF SOVIET COMMUNISM: The years from 1989 through 1992 were pivotal in the nation-state's demise. Soviet hegemony and Soviet-style communism collapsed in eastern Europe by 1989. In 1991, the Soviet Union deconstructed, to reassemble as the decentralized, ineffectual Commonwealth of Independent States, formally non-communist and several republics shy of the former Union. The collapse of Soviet power from 1985 to 1991, and the subsequent degeneration of the former Soviet territories into civil war, social chaos and barbarism presented a dangerous political, economic and social vacuum. It heralded a partial collapse of the socialist bloc, of the "socialist world" alternative to capitalist development for the Third World to emulate, eliminating the most developed sector of the socialist camp. As such, it

44

contributed to the sense that "things fall apart, for the center will not hold" in the world at large. The specific dynamics in the sundered "socialist world" are worth noting:

1) EASTERN EUROPE: National and ethnic conflict proved to be the motor force for problems in this region after 1989, resulting in civil war (Yugoslavia), separation (the Czech/Slovak velvet divorce), encroachment (Serbian, Albanian, Greek and Bulgarian dismemberment of Macedonia), unification (Germany's tumultuous reunification), incorporation (Rumanian annexation of Moldova), and warfare (Serbia and Albania, Hungary and Rumania, Slovakia and Hungary). Eastern European instability had two direct consequences by the twenty-first century. Both the shotgun unification of Poland, Hungary, the Czech and Slovak republics, Slovenia and Croatia into a European Economic Commonwealth by the European Economic Community, and the tacit acknowledgment of Greater Rumania, Bulgaria, Serbia and Albania as a partial, if unstable buffer to the whirlwind of violent upheaval further east, undermined the nation-state paradigm.

2) COMMONWEALTH OF INDEPENDENT STATES: The former territories of the Soviet Union have become an immense charnel house for far more complex reasons, beginning (a) with national/ethnic conflicts more fractious than eastern Europe's. If a national republic could declare its independence from the Soviet Union, then a national minority could seek its sovereignty from its mother republic. Secessionist movements (Moldova from the CIS, Cossacks in the Ukraine, Tatars in Russia), civil wars (Georgia), pogroms (anti-Jewish/anti-Armenian massacres across Russia and Ukraine, 2000) and incorporations (Nagorno-Karabakh into Armenia) were rife, further complicated by civil war within civil war (secessionist Volga German/Tatar wars within Russia, 1999-2000). Border disputes and international conflicts festered throughout the former Soviet imperium as well, occasionally flaring into armed skirmishes and open warfare (Polish, Byelorussian, Russian altercations; Uzbeck-Tajik tribal wars, ongoing Russian-Ukrainian Black Sea quarrels with armed hostilities 2003 to present). (b) Russian attempts to maintain a position as the region's strongest power lended greatly to the international and ethnic tensions (abortive intervention in Moldova, quiet pressure on Ukraine, strong arm tactics in the Baltic states, clandestine efforts in Georgia). Russian government intervention abroad ostensibly on behalf of foreign Russian minorities, and ever more authoritarian methods to repress internal secessionist movements to delay civil war at home, reflected the Great Russian imperialism known all-to-well by the peoples of the region since Tsarist times.

END TIME

Other contributing elements to this disintegration proved to be (c) the failure of western aid to materialize in any appreciable quantity and the collapse of the region's economy (lines for basic necessities, rationing, unemployment, black marketeering, currency fluctuations, harsh winters, poor harvests), not to mention (d) the economic stranglehold held by regionally based mafia monopolies (St. Petersburg/Moscow gang wars, 2000-2001). In turn (e) as former Soviet bureaucrats became the de facto owners of business and industry in many of the new nations of the CIS, the working classes in the independent republics gained a wildcat trade unionist militancy that took on unruly syndicalist, councilist and anarchist directions (1999 Russian All-Workers General Strike). Beneath all of these currents ran another, sometimes contrary, but equally disruptive flow; (f) that of vestigial Soviet power. The Soviet military, formally divided up among the independent republics, remained staunchly Stalinist in its conservative upper echelons, with the entire military resistant to post-Soviet realities. The Communist Party, outlawed in some republics, barely tolerated in others, and the mainstream of politics under a different name in still others, was by origin a cellular, clandestine, conspiratorial paramilitary organization with dictatorial and internationalist aspirations. It absorbed disaffected elements of the secret police and, after the 1993 *putsch* which permitted then Russian president Yeltsin to assume dictatorial powers, the party continued an underground organizing principally in the post-Soviet military, fractions of the Party taking advantage of troubled times and a regional economy in ruins, using assassination, military putsch and red terror to further political instability and social chaos as precursors to Party takeover and a "second Soviet Revolution" (unsuccessful February, 2000 coup d'état in Russia, Ukraine and four other republics). Finally, (g) the presence of nuclear weapons arsenals (Russia, Ukraine, Byelorussia and Khazakstan), (h) the spread of a virulent youth counter culture encouraging drug abuse, nihilism and social desertion, and (i) the expiration of the Volga River and Lake Baykal ecologies, choked by industrial pollution (1999-2000), must be factored into any equation that attempts to explain why the territories of the former Soviet Union disintegrated into brutal civil war. The post-Soviet crisis in the nation-state, culminating in the "Time of Troubles" (1999-2002), contributed directly to the Chinese 2003 invasion of western and eastern Siberia to settle long standing border disputes with Russia; an undeclared war that drew in Mongolia, and is rumored to have escalated from conventional to ABC warfare.

3) REMNANT SOCIALIST BLOC: China's difficulties in absorbing Hong Kong (1997-1999) and ongoing internal strife, Vietnam's con-

46

tinuing war in Kampuchea, North Korea's problematic development of nuclear weapons, Cuba's stubborn atrophy under Castro's geriatric rule, Peru's auto-genocide after PCP/Sendero seizure of power (1999-2003), the problematic return of Sandanista rule to Nicaragua (1998), the Angolan government's final pyrrhic victory over UNITA (1997), and Mozambique's off again-on again civil war amply demonstrated that the remnant socialist camp was not immune to instability and chaos. The socialist bloc's desperate retrenchment and consolidation in supranational alliance, brilliantly engineered by China's post-Teng leadership at the 2002 Azanian International Conference on Socialism with the negotiation of the Azanian Compact of Mutual Socialist Assistance and Trade, helped protect these regions from being savaged by the holocaust enveloping the former Soviet Union and most of the Third World, nothing more. In turn, the mixed economies to most of the severely authoritarian socialist regimes in the Compact, the terms of which invited core capitalist penetration in gradually opening markets and liberalized foreign investment, seriously eroded the remnant socialist bloc's claim to be a qualitative alternative to capitalism for a Third World in flames.

E) THIRD WORLD HOLOCAUST: Eastern European/Soviet socialist demise and Soviet disintegration, in pulling down the sole bridge of semi-peripheral economic development out of Third World peripheral destitution, sealed the world-system economic alignment evident by the end of the twentieth century. The regionally consolidated, developed capitalist core to the capitalist world-economy in the northern hemisphere (North America/Europe/Japan) viciously exploited southern hemisphere Third World markets, labor and resources; finding it advantageous to undermine the Third World nation-state and keep this periphery in a constant condition of internecine conflict to further its exploitation. As a consequence, the Third World burned throughout the 1990's and into the twenty-first century. Not only did Soviet collapse and subsequent civil war feed into this Third World inferno in the abstract, by example, but the black market in post-Soviet weaponry directly fueled a social carnage and destruction spreading worldwide. The number of wars between Third World nations were legion (Myanmar-Bangladesh-Thailand, India-Pakistan, India-Tibet-China, Turkey-Iran, Turkey-Armenia, Azanian Boer secession, Egypt-Libya, Peru-Bolivia, Brazil-Argentina, etc.). Divided, conquered and disenfranchised nations continued bloody liberation struggles (Kurdistan, Tamil India, Palestine). And the fragmentation within Third World nation-states was sometimes violently granular; with religion battling religion as faith divided into sects, class attacking class as social strata crumbled into mafias and gangs, and ethnic group fighting ethnic group as nationalities fragmented into tribes. Tribes with flags, gangs with

END TIME

vendettas, and sects with divine sanction fought each other, plundered each other, ravaged and scorched the earth in a "war without end" (India, Afghanistan, Iraq, Algeria, Zaire, Colombia, Brazil). Volatile supranational Third World movements (Pan African and Arabic movements, Islamic and Hindu fundamentalisms) failed to stem this devouring global social chaos. Indeed they often contributed to it. Population ballooned across Latin America, Africa and Asia. Climate and weather patterns shifted with incremental atmospheric warming. The Sahara and other deserts expanded. Whole species continued to die off. Increased ultraviolet radiation due to atmospheric ozone depletion (1996-2002 northern hemisphere ozone hole) cut into agricultural production, and began to play havoc with the ocean's phytoplankton, disrupting fish supplies. Starvation, deforestation, massive erosion and famine followed. Diseases spread; the new in cancers and AIDS mutations, and the old in cholera and malaria. Pollution from toxic and radiation dumping, not to mention warfare, poisoned large regions of the periphery. Billions of people have died since 1991. All the while, the capitalist world-economy's core maximized its exploitation of the peripheral Third World's cheap indigenous and migrant labor, ample exportable resources, and war-hungry markets; establishing a permanent indenture upon the periphery with the 1998 Third World economic collapse.

F) GLOBAL CAPITALIST CONSOLIDATION: The capitalist-world economy, inclusive of the socialist bloc prior to Soviet communism's demise, achieved the global penetration of multi-national corporate capitalism with the partial collapse of the socialist camp. With the Warsaw Pact and COMECON eliminated, and the remnant socialist bloc interested in capitalist investment, the "strong force" (multi-national corporate capitalism) holding together the core's several national centers of competing capitalist power attained a fully global reach. This heightened the wave of regional supranational capitalist consolidations out from the North American Trade Zone and European Economic Community, somewhat forcefully in eastern Europe (with mutual development/preferential trade treaties binding Community and Commonwealth into a continental system of slow economic development), and eagerly in Asia (South Korea/Japan trade pact, Taiwan/Philippines/Singapore economic alliance, India/Australia/New Zealand commercial confederation). It proved increasingly advantageous for the national centers of capitalist power in the capitalist world-economy's core to consolidate supranational "co-development spheres" (to include developing and undeveloped peripheral regions), in order to secure stable, regionally diverse economic communities that could sustain a measure of internal market expansion and development. These consolidated capitalist regions served as bulwarks against the slow-motion Armageddon overtaking the former Soviet territories

BABYLON BY THE BAY

and much of the Third World. Finally, the collaboration between multinational corporate capitalism and regionally consolidated supranational capitalism to destabilize, shatter, ignite and loot the peripheral Third World completed the former's global reach while minimizing conflicts in the Third World between the competing national centers of capitalist power through a division of plunder. The US continued to act as the "center of the empire" (dominating the world-system's core even in decline, leading two wars against Iraq in the Persian Gulf, intervening in east Africa, the Balkans, central America and northern Asia) even as the capitalist world-economy became more polycentric. Nevertheless, the contradictions involved in US sponsorship of north American economic consolidation are illustrative, and worth detailing:

1) NORTH AMERICAN CONSOLIDATION: US INTENTIONS: America's ruling circles developed plans for supranational continental economic unification chafed by the Japanese miracle, anticipating unified Europe's economic power, and taking stock of widening world chaos. US sponsorship of the North American Trade Zone, via the Free Trade Agreement and subsequent, more protectionist amendments of the Continental Trade Agreement, was inclusive of Mexico, an unstable, poverty-stricken Third World country, and intended to be open ended in membership, focusing on the western hemisphere. American business and industry intended to practice its cowboy capitalism well into the twenty-first century. Neither incorporating unions into the social governance (Germany), nor treating workers as family (Japan), nor even providing basic social services (child care, universal health care-Britain) fit the John Wayne style of US corporate capitalism. US capital's strategy to compete with Japan and Europe was simple; promote rapid continental economic restructuring and trade to launch a burst of economic prosperity that staves off the labor organizing, social ferment and tax burden that a true "social contract" entails. The Trade Zone was intended in particular to end the threat of organized labor. The strong Canadian unions were expected to crumble as US corporations bought out the Canadian economy. Mexico's insurrectionary unionism was expected to evaporate with the increased opportunities and prosperity for its working class, and the increased stability of the country as a whole. And US unions, barely 10% of the work force, widely despised for their privileges, were intended to disappear entirely under the competition. A vast, continent wide pool of surplus labor, much of it migrant, was eventually to be created to fuel north American economic expansion. (Compare with European Economic Community use of eastern Europe as Third World region and as competition to attack western European unionism.)

END TIME

2) NORTH AMERICAN CONSOLIDATION: THE RESULTS: US ruling circles, with the aid of their Canadian and Mexican counterparts, did their best to weave together the separate national economies of the continent into supranational whole cloth before the close of the twentieth century. And the middle years of the 1990's did experience unprecedented economic reorganization across north America with a climb out of deep structural recession into a modest prosperity. However, the transnational ruling elite of this new continental economy was never more surprised than when militant labor organizing increased. Canadian unions in the CLC, seeing the writing on the wall, took the initiative and dispatched organizers and mutual aid to their US working class fellows in the AFL-CIO by the end of the 1990's. Wildcat strikes, sit-downs and secondary boycotts re-emerged and were combined with new tactics; data and information system sabotage, high-tech muckraking, and molecular strikes (the 1998-99 US/Canadian 48-hour "slinky strikes" covering up to 80% of truckers, dock workers and merchant marines, railway workers, airplane mechanics and flight crew). Purely economic demands were being supplemented, and sometimes supplanted by political demands. Organized labor, the unions proper, did not sponsor these new campaigns of economic direct action. Instead ad hoc, extraunion and extra-parliamentary, transnational workers organizations, in the form of independent industrial committees and councils, took responsibility. The complexities of litigating labor law across national borders in the Trade Zone were key to this new labor militancy's initial successes. US dominated continental capitalism fought this resurgent unionism tooth-and-nail through the turn of the century. Ultimately, the continental ruling class resorted to war in southern Mexico and patriotism to split militant north American labor into conservative, pro-war AFL-CIO/CLC/CTM majority unionism opposed by minority anti-war, independent unionists. The US government's reinstitution of a limited conscription has fueled antidraft sentiments as well as a continental anti-war opposition, particularly among the young. (Compare to transEuropean democratic trade union movement; European peace movement.)

3) NORTH AMERICAN CONSOLIDATION: SOUTHERN MEXICAN SECESSION: Mexican unionism, subject to chauvinism and racism from its northern "class comrades," nevertheless provided stunning, charismatic leadership and ultimately the most powerful challenge to the North American Trade Zone. Mexican unionism took its spark from labor struggles further north; Mexican farm labor unions joining up with the resurgent United Farm Workers which spearheaded a reverse, migrant worker organizing drive into Canada. But the Mexican government's propensity to resort to the

BABYLON BY THE BAY

Federales and unofficial death squads (Guadalajara, 1998; Oaxaca, 1999) created labor martyrs which, given the minority migrant Mexican populations in the US and Canada, provided much begrudged legends for all of north America's labor struggles. The radical Mexican working class, in looking up to the accomplishments of the US/Canadian labor movement (which by and large shunned class struggle "south of the border"), ultimately made the qualitative leap that started unraveling the fabric of North American economic integration from the bottom up. The Union de Trabajadores de Mexico was founded in late 1997, to grow by leaps and bounds through the corrupt, PRI-purchased 1998 elections, to become Mexico's largest libertarian trade union. The UTM organized the post-election protests which brought down a bloody response from the government and drove much of the union's leadership underground. Sparks from UTM's example flew about the country, creating numerous labor organizing brush fires that consumed the government-sponsored unions in the CTM before culminating in the formation of the multi-union Confederacion del Trabajo by mid-1999. The CT's first action, the calling of the November 1999 General Strike, precipitated a full state crackdown, declaration of martial law, brutal military and death squad repression, and covert CIA intervention. Driven underground once again, Mexico's revolutionary forces regrouped, established the Zapata Liberation Front, and launched the historic August 2000 Uprisings to establish the Meztican, Mixtecan and Mayapan Liberated Territories. The uprisings succeeded in declaring the latter two Liberated Territories by force of arms in the south by October. Thus, they founded a libertarian secessionist movement opposed wholeheartedly by the Mexican and US governments, and by the Canadian government only reluctantly (Quebec and aboriginal secessionism). When southern Mexico withdrew by insurrection from the North American Trade Zone, seceding from Mexico as the consciously anti-national Liberated Territories, the principle contradiction of the post-Soviet, capitalist world-system at the core played itself out. The "scorched earth" and "war without end," promoted by core multi-national corporate capitalism and regionally consolidated capitalism in the peripheral Third World, had come home to roost. The ZLF defiantly picked apart the weave of continental economic unity from revolutionary southern Mexico, in the US's own back yard, and US/Mexican military intervention was all but inevitable. But US/Mexican military war against the Liberated Territories is fast becoming an "endless conflict" between technomilitary counterinsurgents and brutal death squads on the one hand, and firmly entrenched, peasant guerrilla and popular forces on the other hand. (Compare to western European Basque and transEuropean Romani problems.)

G) WORLD SYSTEM, 2002: Capitalist world-economic core consolidation in its multi-national corporate and regional supranational dimensions was both the product of and a factor in Soviet collapse and Third World holocaust. Soviet collapse and Third World chaos were simultaneously a ripe harvest for consolidating capitalism and its Achilles heel...

TEN

DL pounded the raised, paved walkway surrounding Lake Merritt's somber waters. The sun of a new day had not yet cleared the dark, sullen Oakland hills, though its violent aura sifted through drab clouds, broken after a brief rain. The morning was brisk. He could see his paced breathing in the air before him as he ran, careful to avoid the heroin syringes, crack viles, Elysium caps, Ynisvitrin baggies and 999 bindles littering the ground he had chosen as his track. An oily sheen lapped with the tiny salty waves onto the shore. A small flotilla of ducks, permanent lake residents, cruised the still surface. He inhaled the air of his relative freedom with relish, and determination.

Prison's only gift to those doing time was time. It was up to the prisoner to find the self-discipline to use it wisely. Fortunately, DL had befriended a couple of powerful mentors to help him onto a productive course during his incarceration for accessory to auto theft; Askia of the New Afrikan Liberation Army and Isaak of the Nation of Islam. Despite their vast political differences, both had worked together in prison to punch out a small Black liberated zone behind bars. They conducted study groups and prayer sessions, and suffered long spells in solitary lock down for their efforts. Short-timer DL had gang money outside, so he did what he could for Askia and Isaak. They, in turn, gave him books to read and seminars to digest. Besides pumping iron, which almost everybody wound up doing, he had read volumes and developed his political consciousness. He had converted that prison self-discipline into habit once out, one as strong or stronger than his former crack habit. He had done the Black Panther thing; replaced his drug abuse with revolutionary zeal and commitment to "picking up the gun." Each morning, every morning, he ran fifteen miles and hefted weights for an hour to keep himself in shape. Between politics and working out, DL had no time for anything else, let alone romance. Besides his gang girlfriend, Winnona, had kept on the pipe while he was doing time, and had been shot by her dealer for stealing from him.

His Nike Superair's crunched into the walkway's damp gravel as he ran. DL wore a pair of headphones, but no matter how he ran or held his head, he could not seem to hold the signal from Liberation Station Afrika. DJ Elijah ran the pirate radio station single handedly; playing all types of African music from the Americas as well as the motherland; replaying the speeches, prose and poetry of famous Africans and African Americans; providing educational and self-help programming for the community; and broadcasting his controversial Liberation News Service comprised of international, national, state, city and neighborhood stories rarely, if ever, covered by the official media. Properly speaking, Elijah was an "African Zionist;" a Monophysitic, Gnostic mystic who belonged to an obscure sect of the Ethiopian Coptic Church and who preached a "black Christ/back to Africa" line. Rumor had it that he was a blind Persian Gulf vet who had kept his uncompromising pirate station operating for the past three years by using military surplus and a clever system of transmitters scattered about the city to avoid detection. DL also wore gray sweats, with a distinctive patch sewn into the long sleeve arm at biceps level.

Ahead, a dark shape, that of a man, loomed out of the morning.

"Yo, Snake Boy," DL stopped in his tracks, "How you doin'. Long time."

"DL, dat you?" Snake Boy cocked his head, his eyes glazed and bloodshot. "Ya out o' jail man?"

"Been out almost a year," DL stretched to keep from cramping, "How you been Snake?"

"Not too good," the decaying young black man grinned a feeble, gaptoothed smile. "Dey be cuttin' da street shit 'gain. Can't get it strong 'nough. Ya still wit' da Lords?"

"Got back into it," DL was sketchy, acknowledging the other's mention of his gang, the Young Afrikan Lords. "Things gonna be different."

"Better be," Snake Boy sniffled, then coughed, a deep, phlegm-rasping cough. "Dey be da main ones puttin' out dat weak shit."

"That ain't us," DL grimaced, "Some of the gangbangers from the Lords are still runnin' the streets, but not under our name. The Lord's ain't sellin' no shit."

"Huh?" Snake Boy tweaked up his eyes, "DL, ya get religion in school?"

"Something better," DL said, ignoring the street reference to jail. "Got liberation politics, boyeee."

"Pie in a sky," Snake Boy simply shrugged. "Ain't gonna do nothin' for ya but get ya killed."

"Maybe. But I'm too proletarianly intoxicated to be astronomically intimidated," DL laughed over his favorite quote, "Besides, its betterin' killin' yourself, like you doin' Snake."

"Ya just buyin' inta Da Man's rotten political system," the addict bristled at DL's remark.

"Fightin' the powers-that-be is politics, but it ain't sellin' out," the Young Afrikan Lord shook his head, "So what you contributin' to the race with your crack pipe?"

"Man, I just tryin' ta get through dis life," Snake Boy was angry, "Just tryin' ta get by dis racist system."

"Racism's cold truth, man," DL preached, "But you don't got to react to the system by doin' Whitey's work for him by killin' yourself."

Snake Boy did not answer. Instead, he turned abruptly and walked away. DL shrugged and started running again. As the two men separated, each thought of the other as deluded, a chaser of illusions.

***

The cold morning air slapped Greg's face on his drive south to the city. He had a headache from the night before, two if the riemanium were counted. Sunrise wrinkled through clouds and spangled across the rain-wet new day. His brooding over Janet was dulled by the touch of hangover. He wanted to hurt her. He wanted to smash up her life as she had broken up his. Wounded self-pity invariably gave way to a fist clenching anger. A desire for vengeance.

He caught an expansive view of the city on the turn approaching the Golden Gate, above Sausalito. Reborn once from ashes and recently twice shaken by seven-point-plus quakes, the city rubbed its back, the peninsula's spine spiked with trees and communications towers, up against thick clouds. The eastern lowlands and landfills built up into skyscrapers and arcologies in disregard, if not defiance, of the trembling land. The Transamerica Pyramid was still prominent. To the south the Pleiades Platform climbed into the new day sun. Steel, cement and reinforced concrete, glass, plastic, experimental plasglass and plasmetal fleshed out the body physical of the voracious, computerized global capitalism gripping the peninsula, the tentacles of which he imagined reaching off in every direction. He envisioned a fission sun going nova in its midst, shredding the buildings with nuclear tracery, folding up into an orange cored mushroom cloud, finally forming out into a lightning wrapped human skull teethed in ruins. Then, against his conscious will, he materialized a vision of Janet squarely in his fantasy holocaust, fascinated and horrified by the juxtaposition.

He had driven down early to miss the traffic and so had to wait for the stores to open. Shopping for software only took an hour and a half. It kept his mind off the ugly thoughts and feelings he entertained. He and his dad had talked about what the house needed in the way of a software update, as well as what each of them wanted in a new pro-

BABYLON BY THE BAY

gram package.

"We've got an Einstein," he told the sales clerk in the third software shop he had visited that morning, "The home 'some needs something for compunet operations. It now coordinates four smaller computers. We need it to handle twelve. My dad wants augmented verbal transcription capabilities, with advanced legal dictionaries and case indices. And I want full 3-D CAD/CAM. Currently, I'm using a quick layer effect."

The clerk recommended the NOOSPHERE 5.0 package with a compatible GODEL application and a couple of Law Data Extensions. Greg priced the hot selling CASE software series; universal translation modules for computer operating systems produced by NishiCorp. Too expensive, so he settled for the other items, paying for them with his father's credit card.

Without a doubt, Greg needed a reality check. Janet was a continuous slam to the jaw, but the riemanium was...what? He knew it was enough to make a bomb. The media had made that clear with constant repetition. It was a quintessential of America, a distillate of the evil of which this country was capable. But what was he to do with it? He did have it in his possession, a fact that still rattled around loose in his mind. Time to talk to Larry, Greg told himself.

The day's chances for rain broke up, patching the cold chopped bay with swatches of creamed sun. On the drive back, he checked out the city's latest sight, the Pleiades Platform off Potrero Hill. Seven large pylons, each a sleek skyscraper of plasmetal and plasglass, chrome by day and matte black by night, rose in a cluster from the bay floor into the sky, equal in height to anything downtown. Thin, gardened spans, decks and platforms interlaced the pylons at various levels, and sophisticated pneumatic causeways connected the Pleiades to a large parking structure on land south of Market. In the scheme of Bay Area capitalism, the Pleiades was not so much its heart as it was its penis. It was an American/Japanese *zaibatzu*; the Bay Area's multinational redevelopment corporation.

California's economy had suffered a number of shocks toward the end of the 20th century. Drought and imported pests played havoc with the state's legal agriculture. Defense spending realignments threatened the aerospace industry with severe cuts and the military with draconian reductions. Various voter referenda, state laws and taxes, and state judicial decisions leant to corporate flight. Earthquakes—Los Angeles in 1998 and San Francisco in 1989 and 1999—turned in heavy loss of life and property damage. California, once the sixth largest economy in the world, reeled from such blows.

A governor with her own vision for California then stepped in to turn catastrophe into opportunity. As the Federal Government delayed on

55

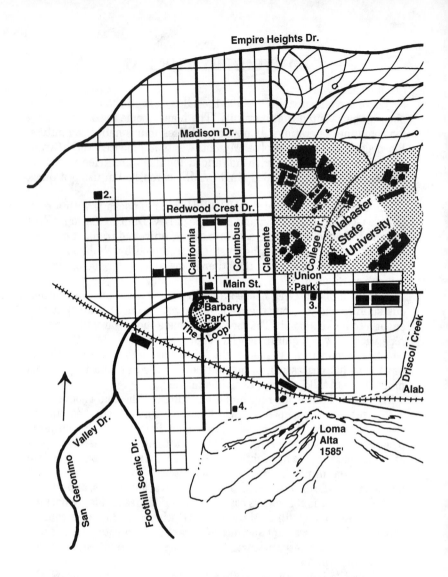

ALABASTER
1. Peregrine's apartment
2. Gregory Kovinski's home
3. Marcus Dimapopulos's cabin
4. Larry Reed's house

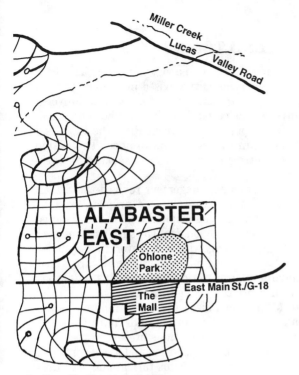

Miller Creek

Lucas Valley Road

ALABASTER EAST

Ohlone Park

The Mall

East Main St./G-18

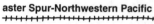

aster Spur-Northwestern Pacific

Tarry Rd.

CALIFORNIA

ALABASTER

Lucas Valley Rd.

Woodacre

Fairfax

Marinwood

101

Sir Francis Drake Blvd.

W. Peak ▲

E. Peak ▲

Mt. Tamalpais

San Rafael

PACIFIC OCEAN

Mill Valley

Corte Madera

San Pablo Bay

101

Sausalito

San Francisco Bay

Golden Gate

Angel Island

580

Richmond

San Francisco

water legislation, and hemmed and hawed about supporting aerospace industries or subsidizing winter agriculture based in Salinas, Central and Imperial valleys; and while the multi-nationals steeped in North American free trade diverted, doled out and delayed the State's economic recovery; the governor opted for the Pacific Rim. The Japanese-financed Pleiades Consortium was the consequence. The Waldo Tunnel's darkness swallowed Greg up, only to spit him out into Marin County's affluence.

Bioengineering and water micro-management revived the State's agriculture. Joint Japanese and EuroAmerican projects brought California aerospace back to its feet, and inspired related heavy industries—shipbuilding, electric car production, etc. The surplus of military and weapons expertise came to terms with a new world order and a new world war; fractious, decades long military brush fires throughout the developing and underdeveloped world. New weapons industries tooled up, and counterinsurgency consulting became a rage. The undeclared war in southern Mexico revitalized the state's military sector, allowing both the Alameda Naval Air Station and Treasure Island Naval Base to reopen. High tech, always the state's strongest suit, managed to give the Japanese strong competition and a few surprises. The Pleiades was instrumental in much of this turnaround, and thus spearheaded the state's physical reconstruction, infrastructural rebuilding, and informational rewiring. Besides the towers in San Francisco Bay, another Pleiades Platform rose from the Santa Monica mountains overlooking LA.

As the United States moved to integrate with Canada and Mexico, California moved to integrate with the Pacific Rim economy. The state was also a majority "minority society" by the turn of the century. California was properly a Pacific Rim power, not a North American power.

He crunched into his driveway before 11. Larry's answering machine picked up on Greg's call. Greg piled the software onto the Einstein and fixed himself a sandwich. He had a fax, from his listing in *Hemming's Motor News*. Greg read the request for his estimate on rebuilding pistons, cylinders and heads for a '64 Cadillac V-8. He called Larry again, and again got his friend's machine. He remembered another place his friend might be. Before leaving for his car, he recovered the riemanium from the basement, wrapped it in a blanket, and fit it into his trunk.

"Greg, yo! Party tonight at my house," Larry said as the two high-fived.

"I remember. Got your fax too. Also got to talk to you after the meeting." Greg whispered. "Serious business."

The meeting in question, and in progress in the Campus Student Union Building, was that of Alabaster State Students for Peace. ASP

58

for short. It was the day before the beginning of second semester, and the student lounge was not yet littered with stacks of newspapers, coffee cups, full ashtrays and soda bottles.

Greg found a seat next to his friend Larry Reed, a prematurely balding, pudgy, scraggly bearded, stringy-haired young man a year older than Greg. Larry had been orphaned at 16 when both his parents died in an automobile accident. Retaining some presence of mind after the tragedy, Larry moved quickly to declare himself an emancipated minor, and to secure his claim to his inheritance. He actually employed Greg's dad to add weight to his case well before he and Greg became friends. Social security, life insurance, and company retirement and insurance benefits all compounded to secure him a comfortable financial independence. Larry in turn had invested a portion of it into a future of suburban agriculture. Indoor marijuana cultivation to be precise. As the meeting proceeded, they whispered rude gaffs to each other about the principals.

Close to sixty people jostled for seating around a report being given on San Francisco's demonstration the day before, representing a good cross section of youth under the gun of the draft. Aside from the conventional few, here were punks, dreads, metalheads, mods, at least one skinhead, and a sprinkling of neo-hippies and neo-neo-beats in the retro category. Raspies, Ferrels, Spooks and even a few Nulls occupied the moderné. Smoke's transcendent, and therefore somewhat scary MayDay Revolutionist Gang, had not made their entrance yet.

"...Some of us stayed at the rally," Mitch Skyler said. A sophomore, he was a prep, a dap, a yup in training, his attire natty and his grooming impeccable. It was rumored he was heavy into "cognitive performance enhancement substances." In other words, smart drugs. "Others in the Students for Peace contingent either stayed with the splinter groups who broke off from the march down Market or left the rally once the rioting started. I was one of the one's who stayed. There were lots of good speeches and literature. ASP had its own table. Also, I got to speak for the organization toward the end of the rally. It seems that our 'scheduled' speaker wasn't 'available' at the scheduled time."

"Sniff, sniff," Larry said. Lori Turnage laughed out loud. She was a senior, a brassy, long-haired strawberry blonde, cheeky, and zaftig. She was post-Rasputanic, though she still wore the characteristic black clothes streaked with red to resemble blood.

"You bet I was doing something more interesting than hanging around a stodgy old PEACE rally for the 'opportunity' to speak to a bunch of people too chicken shit to take to the streets and try shutting down the city," Lori stood. She had been born in Texas and had grown up in the south. Her accent was not noticeable, unless she wanted it to be, and now Lori drawled. "The Hooligans were everywhere; turning

END TIME

over cars, breaking storefront and bank windows, setting intersections on fire with dumpsters full of trash, street fighting with the cops or leading them on a merry chase. Now, that's how to have an ANTI-WAR action! Those of us who weren't masked or organized, all we could do was stay out of the way, on the sidewalks. But the cops couldn't ignore us. They busted heads among the bystanders too. The Hooligans kept regrouping and running off in unexpected directions and we kept backing 'em up. For the next mass demo I propose that ASP organize our own autonomous cells and kick some ass."

"And she calls us macho," Greg commented. Larry snickered. Lori lit a clove spice cigarette.

"That's not the issue," Mitch snapped back. "You took the responsibility for being the ASP speaker at the rally."

"That was before the demo got militant," Lori lashed back in return, taking a drag on her scented smoke, her cozy southern accent fast evaporating.

"Militant or not," Mitch took a steadying breath, "Our contingent was depending on you to speak."

"Half the contingent was watching Hooligans fight cops up and down Market," Lori flared, "While you all were sitting on your butts, pretending you were accomplishing something."

"OK, ok," David stood, holding up his hands to break up the verbal fight. "Can we have a little process here. For a minute. Please."

"End of round one," Larry whispered.

David Weinstein, with Beth Roland, were Mr. & Ms. Coop on campus, a couple of sorts. Thanks in part to their energies, an amalgam of coop restaurant, general store, book shop, food store, bike shop, computer exchange and recycling group were giving the University a run for its money in economically providing for student services. Greg himself did volunteer work for the recycling enterprise; renting and driving University trucks to carry the campus's recycled newspapers, computer paper, bottles and cans to the yard in San Rafael.

David, like Beth and others in ASP's leadership, was a perennial senior, always on the edge but never quite graduating from ASU. Coincidentally, many of these old timers were also prominent in ASP's leadership. David was short, of stocky build, 26, and balding in a rabbinical manner that demanded a skullcap. He also had a lecherous eye for the young stuff, and the nubile 17-year-old coeds entering ASU every year as freshmen without a doubt were a factor as to why David cultivated his perennial senior status. Beth, his main squeeze, was David's height, plump, attractive, with short black hair and clear blue eyes behind stylish glasses. In addition to attending ASU, she had a legitimate job doing community development in the small Latino/migrant barrio in southwest Alabaster.

60

BABYLON BY THE BAY

"OK, let's just begin with the obvious," David folded his hands. He was always deliberate in his conversation and mundanely methodical in his thinking, "There are many kinds of action. Education, civil disobedience, street fighting, etc., etc. I mean, the night before yesterday's demo, someone broke into the biggest police parking lot on the peninsula and flattened every tire on 240 police vehicles. And I'm still trying to get people interested in forming a mobile guerrilla theater troupe to perform on the street and at demos."

Groans came from around the room.

"OK, my point is, there's lots of ways of expressing our anti-war protest, and ASP doesn't necessarily favor any one of these strategies. I personally would like to see our group get a little more militant about things, but the whole organization needs to decide democratically what direction to go into. By the same token, ASP runs entirely on volunteer labor. No one gets paid here, and no one can take up the slack when someone else is irresponsible. At least, they shouldn't have to. If people take responsibility to do something for the organization, they fuck up ASP's organizing efforts toward peace when they don't live up to their responsibilities. It's like working at the coops. If I'm supposed to open up, say, the Zapata Cafe in the morning, and I don't show up with the keys, that inconveniences everybody and fucks things up for the restaurant. George."

Consensus for that meeting had been that each speaker would call on the speaker to follow. George Meternich, at 33, was the seniorest of the seniors present, short haired, steely eyed, and the group's most likable Marxist-Leninist. Unlike the Revolutionary Socialist Vanguard Party and Communist Unity League reps who irregularly attended the ASP meetings, George was truly independent of party, and somewhat principled in his organizing methods. A thinking ML in search of that elusive, true vanguard party.

"I see it as an issue of self-discipline," George was much more soft spoken, "I mean, all of us could be doing something else, something more enjoyable, like going to a concert or drinking beer, or whatever. We've taken on working against the war because we think that work is important. Not necessarily pleasant or glamorous. Going to meetings isn't 'fun.' A lot of this basic organizing requires self-discipline, and living up to responsibilities. I'm afraid there's a tendency to get a little adventurist and romantic. I get the feeling that something is seen as more fun if its more militant, which I think can be a dangerous attitude. 'Sitting on your butt' listening to speeches at a rally may be an appropriate action at a certain point in time, and street fighting might be an appropriate action at another point in time. In either case self-discipline, carrying out the responsibilities we take on, is important. More so, I suspect, in street fighting than in going to meetings or speaking at rallies. If we can't be self-disciplined about a rally, then I don't think we should be considering street actions at this time. I mean, we need to analyze the conditions of our society, our movement, and our own group, discuss it thoroughly, debate out the various positions and struggle toward common ground if we're going to change ASP's work and focus. Joseph."

"This is gonna get deadly fast," Larry mumbled, screwing his face up unpleasantly.

"Meetings can be such a bore when these guys get going," Greg seconded the thought.

Joseph Curlew didn't look to make it any better. Joseph, with Nina Shaw, were neo-hippies, though so old that most considered them just hippies. Joseph had long wiry hair, a thick, full beard and a set of wire rimmed glasses. Sturdily working class, a carpenter with general contractor skills, he nevertheless seemed a little too spaced on drugs, or New Age religion, or utopia. He wasn't a perennial senior so much as a perpetual student; taking two years of something and then changing majors, taking a couple of years off to work and travel, finishing vocational training on his own by apprenticing out to a licensed practitioner, and the like. Nina, invariably attired in peasant dresses with floral prints, rarely spoke at meetings.

"Now, I might be wrong," Joseph often emphasized a folksy, rural air. "But as I remember the name of our organization, its Alabaster State Students For Peace. Not Students Against War, although I'm also against war. I'm for peace, and peace to me is not just an absence of war. Peace means making new relationships between people, relating to each other non-violently and with mutual respect..."

At that moment, Smoke entered the meeting with three of his MDRG boys. The "yo's" and high-fives momentarily disrupted things as the meeting's silent mass came to life. No doubt about it, they were popular if only because folks did not want to risk not being their friends.

Leather jackets and military overcoats, heavy black boots and Creepers tennies; they were outlaw to the core. The skinhead, Darrel, popped a Rolling Rock as they got settled, swigged it and handed it to dreadhead Eric, who in turn passed it to Jim in rat tails and shaved patches. Their casualness with alcohol in this part of campus where it was forbidden was a clue to their attitude. Smoke remained standing, casually leaning against a wall with cool approval for the disruption they had caused. Of indeterminate age, he was average in height and build, red hair cut very short, freckled, and always wearing mirrored sunglasses. Smoke was not now, nor was anyone certain he had ever been a student at ASU.

The MDRG boys used more "controlled substances" than any dread, neo-hippie or Raspie, and did so in highly uncontrolled ways. They ran the smoke-ins, psychedelic "mushroom madness" festivals, and anything goes liberated zones on the campus as mass, spontaneous, theatrically catalyzed events outside of all channels and permission. Guerrilla theater gone ape shit. At the same time, their aggro levels exceeded any of the punks or skins left around, and the MDRG walked like they talked. For instance, there was the time when an alliance of Woodacre Boot Boy skins and Marinwood Death Wish Kid Nulls named The New Order called them out for war in Barbary Park at the Loop. The New Order outnumbered the Gang two to one, but they had not figured on master strategist Smoke. MDRG's fifteen-odd crew arrived early at the park to take up positions, and when The New Order mob arrived the Gang immediately attacked, giving their enemy no time to reconnoiter on unfamiliar turf, let alone to dig in or to bluster. Billy clubs and bottles routed the young fascists from Alabaster, Smoke even recruiting some of the local high school crowd to chase after the fleeing nazis with their vans and cars to further scatter them. Smoke cultivated the MDRG's no nonsense, kick-ass, street fighting image. Gang members also seemed to get laid more often and more creatively than the best of the Ferrels. In short, they were so bad, so absolutely on-the-edge all the time, they created their own time and space out of their very presence. More real than reality; in fact they were reality guerrillas.

Larry was tight to a degree with Smoke because the MDRG's "events" always swam in cannabis. Marijuana that Larry supplied.

"It's like the hippies and the Hell's Angels," Larry had explained how he saw the MDRG in ASP. "The hippies looked at the Hells Angels, saw that they had the same long hair and did the same drugs, but they knew in their hearts that the Angels weren't hippies."

"Flowers die too easy. Even if they have thorns." Smoke had said that once, quoting somebody.

"Didn't see you there yesterday, at the SF demo," Lori smirked, one of Smoke's ex-lovers, her cigarette poised.

"The gang don't like crowds much," Smoke smiled broadly, "We did our important work the night before. And those of us who did go on Saturday did so masked."

The suggestion hung there, suspended in the meeting's air, for folks to make their own connections.

"I don't know where things were before we got here," Smoke easily assumed the floor. "But maybe we should talk about taking the next step. There are things on this campus; departments entirely devoted to military-related work and buildings substantially committed to the same work. Perhaps we need to call our own demo at one of the sites on campus. You know, maybe walk through and tour their work, make it impossible for them to go about business-as-usual..."

To say that all hell broke loose would be an understatement. It was clear in the raised voices and arguing that followed that Mitch, George, Joseph and others did not quite trust Smoke and his boys, even if some had sympathy for Smoke's idea. David seemed to have an out-and-out, old fashioned male rivalry in mind every time the two sparred at a meeting, and it sometimes seemed he dug for things to disagree with in order to challenge and fight with Smoke.

"I think Smoke's being excessively paranoid about the media," David said to the meeting. "We can notify the media fifteen minutes before our demo without worrying that they'll tip off the cops about our plans."

"And who said the Revolution will not be televised," Smoke smirked and stage whispered, giving the meeting a sly wink.

In turn Lori, Smoke's former lover by his choice, often sided with him out of the sheer spunk and cussedness of Smoke's stance. And, often as not, Smoke was able to strike the sympathetic chord in a meeting's silent mass. In the end, the meeting agreed to a watered down version of Smoke's original proposal, a mass student rally on Wednesday the first week of school, in Remley Plaza next to the Science and Engineering Complex to emphasize the University's complicity in the war. Lori's original proposal was incorporated as a task force created to study the possibility of further, future direct action, a grouping in ASP some were already calling the organization's "action faction." Smoke and the MayDay Revolutionist Gang left for the campus pub with a good portion of the ASP meeting in tow, leaving the heavy rads remaining to wonder out loud if the Gang had any tricks up their sleeves.

"So, what's serious business?" Larry asked, as he and Greg wandered away from the Student Union, among the bizarre public art pieces semi-randomly littering the campus. ASU had been a sleepy community college in the 1970's, until the baby boom's baby boom converted it into an expanding State University serving the northern peninsula and wine counties in the 1980's and thereafter. The bad, mostly abstract public art, had been donated to inaugurate the new SU by other California SUs, an unconscious act of hostility if there ever was one, given Alabaster's practical educational focus.

"Janet and I, we're not together anymore," Greg jammed his hands into his pockets as both stepped around a triple pyramid sculpture in translucent shades of blue-green plastic, the top fifth of each pyramid suspended above the rest of the structure, as on the dollar bill, only sans eye.

"Whoa," Larry stopped, "Why's that?"

"She started seeing someone in Boston," Greg looked away, afraid his eyes would reveal too much. A distant line of geese, black specks above the coastal ranges, flew south beneath the occasional puffed up cloud.

"Said she's in love with him."

"When did'ja find out?"

"Yesterday. She wrote me a letter."

"'Dear John'," Larry shook his head and stroked his beard, "That's cold. And she was here for Christmas. You two've been together for a long time. Kinda thought it might last. I'm really sad to here it."

"Yah, well," Greg slammed back his welling tears, and started to walk again, steering toward the parking lot, around a bulbous bronze that vaguely resembled a voluptuous reclining female form, or else a Dali soft billiard game. "Glad it happened now, instead of when we got married and had kids or something. Anyway, I've got more important things to deal with. You heard about the riemanium stolen yesterday, right?"

"Yeh, they still haven't found it," Larry was still mulling over his friend's newly shattered relationship.

"Well, I did," Greg dropped his second surprise.

"Huh?" Larry grunted, not comprehending.

"The riemanium," Greg smiled wanly, "I found it. Yesterday. On Foothill Scenic Drive near Mount Tam."

"You're shitting me?!?" Larry's jaw dropped.

"Not at all. It's in my trunk right now."

The two crossed the remainder of the lawn, past a concrete monstrosity resembling a giant stalagmite of melted wax, to the parked Spitfire. Sure enough, when Greg opened the trunk, the gray case with its ten smaller containers and yellow warnings waited, wedged in next to the spare tire, nestled in blankets.

"Jesus H. Christ!" Larry exclaimed, clasped his head, and then glanced about to see that no one else was watching, "This thing is hot, and I don't just mean radioactive. What the hell are you gonna do with it?"

"Don't know," Greg admitted, "Hadn't thought that far ahead."

"Everybody is looking for this stuff," Larry emphasized, still not believing his eyes. "The cops, the FBI, everybody wants this pup. I bet there's a reward out."

"Probably. But couldn't we do something a little more 'creative' than that with it?"

"Such as?"

"Oh, I don't know," Greg shrugged, "Maybe use it as a prop in a demo. Build it into a fake atomic bomb and scare the shit out of the powers-that-be. Something."

"Yo!" Larry's eyes brightened. "I just got a flash. Drive me to my car."

Greg did, though his friend refused to let on his idea.

END TIME

"Drive to my house," Larry said, and backed his electrically converted white VW microbus out of its space.

Larry lived on the south side of town, across the tracks, in the three bedroom ranch-style house he had inherited with his parent's death. He operated a large, central sensimilla core in his father's old orchid greenhouse, experimental batches of African kief and pure indica in the 1950's bomb shelter, a commissioned crop of Kajan in the basement, and cloned stocks of deep Jamaican, Hawaiian, Thai and Borneo bud in a sealed room inside the house. He used both conventional and hydroponic cultivation techniques. The house was ideally suited for Larry's agricultural venture. Insulated by an acre and a half of land, it was backed against Driscoll Creek and a low set of forested hills, part of the Lomas Alta peak further south east. Larry had also selectively seeded those hills, entirely out-of-the-way places that might also support wild marijuana with not a lot of backup care. He intended to visit around harvest time next fall to see what had survived and what had not been discovered by hiker or cop, sort of his "offering to the gods" to spiritually protect his in-house operations.

Greg arrived well before Larry and did not bother to get out of the car. Instead, he enjoyed the pine and farm smell of Larry's spread. His friend's house was penetrated with massive security and jerry-rigged utilities. Larry tied into the Marin County power grid, then used a sophisticated subsystem of electrical regulation, storage and amplification to maximize its use. He supplemented this with solar cells and panels, two windmills, and unobtrusive paddle wheel water generators when the creek ran high; all to minimize his visible use of power. The same with water; backed by rain catches, cisterns, and a seasonal, incremental diversion of the creek. He even vented off and stored the methane from his composting and human waste recovery unit which contributed to his fertilizer, using the methane to supplementally heat his crop to a ripe temperature.

Larry also maintained a far reaching security and surveillance system to guard his realm, consisting of a 24-hour compunet with a mainframe media server, video monitoring, trip wires, heat sensors, pressure pads, motion and pattern sensors, robotic surveillance insects, and backup gasoline generators. The spread included a mini-grove of oranges and one of walnuts, a few rows of healthy grape vines, plots of drip-irrigated French intensive agriculture abundant with vegetables, a rabbit hutch, a chicken coop, and an indoor/outdoor lily-dense fishpond stocked with edible trout, bass and catfish; legitimate farming, husbandry and aquaculture to camouflage his illegitimate crops. The whole setup supported his autonomy and peace of mind. An array of antennae and satellite dishes, a two-car garage outfitted to make auto repairs, and a decorative gazebo situated to conceal a recently built, underground warehouse stocked with additional supplies, filled out the picture. That Larry often rearranged and updated his interconnected security system kept Greg in his car until the dusty veedub pulled alongside.

"Get that pup. Wrap it in a blanket. I'll be out in a moment." Larry ran off into the rambling one-story house.

Some time later, Larry ran back out, dressed in camo pants and laced-up Army combat boots, and carrying an instamatic.

"This way," Larry gestured. He took off across his land, down and across a rocky, modestly full Driscoll Creek, and up into the hills. Greg lugged some sixty pounds of deadweight behind. The mocking rended brass caws of a murder of crows ricocheted among the sun dusted pines.

"Larry. I'd really like to know what this is all about," Greg panted finally.

"Guess this is as good a place as any," Larry glanced about.

He set the riemanium case framed by ferns against a tree, took a picture, opened its lid, took another picture, and turned the case to take yet another picture from a different angle.

"Here," Larry handed Greg the camera while keeping the developing film. "Take a picture of the case, with my foot next to it. Another. Now another."

Larry changed his footwork as Greg snapped away. Larry then laid out the six pictures, in various stages of development, on a nearby log.

"OK, now imagine the following 'communiqué'," Greg's friend grinned. "'We, the Ecotopian Liberation Front have expropriated sufficient riemanium from the fascist AmeriKKKan state to construct a nuclear weapon capable of devastating California's San Francisco Bay Area. If the imperialist forces of the United Snakes of AmeriKKKa do not withdraw immediately from the revolutionary territories of southern Mexico, and if all political prisoners in AmeriKKKan jails are not immediately released, we will build and detonate this weapon in the city of San Francisco on May 1.' Now, picture that xeroxed message superimposed over a color xerox of these pictures."

Greg stood, stunned silent for long minutes, speechless from the audacity of Larry's suggestion.

"We...we couldn't do that!?!" Greg breathed, his voice decibels below his friend's enthusiasm.

"Sure we could," Larry's grin turned Cheshire, and stretched into the absurd, "We might even be able to recruit some ASP heavies to back this little scheme."

Greg's thoughts expanded around Larry's idea, and a small, dim image of Janet hovered about the edges of his imagination. "You'll see," Greg said to himself. "You'll hear about me. You'll want me back."

END TIME

ELEVEN

BBC World Service Special Report
"Modern Counterinsurgency: The Weapons of War"
BBC Reporter: Nijal Thomas [1-13-2007]
(Electrostraca #: RNB/GM-113007-375-789-0376)

Exactly how arms and supplies flow into the Yucatan, and exactly how guerrillas of various organizations belonging to the ZLF move about the countryside, is critical information for the Pentagon. To this end the U.S. counterinsurgency effort in southern Mexico employs the latest in sensopic technologies, to directly gather what information it can on guerrilla military movements in the Yucatan. The Argus Net well illustrates the sophistication of this information collecting operation.

The Argus Net is delivered by cruise missile, one hundred thousand bundled sensopic sheaths to the largest package. Some three hundred meters above the ground the Argus payload mechanically fragments into a thousand million needle-sized sensing devices that pattern-spread across the terrain according to factors such as the angle of delivery, missile spin, and weather. A single Argus payload can blanket a maximum of 1,400 square kilometers, though smaller delivery packages and one's designed to cover specific terrain, are also employed.

Each sensopic "stik," as they are called, is shaped like a double pointed toothpick, only much smaller, and is composed primarily of carbon and silicon. Each is a basic, miniature computer, containing almost microscopic microchips and sensory "nerves," thirty day power nodes and, in combination with other "stix," radio transmission capabilities. These precision needles sometimes catch in vegetation, but most of the time they fall to the ground where their strict earth tones camouflage them.

Thus a subtle electronic net is dropped for a month, say, over the south eastern Mexican/Guatemalan border. The stix detect human and mechanical heat sources, the presence of certain airborne chemical compounds such as human urine and sweat as well as gasoline and motor oil, not to mention radio, microwave and laser signals. A satellite can receive the Net's collective broadcast, and computers in the Pentagon can image up a map of human activity through the area from the data. This can then be superimposed on the known topography to build up clear patterns within weeks. The Pentagon evaluates this information in planning its military campaigns. Finally, the Argus Net can be used to guide in smart weapons, troop intervention or even carpet air strikes, all precisely targeted. Then, in forty-five days, the Net biodegrades.

The negative side to the Argus system, and indeed to all sensopic technologies, of course, is that the thousand million computer sensors, shaken across the Mexican jungles like so many divining straws, cannot distinguish between armed guerrillas and simple peasants. The U.S. counterinsurgency war drives the migration of civilian populations across borders, as does starvation, misery and economic opportunity. Even for trade and commerce, local peasants are required to travel different routes weekly, in hopes of outguessing American air power. But there are only so many ways across the land.

What is more, the ZLF guerrillas are fast becoming wise to ways of tricking such sensopic nets; hanging buckets of urine and motor oil along unused trails, setting off decoy radio transmissions, running car motors in deserted stretches of jungle, arranging controlled jungle burns, using EMP generators, and the like. Advances in counterinsurgency strategy, tactics and technology are therefore frequently matched by insurgent ingenuity.

TWELVE

Marcus parked in the Motel 6 parking lot at 5 p.m., the 1996 MitsuChrysler mini-wagon's back filled with eight hastily packed suitcases. The motel's aged sign hung off Main Street, in central Alabaster near the courthouse and the police station, and across the street from Union Park, a block from Alabaster State University. Gwen was not pleased at all. She was hungry, and while she had accepted her husband's job proposal, she had not anticipated his hurry, particularly after Neal Emerson's late morning delivery. What's more, she did not like the motel.

"This looks a bit run down," Gwen frowned, "I hope we're not renting this just because of the price?"

"They have cottages in the back you can rent by the month," Mark massaged his temples, "Neal and I rented here when we went fishing. When we were at Bridgeport. Stafford, Alpine and Kent Lakes are near here. So's the Nicasio Reservoir. One bedroom cottages, so we'll have some space and privacy. And, a private phone."

"Do they have buses in this berg?" she wondered, glancing critically along the Main Street. She was an attractive older woman, silver hair styled short and cool green eyes now critically appraising their surroundings.

"I suppose they do," he yawned, "We're still in civilized Marin County."

"Can we go back to Santa Clara tomorrow to get my car?" she asked.

"Yes Gwendalyn," he looked over at his wife, "I hadn't intended this to be a chore for you. More like a vacation."

"A working vacation," she pointed out. In fact, Marcus frequently employed his wife in his business, and if the truth were known, her skills had underpinned the success of his agency. "It's just that your

69

hurry to get here has been a little disconcerting."

"I'm sorry dear," he touched her hand, "I needed to get on this trail while it was fresh. Peregrine is here in Alabaster. I have a feeling he's still in the area. And, even if he has gone, he was here last and we'll pick up his trail here."

"Guess we'd better check in then," she knew better than to argue with his professional enthusiasm as she reached for the door handle.

"Gwen, we could secure our retirement in comfort with what we'll be making on this case," he sighed, pleading with his eyes, "We could have a nest egg to cover any and every contingency."

"You could retire tomorrow, Mark," Gwen gave him a mock angry smile, "You'll never retire because you can't *not* be a detective. We have investments. Good life insurance and medical coverage. IRA's, T-Bonds, our own house free and clear, two independent children. There's not enough money in the world to cover every 'contingency'." The bigger our nest egg, the more contingencies you find that we can't cover. That's how it always goes."

"I've always believed in an active retirement," Mark frowned, "I wouldn't last five years hanging around the house, puttering at one or another hobby. Investigation always kept my blood circulating. Kept the arthritis away."

"I just wish we could do some traveling now and again," she shrugged in resignation, "Maybe you don't have to retire. Fully retire. But you could take some time off. Europe might be nice. Or the south Pacific."

"Aha," Mark's eyebrows faked an inspiration, "Marcus I. Dimapopulos, international private eye."

He barely ducked the wadded up napkin she tossed in getting out of the car. They rented a cottage for February, paid for phone service for that time, and brought in their suitcases. Gwen unpacked their clothes and other personal items while Mark set up, first their security box in the frame of one of the twin bed's box springs, and then the OXO communications center connected to the telephone line. Mark sent a fax to Neal's answering service in order to test his hookups, with confirmation in the reply, then called Sampson's office to leave the message he would be around the next day for the case report.

"How about checking out whether this 'berg' has any good restaurants," Mark smiled when they were settled. "Maybe a little Italian?"

"Now we're talking vacation," Gwen said.

THIRTEEN

BBC World Service Special Report
"Modern Counterinsurgency: The Weapons of War"
BBC Reporter: Nijal Thomas [1-13-2007]
(Electrostraca #: RNB/GM-113007-375-789-0376)

BABYLON BY THE BAY

CG30 is called shudder gas because of the epileptic-style seizures that it produces in its victims. This gas is considered a fast liquid. To understand this, consider that glass is a slow liquid. Glass appears solid, but the fused combination of silicates in a window, for instance, will puddle over several thousand years.

CG30 is created by the initial combination of precipitants sprayed from B-52 delivered cluster bombs. Detonated one hundred meters above the ground, the cluster bombs spread their extremely reactive compounds over wide areas, falling as a thick, wasabi-green fog to pour through the Yucatan rain forests. Heavier than fog, it behaves in most respects like an atmospheric liquid, pooling in the lowlands. It has a distinct honey-bitter smell, maintains a measurable surface tension in "flood" or "pool," and carries a sapient specific neurotoxin in its loose waves and currents that immobilizes humans and many types of monkeys for six to eight hours.

A person walking through a CG30 puddle sublimates enough fast liquid into gas to have an immediate effect. Because CG30 as a liquid is lighter than water yet only minimally soluble, it hangs about the wet Yucatan lowlands often for days, only gradually biodegrading into harmless compounds. Only two to four percent of those immobilized by the gas die of complications, according to Pentagon sources, so it is ideal for sweeps into territory firmly held by the guerrillas, or frequently traversed by them, as a "humane" form of "mopping up." It is not effective in the mountainous strongholds of the ZLF, and the insurgent peasants in the lowlands are finding ways to counteract the gas using trenches and elevated dwellings.

FOURTEEN

Greg returned home with the riemanium and pictures.

"I'll have to think it over," Greg said to Larry before leaving.

He placed the case and the Polaroids in the locking cabinet beneath his laser lathe. Then he drank a beer before a quick shower and a change of clothes. Larry's parties were famous in Alabaster's youth folklore. Beyond rage, rave and ragga, his parties qualified as masqs; slang from the word masquerade for monster events incorporating several youth scenes and strains of youth counterculture. Thus his parties required that he partly disarm his security and entirely lock down his dope operation, so Greg returned early to help with the task. Other things needed attending to as well. Joints needed to be rolled from Larry's party stashes, the music had to be lined up, the munchies needed preparation, and all other non-crop, yet unauthorized areas needed to be battened down. Kitchen, bathrooms, living room, dining room, porches and the great outdoors not fenced in for gardens were the party territories, as well as one bedroom, a "back room" for esoteric drug use. Even the music, Larry's semi-automated home entertainment complex, he locked behind his bedroom door. Larry had the system on the radio, tuned to Liberation Station Afrika for DJ Elijah's Blues Hour, while the two worked. About fifteen minutes before the party's official 9 p.m. start, some of the MDRG boys showed up with four kegs, and about fifteen minutes after the hour, the first partygoers arrived.

Greg did a lot of beer and smoke first off as anesthetic, and kept his level of intoxication plateaued just shy of severe memory loss thereafter. Simply, he felt miserable, unsociable and awkward. His friends were often Janet's friends, and as he helloed some of them on their arrival he wondered who knew. Who had Janet told over Christmas? He tended to withdraw as the party progressed, to nurse his own wounds, ultimately taking over the task of sustaining the music level with the key to Larry's bedroom. He would stack up the next sequence of multi-media selections, and feed the home entertainment computer the program card Larry had imprinted. Then he would retire to one of the couches in the living room with beer and smoke until the music needed him again.

The south end of the living room had been rebuilt with glass walls and partial glass roof so that it overlooked the creek through a tattered line of planted eucalyptus at the end of Larry's lot. Heavily ferned and exotically house planted, much of the floor at that end of the room was a dark green pond. His fish farm was perfumed with water lilies, crossed with narrow wooden catwalks, festooned with hanging vegetation, bird cages and candles, and occasionally sparkled with the scales of a languid fish or two. Incense roped the air, and a parrot squawked from a ribbed cane cage. The pond extended beneath the glass and out into the yard, where botanical garden landscaping complimented the affect of bridges and fronded, horse tailed islands. The couch inside next to the pond was more often Greg's choice as the evening deepened.

"You're in Students for Peace," a cute girl said, sitting next to him on the couch, a wine cooler poised before full, kissable lips. She was perhaps a quarter Asian, her eyes and hair black and her figure petite. He had seen her before, probably at school. "My name is Margaret. Did you go to the peace demo in the city yesterday?"

"Greg," he said, accepted a joint from the crowd, hit it, and then passed it to Margaret, chasing the smoke with a long swig of Elephant malt liquor. "Yah. There was over a half million people. The street fighting got pretty radical."

"You were in on that?" her eyes widened. She was dressed Mod, with an emphasis on black and white, her hair smartly bobbed.

"Some of it," Greg stood, looked about to see who might be listening. A pair of parakeets in a bamboo cage above the pond chirped. "Gotta set up some more music. Come along?"

72

BABYLON BY THE BAY

She did.

"Yah, the Hooligans were real aggressive," Greg fabricated as he opened Larry's door. "I didn't have a mask, so mostly I just hung out on the sidewalks. Got in a few good hits though. Broke a Chase Manhattan glass front door. Also slammed down a cop trying to subdue a Hooligan girl."

"Weren't you afraid of getting arrested?" she gave him a sideways look.

"A little," he faked it, "But there was too much happening. The Hooligans had the cops preoccupied. They busted the bystanders only when they got too frustrated from not being able to take out the street fighters."

"I think I'd be too scared to do anything like that," the girl looked down, fidgeted with her hands. "Probably couldn't join in. Besides, I'm not sure that the Hooligan stuff is such a good idea. Its not a very peaceful way to get peace."

He pointed out Larry's vast collection of tapes, records, CD's, DAT's, videos and holos and she was snared. She had better taste in music than her retro clothes suggested. Besides the ska, funk and punk he had expected her to pick, she also chose some quality Spook, Null and Raspie, with some precursor source music to all three. She was particularly excited with a "best of" compilation by Tit Wrench with Bob Barley called "Baseball Cards, Sex & You," including songs such as "Pit-Bull with AIDS," "Life Sucks, Do Me," "Reh-Reh," "White Punks On Rap," "Revenge of the Partridge Family," "Violet Flame," and "Go Back To Europe," among others.

"I know this guy," Greg mused, speaking the truth now.

"Yeh?" she looked up at him, skeptical.

"Cowboy Bob, the Chula Vista Commie?" he laughed, "Sure I do. I attended the 'Death of Gilman' show in '97 when he played. My very first show. Also, he played at my house in '98 on their reunion tour, just before Bob went off to live in Ireland. The show thrashed two garage walls and the washer/dryer."

Actually, he had been a scruffy SxEx skate punk at the time, part of punk's last gasp, wearing his backwards baseball cap and his baggy shorts cut down from pants, as was the style. He had actually gotten to know Bob Barley through the mail as both had been avid baseball card collectors.

"That's roots," she exclaimed, "Want to smoke some Kajan?"

"Sure," he said, and started to stack his and her selections into Larry's servo mechanisms. Greg punched up a sequence into the computer, and things were ready for another hour plus of music through automated DJing. Borneo grass was legend, and Kajan weed was God. She pulled a symmetrically rolled joint from her blouse sleeve.

73

END TIME

"Match?"

Greg produced a lighter. The resins spluttered violently, attacked his lungs with his first hit. He coughed, trying to hold it in. The high pierced through the murky beer/street grass sludge consciousness as had no other grass he had smoked that evening. They talked about music some but Greg knew what she was interested in. Knew what she was offering and, with Janet firmly in mind, he took Margaret's offer. He leaned over and kissed her. They sat in Larry's bedroom for a half hour making out, steaming each other up.

"Will anyone walk in on us?" she whispered.

"My dad's not home," he breathed, "Want to have breakfast at my house?"

"If you help me work up an appetite," Margaret smiled coyly.

The two stumbled back into the party.

"Larry, you'll have to find someone else to tend the music," Greg said, placing a hand on his friend's shoulder.

"Oh?" Larry glanced away from his conversation, caught Margaret on his arm, and winked at Greg, "That was a quick recovery. Guess its good night."

"Guess so," Greg grinned. Emboldened with Margaret at his side, in fact intoxicated by the evening's turn of events, he suddenly pivoted back to Larry. "And about what we were talking about earlier, why don't you put out some 'feelers' to the right people and see if there's any interest in our idea."

The two then careened, giggling, out of the house and into the Spitfire, kissing and feeling each other up shamelessly along the way. Greg drove to his house in lightning time, and she pulled him down onto the hall rug when they entered the door. Greg barely managed to kick the front door closed with his foot before she started tearing off his clothes.

"Condom?" he asked.

"I'm on Time Release," she said.

Their sex could hardly have been called lovemaking; raw, unfamiliar, clumsy and rough it was instead. Greg intended this for Janet, to get back at her as he pawed Margaret's smaller breasts and larger nipples, and slipped his other hand down her pants and panties into the wetness between her legs. There was little tenderness or grace involved, only a need for revenge. He was not very gentle. Above her, pounding into her, he thought: "Fuck you, you bitch," thinking of Janet with each aggressive thrust. Margaret groaned, wrapped her legs around his back and dug into his ass with her fingernails, and he came.

They fucked all around the house, in a half dozen rooms and a dozen positions, two young animals in heat to make even a Ferrel blush. Finally, several climaxes later and scraped raw, Greg collapsed in his

74

bed, Margaret in his arms.

She woke him playing with his morning hard on. Before he could protest, she mounted him and rode him hard. Sunrise sprayed up into his window, silhouetted her grunting, shaking form, and illuminating his shelves of books, transparent computers, mounted circuit boards, a half dozen signed baseballs, and pictures of him and Janet, or just Janet. There was something missing. He was missing, or rather, he was a distant observer to Margaret's buckling orgasm. Yet, he did come.

"Morning," she said.

They quickly showered, and went down to the kitchen, by which time Greg thawed a little. He cooked breakfast, scrambled eggs with onions and cheese, bacon, buttered toast, orange juice and coffee as they chatted on the courses and instructors for which they had signed up.

"Thanks," Margaret said, accepting an aromatic plateful, "I got a class at ten this morning."

"Got one at eleven myself," Greg said, "Need a ride home?"

"If you could," she kissed him, and let her hand wander into his pants.

"Keep that up," Greg returned her kiss, "And you'll miss that class."

She laughed and they unclinched. Both hurried through breakfast. Greg not only drove her to her apartment for her books and a change of clothes, but also to ASU.

"Call me tonight," she blew him a kiss and walked away, around a statue of wildly welded thin blue metal poles that imitated the shape of the Cat-In-The-Hat's hat.

FIFTEEN

BBC World Service Special Report
"Modern Counterinsurgency: The Weapons of War"
BBC Reporter: Nijal Thomas [1-13-2007]
(Electrostraca #: RNB/GM-113007-375-789-0376)

A conventional surface-to-surface, or air-to-surface missile delivers the Zeus over its target. As the Zeus payload detaches from its rocket, stubby wings emerge for its descent, giving the smart "hive" bomb the measure of maneuverability in pinpointing its precise attack zone. Between three and two hundred meters from impact the Zeus splits along precise fracture lines, cleaving cleanly over and over until a total of five hundred "boomerwings" shave off.

The Zeus is a puzzle-fitted bomb. It descends like a shot and forms into a vicious cloud of flying microwings, each the size of an old fashioned gold dollar. Each individual razor edged, aerodynamic boomerwing is equipped with optical gestalt targeting, microfoil maneuverability, and a gram of CTX-X plastique. Enough explosive to take out a large tank, a medium sized boat or building, or a small government. Each boomerwing has a share of the overall bomb's momentum and intelligence, and as a total swarm, the microwings are capable of networked guidance and a limited, coordinated attack. Singing through the rain forests like a fevered, golden metallic horde, the Zeus Cloud is a terrifying weapon.

The Zeus can be used with effect against a concentrated objective in jungle low lands and against dispersed targets in highland or mountainous terrains. The Zeus's swarm can be focused or allowed to shotgun. And, as the guerrillas become more expert in building decoys, the U.S. military continues improving the visual targeting of each boomerwing and the collective intelligence of the entire cloud.

SIXTEEN

"I had a long talk with Darby Holbin yesterday," Edward Sumner said, making himself comfortable in a chair in Captain Sampson's San Francisco office early on the week's first working morning. "He said I could depend on the full cooperation of the Highway Patrol in my work. He also informed me that you were managing the investigation for the department."

"Yes I am Mr. Sumner," Brian said, hefting his mug for the necessary working coffee. He chose to ignore the FBI agent's mention of his boss, as he chose to ignore the not-so-subtle ranking it implied. What was the new FBI West Coast Field Office Director's purpose in checking up on the Patrol's street-level investigation? "Care for some coffee? Fresh pot."

"No thanks," Sumner waved away the offer, "I've been up since 4:30. I'm afraid I'm already swimming in it. By the way, call me Ed."

"I have an up-to-date report on the case," the Captain did not feel comfortable with such instant familiarity, not with Sumner at least. Instead, he handed a thick manila folder across his desk to the young suit. "You'll notice I've also tried to collate other reports from the other police agencies working on the case. They're appendixed, in the back."

Sumner thumbed through the file, stopping now and then to read.

"You see this as a jewel theft," the agent finally said, closing the paperwork. "With the riemanium figuring in as an afterthought. A complication."

"That's the simplest explanation," Sampson poured himself a refill. "At the end of the report, I go into a list of possibilities. This department's working assumption is that the Diamotti gang either tossed or stashed the riemanium, and that it either hasn't been found yet, or our fifth suspect has recovered it. On an outside chance, someone else has found it, and for one reason or another, hasn't yet brought it to the attention of the authorities. Occam's Razor."

"What?" Edward frowned a bit.

BABYLON BY THE BAY

"Use the simplest theory to fit the facts, because that theory is probably the closest to reality," the Captain said, "A thirteenth century philosopher, William of Okham said: 'Entities must not unnecessarily be multiplied'."

"So, speculating that this case is perhaps a riemanium theft, with the gems as a diversion, and the riemanium possibly in the hands of domestic terrorists," Sumner sketched out his position, not sure how to handle a cop who quoted 13th century philosophers. "Such a theory would violate this Occam's Razor of yours?"

"Not just my principle," Brian said, and thought better of describing its scientific applications, "That's what I've called the two gang or riemanium buyer options in the report. We know the thieves drove from the central Berkeley/Oakland area to the east Mount Tamalpais area, with a change of vehicles, in a fixed time. The time frame and numbers don't fit either of these options well. Then, there's the gang's profile, evidence at the safe house and on the corpses, evidence at the warehouse where we believe they kept the truck, a lot of things. I consider those very remote possibilities."

"Did Holbin tell you of my little talk to the heads of local law enforcement on Saturday?" Sumner's frown deepened.

"Yes, he did," Brian said simply. The second mention of his boss's name, meant to put Sampson in his place, rankled him.

"Does it make any difference to you to know that the President and the National Security Council are taking the possibility that this theft is the work of domestic terrorism completely seriously?" Edward asked gravely.

"Whether we assume it is a jewel theft, or an act of terrorism, it doesn't seem to me to change this department's prosecution of the case." Sampson decided he did not like Sumner, but he also decided to be careful with his words.

"You mean you wouldn't shift personnel assignments and work priorities if it turned out to be a threat to national security, instead of a jewel theft?" the agent's question was weighted.

"At this time," the Captain felt his anger flare and as quickly he throttled it, "I have every available officer out looking for the fifth suspect around the clock. Police agencies around the Bay area are working with us, and the Governor has offered us every resource of his office and of the state. I don't see what more we could be doing."

"To begin with, don't put all your resources behind the hunt for this fifth suspect," the agent slammed his point home, "There's a high probability that the riemanium is already in the hands of a second party. The gang might have hidden it, and by now your fifth suspect may have recovered it, sold it to an eager buyer, and skipped the area altogether on his gains. There's also a strong possibility that the second party in question has some dangerous political intentions in holding the riemanium. A little intelligence gathering, say, on the better known radicals and revolutionary organizations in the area might be in order."

So this was it, the Captain thought. The bottom line.

"We're the Highway Patrol," he stiffened, "Not the FBI."

"Quite true," the agent's smile was ugly, "However, on an issue of national security, perhaps your department could see its way toward 'modifying' some of its procedures."

"My officers are trained to do the very best jobs they can," Sampson folded his hands, "But they are trained strictly as police officers. I need all their skills devoted solely to the tasks for which they were trained, in order to get my department's work done."

"I see how the land lies," Edward said sarcastically, "I'm sure you do keep files on such activities and individuals, and I'm sure you would gladly provide the Bureau with copies of them, upon request."

"We maintain files on some individuals who've given us trouble in the past," the Captain was all business now. "We're not in the habit of singling out specific organizations or activities. In the spirit of cooperation between law enforcement agencies on this matter, my office would gladly provide your Bureau with copies of the files on anyone you name. Provided that is, we have them."

"In the 'spirit of cooperation,' I'll be sending an agent over this afternoon with a list and a truck," Edward stood abruptly, "Thank you for your time, Captain. I'm certain Chief Holbin will be most interested in our conversation."

Edward extended his hand. Sampson rose, but did not take it. The third mention of Holbin's name had been the final straw.

"Thank you for dropping in," the Captain refused to conceal his disdain, "Chief Holbin understands the job I was hired to do."

Edward exited, leaving a bad smell in Sampson's office. Brian fumed inwardly as he sat back down. He had wanted to punch out that bastard FBI man, no doubt about it.

Brian realized that police agencies in large metropolitan areas maintained black files and red squads to keep track of troublemakers, particularly with the growth of anti-war sentiment and protest. Undoubtedly, Edward would ferret them out and utilize them to the Bureau's advantage. But to honestly suggest that the Highway Patrol put together some type of red watch to help out the FBI? Sampson could only chuckle softly to himself.

"Hey Brian," Marcus knocked on the Captain's doorjamb, "Are we still on for some conversation?"

"Sure," Brian smiled despite his memory of Edward, "Just got done talking to the west coast director of the FBI. The goddamned jerk."

"Guess I passed him on the way in," the PI took the chair recently vacated by Edward, "How'd the Fed get you so steamed?"

"Damned arrogant asshole," Brian searched across his desk, "Tried to get my boys to do his job for him."

Finding what he was looking for, the Captain handed Marcus a manila folder, duplicate to the one he had given Edward.

"That should be everything you need."

"I appreciate it," Mark said and glanced through the file, "Me and the missus have taken up temporary residence in Alabaster, to get as close to our fifth suspect as possible. Here's how you can reach me."

He scribbled new address, phone number and FAX on the back of his business card and handed it to Brian, who methodically placed it in his wallet.

"Anything new on your end?" the detective asked.

"Not a thing," Brian confessed, "It's damn strange that two pounds of bomb grade riemanium could just vanish into thin air so quickly."

"Hopefully, it's lying on the side of some road somewhere, under a bush or in a ditch. If it is, it'll be found. And if this Peregrine has it, then we'll find him."

"Now that you've relocated to Alabaster," the Captain said, "I think I can arrange for some help for you. We have a team of officers assigned to Marin on this case. That information is in the file. I also know someone on the Alabaster police force. Joe Manley. He's an excellent officer. I'll give you his name and number now, and I'll call him this afternoon to tell him about you. What are your plans?"

"First, I'll interview Rosanne Casey," Marcus said, "I know you all did a good job, but I need to cover all the bases. Just the way I work. Then I'm going to make copies of your sketch of Peregrine/Baumann and take them around to the places in Alabaster for which we have numbers from the safe house. I'm also going to do some computer hunting through a few data bases I've used in the past. Then it will be old-fashioned gum-shoe work. It still surprises me that our fifth suspect's fingerprints never made a police record. That strikes me as odd, especially if he's a professional, as all our other evidence indicates."

"Good point," Brian smiled, "What's your theory on that?"

"He could have been a juvenile when arrested," the detective picked off the points on his fingers. "Had his records sealed or expunged upon turning eighteen. Then again, he could have been outside the country for most of his life, either from birth or from his family living overseas."

"Interpol might have something then," the Captain considered the idea.

"I'm planning to check. Finally, and aside from the possibility that he was never arrested, Peregrine or someone he knows might have removed all trace of his criminal record wherever he had one. These days, police departments are putting records on microfilm and in computers. A knowledgeable hacker, or someone with inside connections, could quite literally erase his own criminal record, even his identity."

"An intriguing possibility," Brian said, interrupted by an intercom call. Once done with business, he turned again to Marcus. "I guess I've got work piling up out there. Marcus, watch out for this Edward Sumner. He thinks all of this is "domestic terrorism." He's a prick. I've got a feeling he won't like any independent investigation on this case. He doesn't know about you yet, and my advice to you is don't introduce yourself. I'm certainly not going to tell him you're Neal's hired PI."

"Thanks," Mark stood to leave, folder under his arm, "And thanks for the warning."

"One more thing," the Captain said, standing as well, "I know you're answerable and accountable only to Neal, but I'd appreciate you keeping me up to date on what you uncover. I'll do the same for you. I don't want to steal any of your thunder Marcus, but you're working on this twenty-four hours a day. I can't. You'll probably solve this before we do. If you do, put me in the picture somewhere. Somewhere in the background will do just fine. Edward is going to try and read me wrong to my boss because I won't turn my department over to him. Any surplus glory you could throw my way would be greatly appreciated."

"If I do crack this, I'll do that," Mark smiled and the two men shook hands.

Marcus had dropped Gwen off at home bright and early that morning for her car, so he had all day to pursue the case. Thick fog clouds rolled over the UC San Francisco campus near Golden Gate Park, alternating with crinkly cool, late morning sun amidst airy California architecture and trees leaning on the breeze. It reminded Marcus of his own school days, so long ago, on the GI bill. He noted that fashions were certainly different as two coeds in shorts and form-fitting spandex sauntered by. He located the administration building despite such distractions, and with a little persuasion, and the lie, based on the police report's profile, of being a visiting relative, he managed to ferret out Rosanne's schedule for the day.

"Hello, Rosanne," Marcus said as she left her nursing class for an hour's break, recognizing her from a picture in Sampson's file.

"Police, right!" Rosanne bristled.

"No," Marcus found his ID, "Private investigator. Can we talk?"

"I've told everything I know to the police," she started walking briskly toward the campus library.

"It's important. I'm trying to find Michael before the police do," he said, true as far as that went.

"Do you know Mike?" she asked.

"Not personally," he said, "You know he's suspected of being in on

BABYLON BY THE BAY

Saturday's theft."

"And of taking the missing riemanium. I know." she sighed. "Mister, I know Mike and he didn't do it."

"Marcus Dimapopulos. Mark." he offered, "Have you heard from Michael since the robbery?"

"No," she frowned, "But I'm sure there's a reason for that. Mike did not steal any gems or any riemanium. I'm sure of it."

"What makes you so sure?" Marcus said.

"I...I just am," she was firm. "I was his lover. I knew him. I knew his soul. He could no more commit that robbery than I could, well, kill you."

"And if I were attacking your mother and you had a gun?" Marcus offered.

She looked baffled for a moment, then bit her lip.

"You're saying there might be 'extenuating circumstances' then?"

"I'm saying that no one can say what another person will do in this life, no matter how well you know that person," Marcus matched her now slowed pace. "I'm not trying to harass you, Rosanne. But I still want to interview you."

"All right then," she sighed, resigning herself.

They did not go to the library. Instead, he took the interview on the cafeteria's outside terrace. Seagulls glided above a view of the Golden Gate, the park frayed by traffic and the bridge laden with cars. Sooty white buildings and harshly colored billboards down the hill played hide-and-seek with the fog. Telephone pole transformers fizzed when hit by a fog bank, an occasional undertone to the ever present din of traffic. She spent about thirty minutes going over her and Michael's two month relationship. Marcus took notes and asked questions, but failed at first to uncover anything beyond the police sheets.

Peregrine, aka Michael Baumann, passed himself off as 22 years of age and an independent computer programmer/consultant. The address and telephone number Rosanne had for her "Mike" were correct enough, a now vacant SRO near Washington Square Park rented by the week, until recently, under yet another pseudonym, a Robert Fitzooth. The room yielded the same set of enigmatic fingerprints. Not only had Diamotti bankrolled his Peregrine's cover, but "Michael" had spent the time needed to flesh out that cover. The gang had invested a good deal in Rosanne Casey, in setting her up as the gullible, unwitting access person into Security Pacific.

"When was the last time you saw him?" Marcus asked.

"Guess it was the Friday night before that robbery," Rosanne sipped a soda, "Actually, it was Saturday morning. He came in around 12:30, and I was already in bed."

"You weren't expecting him then?"

"He said he'd be over. But he also said he'd be working late."

"How was he dressed?"

"Hmm, let me think," she paused and crunched on a potato chip. "He was dressed in black. Black canvas shoes. Black pants and black sweater. Even his t-shirt under the sweater was black. He also had a black bandana, and his black bag."

"Bag?" Marcus noted. Not in the police report, he also noted.

"Yes. He always carried this black bag," she remembered. "Canvas bag, about two maybe two and a half feet long, with a shoulder strap."

"You didn't mention that to the police," Mark pursued.

"He always had it with him," Rosanne shrugged, "Guess I just forgot."

"Anything you can tell me about the bag?" he wrote in his notebook, "Anything in it? Any tags or initials on it? Anything at all?"

"I guess he kept a change of clothes in it. Or could." she said. "When he left in the morning, he was wearing a dark brown sweater and his red high tops."

"Anything else?"

"Can't think of anything else. He kept it zipped most of the time. I remember once, when we were on the BART, going to a movie, he took out a little black appointment book from the bag and wrote something in it. Oh yes, and I remember seeing some embroidery, in yellow thread, on the shoulder strap. Kind of an 'X' with some letters on it. A 'B' and an 'N'..."

Marcus sketched something on a napkin:

"Yes, something like that," Rosanne said. "Is that significant?"

"It's a good lead," the detective admitted, chewing on the pencil's eraser. "What did you do after Mike arrived?"

"We made love," she blushed, pleasant for Marcus to watch. "Then we slept. He got up real early, around six, showered and dressed and left before six thirty. That's the last time I saw him. Do you know anything more about Mike?"

"The police haven't found him yet," Marcus closed his notebook, "And no one's renewed the rent on his room. It doesn't look good, him not being around, if he didn't have anything to do with the robbery."

"I know," Rosanne bit her lip, "I don't know what's happened to him, but I'm sure he has a good explanation."

"I hope so," the detective smiled wearily, "Since you've been so cooperative, you'll be one of the first people I call when anything breaks."

"Thanks," she looked forlorn, "I just can't believe he'd be involved in that jewelry theft. None of this makes any sense to me."

They made small talk until she had to go to her next class, about her studies on a UC scholarship for returning women students 30 and over. She showed him her talented anatomical sketches, and spoke of perhaps pursuing medical illustration. Currently, she was looking for another part-time job after being fired from Security Pacific. Not wishing to reveal his employer, he said nothing. He excused himself when she stood for her class with a thank you and a promise to keep her informed.

He pondered the clue she had provided him as he reached mid-span on the Golden Gate driving north, parts of the bridge still enshrouded in fog. Black dada Nihilismus was one of the most extreme of the Hooligan groups to emerge with the start of US intervention in southern Mexico after 2001. Clandestine and cellular in organization, virtually none of its members had been arrested to date, despite the massive property damage attributed to the BdN. One brick wall off Telegraph near Berkeley's former Peoples Park displayed the group's abbreviated five point program:

MAXIMUM
Self-Direction
Protest
Resistance
Direct Action
Take-Over
BdN

He did not know much more about BdN than that, though he was sure to learn all he could. What the association between Peregrine and BdN did was to expand Marcus's mental image of this fifth suspect. The Alabaster area night club phone list said that he hung out with young people, and the BdN connection further delineated his milieu. If he were an anti-war activist, associated with a dangerous fringe group, then perhaps he could be found in photos or videos of Bay Area peace demonstrations. The detective made a note to hunt down such material—police, press and private—to aid his investigation. Briefly, he wondered if the FBI was onto something with its terrorism theory.

It was sunny and warm in Alabaster, and Gwen's old Ford Taurus was parked in the motel lot. So was a familiar Mercedes. Marcus smelled his wife's cooking upon entering the cottage; lean hamburger, garlic and sautéed onions simmering in a tomato-based sauce. Neal waited for him, seated on a chair in the living room.

"Honey, I'm home," Marcus said in the direction of the kitchenette, "Well Neal, I take it you remember these cottages from our bachelor days. Caught a two foot bass at Nicasio as I remember."

Neal barely nodded. He was clearly agitated.

"Any breakthroughs?"

"A couple of very promising leads." Marcus removed his jacket and hung it in the closet. "But we haven't caught Peregrine yet, or found the riemanium."

"Mark, the FBI is on my back. They're threatening an investigation." Neal clenched his hands.

"Don't tell me," Mark said, "A guy named Edward Sumner."

"You know about him?" Neal's worried eyes widened.

"Our friend, Brian Sampson, warned me about him. Said he was bad news."

stepped momentarily into the kitchenette to give Gwen a appropriate two glasses as well as the bottle of wine with e had been flavoring their dinner.

..." the detective offered, "I don't drink anything stronger these days.

"Thanks," Neal accepted the full glass of rosé, "I was hoping you'd come up with something to get this guy out of my hair."

"Skeletons in the closet, Neal?" Marcus poured himself half a glass.

"My personal life, no. It's business I'm worried about, but not on this shipment," Neal was not in a sipping mood, and his glass was soon empty, "Not in the last twenty years either. But when Security Pacific was a struggling business, well, I can't claim the same. I don't think Sumner is going to limit himself or the Bureau to the last two decades."

"Better start your damage control," Marcus suggested, refilling the corporate president's glass.

"Already have. But the best damage control would be a quick resolution to this theft. Then I could easily convince friends in Washington to quash this investigation."

"I have a feeling that this case is not going to be solved quickly," Mark said, and seeing the flash of sheer panic on Neal's face, continued, "But with any luck it'll be resolved sooner rather than later. I already have everything the police have found out, thanks to Sampson, who is also arranging some local help for me. And, I've started interviewing the principals. By the way, I'll need a 1200 dpi color multimedia scanner and a gestalt pattern-matching computer program to help with some of the research I'll be doing."

"It's yours," Neal gestured for a third glass, "By the way, what do you know about my former scheduler?"

"Rosanne Casey? Talked to her today. Nice girl."

"I found out she's the one who tipped off the media too. Cost me a bit, but the TV reporter revealed his source. Mark, she's involved in this in some way."

"I tend to doubt it," Mark sipped his wine, "She still can't accept that her boyfriend was involved in the theft. She's just confused, and maybe a bit naive."

"I don't know about that. I could see her accidentally revealing the shipment to her lover or the riemanium to the media, but slipping up on both...its too coincidental for me."

"What did the reporter say?"

"He said he'd tricked her out of it, but I just can't accept two such mistakes. The odds don't cut it with me."

"I tend to believe that reporter," the detective said, "Peregrine's shaping up to be a true professional. I tend to think he just used Rosanne to get access to your building. In any case, I hope you haven't gone and done anything, um, stupid. Like when you fired her."

"I've taken what action I thought appropriate," Neal straightened in his chair, his umbrage unfurled by the alcohol.

"As your friend, not to mention the detective you've hired to crack this case," Marcus put down his glass, still a finger full of wine, and decided for honesty, "I'm getting annoyed with this vengeful side to you, Neal. It's knee-jerk. You have tremendous power. You're injured, upset by the theft and embarrassed by what Rosanne's done. Granted. But you ignore the evidence that her actions weren't intentional and you lash out, not once but twice, to squash what's accidentally hurt you by crushing someone as powerless as Rosanne. You're not thinking, Neal. And your mindless actions are making my job a hell of a lot more difficult. It's as if you're working against me solving this case."

"Sorry," his old friend slumped back into the chair, deflated by the detective's sharp, accurate words. "This whole thing has me over-wrought. I haven't been sleeping well. Or thinking too clearly."

"So, what did you do to Rosanne this time?"

"Wrote a letter to the UCSF Chancellor," Neal was sheepish now, "I'm sure nothing will come of it. After all, she hasn't been accused of any crime by the police."

"Let's hope so," Marcus shook his head.

Security Pacific's president excused himself soon thereafter, leaving Marcus and Gwen to a tasty spaghetti dinner, complete with tossed vinaigrette salad and garlic bread.

"Overwrought is not the word," Gwen commented, following a mouthful with a sip of wine, "Neal's likely his own worst enemy in this situation. You might want to suggest that he leave town for a little while, to cool down."

"He can't," Mark smiled ruefully, "Not with Sumner on his ass. But with any luck, we can wrap this up in a couple of weeks, and save Neal's butt. Still, I can't get over how petty Neal's being with Rosanne."

"Will closing this case derail the FBI investigation?"

"Neal has more than his share of high-placed influence. He wasn't lying about his friends in Washington." Mark helped himself to more meatballs and sauce, "Excellent meatballs. Anyway, if I nail Peregrine, and Neal gets the riemanium back, he'll be telling Edward to take a flying leap. Gwen, would you mind it if we talked about work over dinner?"

"I thought that was what we were doing," she teased.

"I mean, your work," Mark chuckled, "I have the police file to date and it is extensive. Also, Captain Sampson promised regular updates. I have some evidence that Peregrine might be involved in ultra-radical antiwar activities. The scanner Neal's getting is to try and match the police sketch with characters in whatever local anti-war footage I can round up. We need to find out who this Peregrine really is. That means you'll have to access our regular, alternative data bases. Interpol, the Fortune 500 Blacklist, Credit Nexus, Celebes Data Board..."

"Black Talon," Gwen shuddered.

"Yes. Black Talon included," Mark said.

The sophisticated followers of neo-Satanist Anton LeVey had been able to compile THE most comprehensive extralegal database around. The Black Talon Board was so thorough, so accurate and so up-to-date that Marcus, as a private investigator, often wondered how they managed to collect and update it.

"Anything else?" Gwen asked.

"No." Mark poised his fork over his last cache of meatballs, "I need a list of every rental in Alabaster, but I'll get that from real estate offices in town. There'll be no substitute for door-to-door on this case."

They finished their meal, savoring moments of silence as much as the food's rich flavors. Mark collected and washed the dishes. Then he called Joe Manley.

"Sure, I'll help," Joe's voice boomed, "Might even get it approved by my Supervisor."

"Did Brian fill you in?" Marcus asked.

"Sure did. Our station got a copy of the sketch on that suspect. If you want, I'll take a copy of it to those Alabaster area nightclubs."

"Deal. How about a meeting?"

"I can drop by today, after work. Around 3 this afternoon."

"That'll be fine."

SEVENTEEN

BBC World Service Special Report
"Modern Counterinsurgency: The Weapons of War"
BBC Reporter: Nijal Thomas [1-13-2007]
(Electrostraca #: RNB/GM-113007-375-789-0376)

The dark side to the U.S. counterinsurgency campaign in southern Mexico raises an unseemly interest in a zoology of weapons and war-

BABYLON BY THE BAY

fare, both natural and artificial. The preferred assassin doing US/Mexican counterinsurgency work in the Yucatan, for instance, is not human, and not even alive. Rather, it is the Subucu Spider. Take a ZLF terrorist into custody for interrogation. Make sure to get a skin sample for genetic fingerprinting before releasing the known guerrilla. Then, use the Subucu.

The Spider is a Japanese manufacture on a CIA commission; a body the size of a child's fist crafted of plasteel and superb silicon/carbon/photon microelectronics, and eight expertly micro engineered prehensile tensor legs. Feed in the required DNA fingerprint, then let the spider loose in the countryside, in a village, town or city. During the day, a Subucu tucks into a nondescript, soil colored lump in a sunny, obscure spot to recharge its photovoltaics in order to supplement its radiation decay energy cells. During the night it uses the cover of darkness, fuzzy mapping, sensopic antennae, and infrared cluster-eyes to locate sleeping humans. It extrudes an extra fine needle, sheathed in local anesthetic, and inserts it into the slumbering flesh to take a DNA sample. No match, the spider scuttles on. A match, and the Subucu injects either shellfish toxin or a highly concentrated arachnid poison. Simple, and deadly.

The spiders are methodical. They can be coordinated with other spiders to cover a wider area. They can be homing invested. They are non-emotional, self-recycling, reusable 21st century assassins. And they are one of a growing phylum of robotic arthropods, used primarily in military capacities. Subucu also offers the Subucu Scarab, a large dung beetle outfitted principally for photoelectronic spying. Benderz of Germany offers a spy-mantis and a plastique warheaded cockroach smart microbomb. The US based Singer Syndicate rounds out this arachnid/insect schema with a multi-use land crab; a robot crustacean with interchangeable intelligence gathering, explosives carrying, and poison delivering modules.

Through recombinant DNA, bioengineering and advanced biological sciences, the U.S. military has attempted to turn even the natural world against the ZLF insurgents and their supporters. Sterilized, genetically modified super caribe fingerlings are regularly released in schools along the Usumacinta, Candelaria, Grijalva and other rivers in guerrilla liberated territory. They eat their way upstream in their brief six month, bioengineered life cycles; through fish, birds, river creatures and drinking animals as well as playing children, women washing clothes, farmers irrigating crops, fishermen catching food, and guerrillas wading water.

Most bees and wasps are solitary insects, the exceptions being social honeybees and hornets. With invariably social ants, they form the order Hymenoptera, and all share a genetic trigger of primeval origin called "defense swarming." A complex pheromone trips this reaction which, in the hive-oriented, amounts to frenzied nest protection and reinforcement. In solitary bees and wasps the mechanism is regressive, but the reaction is profound.

Bechtel manufactures a synthetic pheromone which can be dusted over hundreds of square miles of Yucatan forest in spring bloom by cruise missile or helicopter gun ship. The solitary bees and wasps start chasing each other in buzzing lines. Lines loop, and humming loops accrete into thrumming whirlwinds. These angry, stinging insect storms attack anything in their paths, slaughtering animals and people indiscriminately as they zigzag through jungle as visible, killing thunder. Finally, they break up from exhaustion and die by the thousands. Dow Chemical recently completed the research on a similar process to trigger hummingbirds into scream winged, needle billed, killing swarms. And plans exist to study inducing close-to-shore shark feeding frenzies.

Bombers selectively spray millions of gene designed caterpillar larvae across the rain forests in lieu of more toxic herbicides. The voracious creatures eat through vast swaths of jungle and farmland as they expand out from their drop sites, each growing to the length of an adult hand before metamorphosis sets in. Wide gray curtains of pupae then hang in the forest's gloom, colony shrouds fed on immense deforestation. When these *papillion de la meurte* split open their cocoons, they are asexual red and orange butterflies that live only three months more.

The guerrilla forces, as well as the civilians in the self proclaimed Mixtecan and Mayapan Liberated Territories, as yet are unable to counter these sometimes gruesome, planned epidemics of natural and artificial pestilence.

EIGHTEEN

Peregrine quietly and expertly disarmed the alarm, then eased open a window with a craft set of tools. He'd gone to this bar infrequently, and only because it was close to his apartment. A gaggle of local old time regulars had made it conservative and uncomfortable, nothing more than a place to go when every other place was closed or too far away. He felt no qualms about burglarizing it.

The safe beneath the bar was old, so the tumblers fairly shouted falling into place. He didn't need an augment to crack it and collect the $540 in cash. He left the change and the revolver. He'd never owned a gun, let alone carried one on a job. Quietly, Peregrine disappeared into the night before dawn.

***

Greg assumed that sleeping with someone else would somehow, magically take his mind off Janet. It did not. She had been his best friend while in Alabaster. Her betrayal still cut him like a knife. He wanted to get the word of his sexing Margaret back to her, to provoke what he could, hopefully some jealousy. They had talked, swum, studied, seen movies, gone to concerts, fixed each other's cars, and done most everything else together for the past five years. He felt her absence in his life as a deep hole cut into his heart. Margaret had no way of filling it for now. No one could.

He walked down to Remley Plaza after his first class in Intermediate Statistics, gathering clouds of dark emotion about him. Monday/Wednesday/Friday were Greg's short days, just two classes. Typically, the beginning of a semester figured as MallTime, with students shopping for classes down to the administrative wire. Two large ravens, Hugin and Munin, seemed to touch wings in their flight above and across his path, tossing their shadows briefly onto him.

The plaza was the largest gathering area on the campus. It was pentagon-shaped, with a now quiescent fountain off center. The low redwood student center and student coop enterprises occupied one side. The central library's reinforced concrete arcologies commanded another, flanked to one side by the sci-fi stacked waffle architectures of the Physics and Mathematics Building—part of the Science and Engineering Complex—and on the other side by the fluted Humanities/Social Science Complex spires. The brittle, concrete Administration fortress walled off the pentacle on its fifth side, part of a cluster that included the Student Union building. Garish, "arty" sculptures accented this star-shaped pattern. ASU's three cluster colleges—Warhol (art and music), Cookes (premed), and Merrick (vocational high-tech)—were scattered on the southern and eastern peripheries. ASU was a commuter campus, with over half of its students traveling to attend from outside Alabaster proper. Greg, a third year student, no longer noticed the details of his school.

In addition, he was engrossed in his own misery. So engrossed that he was virtually in the midst of the MDRG smoke-in before the pungent smell of burning marijuana brought him out of his own cloud. He looked up surrounded by people smoking dope. Smoke and two other MDRG lads tossed joints into the crowd, perhaps five hundred strong, like farmers seeding an alfalfa field. Someone handed Greg a joint and he accepted it. The fragrant cloud of combined smoke drifted off toward the library.

"Greg," the familiar voice piped up behind him. He turned to find Margaret, books in hand, smiling at him. Damn, Greg wanted to remember where he had originally seen her. Certainly before Larry's party. Instead, he smiled back.

"Care for a hit?" he offered her his smoldering joint.

"I try not to smoke during the day," she waved it off, "Do you know the people who put this on?"

"Smoke? The MDRG? Sure." Greg said and watched her eyes widen a bit. "Um, how about a movie tonight?"

"Will your dad be home?" she wiggled closer.

"No, he won't be home until Wednesday."

"Then why don't we just go to your house." Now very close, she looked up at him coyly, her lips pressed together. "Stay home tonight. And *fuck*."

She brushed her hand along his crotch and giggled. When the bone gets hard, the brain gets soft.

"Sounds great to me," he grinned, blushing with her boldness.

"Pick me up around seven," she said and turned, "Got to go to class."

"I see you're making up for lost time," Larry stood at his elbow.

"Just a diversion," Greg said, watching Margaret sashay off.

"Nice diversion," Larry laughed, "Quite EM. By the way, I've sent out certain, shall we say, probes to certain ASP folks, about you-know-what. There's interest. A meeting's been suggested, tomorrow, around two. Place to be told me."

"I'm still not 100% sure about this," Greg frowned, remembering his words from the night before and nervously raking his hand through his hair. "I mean, I like the idea. In principle. But I can see it easily getting out of hand."

"True," Larry hit off a joint and gave it to Greg. "I was thinking we go in with the position that the, um, item remain hidden, known only to you. What we're going to ASP for is their political savvy in setting this up. We want to pose a credible threat, so we need to project a credible image. That's what we're asking ASP's help on."

"And if I don't agree with the way ASP wants to handle things?" Greg asked.

"Then, its off. Clearly." Larry said with finality, "You have the last word. If you're not comfortable with it, it doesn't go down."

"One more thing," Greg grasped for his idea, "Can we distance ourselves a little more? I don't know. Say we don't have it directly, but that we know who does?"

"Tricky," Larry stroked his beard, then glanced about, lowering his voice, "They're still looking for that guy, Peregrine. Maybe we can say he has it and is actually a politico, and he wants to use it to its best political advantage."

"That's an idea," Greg said, then glanced at his watch, "Time for my next class. Let's give this a tentative yes. And lets make it three tomorrow. I have classes solid until then."

"Check," Larry said.

Greg normally did not smoke in the day either. His next class, in Humanities entitled "Anglo-American Cultural Traditions," fulfilled

90

his breadth requirements. It was also irredeemably garbled, thanks to the grass.

"If you will, consider for a moment the difference between 'paradise' and 'utopia'," the Prof., Stewart Holmes, paced as he introduced the course. "Paradise comes from the old Persian word *pairidaeza*, meaning an enclosure, or park. The most famous paradise in western tradition, of course, is Eden, Hebrew for delight, and actually a garden planted by God eastward in Eden. The garden of Eden shares with the more general concept of paradise the feature of cultivation. Both a park and a garden are planned plots of land; prepared, planted, and landscaped by an intelligent agent. The Persian *diz* means to mold, and *pairi* means around. So paradise, literally, is a defined and designed area. As such, paradise can and does exist, in as much as any garden or park exists.

"Utopia is also a construct, a deliberate creation. It is the perfect social order, a sociopolitical realm without conflict or strife. But it is intended not to possess any substance. Coined by Sir Thomas More in a romance of a perfected island society with the same name, utopia comes from the Greek, *ou* meaning not plus *topos* meaning place. Literally, utopia means no place. Samuel Butler wrote a utopian novel called *Erewhon*, the perfect society of which is nowhere spelled backwards. William Morris continued in this vein with his *News From Nowhere*. The ideal state then, the just society free of internal strife, is nowhere.

"Pre-modern civilizations thought it enough to win the struggle with nature and to cultivate the perfect garden or park in order to create paradise. Remember that the Judeo-Christian 'Fall of Man' occurred in the Garden of Eden and that the serpent also resided there. Paradise did not prevent sin, even in the conception of pre-modern civilizations. Perhaps the modern world is just that much more cynical in that paradise has been replaced by utopia, and that utopia by definition does not and cannot exist."

Greg had not needed the marijuana enhanced confusion. Give him a wiring diagram or circuit board and he could read it. But with Shakespeare, Plato or de Tocqueville he was lost. This was actually his toughest subject, something that Janet would have found a breeze. Trying to do homework in the library after the class, in turn, proved slow and sloppy, until the high wore off. He found he could keep his mind off Janet by hitting the books, however, and so he promised himself not to push it stoned anymore. By 6:30 he was on the road to Margaret's apartment. By 8, four Guinesses and a joint of kajan later back at his house, Margaret and Greg were doing their best to fuck each others' brains out. Greg still burned with the desire to get back at Janet with his more than willing partner.

END TIME

Oakland was quiet. Leon and Snake Boy cracked the Rexall on Telegraph that Monday night, high on PCP, Elysium and crack; the preferred 21st century street speedball. Two black-and-white's responded to the silent alarm in time to catch the young black men taking flight down the alley. Four cops jumped, revolvers drawn, and two shouted "Halt!" Snake Boy whipped back his own piece, squeezed and pounded the black cop. The cops' return volley splintered concrete and plaster as the two thieves leapt into a hole in the wooden fence.

One cop went to call for backup and an ambulance. The remaining two gave chase. They caught up with Leon and Snake Boy and again yelled "Halt!", this time from behind parked cars as the two black men ran across the street. Snake Boy tried his magic once more, got off one wild shot, and was instantly shredded into blood, bones and guts in Leon's sight by the police response. Leon skidded to a stop, raising his hands.

"Don't shoot," he wailed. "I give up. Don't kill me."

Within seconds the two white officers stood on either side of him, guns leveled and cocked. Within the minute a black-and-white screeched to a halt blocking the street in front of this tableau. The white cop who jumped out whipped into Leon with nunchucks, and slammed him over the police car's hood for a search. Leon freaked big time. He tried to roll off, inspiring the cop with the nunchucks to throw a choke hold on him while the other two cops beat him on his back, chest, arms, legs and groin with their nightsticks until he collapsed. Then they brutally handcuffed Leon's wrists and ankles and tossed him into the back of the cop car.

The three cops stood out on the street discussing the situation, waiting on the report of the downed officer's status, as Leon raged into his final act. He turned with excruciating pain until he was on his back in the back seat. With one kick of his cuffed sneakered feet, he knocked out the side back window. It shattered, and showered the police outside with glass shards.

"That's it, mutherfucker."

The cops dragged him out of the car, the nunchuck cop once more in choke hold while the other two slammed him over and over with their batons for close to ten minutes, ensuring Leon's respiratory collapse. The paramedics could not revive him. He was pronounced DOA at Highland General.

News traveled the streets like electricity, aided by broadcast of the story on the Afrikan Liberation Station news and the telephone work done by the New Afrika Center's switchboard. Two of Oakland's council of Baptist ministers were the first to arrive on the scene. An angry mob, over five hundred strong, railed against a line of nervous police blocking off the shooting site at two in the morning. Then, important members of Oakland's Black Unity Front, Black Panther Party, New Afrika People's Movement, All-African Peoples Socialist Party, African Peoples Revolutionary Party, African Peoples National Party, and Nation of Islam—some with offices in the New Afrika Center—arrived soon thereafter. DL made it in time to see thirty cops sweat as the crowd doubled in twenty minutes. Then, reinforcements arrived; Oakland PD and Alameda County Sheriffs. Tensions, in a word, escalated.

The community heavies arranged an impromptu street corner meeting. The meeting decided to call a rally and picket in front of the central police station on Wednesday at four to protest Leon's and Snake Boy's deaths, and police brutality against the community in general. DL offered the New Afrika Center as an interim meeting place. The word spread. Reluctantly, grudgingly, the crowd dispersed, leaving the smell of their anger in the air.

***

Peregrine sat on his windowsill, one foot on the sill and the other foot on the fire escape's creaking metal. A half empty beer, his third, rested on the ledge next to him. He had a clipboard and a pen, and he pondered over the letter he was composing to his brother. Monday evening curdled into night. Gondwana was starting to jump, the usual crowd of scene makers occupying the most prominent tables. The high school crowd assembled in their cars and vans around the Loop. And, on a street corner in the waning light, a preacher tried to cut through their youthful attempts at decadence.

"It is not too late to repent!" the man in a badly fitting black suit spoke. He held up a dog-eared, hand-worn, leather-bound black Bible. "It is not too late to be cleansed by the blood of the lamb, our Savior, the Lord, Christ Jesus! Heed the Lord's call now, because His Second Coming is near. When the suffering servant, when our glorious redeemer returns He will reign over earth for a thousand years with His Elect before the Final Judgment. You can be a part of the Lord's Elect and you can rule with Him. It is not too late."

As usual, he wasn't attracting much of a crowd. The apocalypse, the traditional four horsemen, were not a big seller. Not cyberpunk enough. Not enough gore. Too predictable, and the most interesting side, the Dragon's side, was predetermined to lose.

Peregrine no longer went out much nights. This was not due to any "low profile" strategy. In fact, he subscribed to the notion that the best place to hide was out in the open. Right under the noses of his pursuers. The idea was as old as Poe's "Purloined Letter," yet it continued to work. If anything, he'd intensified his undisguised public presence in the wash of the media's constant broadcast of the police's flawed sketch and description. No, he needed to consolidate his resources, and the letter was an important part of that effort. His mini-arsenal buried in the mountains, plus the satellite hacker box but minus the ID, would collect a tidy sum from the right buyer.

I've recently begun working a new job, Peregrine started out his third paragraph. This paragraph they reserved for such clues as his that he'd started back with second-story work. *And I'm trying to sell my car. It has LOTS of accessories, really an excellent buy, so I hope it doesn't take long to sell.*

Brothers, they'd worked out intimate signs and codes to get by first, their parents, and now his brother's keepers. His bro would know that he had a modest cache of sophisticated technologies and armaments for sale. From jail, he would manage to connect up with both prison and street grapevines for Peregrine; put the word out and screen most of the inquiries. The Hawk was very well connected. He would watch out for his younger brother, for a healthy percentage. One that Peregrine was glad to cut in order not to have to do it himself. A scene from childhood, him and his brother building forts out of the furniture in the living room to his family's poor, tidy Flatbush brownstone, wandered through his thoughts.

He played with his ring, the clipboard in his lap and his eyes on the bright, vibrant cafe kitty corner across the street. Peregrine knew the Gondwana's owners. They had often contributed to the political work he maintained in his surface identity. That he contemplated making the cafe his next job sent a spike of regret through him. He flashed on the memory of a roommate he once had, a girl first time away from home to whom he'd rented a room. She'd kept all her money tied up in her socks in a clothes drawer. In stealing her savings, Peregrine had dashed all of her hopes and plans, forcing her back to a bad family situation.

Immediately, he squelched the guilt now turning in his mind. She'd been stupid to leave her money in so obvious a place. And the Gondwana's owners would not be badly hurt by his theft. They did a brisk business, and he needed the money. This would be just another contribution to one of Peregrine's causes, this time himself. He yawned, then wrote a closing paragraph. He signed the letter. He folded it and slipped it into an envelope which he addressed, sealed and stamped. No job tonight. He intended to get a full eight hours sleep.

***

Sumner did not like independents. Nor did he like running down loose cannons. The local police, Sampson in particular, would be brought into line, given time and attention. Now there was this PI that Emerson had hired and so far refused to fire. Edward cleared the Stack's gloomy pre-dawn mass, cruising up 880 from home base in San

BABYLON BY THE BAY

Jose in his Dihatsu Chrysler Royale. He had checked out Marcus Ira Dimapopulos. Impeccable. All the more reason to bring him into line, if not onto the team.

Sumner was Nebraska born and raised, a USMC veteran of the first Gulf War, and a University of San Diego law school graduate. He had joined the Bureau after completing school, distinguishing himself as a regular field agent in LA's smog-bound sprawl. The Bureau's anti-terrorism work had been his first choice, having trained in counter-insurgency warfare while a Marine at Quantico. So, after taking several additional FBI training courses, he applied for and received a transfer to the West Coast Anti-Terrorist Command Headquarters. Brilliant performance and several promotions later, he was in charge of Headquarters. The Bureau's reorganization in the wake of the Heidelberg scandal, in turn, handed him his present position, a mixed blessing at best.

Seared golds played behind industrial landscapes to his east. The entire western bay, peninsulas north and south, were enshrouded with fog. He enjoyed the time to think given him by the drive, his cellular, lap top, car fax and scrambler at his fingertips. He still needed to get used to his appointment, meaning he was still hard wired with the instincts and habits of a field agent. Witness the visit to Sampson yesterday and now his intention to meet Dimapopulos. He needed to delegate more, even though he preferred handling things one-on-one. The confrontation with Sampson in particular had been a mistake, and entirely unnecessary. Edward had new powers and greater authority. He had to learn to wield both effectively.

Before the promotion to West Coast Director, he had been one of the Bureau's more prominent internal gadflies as well. His sense of patriotism had motivated his scathing off-the-record criticisms of the FBI and some of its policies, not to mention of the Justice Department's use of the Bureau. Fighting Saddam Hussein, Round One, as a Marine had opened Edward's eyes. Most of the world did not like the United States. Part of the multi-national coalition organized to protect Saudi Arabia and liberate Kuwait, Edward had been stationed in Saudi Arabia; a country that did not permit his Christian worship, refused to let him get drunk on a Saturday night leave, and privately considered him an agent of imperialism and Zionism. His patriotism had only grown stronger. He had wholeheartedly supported the U.S reassertion of its global power. America was a country worth defending from attack, foreign or domestic. After his tour of duty the FBI had seemed the best place from which to protect it.

His years in the Bureau had given him insight into the politics true patriotism was up against. It had made him cynical. Congressional investigations and oversight committees, internal Justice Department

95

probes and reorganizations after contentious Presidential elections, citizen class actions, traditional rivalries with the CIA and other security agencies, NSC "coordination;" Edward could understand in the abstract why some special agents, even some field office directors, had felt the need to go solo, literally to conspire to protect the nation outside of this straitjacket of political restrictions. Independent of all the political bullshit.

Highway 880 became 580 amidst WWII vintage military base and industrial neighborhoods. The old Bureau structure, DC headquarters and subordinate field offices, as well as the old Bureau policy of routing promoted field agents through a grueling tour-of-duty in the national bureaucracy before assigning them to head local field offices, had not prevented rogue activity. The Puerto Rican field office cabal around Frank Heidelburg was only the most obvious example.

Heidelburg's conspiracy had amounted to a death squad operation against PR nationalist elements, in particular the Movemiento Liberacion National Puertorriqueño—MLNP. Two of his operatives had even employed the white hand symbol, painted on public walls after each of their jobs. And because Heidelburg had been a brilliant Washington man, knowledgeable of the ropes, he had managed to keep his clandestine Justice Teams operational for close to two years, running San Juan's streets red with MLNP blood. Yes, Edward intellectually understood the actions taken by Heidelburg and others even while he could not condone them. The whole scandal had wrought havoc with the Bureau's operations across the board. He could not help thinking that FBI disorganization had also allowed the riemanium theft to occur, if not worse things to come.

He would be the first to admit that the Bureau was America's political police. What is more, he often argued that, in a world with a substantial communist bloc residue, plus ever more numerous out-and-out maddog states like Peru and Myanmar, a strong, effective political police apparatus was even more necessary than during the good old Cold War days. The model could no longer be based on polarization between two global superpowers. The points of conflict around the planet, as well as the sources of terrorism had fractured, multiplied and become far less predictable. The new reality was now solidly center versus periphery, and the center must hold as his friend, David Burns, liked to say. The Bureau needed to adapt strategies to deal with the sheer chaos internationally that continually spilled into domestic affairs.

He supported the proposal, so far privately circulated in the Bureau, to consolidate a wing of the FBI with that of the CIA as a prototype interface intelligence agency. Edward was a Bonapartist, however. The Bureau needed a strong, innovative director, on the lines of J. Edgar

BABYLON BY THE BAY

himself, to take command; push through an FBI-CIA experimental merger; reassert FBI counterintelligence work against the peace and anti-war movements; and rebridle the nation to the task of keeping America Number One.

Until now he had been satisfied with bitching about the Bureau while remaining a top ranking loyal agent. He had looked forward to devoting his skills and talent in service to his ideal Director, if one could ever be appointed by the politicians. The council of regional directors he belonged to, and other reforms, had come out of a committee appointed by the current Director; not the type of leadership Edward respected. He reserved his judgment on the restructuring, even as he participated in it. The Bureau was in deep trouble, better make that out-and-out crisis. Sumner would do what he could to help restore the FBI's credibility and performance.

The West Coast Directorship promotion, in turn, gave him pause. Perhaps he could be his own ideal FBI Director, the first to be appointed from within the Bureau since Hoover's death. Both the Bureau and the country needed a good, immediate sweeping-out. If no appointee capable of strong leadership was forthcoming, perhaps Edward could prove himself yet again, using the riemanium theft this time. This case was a set up for further promotion, if he ran things right. In private fantasies, Edward anticipated the coming political purges, to make Palmer and McCarthy look like Boy Scouts. He briefly played out his own potential roles in them, adding this one to the list.

He remained on 580 when it split with 80. The depressed, dingy industrial skyline of Richmond stained the morning around him. One thing he knew, many of his field office directors were having a hard time accepting Sumner's upstart command, themselves the product of years of duty in the Washington bureaucracy. He had gone from critic to "The Boss" of some of those he had criticized, responsible now for keeping them in line where once they had run point on him and his sometimes cavalier behavior. This switch, this turn of the tables also made him uncomfortable. He hoped it was only a matter of time and on-the-job experience before he became adept at using his new position. However, to face his first crisis, so soon in office...

The war, despite low American casualties, had given new life to Leftist virulence, a layer of clandestine activity parallel and sometimes in contact with crime, yet its own creature. With such anarchic proliferations as 'Core 'Gainst War, Hardcore Autonomy, Black dada Nihilismus, Black Gang, and Maximum Attitude in recent years, the potential for domestic terrorism against the war effort, a la the Weather Underground, had increased astronomically. That the riemanium might have been sold to a hostile power, and destined to be smuggled out of the country, was also a working possibility for Sumner

97

and his superiors. Therefore, he needed to frankly question why it seemed so difficult to sell the idea of internal terrorism to Bay Area law enforcement and government.

It had been two days of every police agency in the Bay Area scouring every lead, every snitch, every source, every back road, every vacant field, every vacant house and every vacant alternative. The media still regularly broadcast calls for public help in the case. Still, no riemanium. The domestic terrorism option figured more and more prominently in this case. The evidence so far spoke to this theory. The riemanium had never been at the safe house, and it still had not been found despite massive effort. Nobody offered to ransom it. It was as if a black hole had swallowed it. Or the political underground now had it.

Aside from a minority of dissenting opinions in the NSC, the chain-of-command all the way to the top supported the Bureau's investigation into the potential political dimensions to the theft. This insured that the local political establishments would eventually fall into line, despite their protestations and claims of local prerogative. The local police still treated the theft as a non-political crime however, as all their training and experience dictated. That he needed to change. But it was more than simple, conservative training that held law enforcement back, he felt. It also involved wishful thinking. Nobody wanted to deal with the terrorism option. None were comfortable with seeing the theft as a political issue. He needed substantive evidence, and soon, to continue what, privately, he now termed Operation Anvil of God.

He trundled across the Richmond-San Rafael Bridge, bay waters steeped up with smoggy blue sky, and turned north on 101. Edward had cut his teeth and made his name in the Bureau on homegrown terrorism in the last third of the '90's. The issue of abortion had remained a battleground throughout the 1990's, with anti-abortion forces resorting to extremes confronted by the Clinton administration's laws, regulations and Supreme Court appointments. California, the land of weirdos, UFO's, and mass murderers, with a State constitutional privacy clause guaranteeing abortion; California turned up ground-zero for this extremist fringe's more harrowing actions. A Catholic-based pro-life splinter group out of El Cajon, alienated by the Protestant fundamentalism of the anti-abortion mainstream such as Operation Rescue, took what they considered to be the next step. They formed the Revolutionary Army of the Infant Jesus and in late 1998 the RAIJ bombed abortion clinics across the state, a campaign that culminated in kidnapping California's Attorney General as the Devil's Right Hand in March, 1999.

One of those the Anti-Terrorist Headquarters assigned to crack the RAIJ had been a rookie named Edward Sumner. He himself was pro-life, but in this terrorist splinter, the anti-abortion movement had gone

BABYLON BY THE BAY

too far. Special Agent Sumner proved instrumental in tracking down and hammering the RAIJ, spotlighting himself in the FBI's Operation Final Thunder. He earned his first big promotion at Headquarters. Too bad about the Attorney General.

After the RAIJ case, Sumner helped to work up the Bureau's initial post turn-of-the-century counter-intelligence programs directed against the anti-war movement gaining momentum. But Anti-Terrorist Headquarters was also worried about US Leftists sympathetic to the Mexican revolution giving "religious refuge" to Mexican politicals and terrorists who managed to sneak illegally across the US southern border, sometimes to disappear into this country's seething Latin immigrant mass. So they assigned him the Sanctuary Movement. Edward called his campaigns of infiltration, disruption, legal prosecution, and extra-legal intimidation from the Rio Grande river to the Tijuana River and deep into Colorado Operation High Borders. Not only did High Borders decimate and fragment the Sanctuary menace, it slashed all illegal immigration across the US/Mexican border in half as well. His methods had been so effective that the Border Patrol adopted them in the face of the growing number of regular economic illegals fleeing poverty in northern Mexico and Central America. Kudos from the Director, and Sumner had snapped up the head position at Headquarters.

He turned right, onto a Lucas Valley Road immersed in security suburbs, while running down to himself how he had used the last two days to seal off the Bay Area. FBI agents monitored every airport, train station, bus station and docking around the clock with portable radiation detecting equipment. The Bureau had just completed installing sensitive radiation screens along key highways, with any increase in background radiation levels triggering armed pursuit. He had muscled the Teamster's, and the union was now muscling the membership on the riemanium. Edward had had the good sense to turn this perimeter work over to Marable for maintenance, concentrating his own efforts now on turning up the heat within that perimeter. Agents from other west coast field offices, arriving since last evening, would fan out across the Bay Area with the remaining local special agents, after Edward's orientation at noon. He had to pull bureaucratic teeth to set this into motion, and he vowed to himself that this was merely the first wave. In all, he had mobilized a lightning response and show of strength, with the prospect of getting some sleep tonight.

It is not just field agent wiring, he told himself. He was not delegating more because he was short-handed, and without anyone trusted enough yet to act as his lieutenant. Marable was adequate with handling the daily Bay Area and perimeter operations assigned him, but Edward was certain the old Negro had his job out of the affirmative action suits of the last decades. In any case, he had no intention of promoting Marable to San Francisco as was within his power. Washington appointed in all other circumstances. That process remained tried-and-true, with candidates culled from the ranks of the national bureaucracy on criteria more political than professional. Bottom Line it meant San Francisco would remain vacant for another week, perhaps two, while the wheels in Washington slowly turned. Bottom Line it meant, he had to cover.

He had married twice and divorced twice, a child with each ex. Deftly, as if he had driven this way dozens of times before, Edward turned west just past Marinwood on County Route G18 for Alabaster, oaks and pine framing the road. He had never been able to make the family thing work, not even with his own family. He had joined the military to get away from his tyrannical father, a sensible alternative to patricide. He still kept in touch with Jane, his mother, but his father was as good as dead in his life.

Edward pulled into the Motel 6 parking lot at 7:55 a.m. The bungalow was easy to find, thanks to Emerson's directions. He could see two somewhat elderly individuals, a couple breakfasting, through the open curtains of the front window as he knocked on the door. The man, in his robe, answered the door.

"Edward Sumner, FBI," Edward almost said special agent. Instead, he produced his new credentials. "Are you Marcus Dimapopulos?"

"Excuse me," Marcus said, and reached for something on a table by a chair next to the door. He handed Edward a business card and shut the door. It read:

MARCUS I. DIMAPOPULOS
PRIVATE INVESTIGATOR
HOURS: 9 AM-5 PM, MONDAY-FRIDAY
CALL FOR APPOINTMENT

And then it provided a telephone number. Puzzled, Edward knocked on the door again. Again, Marcus answered.

"I don't believe you understand," Edward straightened his tie. "I would like to speak with Marcus Dimapopulos."

"That's me, and I'm in the middle of breakfast," Marcus said gruffly, "You did not make an appointment, so please return at 9 when my business hours start. I'll talk to you then."

He shut the door again. Edward boiled up. His arm jerked up to knock a third time, until he thought better of it. The old goat was a stodgy, geriatric, old school PI. Edward realized he needed to humor him if he wanted to get anywhere. Part of having power was knowing how, and when, to use it, he realized. He left, got into his car and drove back across Driscoll Creek Bridge, to the Denny's on East Main. He spent about twenty minutes on phone and fax transmitting instructions and orders around the Bay Area. Then he stepped into the diner for coffee and a poached egg on toast. When he returned at 9, Dimapopulos was exiting his front door, clipboard and pen in hand, dressed in a frumpy brown suit.

"Ah, Mr. Sumner," Marcus greeted the west coast director amiably, "You're just in time to accompany me on my door-to-door."

"Excuse me," Edward was again momentarily puzzled, "But didn't Neal Emerson hire you to find the stolen riemanium?"

Marcus proceeded to his car, and Edward had little choice but to follow.

"A bit more mundane then that," Marcus was quite cheerful, "Actually, I'm looking for the fifth suspect in Saturday's robbery. Peregrine, or Michael Baumann, or whoever. Emerson and I are working on the assumption that when we find him, we'll find the riemanium. Or, at least be several steps closer to finding it."

"By going door-to-door!?!" Edward was astounded. The detective opened the passenger door for the FBI man.

"From everything we know, this was his home base." Marcus continued, his mood jovial. "So I'm taking the police sketch around to the local merchants and rental managers. Either he's here, laying low, or he's skipped and we can pick up his trail here. Either way, that means legwork in my book. Mr. Sumner, if you want to continue our conversation, hop in. I like getting started early."

Marcus did not tell Edward about his connection with Sampson. Or about all the work Gwen was doing sifting through computer data bases and media images. Or about the favors he was calling in right and left to push the investigation forward.

"Oh, no thanks," Edward smiled, queerly, "I believe I've heard all I need. Thank you for your time, Mr. Dimapopulos."

Marcus shrugged, happily, and closed the door.

"Anytime you want to call," Marcus said, smiling, climbing into the driver's seat, "You have my card. And my hours."

Edward walked to his car as Marcus started his. The old bugger was classic, Edward thought and shook his head. He got in his auto as the PI drove out, waving at the FBI man. Let the old fart go door-to-door. The town undoubtedly had a peace movement. By second wave, Thursday, two special agents would be assigned to Alabaster, one to the community Left and the other to the state university Left. Edward would cover more ground in a day doing so than the old duffer would in a month. As he sped back down to East Bay, he worked the phone mercilessly.

***

Greg woke before the alarm, Margaret's fragrant warmth next to him. It was still before sunrise. A street light splayed through the parted curtains of the room's window and over a collector's item Toothless Mood poster. He had waken out of a dream, and could still grasp its outlines. Reverse Orpheus. He followed a woman in a long flowing dress up a long dark tunnel, toward a distant slice of sky. He felt, somehow, that he knew the figure ahead, a kind of "dream knowing" as he could not see her face no matter how fast he walked to catch up with her. Margaret? Janet? Rachel? With every step she was two further ahead and more gnawingly familiar. The alarm buzzed.

"Got a class at 7," he groaned.

"No morning delight?" she pouted.

"Hop into the shower with me, and we'll see."

The fax from Larry read: 3:30, Redwood Eatery. Greg drove her home as her first class was not until noon. He let her off with a promise to call. As it was, he was five minutes late for his first class. Then school took over, solid and technical, until 2:50. He found Larry in the Redwood Eatery, the campus pub and one of his regular hangouts, propped at an inside table with a pitcher of beer, half consumed.

"Bacon cheeseburger, quarter pound, double fries, and a coke," Greg ordered before he strolled over to Larry's table.

"Grab a beer Greg," Larry smiled, "Bring the pictures?"

"Got em right here," Greg patted a pocket in his backpack, "But no beer. Gotta study after this."

Halfway through his meal, he did take a glass and some brew.

"What's the plan?" Greg washed down the food with the beer.

"ASP folks oughtta be here any minute," Larry snuck a few fries, "Then we'll 'retire' to an outside table. An outback table, for a little discussion."

The ASP crew—David, Beth, George, and Lori—sauntered in about 3:40. Greg and Larry stood, and their enlarged group walked out onto the pub's fenced in yard. Larry had ordered another pitcher, and he carried it out with him, to George's barely suppressed disapproval. David led the way up wooden stairs to the patio's upper terraces. The sun warmed them through groved green pines, their needles and branches severing its light into dusty rays around them. A jay darted; a flash of blue. From a distance, ravens cawed. The upper terrace, the Pub's outback, was actually three small platforms half-stepped up into the hill, and they climbed to the highest.

It was not empty. Yakubu Tsikata, head of the ASU Black Student Union and a staunch cultural nationalist, Hector Guellermo, chair of the ASU MEChA and a worshipful Fidelista, and Chin Lee, President of the ASU Asian Pacific Student Alliance and a reconstructed Maoist, waited for them at one of the tables.

"Welcome to the Mountain," Yakubu grinned and broadly gestured with two hands. Only George caught the Jacobin reference, smiling slightly.

"David invited us to sit in on your discussion," Chin said, "As, um, revolutionary consultants."

"More like white middle class bullshit detectors," Hector smirked.

Greg gave Larry a strong, wary glance, and his friend shrugged. The PC police. The six white newcomers found chairs and arranged themselves around the table. The enveloping pines striated needles and sun up into sky lightly touched with clouds.

"Now then," David knitted his hands, "Larry says the two of you have something extremely important to share with progressive leadership on campus."

"First, I have to have everybody's word that what we're going to discuss won't go beyond the people around this table. This is crucial. If word one gets out about this, we'll all be in big trouble." Larry said. When everyone verbally agreed Larry gestured to Greg, who unzipped his backpack pocket to pass around the pictures. Larry spun their fabrication about media-prominent Peregrine and "his riemanium." A hawk's cry screeched through the trees.

"Why did this Peregrine contact you?" Lori's eyes narrowed with suspicion, striking a match for her clove cigarette.

"Um, he was, uh, one of Larry's 'customers'," Greg thought fast. Since not everyone knew Larry's business, some side conversations were required. "Real clandestine type otherwise."

"And he's willing to let us make political use of the riemanium?" Beth asked.

"To be precise," Larry responded, "He's willing to let us design a political package around the riemanium."

"What's your suggestion, or his suggestion as to how we might, uh, 'package' this?" George asked, carefully studying each picture.

"Put out a communiqué, say, from the Southern Mexico Solidarity Force," Greg said. "Demand an immediate withdrawal of US troops from the Yucatan in exchange for return of the riemanium. Otherwise, the SMSF threatens to convert the riemanium into a nuclear weapon and detonate it in the Bay Area. To give the US a taste of the total air war we're raining down on the Mayan peasants."

Clearly, the riemanium, and the prospects for its use, were a show stopper. The pictures passed from hand to hand. Silence congealed around the table.

"The intent of this, I take it," Hector finally spoke, in meditative pose, "Is to throw a monkey wrench into the workings of the powers-that-be. Increase the disruption and chaos on the home front. Unfortunately, this might result in just the opposite. A full-blown clamp down. You release that communiqué and for certain every Federal pig west of the Mississippi will be in the Bay Area. Enough pigs to give each Bay Rad his own personal shadow. Then again, increasing the repression might just spark a full-scale insurrection that much sooner."

"I know that the war is the big issue," Yakubu took his turn, "But the war is an abstraction to a lot of people living in this country. It's a TV war. A movie re-run. A nintendo game. It'd be real intelligent of you all to link this up, not only to the war, but also to the shit coming down in this country right now. I mean, brothers are dying nightly on the streets o' Oakland 'cause of trigger happy pigs. The war in southern Mexico could end tomorrow, and the war in this country's ghettos would go on without a pause. Thanks to the occupation army o' pigs holding down people o' color here at home."

"One question," Chin asked, "If the US military did miraculously withdraw from Mexico, would this Peregrine return the riemanium?"

"Yes," Greg said, "I think so."

"It makes me uncomfortable," Chin continued, "After all, you don't have the riemanium. You're not in control of either the riemanium or this mystery man. What if this Peregrine is arrested? He is wanted. A good bluff is a useful tactical ploy, but this goes beyond a bluff. Not only can't you deliver on the threat of a nuclear weapon, you can't even deliver on the riemanium yourselves."

The white students digested these criticisms for some minutes before Yakubu stood.

"I know Hector an' Chin an' myself got a Cal-EOP battle we got to fight in fifteen minutes," Yakubu announced. "They gutted the program last year. Now they wanna' finish it off. So we'll leave you all to your own devices."

Beth was the first to speak after the Mountain descended from the hill.

"Well, what happens if Peregrine is caught?"

"He doesn't have the riemanium with him," Greg improvised. "He's got it stashed. If he's caught, well, we can be the ones who recover it for him."

"If he's caught, won't he want to use the riemanium as leverage to spring himself?" George pressed the point.

"Maybe," Larry said, following Greg's lead, "He's a real political person, and this cause is important for him. But even if that happens, what do we lose? Nobody but us knows who's behind this thing. It's not like we're sticking our necks out by putting our name on this. So, if something like that happens in the long run, what do we lose? Until that happens, if it happens, it's a great opportunity to make a political point."

"First off," David said, "We need to decide if we can accept the general spirit of the proposal before us. Do we agree to put together an anti-war 'context' for the riemanium?"

They went around the table and each agreed. Only George expressed strong reservations that matters could too easily degenerate into adventurism, but in the end, he too agreed. Beth then volunteered to put together the communiqué, with Larry's help, and the suggestions followed hot and heavy.

"Don't be too specific about how the riemanium was obtained."

"Use desktop for the type. Better yet, cut words out of magazines, punk style."

"Color xerox the pictures. Xerox the type over the pictures."

"We'll need a snappy name. I don't like the one suggested."

The latter provoked a long discussion, as various proposals were batted back and forth. Finally, the Mexican Revolution Solidarity Brigade was chosen, "brigade" being more militant than "committee" or "organization."

"Absolutely no fingerprints. Use gloves."

"Don't lick the envelopes. Use a sponge."

"Get a media list from the library. Hit radio and TV as well as the papers."

"Let the cops get their story from the media."

"We don't even have to threaten to make a bomb. The smallest particle of riemanium can cause cancer. We can threaten to dust the City."

This also provoked debate, over what demands to be made backed up by what threats. They reached consensus to make US withdrawal from Mexico and an end to the war the focus while making the language as non-sectarian as possible. No direct threat would be made, although both the potential for a weapon and a dusting would be outlined in the communiqué.

"Mail the letters from the central Bay Area. No Alabaster cancellation."

"Buy generic stationary. Five-and-dime."

As the rounds continued, Greg leaned back in his chair and gazed up into the green canopy above. His eyes gradually picked out an object he first took for a knot of debris, litter of some sort somehow hung up in the tree. Suddenly, he realized it was a ball of feathers. It was a bird, an owl perched on a branch, its eyes closed, asleep until dusk allowed it to hunt. He glanced back down from the owl to catch Lori staring at him with curious, hooded, hungry eyes, scented smoke escaping her lips. Greg and Larry made their way down the hill after the meeting of this, another "mountain," a potential volcano, adjourned, only to have David sideline them.

"Larry, Smoke doesn't know about any of this, does he?" David asked.

"No." Larry answered.

"We'd prefer you didn't tell him." In the background George, Lori and Beth indicated agreement with David.

"Why?"

"'Cause Smoke is a little, shall we say, erratic. Unpredictable. Not dependable."

Smoke was an *Enrage*, and David et al were Jacobin wanna-be's. Larry and Greg, lost in their own machinations, did not pick up on David's. Greg walked with Larry to the south parking lot, passing a metal-based ceramic sculpture, a stylized, off-white sperm whale.

"We're riding the tiger now," Larry breathed.

"You'll keep in touch with Beth about the final details," Greg said, hoping his friend would take the responsibility seriously. "School's heavy for me this semester."

"Sure, no problem." Larry hesitated as Greg reached his car.

"Keep it conservative and general. Nothing we can't back out of. You know what I want, but if you have any questions about what Beth comes up with, get hold of me. David's probably going to ghost write on this thing."

"Man, I hope we're doing the right thing."

"You and me both, brother."

Greg drove home, old broad leafed trees arching over his speeding spitfire in the dusk. The maid, Consuello, was there and the house was spotless. She gave the young man a disapproving look, having had to clean up the debauched remnants of his orgies with Margaret. Consuello was from Panama, on Green Card, with a sister and her family in this country. She worked four days for the Kovinski household as a live-in, helping with her sister's housecleaning business the other two, to leave the Sabbath holy. He called Margaret, but her female roommate answered.

"No, she's not home. I don't know where she is or when she'll be back."

He was irritated at not getting hold of her. They had no commitments, no responsibilities to each other, and certainly nowhere near the depth of relationship he had shared with Janet. Yet it irked him that she was not home, waiting on his call. A pang of intense loneliness overwhelmed him. He wanted a lover, not just someone to screw. He, wanted a partner with which to share his life.

Greg fixed himself dinner, more pizza and burgers, while avoiding Consuello's judgmental gaze. And, when she was not watching, he snuck a couple of beers. He ate in his room, doing homework until the beer caught up with him. He slipped on a basic glove and just the goggles to walk through his pc 'some in MC Escher virtual to figure out the cost of the *Hemming's* engine job. He added a materials rough from his on-line mechanics database to his guesstamation of time on the lathe multiplied by $50 an hour. He wrote a letter on his computer, accessed the Einstein in the den downstairs through the home 'some (set on low key Peter Max by his father), primed the OXO's fax, and sent his estimation regular priority to his potential customer's fax message cache.

Then he wandered down to the Einstein, and the stack of new bought software Consuello had straightened up beside the computer. With a couple of his own disks in hand from the house software library, he began the routine install of the NOOSPHERE and GODEL programs into the home 'some's compunet. He piggy-backed his own anti-Spook program at the right time onto the new software's already formidable anti-viral/counter-hacker defenses. Not all Spooks were hackers and not all hackers were Spooks. But when a Spook was a hacker, the individual tended to be a brilliant pain in the butt.

Some of Greg's friends were Spooks; Spook being where techno went musically. Smart drug-XTC-Acid House-Rave 20th century techno easily evolved into techno's 21st century masq-digital-Spook-999-brain stim on that relentless neo-disco beat. It was evolution further along in what a few Spooks were calling "digital dreamtime;" the artificial electronic reality they claimed to be creating not only with direct brain stimulation, but also with attachable computer symbiots for mental amplification. And not just with Love 999, but with newer generations of designer drugs as well. Drugs tailored for effect to individual body chemistry, as well as bio-drugs of genetically engineered neural enhancers. The Spook slogan "everything's digital" meant designing digital audio and video art, and making them mutually translatable; saying "digitized" for stoned and "analog" for straight; developing neural shows; doing deep VR and kything... Spooks had *invented* Emo-Tech.

Pale as the grave, dressed in pure black so as to disappear by night, some with brainstim sockets; Greg only worried about Spooks when they became kythers, the Spook term for hackers. Greg and his dad subscribed to Internet, AT&T Mail, NoloLine and EcoWeb. The Einstein in turn managed the house phone, modem, fax, fibre and cable via the OXO. A clever hacker could gain electronic entrance into the home 'some through these connections to the outside world. Sophisticated compunet software came with killer virus and hacker defenses to prevent just such penetration. Spook hackers, however, walked through electronic walls on digital juju. Once in a computer like the Einstein, an aristocratically arrogant Spook kyther had access to every other networked computer in the house, Greg's included. The potentially endless havoc and permanent damage that even one such electronic "break-and-enter" could wreck in the home 'some had grabbed Greg's attention by the short hairs.

END TIME

He did not approach it in terms of competing with the Spook. He had no hope to out hack the hacker. Instead, his anti-Spook program was a simple, effective shutdown device that worked on the "seven second delay" principle, on the order of seven nanoseconds. It looped all incoming electronic transmission, in effect creating a time delayed electronic front. A Spook hacker either would start right off cutting into the Einstein's defenses, triggering a shutdown, or would take notice of the piggy-back program and in disabling it, trigger a shutdown. It was an early warning device, telling Greg to take the Einstein in for diagnostics and some serious discussion of higher level defenses. Larry, who practiced far more stringent prophylactic measures for his home compunet, had turned him on to the two original software templates, which Greg combined and modified for the Einstein's operating system. To date, it had never cut in to cut off the Kovinski compunet from any intruders.

He ran diagnostics on his installation, then detached from the cyber reality that he and his father defined with their computers. He grabbed another beer on the way up to his room, downing it as he smoked a joint and listened to Sonic Toe Jam Death Cult at considerable volume over his earphones. His father would be home tomorrow, and he would have to tell him. He carefully removed all the pictures of Janet from around his room, taking them out of their frames and sliding the photos into a folder in his desk. When, he wondered to himself, when would Janet's memory stop haunting him?

***

Peregrine entered the dark Gondwana Cafe with ease. The roof trap into the back storage room jimmied easily with his tools. He knew how the business operated and didn't expect much. The ease of entry and proximity were the benefits. Ferns cast eerie shadows across the floor from street light. The cash register's safety drawer yielded up $240 some odd in bills. Then, he was gone, leaving any guilt behind.

***

Greg hurried to Remley Plaza after statistics to find the ASP peace rally still in progress. Over two thousand students crammed into the plaza, focused on the stage and PA setup in front of the Student Center. An assistant professor, his prospects for tenure long ago blown by his proclivity for sleeping with his female undergraduate students, droned on about the university as a knowledge factory, students as proletarians and the need for a new type of class consciousness to begin to halt the university's complicity with the war machine. Close to three hundred flag waving jocks and frat boys, with a sprinkling of girls and the odd skinhead and Null, clustered in front of the library, shouting counter-slogans in a feeble attempt to compete with the booming PA. Most of ASP's peace monitors formed a line between the crowd and the

108

counter demonstrators to prevent trouble. They were supplemented by a half dozen campus cops.

Greg half expected the Movement's ass-kicking members also to be hanging out near the counter demonstrators, waiting for the chance to rumble, but none were evident. Looking around he found close to a dozen MDRG boys loitering nonchalantly all about the steps of the Physics and Mathematics Building, only one campus cop anywhere near. He had not made any of the ASP "action faction" committee meetings, but he knew something was up.

The speaker finished, the crowd applauded, and an MC took his place at the microphone. As she made several announcements, Greg caught Beth's eye, standing next to David near the stage.

"We mailed them out this morning, before the rally," she whispered, "Larry looked it over and approved it before we did."

Greg had Larry's faxed copy of the communiqué folded in his shirt pocket.

The MC said it was time to hear from the next speaker. Smoke bounded on stage, the ever present sunglasses capped by a black toque and underscored by a black and red kaffiyeh. He popped the microphone off the stand and paced the stage, holding the mike like a rock star.

"I'll be real brief with this," Smoke cleared his throat, "I'm just gonna run down some of the Department of Defense grants and contracts that professors in the P&M Building are working on even as we rally here in this plaza.

"Number one. Professor Douglass Faber is currently modeling the dispersal of 'factor three volatility' heavier-than-air gas over a given territory of torrid forest vegetation. Read tropical Yucatan jungle for that, and the Pentagon's new arsenal of 'non-lethal' nerve gasses for the other."

Hisses and boos rose from the crowd.

"Number two. Professors Alden Milikan and Stephen Bullock are currently studying whether coherent, modulated electromagnetic pulse effects can be employed to disrupt advanced mammalian neural activity. We're talking here about using a side effect of nuclear explosions to paralyze human nervous activity over wide areas."

More hisses and boos. A chant started: "Stop The Air War! No More Genocide!" Smoke cut in.

"Number three. Professor Kelley Strong is now patterning the more effective pancake dispersal of 'high velocity micro projectiles.' This university is researching how to make more effective anti-personnel bombs, the same bombs we're dropping all over the Yucatan to terrorize and maim innocent Indian children and other villagers not a part of the Zapata Liberation Front."

"Lesco! Resign!" the crowd bellowed, this for ASU's president. Peace signs and fists rose to shake in the air.

"All of you," Smoke yelled over the mike, "Look at your hands. Those of you who are students at this university, your hands are covered with blood." The crowd started quieting down, the counter demonstrators included. "When you paid your fees to this so-called institution of higher learning, you dipped your hands in the blood of slaughtered Mayan women and children." Complete silence now, waiting for a pin to drop. "There's only one way to wipe the blood off your hands. Only one way to stop the rivers of blood flowing through the Yucatan."

Smoke stood stock still and dramatically raised his right arm, finger extended, to point at the waffled Physics and Mathematics Building.

"SHUT THE FUCKER DOWN!"

The MDRG moved then, up the steps with about fifty other students. The crowd, directed by Smoke's theatrics to look, responded viscerally and surged forward. The one campus cop was overwhelmed. Within minutes, doors were jammed open and students flooded into the main lobby and down the building's radiating halls until the entire ground floor was packed.

"Lesco! Resign!"

"1, 2, 3, 4...We Don't Want Your Fucking War..."

"Stop The Air War! No More Genocide!"

"5, 6, 7, 8...We Don't Want Your Fascist State!"

Fire alarms rang out, by design. The building's labs and classes disgorged. The students and professors evacuated through the occupation, many joining though most exited the building to further disorganize the confused squad of campus police trying to get a grip on the situation.

"No Draft! No War!"

"No War, No Way..."

"Peace Now, Peace Now!"

"...No Fascist USA!"

Someone hauled a portable, amplified lectern out of one of the lecture halls and set it up in the lobby. The speeches—rabble rousing, lecturing, inspirational, rhetoric laden—began.

Greg quietly left the occupation around 4:30, past a loose line of cops who had a hard enough time keeping people from casually walking into the sit-in, let alone to arrest or harass those leaving. As he drove home, he shifted gears mentally for what was to come.

"Evening Greg," Andre greeted his son from the living room.

"Hello Dad," Greg put down his books, "How was New York?"

"Tiring," the distinguished man, dark hair silvering in streaks, hugged the young man briefly, "I'm glad to be back. I hope you haven't gotten into too much trouble in the peace movement. Ready for some

BABYLON BY THE BAY

dinner?"

"Sure."

Andre selected the Revelle Italian Bistro on the Loop. The father had the linguini in mushroom and clam sauce, and the son had the meat and sausage three cheese lasagna, both starting off with soup, salad and garlic bread. Greg noticed through the window that the Gondwana Cafe across Barbary Park was doing a brisk business with ASU students, despite the occupation on campus.

"Dad, Janet and I have broken up," Greg announced, between bites of his meal.

"Oh?" his father gave him a glance, eyebrow arched, "How did that happen?"

"She wrote me a letter. She said she's seeing someone else."

"Did Janet break it off?" Andre tried to zero in gently.

"She still wants to be friends," Greg played with the remainder of his salad, "But I don't know if I can. We had lots of plans. I thought we meant a lot to each other. I really don't understand how she could do this to me."

"I see." Andre used fork and spoon to expertly devour his meal. "It took me a long time to be friends again with Rachel. And I'm still not a very good one, I'm afraid."

"Dad, is it even possible these days to have a long lasting relationship with anybody?" Greg bleated, "I mean, you and mom. Janet and me. Everybody's parents I know, most of them have been divorced before. I mean, should I just give up on expecting any kind of long term thing with anybody?"

"My mother and father, your grandparents, are still together," Andre sidestepped his son's pain, which struck too close to his own conclusions about male/female relationships in the modern world. After Rachel, Andre's relationships had been fleeting and unsatisfying; more like brief affairs. Work was his only true solace. Rachel, who now ran an award-winning *LA Times* city desk, had never remarried.

"But they're so old. They're from another time altogether. They came over from Europe after the World War. It doesn't seem that anybody younger than they are values that type of relationship anymore."

"You obviously do. Greg, to be honest with you, I don't know if a permanent, long-term love relationship can be sustained these days. I do know that life goes on. How do you feel about this?"

"Angry. Sad."

"Depressed?" Andre probed.

"Yeh, I guess," Greg admitted, "I mean, we were just so close. It hurts a lot."

"I know," Andre said, again gently, and waited out the long silence that followed.

111

END TIME

"Is this how you felt when mom left?" Greg finally asked.

"Yes," Andre said, simply. Another, shorter silence, and Andre spoke again.

"Except that before your mother, I'd had a couple of girlfriends, one pretty serious. Janet was really your first girlfriend, so I know you're feeling things a lot more strongly." Andre ordered coffee at the end of the meal. "It may take you a long time to find someone else you feel as deeply about as you still do about Janet. And when you do, there will be no guarantees that your next love will last forever either. Or even as long. It may be that all we can do in this life is to accept the brief moments of happiness, and learn from the pain. Life is larger than Janet. Greg, you rebuild classic car engines and get a lot of satisfaction from it. You've burned up weekends on that lathe cutting obsolete parts. I've seen you spend eight hours straight reprogramming your computer or building some solid state hardware to augment it. I know you like school and I know you've got other good friends."

"Dad, what went wrong?" Greg glumly finished off his lasagna, "I mean why did Janet do this?"

"Nothing necessarily went wrong," Andre sighed. "Sometimes things change is all. Janet could have fallen in love with somebody else, yet still care for you, even love you in a way. Maybe not in the way you want to be loved by her, but that's for you to decide. Things change. You might think I'm being cliched, but you're still very young. Both of you. Maybe Janet felt that she was just too young to be committed to someone else for the rest of her life. Maybe she wanted to explore other people, and maybe you need to also. Believe it or not, you might be hurting badly now, but with time you will heal. That is, if you don't become obsessed by it."

"Why did mom leave, dad?" Greg asked, "She told me once it was to find her own life."

"Because she couldn't find her life with mine. Or in mine." Andre interpreted, "She told you the positive side to her actions. Basically, she was trying to stop from being smothered by my career. She told me once that she felt like she was suffocating. I think that's more accurate."

"Do you think Janet felt suffocated?"

"Maybe not suffocated," Andre left a credit card with the check, "Maybe more like confined. Alabaster is a small town, and even if we do live near the 'big city,' neither you nor Janet were raised in the city. You like Alabaster, but Janet, she's now three thousand miles away, on another coast, in a big city. She's looking back here from a long distance. Sometimes that can be a distorted point of view in its own way, even if its somewhat broader. And if it had been you who'd fallen in love with someone else, how would you have told Janet without hurting her?"

"I wouldn't have fallen in love with someone else."

"You didn't fall in love with someone else," Andre made the distinction as he signed the slip and initialed a gratuity, "Don't be so sure you wouldn't have, under the right circumstances. So, I shouldn't get too worried about the hole in my beer supply?"

"No," Greg was sheepish, "Just had a few friends over, after I found out. Talking things through."

Greg did not mention Margaret. In turn, Andre did not mention that he had met Janet's mother, Beverly, shopping at a department store before Christmas. She had given him several not so subtle hints as to this impending breakup over a little cafe coffee. He also realized that most of his words would be lost on his son, for the moment.

On the ride home, Greg sketchily described the campus occupation.

"We've got some sleeping bags in storage, don't we dad?"

"Some," he crossed Main. "We have two of your old Boy Scout bags. Then we have my bag and your mother's. Also, we have the extra one we bought when Uncle Will stayed with us that summer."

"Can I give the one's we don't need away?"

"Sure," Andre smiled, the shadow of memories in his eyes.

"I'll keep the best three for us," Greg said.

"Funny," his father mused, "The more things remain the same, the more they change. When I was your age, little younger, we were also protesting against a war. The Vietnam War. Not me so much. I was only 13 when the war ended, but I'd been sympathetic. My older sister, your Aunt Francie, took me to demos when I was ten. Those days, the last thing anyone wanted was commitment and monogamy. Strange."

Needless to say, Greg did not reveal that two pounds of riemanium were hidden in the basement of his dad's house. He excused himself when back home, dug out the old sleeping bags, and piled them into his car's passenger seat. He was determined to re-enter the liberated zone that was the P&M Building that evening. The guard, one of six standing in a semi-circle about the lobby entrance, objected when he tried to do so with four sleeping bags in tow. There were fully a hundred plus students hanging about outside the police line, on the steps and across the plaza. He found Eric, from the MDRG, and convinced him to momentarily neglect a beer and a girl to help Greg. They catapulted three of the bags over the campus cop line and into the building occupation.

The occupiers hooted and cheered as they accepted the sleeping bags. Greg shook Eric's hand for a job well done, waved at the cop and circled off into the night, the remaining sleeping bag under his arm. The large vents on the long side of the P&MB were completely unguarded, and were where Greg had tasted his first Kajan, one of

Larry's imports, after school his freshman year. They had smoked the pinner in the manicured hedges and cypress trees where the vent fitted into the wedge of the building's architecture at ground level. It was then that they had noticed that the campus gardeners kept the narrowest of paths open between the landscaping and the building's walls, perfect now for allowing Greg to sneak in behind the campus cops. Once safely within the police line, safely in the occupation, he made a point of "thanking" the cop who had blocked his way before.

***

A lot of people did a lot of legwork. The Oakland demo was remarkable. Fifty thousand from the community thronged the sidewalks around the downtown police station massively protected by police, who were a bit chagrined by the crowd's size and solemnity. Slogans were shouted, but curses were not. Black arm bands, and a theme of mourning pervaded. Some participants even carried candles. The rally's sponsor, the ad hoc Oakland African American Alliance Opposed to Police Brutality included numerous local ministers, the spectrum of Black/African nationalist groups, the African American GI Organizing Project, even the more conservative Black civil rights groups such as the Urban League and the NAACP; the Alliance organizing from the New Afrika Center, heart of the Black nationalist fringe.

The rally lasted from 4 until 8, and community leaders violated noise laws to speak to the multitude over portable PA's. None were hassled by the police. The cops did not dare. The entire event was peaceful. A young representative from Liberation Station Afrika named Leo ran around interviewing folks. A lot of Oakland, only minimally patrolled with the PD's concentration in the four-block area around the station for the rally, proved an ideal situation for the city's gangs. Then there were the Young Afrikan Lords doing security.

DL was the Lord's warlord, gang president, head man, and he did as the other brothers did; Jack'o'Hearts, Hakim, Killah Samuels, Captain Zero and the rest. Two dozen Young Afrikan Lord members, each dressed in black clothing and leather, and each sporting a black beret with a red-green-black-gold patch, stood in a solemn, disciplined line between the demo and the PD. They had their backs to the police. Yes, it was the same Oakland PD who had busted each at least a half dozen times before. They now itched to get their hands, or rather their batons, onto the proud, perhaps arrogant Lords.

A lot of the community at the demo were also leery, at first, of the strutting Young Afrikan Lords. Up until six months before, the Lords ran east Oakland turf; drugs, numbers, prostitution, protection, auto theft, the usual. They had been one of Oakland's most powerful gangs, not gangbangers as much as entrepreneurs with uzis. When DL got out of jail at the beginning of last year, he had sought to reclaim his gang on the advice of Askia and Isaak.

DL had spent the first months out in the community talking with the numerous, fractious nationalist organizations ranged across Oakland, learning from everyone before making his move. And of course, he had talked with the brothers, the baddest as well as the most receptive, teaching what he could, for without them he could not make the move. About half of the Lords wanted to go with DL, so he gave the other half the gang's entire operation—contacts, fences, bookies, rackets, the works—while keeping the name and treasury to date. Fair deal, all agreed and no friendships were severed.

"You pick up the gun outright," Askia had warned him when DL visited him last, "And you'll be dead before the year's gone. Pigs will see to that. They don't mind you being a gangbanger. That's blacks selling to blacks and brother killing brother. S'long as you be doing that, they even help you. But you take up the gun against the powers that be, they gonna try and swat you like a fly. Ask the Panthers about it. Ask Malcolm. Ask the brothers in the Liberation Armies.

"And yah, maybe some of us want to be insects stinging and bothering this beast if that's all we can do now. But there's intelligent ways to be an insect. I learned that. You can be the mosquito, what comes out to sting at night and gets away. You can make yourself a scorpion and make your sting too strong to fuck with."

Flashing off Askia's words, DL thought about summers long ago, a summer picnic in the park with a dozen families from the same church, when one of the kids knocked down a hornets nest next to the picnic with an errant baseball. The hive boiled out, swarmed up and most effectively broke up the picnic. DL then turned to Isaak's Nation of Islam for inspiration, not that he was religious at all. Their self-discipline and their enterprise—mosques, restaurants, schools, and the like—did speak to him. So DL, with his Lords, gambled.

He rented a commercially zoned warehouse on a year's lease three months before, and the Lords set to work. Using the rest of their money, and then borrowing from businesses and friends, they rebuilt the warehouse up to code and under permit for low rent offices and store fronts. An Afrikan boutique, a Jamaican reggae shop, first a Nation of Islam barber shop and then their restaurant occupied the storefronts alongside DL's own Afrocentric bookstore. And the cheap offices enticed a number of threadbare Black/Afrikan community organizations to relocate. The Caribbean import/export business subletted the remaining warehouse space not taken up by the Young Afrikan Lords' own projects.

The Lords ran martial arts classes with paid instructors, aware that the self-discipline of karate, ju jitsu or kung fu had habit-kicking consequences. They opened a community library. They arranged computer and desktop publishing classes for neighborhood kids using borrowed and rented hardware. They made rooms available for community meetings. And they wooed a Chicano/Mexicano gang, the Latin 38's, contemplating the transition to a political organization. They did better than break even on the rent, so much so that DL shared a paid, full time administrative position with Killah Samuels, while Hakim was now a full time, paid center staffer. They had just put in a community switchboard and were looking into setting up a free community medical clinic. They now debated changing their name to the New Afrikan Lords.

Others often termed DL's anti-sectarianism naive. He was not ML, nor Muslim, nor Rasta, nor cultural nationalist. If anything he resurrected the self-help revolutionist gang ideas of the mid-60's. If it does not work, chuck it. If it works, keep it. And the New Afrika Center worked, at least so far.

"You can't keep righteous Muslims in the same building as pork-eating socialists and ganja smoking Rastas." Isaak had written him from prison even as he thanked DL for the inspiring pictures and the books he had sent. "Shit'll hit at the first barbecue."

So DL organized the first barbecue himself; a vegie and fish fry kosher with almost everyone. It was the first time many of these people had talked to each other. Unfortunately, the Lords were getting to be another matter, with a strong Muslim tendency often blocking agreements and extending meetings until late into the night. Only DL's street charisma and his audacious plans held them together at times.

One of those plans had been to let the Alliance meet at the Center, and to volunteer to do security for the rally. His offers had been much debated by various community organizations in the Alliance until noon Tuesday before both were approved. Silent and strong, and like so many before to include the Panthers and the Fruit of Islam, they stood up for resurgent African people as they held the line, their backs brazenly to the cops in downtown Oakland on that evening become night.

***

The ASU campus bookstore turned into a nightmare. Not only had the alarm been a bitch to disarm despite all his tools and skill, but Peregrine had not been able to crack the main safe in a comfortable time, even with an audio augment. The three cash registers gave him $60 total for his troubles. What's more, in exiting, he was almost spotted by campus cops on their rounds. His hands shook for risking so much for so little. Peregrine cracked a beer on the fire escape to his apartment after the haunted drive home, watching as an ancient super continent's patronage wound down for the night.

He ached, his stomach knotted up tight and not from guilt. He never felt guilt when the target was institutional or corporate. He thought of another, more personal close call, years ago. Once, after a raucous house party, he had lifted the wallet of one of the unconscious guests, boyfriend of someone he'd known who turned out to be a football half back. The girlfriend had seen him wandering suspiciously about, and she'd put two and two together when the half back woke up sans wallet, and the $150 in it. That it had been circumstantial evidence had prevented Peregrine from being pulverized by the angry jock unwilling to be charged with assault and battery. He remembered the furious half back's huge hands clutching his shirt, lifting him up to slam him against a wall. He remembered his legs going numb and rubbery, and his stomach spasming up hard, just as they did now. He went for another beer from his fridge. Still too hyped for sleep, he filled a pipe for a smoke.

NINETEEN

BBC World Service Special Report
"Modern Counterinsurgency: The Weapons of War"
BBC Reporter: Nijal Thomas [1-13-2007]
(Electrostraca #: RNB/GM-113007-375-789-0376)

The guerrillas and general population of southern Mexico have found few ways to deal with newly developed anti-personnel technologies. Derm Ice comes in fine powder dusted from helicopter gun ships. It produces symptoms identical to frostbite, in the tropics. Killing gangrene follows immediately.

Neuro Trace comes in hair fine thread spun off a cruise delivered bindle bomb. It forms a seraphim fine webbing tapestried across wide areas of jungle. Once touched to the skin, it tangles and wraps, its mycotoxin eating down through the nerves with fiery pain. Eventually, it dissolves the nerve trace back to the spinal cord and brain.

Razor Pollen is a large, biodegradable, artificial hydrocarbon that wafts on the breeze and lacerates eyes, even skin, when rubbed in. Once embedded into flesh it quickly dissolves, combining with blood chemistry to cause tissue ulceration, ripe for festering infections.

Besides regular napalm, Smart Jelly is also used. The new gelled fuel can be configured into droplet and string explosions for wider, more thorough impact, coverage and destruction.

TWENTY

Marcus returned for lunch after another routine morning. Thursday morning. He styled himself an insurance claims adjuster to the merchants and landlords he buttonholed on his rounds, seeking a missing beneficiary, one "Drew Silva," in order to hand over a fat check. Then he laid out the description. Peregrine's description. He had redrawn the police sketch to get rid of the cop-art feel, and he produced it. He intended to give merchants his beeper number and ask landlords to introduce him to the tenant in question, if there was a response. So far, nothing.

He piled briefcase and clipboard onto the desk next to the high tech complex he was amassing. Piles of video tapes and photographs were in the process of being run through the multi-media scanner. The photo materials were favors owed him by friends he had in TV, the press and government, as well as Captain Sampson coming through on his connections.

"I found a great little German deli in Novato," Gwen accepted his peck-on-the-cheek over the boiling bratwurst. "By the way, Captain Sampson called. Said to call him back right away. That it was urgent. And, of course, Neal called for an update."

Brian was not in, so Marcus left a message. Neal would want reassurances and the detective was not in the mood to baby-sit. Instead, he settled down to sausage with hot mustard and horseradish, cabbage, a dollop of German potato salad, beet relish and pickled mushrooms. The telephone rang as Marcus considered seconds.

"Hope you're sitting down Marcus," Sampson did not sound pleased, "Got a call at 11 from Shel Waxmann, program manager for KWNE radio. He received a kind of 'news release' in the mail today. From a group calling itself the 'Mexican Revolution Solidarity Brigade'."

"My God," Mark realized, "You mean Sumner was right?"

"Looks that way," the Captain snarled, angry at having to admit it. "Here's what we have..."

Marcus listened to Brian shuffle papers over the phone.

"...The text of what they call 'Communiqué #1' is as follows. *'We, the Mexican Revolution Solidarity Brigade, possess the two pounds of enriched riemanium taken from the Security Pacific Services armored car robbery in Oakland. For the riemanium's return, we demand the immediate and unconditional withdrawal of all U.S. military forces from southern Mexico and northern Guatemala. We also demand that the U.S. government participate in peace negotiations with the Zapata Liberation Front.*

'The present U.S. air war over the Yucatan, with its use of hunter bombs, antipersonnel weapons, and chemical and biological agents, amounts to a fascistic strategy of 'total war.' The Liberated Territories are a modern-day Guernica. The popular struggles and peoples war of the Mayan Indians and other indigenous peoples in southern Mexico are being met by the only strategy available to U.S. imperialism; aerial genocide to compliment the dirty ground war being conducted by the so-called 'Combined Forces' and Mexican military-sponsored right wing death squads. The war must be stopped immediately. All U.S. forces

118

must be withdrawn. And immediate negotiations for peace with the ZLF must begin.

'The Mexican Revolution Solidarity Brigade reminds the powers-that-be that information on how to build a nuclear device can be found in any good public library. The riemanium, converted into a fine dust and spread into the atmosphere, could exponentially increase the incidence of cancer around the Bay. Will it be necessary to give this country a taste of the 'total war' we regularly rain down upon the Yucatan? Or will the U.S. government militarily withdraw from southern Mexico and make peace with its people?'"

"That's it?" Marcus asked.

"Yes," Brian said, "No deadlines, no ultimatums, no mention of follow through; its not an extremely 'threatening' job. It's desktop, and the communiqué part came on a colored xerox of photos of the riemanium. No doubt about it. It's the stolen riemanium all right. I went to get KWNE's copy for the lab. You know Mark, this thing looks almost like an art project. You know the look I mean. What's the matter with me. I'm faxing a copy to you right now. Lots of other media are getting copies today. My phone's been ringing off the hook."

"Fits with the suspect's political associations I told you about," Mark said, "It might still be him, alone, trying to milk this for all its worth. But you're right. The wording is nondescript. Certainly not militant, much less revolutionary. Too academic."

"Sumner is likely to catapult this Peregrine onto the Most Wanted," Sampson speculated, "Which is all the more reason to have you in Alabaster. I'll keep my two cops available as long as possible, but I know Sumner's going to pull rank with Holbin real soon. I may not be able to give you much up front help before too long. Edward, he thinks you're a joke, which makes you our sleeper. Our ace-in-the-hole."

"Virtually the only independent operator now I'll wager," Marcus agreed.

"And you still have Joe," Brian reminded him, "Manley's sharp. Use him."

"Already am," Mark made a note to set up another meeting with Joe, "I'm sorry you'll probably lose your mobility with this."

"No sorrier than I am," Sampson chuckled ruefully, "No pleasure knowing that now the whole Patrol is going to have a hard time holding onto our autonomy. Perhaps if Darby gets a little too much of Edward's boot he'll be open to a little solo action."

Brian did not elaborate and Mark did not probe.

"Damned Feds," the Captain finally grumbled. "They'll be descending like flies on shit after this. Trouble is, the bullshit comes with the territory. I knew it when I accepted the job. Means I'm going to have to fight for anything I can get from here on out."

END TIME

"Good luck," Marcus said.

He recapped the news to his wife and turned on the radio. Sure enough, news flashes of the communiqué were like lightning on the airwaves. He called Joe's home phone, got his answering machine and left a message. This certainly was a new twist. He casually read the dot matrix printout as he hung up the telephone; Gwen's work marked: *Federal Bureau of Investigation Data Base Printout. Supplemented by Black Talon.*

BLACK DADA NIHILISMUS: (From poem, entitled same, by LeRoi Jones [b. Everett LeRoi Jones, aka Amiri Baraka], 1964. Poem noted for ultra-violent imagery and race war themes.) The Black Formation (BF) (qv.) first caucused at the 2001 National Conference of Students for an Anarchist Society (SAS) (qv.) when covert U.S. government aid to the Mexican and Guatemalan governments' counter-insurgency campaigns in the Yucatan was exposed by the New York Times. BF became an autonomous grouping with the breakup of SAS in early 2002, itself breaking up by the middle of 2003 over differences in strategy of opposition to the beginning of U.S. air war. Black Gang (BG) (qv.) supported "open affinity structure" and "alliances in the streets" with other radical elements and formations. Black dada Nihilismus (BdN) promoted "clandestine affinity structure" and "street autonomy." BdN published "Kick It Over: A Maximum Strategy" (qv.) in 8/2003. Between 40 and 60 BdN affinities, each of between 5 and 15 militants, are believed to exist in San Francisco, Seattle, Los Angeles, Minneapolis, Chicago, New York and Atlanta. BdN is strongest in SF Bay Area, and combined BdN actions are estimated to have destroyed $750 million in corporate and government property to date. As a consequence, it has become a focus for the FBI Counter-Anarchist Program (ConAnPro, qv.). Presently, only three BdN members have been arrested, and none of these arrests have seriously hampered BdN activism nationwide.

"Keep plugging away at the work," Mark cleared the table and rinsed the dishes. "I'll know more about any change of direction, if there is to be any, by this afternoon."

Marcus pulled the computer processed fax of the MRSB Communiqué #1 out of the OXO. He then employed his tried-and-true method for provoking thought; he changed into Nikes and jogging sweats and went for a long walk to sort out his own confusion.

First, he dissected the photos. Pine forest: Anywhere, Northern California. The camos and combat boots; that set a tone the detective would have expected to be carried through to the disappointing text.

120

BABYLON BY THE BAY

On one part of the right boot, he discerned letters: SP. His son had gone through a punk phase in growing up and by the style he guessed that the initials indicated a late-term punk band, Small Potatoes.

Then, he analyzed the communiqué's text

All that he had noted with Brian still glared out at him. It did not state how the riemanium was obtained. It did not state that a nuclear weapon or a dusting would be the consequences of inaction, let alone that the MRSB would carry through on either. It was remarkably short and vague, giving a muddled fingerprint, what a criminologist might call a sociopolitical profile.

Supposedly, this was a communiqué from an extreme Left wing political group, if Peregrine's BdN connections were assumed. It's rhetoric was grade C, worthy of a naive college PC Leftist. It showed no ideological punch. There was no mention of "the workers" or "the oppressed" or "capitalism's need to maximize profits," and only one backhanded mention of "U.S. imperialism;" the telltale marks of ML leanings. Nor did it contain diatribes against "state power," "politicians and bosses," and "authoritarianism" to tag it as anarchist leaning. The communiqué was remarkably bland for all the divisions rife on the Left, so much so that Marcus suspected that it had been written by a committee working from consensus.

Marcus stood on the short levee for Driscoll Creek south of Main Street before it crossed the bridge to become East Main, past the PD and City Hall. Across the bridge began Alabaster East; the eastward walled suburban/telescanned mini-mall sprawl built up in the '80's/90's aspiring to connect with Marin County's urban creep. He chose the well marked river bank trail south instead.

If Peregrine claimed BdN, then it would have shown in that communiqué. If it had come from Peregrine, it would have been more incendiary, more defiant. He was getting a sense of the man he stalked, and Marcus was certain enough to bet money that Peregrine had not written it. What he had instead in the communiqué was some memo written by some executive committee.

Had the material been passed on? Had there been another gang? Or an after theft sale? Was searching out Peregrine even worth the effort? Or was Peregrine deliberately disguising his political bent, cleverly submerging his extremism with such general Leftist drek? His theories had become doubts.

"Looks almost like an art school project." He repeated Sampson's words out loud to focus himself, glancing at the fax in his hand. A large black raven drifted lazily overhead. How difficult would it be for some art students at any of the Bay Area's colleges or universities, hell even high schools, to spec and craft an object from repeated newsprint and video images meant to alert the public? Fabricate it out of fiberglass

END TIME

and foam to look like the real thing, then stage a media event. Or, would it be performance art? But how would they have known how the box's contents looked?

The levee graded down to the creek bottom, as had the trail he followed. Water pooled and pearled along the worn rocks and small boulders of the creek channel. Straw dry reeds, brittle sage, and tangled mesquite complicated the way. Marcus stopped for a rest on a small boulder, beneath an overhanging film of evergreen needles. As he wiped his brow, the drama unfolded. A ringed, spindly legged roadrunner darted across a wide, sandy expanse, two long strides behind the lizard scurrying, doing evasive maneuvers, until the reptile achieved brief safety under a thick scrubby bush.

At first, the roadrunner scampered about, trying from every direction to badger the poor cold blooded creature out of hiding. Then the avian seemed to tilt its head for a moment of thought. The roadrunner jumped to the side of the bush the lizard would have emerged from, had it continued clear through, and began to peck and claw furiously. It continued its frenzied assault, trying to uproot the bush, until the lizard leapt from hiding and tried for the way back. Back the way it had come, across the empty expanse of sand. The bird expected it. With one bound of wings and talons, it leaped entirely over the bush, to pounce on the reptile. Lunch.

"Gwen, everything's on course," Marcus returned, full of confidence, "What do you have for me?"

"The deep recesses of Black Talon." She was not smiling.

Nor did he blame her. Satanism, much like Christianity or socialism, suffered from innumerable splits and rifts. Anton LeVey's Church of Satan had considered itself "the thinking man's Satanism," an "eye for an eye" philosophy cloaked in Satanic imagery and symbolism. As such, and even after the "master's" demise, it could be distinguished from coven Satanism, paganism which saw in Satanism a Christian-corrupted nature worship, Mansonesque cultic Satanism, and the pop Satanism which had emerged from heavy metal, glam, and gothic punk after the mid '70's. But the LeVeyites were not a unified whole either. The Black Talon BBS was the neo-cyberpunk tendency in that Satanic sect, as distinguished from the professionals and entrepreneurs who took up LeVey's philosophy as justification for their own ruthlessness. Not that the formal LeVeyites were any more pleasant to deal with, but one of the Black Talon's quiz questions to enter their bulletin board, after logging in on a private account with the appropriate password, was:

You are in the castle en route to steal the King's treasure when you come upon the unguarded chambers of the princess. The princess is asleep so you:

122

BABYLON BY THE BAY

A) *Proceed because the princess is merely a distraction;*
B) *Note her location so that you can return after stealing the King's*
   treasure to take her prisoner;
C) *Take her hostage to negotiate for the King's treasure;*
D) *Rape her and proceed; or*
E) *Rape her, kill her and proceed.*

The correct response was E. Luckily for Gwen, and Marcus, their PC did not have a compatible graphics program.

"You've already read the Black dada Nihilismus file," Gwen handed him another printout in a tagged manila folder, as well as a manila envelope. The folder was marked: *Black Talon Data Base Print Out.*

PEREGRINE; [(per' ∂•grin) adj. 1. Coming from foreign regions: a peregrine bird. 2. Traveling; wandering.—n. The peregrine falcon. Also peregrin.] Handle associated with as-yet-unidentified second story man.

Name circulated in New York City vaguely attached to a number of burglaries of differing MO's in the late 1980's and early 1990's. Never clearly identified.

Recently, name resurfaced in association with Piccoli Gem Heist (qv.) and Diamotti gang (qv.) in Oakland, California, 1/27/2007. Associated with fifth, as-yet-unapprehended suspect from above theft. Reputed to have been Diamotti gang's procurer. White male, 22-28 years old, 5'10", 150 lbs, average build, dark complexion, dark hair, hazel eyes, a.k.a. Michael Baumann and Robert Fitzooth. California APB still in effect. May be upgraded to FBI 10 Most Wanted due to release of Mexican Revolution Solidarity Brigade 2/1/2007 communiqué (qv.). There is no direct link between 20th century Peregrine and present-day Peregrine.

Again, Marcus had to marvel at the brief summary's currency. Black Talon already had the MRSB on file.

"Nothing from Interpol?" Mark asked, dangling a pencil from his fingers.

"Nothing I've been able to track down yet," Gwen said, not taking her eyes off the computer screen or her fingers off the keyboard.

At the same moment, Neal logged onto the company compunet in Security Pacific's downtown SF corporate offices, then used a secondary password, known only to himself, to access an obscure data base. The Security Pacific president copied the information onto computer diskettes, five in all, before irretrievably erasing that well hidden memory. FBI subpoenas, attached to humorless FBI agents, had arrived that morning for everything pertaining to the Piccoli Gem and UC riemanium shipments, as well as the current personnel files, tax

123

records for the previous five years, and working books for the last six months. Neal anticipated a more thorough follow-up search any day now.

Neal cleaned out his briefcase and barely managed to cram it full with four bulky manila files from a separately locked drawer in an already locked filing cabinet in his office. He had accepted a number of shady jobs not only when Security Pacific was a struggling new company but throughout his years in business; transporting several stolen masterpieces in the private collection of a well-known individual of wealth and social position, providing discreet security for a drug and sex bacchanalia of several prominent congressmen, middling an exchange of money for sex between a famous Hollywood star and the wife of an ex-president, etc. In turn, his files and records on these and other less-than-kosher transactions had given Neal an inordinate amount of leverage in Washington. No need to waste it by handing it over to the FBI, he thought. He took the executive elevator down to his car, parked in the basement, the files in his briefcase and the diskettes in his jacket pocket.

Marcus set down the folder, then picked up the envelope. This had only one item, a color glossy 8x10 photo of a peace demonstration. A red ink circle on the photo side enclosed a small face in the throng. The back gave the time and place that the picture was taken, the source, as well as the handwritten words: "75% gestalt."

The face in the photo was young. Had the detective been a liquor store clerk, he would have carded that face. The hair in the photo was not dark, but bright red, and a raft of freckles made the ruddy face appear rounder, the cheeks fuller. An optical illusion; still and all, very young. Three-quarters gestalt with the police sketch was not sufficient to update the police description, not from one picture. But it did provide another clue.

"Thanks for sticking with the Black Talon and digging this up," Mark lightly touched Gwen's shoulder. She gave him a weary smile. He continued to ponder aloud on one of the many puzzling aspects to the information collected so far.

"BdN is a radical youth gang," he sketched out the dilemma as Gwen poured herself a glass of wine, done for the day. "Peregrine's been described as young, and not just by Rosanne. All of which just doesn't jibe with the 'feel' to this guy. If there is a connection between New York's Peregrine and ours, then this guy can't be in his early 20's. Otherwise, he'd have to be the youngest hot-shot second story man on record anywhere. But, leaving that aside, what we know of him from the Diamotti gang also implies that he's older. More experienced. Either that or he's really been around, which doesn't jibe with his lack of a police record. Then there's his sketch and this photo. It's over a year old, but it has a high gestalt."

"Either he inherited his handle from someone else." His wife enjoyed her well-deserved drink in small sips. "A father or a mentor-in-crime. Or, he's a lot older than he appears. That suggests either a naturally youthful appearance, or maybe cosmetic alteration."

Joe Manley called then, and Marcus set up a meeting for the next day.

***

Greg tried studying his biological chemistry with great difficulty sprawled on his sleeping bag in the P&MB lobby. The noise was bad enough, what with people talking, the low drone of several radios playing a weird amalgam of musical styles or covering the latest on the New York jigsaw serial killer who sliced up his victims to mail their body parts to prominent politicians, as well as an acoustic guitarist doing very bad folk covers. The smell of the occupation was even more distracting. First, there was the odor typical of summer camp; lots of sweaty bodies, rancid shoes and socks, and too strong perfumes and antiperspirant. This was mixed with food odors, two distinct burning incense sticks, and a pine sol smell whenever anybody opened the bathroom doors. He looked up from his book, pinching the bridge of his nose to clear his sight. He was not getting a lot of work done when Beth Roland walked through around 4 and zeroed in on him.

"The communiqué's hit the media," she said, her voice low even though no one was immediately about them.

"Yah, I heard," Greg said, "Any response yet?"

"An hour ago. The President said he won't bargain with terrorists. He's ordered the FBI to hunt down 'those responsible' no matter what it takes."

"Now there's a blank check," Greg closed his book and slipped it into his backpack.

"Rumor has it that he's also considering declaring a state of emergency and martial law in the Bay Area." Beth frowned. She did not support the perverse equation that more repression would produce insurrection that much sooner.

"How likely is that?" Greg asked.

"Not very," Beth admitted, sighing, "Some folks were talking about it on KPFA is all. Anyway, I have a couple more things to ask you. The community peace group, the Alabaster Coalition for Peace in Southern Mexico has called a demo downtown on Friday at 2 p.m. I've been calling all morning, and ASP consensus so far is to do some CD. Blockade the Post Office to dramatize registration and the draft. Are you down for that?"

"Sure," he said, automatically.

"Good. There'll be a non-violence training tomorrow at 7 a.m. at the

END TIME

Zapata Cafe. Now, we need a couple of ASP reps to meet with the Coalition tonight, to discuss our CD. We sorta told them that we'd already planned to do it. Feelings are running high that we should keep our independence on this action. The Coalition was blown away by this building occupation. But they also want to channel us into their agenda."

"When's the meeting?

"Seven."

"Okay, I'll go."

"Great," Beth looked relieved. "A lot of the rest of us are busy. It'll be at the Gondwana, upstairs. Lori's also going."

Suddenly a representative for Alabaster Students for Peace, Greg reviewed his own patchwork politics. The word "eclectic" entailed too much choice. Greg's politics had been grafted onto him from his limited life experiences.

To begin with, he admired the vision and courage of a certain type of action-oriented pacifist, though he himself was not one. He had come to appreciate the pacifist point of view while struggling with his decision not to register for the draft. His decision had been made easier by his father's ability to subsidize his education, and a civil libertarian opposition to any form of national ID still extant in society. Greg knew his own limits however, and so knew that there were certain situations in which he would not remain pacifist. He methodically rolled up his sleeping bag before restuffing his backpack with his school work.

In turn, his interest in the practical side to science, in the mechanical and engineering aspects to things, gave him a disdain for PC's extreme subjectivism still rife on most college and university campuses. The equation that, say, a remark was sexist just because a woman said it was (there being no objectivity and the oppressed always being right about their own oppression), made him cringe. He tended to believe that objective reality possessed objective standards. Even when that was not the case, people always defined standards for themselves with each other in a social context. Neither could be as easily dismissed as the PC line might have it.

Greg strolled across the sun soaked Plaza, pack on his back and sleeping bag under his arm. His predisposition toward objective, scientific criteria gave him little sympathy for Marxism however. He particularly abhorred the vile ideological permutations of Leninism. There was a type of reverse romanticism in the latter to which he felt not the slightest sympathy. ML's often took great pride in a clinical, "revolutionary" ruthlessness that to Greg bordered on pathology. History's judgment was all that mattered, and history was not a particularly sentimental or humane force. Millions had died for history to pass its judgment against Nazism for instance. What is more, ML's often took a

126

BABYLON BY THE BAY

perverse carnivore's pride in being agents of history, capable of doing whatever was necessary to bring their communist society into being. Born too late to know of the Khmer Rouge's Kampuchean blood bath, except as history, Greg had followed the Shining Path's Peruvian holocaust as it unfolded to the world via the media.

By the same token, he did not redbait. He had no desire to live in the squalid, repressive "workers' paradise" that was Cuba, China, North Korea, Vietnam, Peru, or any of the other leftover ML regimes reconstituted as the remnant socialist block. But, unlike even a good many anarchists and anti-authoritarians these days, he refused to out-anticommunist the anti-communists. Instead, he preferred to point out the wrongs perpetrated by the US. The anti-communist vehemence of this ultra-Left was a waste of time, according to Greg. The broad concrete steps that he climbed up to the central library's hive-like arcologies, now dotted with casual lounging students, always reminded him of a 20th century sci-fi movie.

He agreed that decentralization was a more humane and creative way to run things; after all, ecologies were most stable when most diverse and variegated. And the new hologramic computers were contrived as decentralized hardware and software webs. But he was not at all sure about decentralized Hooligan revelry in street fighting and violence. This too seemed to be born of a romantic love of violence that used catharsis as an excuse to perpetrate general mayhem. In sum, he described himself as a decentralized, democratic socialist.

He spent the remainder of his time before the meeting studying in the library. He had wanted to drop by home to see if Andre was there. But he met Larry on the way off campus, smoked a joint of dynamite Humboldt, and wound up driving to the Cafe, arriving on time.

Gondwana had been one of his and Janet's hangouts. They had liked the window tables on the ground floor, but were not old enough or important enough to have, de facto, their own table on their own night as did the regulars. At the same time, they had never been intimidated by the Bohemian/intelligentsia types who got irritated when they stayed over at any of the unofficially reserved tables. He felt a little awkward going in solo, a feeling enhanced by being high. He ordered an herbal tea and a toasted buttered bagel with a side of cream cheese, paid and waited, then took them upstairs.

The Cafe had been started by a couple of ASU graduates. They had appropriated the cliched Geology department joke, a favorite of t-shirts, to "Reunite Gondwanaland," as the ultimate expression of the human condition. A "Myth of Sisyphus" to the hundredth power. Perhaps it also had a little to do with their graduating as Liberal Arts majors from a cow-town, agi-college. The service stations on the Cafe floor, in turn, were divided continentally; South America, Africa and

END TIME

Antarctica, with India and Australia combined. Fronds and ferns cooled the raw wood decor with lush greens. The upstairs had been an afterthought, built over the kitchen and toilet areas when the cafe became popular, and crowded. It was more like a loft, an internal balcony with a view of the rest of the cafe and its show. It had the nickname of the Pterodactyl Roost. Once up in the roost, he had no trouble identifying the Coalition folks, even though Lori had not yet managed to make her appearance yet.

Intelligentsia or Bohemian, student or community, the Cafe's patrons were uniformly "in style." By contrast, the Coalition members were downright frumpy; the males mostly bearded, the females without makeup, and both dressed in baggy labor/lumberjack garb. Greg strolled up, introduced himself, and deferred any serious conversation until Lori's arrival. The meeting's context resided in international political developments; events he was familiar with only as history.

The collapse of ML style communism in eastern Europe, and the former Soviet Union's subsequent disintegration into its second civil war, had different political consequences for the rest of the world's Left than it did for the domestic, U.S. Left. The concrete manifestations—shattering of the socialist bloc, ML retrenchment, facilitation of regional and world capitalist consolidation, increased exploitation and ongoing fragmentation of the Third World—were rarely disputed. But the consequences to ideological configurations were in dispute precisely because they differed inside and outside of the United States.

Internationally, Marxism-Leninism fell into disrepute. There existed little in the way of a second world, socialist alternative for the Third World to follow as a model for economic development. Those Third World movements which remained loyal to ML orthodoxy, such as Peru's Communist Party, the infamous Sendero Luminoso, committed mass atrocities once in power to further discredit that ideology. But in a Third World wracked by continuous, generalized civil war, little of the Left remained relevant. Strains of authoritarian capitalism predominated.

Certain revolutionary Marxist strains in Europe—councilism, Marxist Humanism, and some post-Trotskyist sects—managed to hold onto and even modestly expand their memberships. But what benefited most were European social democracy and Left liberalism, when the Left did not lose to capitalist hegemony altogether. European anarchism, autonomism, situationism/post-situationism; that is the anti-authoritarian Left, diminished with the rise of practical and pragmatic political thinking, particularly in a Europe faced with incorporating a devastated eastern Europe into western economic prosperity.

As he spread cream cheese on his bagel, Greg noticed the social dynamics around him. The tableful of politicos and the surrounding

128

BABYLON BY THE BAY

"au courant" each considered themselves the exclusive avant garde, of politics and culture respectively. Clearly, each disdained the other; each group huddling in among themselves as if the other had leprosy. The resulting gap was manifested as a physical space, a no-man's-land the traversing of which had markedly changed Greg's status in the eyes of both camps. Greg had no inkling that his present company, representative of the US Left, was out-of-step with the Left internationally.

Of course the progressive landscape in the US also changed with the socialist bloc's partial collapse, but in ways that reflected the Left's privileged position in the center of empire and North America's modest economic prosperity. Marxism-Leninism declined, but not as markedly as would have been expected. US ML's had often been Third-Worldist in outlook. They could still point to the Third World ML regimes which maintained the remaining fragments of the socialist bloc, as well as the national liberation struggles they supported. Of course US ML's dismissed international events as a turning away from "true socialism." Social democracy lost some ground, but again, not much. Social democratic governments were still being voted in and out of power in the capitalist west. The resurgent north American labor movement of the late 1990's kept both Leninism and social democracy as viable options into the twenty-first century.

The big loser proved to be Democratic Party style liberalism and its overlap with more Leftist politics, as the war drove much of organized labor back into the Party's center, if not further right. US conservatives effectively used international events to decimate the ranks of FDR New Deal liberals. The big winner was the ultra-Left: the youthful, Hooligan amalgam of revolutionary Marxism, anarchism and sundry anti-authoritarian tendencies without the burden of ML socialism's failures, or its successes. With no apparent alternative between capitalist hegemony and Third World immiseration, all manner of utopianism flourished. Outside of this strictly linear spectrum, the numerous branched side movements—pacifism, radical environmentalism, internal nationalism, women's liberation, etc.—also flourished. These peripheral movements grew more widely in the US than in the rest of the world, but not as precipitously as did the ultra-Left.

Lori arrived with a smile for Greg and a cool hard gaze for the Coalition, a Raspie of Amazonian proportions named Mary in tow. Raspie was short for Rasputain or Rasputanic, a youth subculture devoted to Monk Rasputan's notion that in order to be blissfully redeemed, one had to first sin, and sin excessively. Raspie drug, sex and blood orgies were the flip side of an equally crazed mysticism. The Raspie style was black clothes and capes, if not actually caked in blood, then portions dyed blood red, and hung with industrial detritus, hunks of raw meat, embalmed fetuses and the like. The cafe management had banned such costumery as a health hazard, and so Mary wore her earrings of decapitated baby dolls as a Raspie reminder. One positive thing about Raspie was that it had defined the first truly creative musical style after punk; using as its base the hard industrial sound of the early 1990's (Tit Wrench, Lard) while combining elements of glam, worldbeat, funk, hiphop and kayo into a dynamic, aggressive, original gestalt. Raspie combined the sounds of instruments, samplings and synthesizers with the induced vibrational sounds of metal tools, ceramic toilets, glass alcohol bottles, and other common household items into hard, fast music characterized by walking bass lines, quirky rhythms, and occasional stunning melodies pushed forward by unpretentious lead guitars. On the whole, it did not use the new Emo-Sound technologies, though a few bands toyed with some of the audio-neural systems currently on the market. Most Raspie musicians preferred power and originality to what they considered "cheap tricks."

"Let's get started," Lori said, brusquely, as she and Mary took chairs, Lori with beer in hand. Introductions were made around the table.

"The Coalition for Peace in Southern Mexico has permits for a march down Main Street tomorrow at 1 p.m. with a picket at the courthouse." A man called Dannie, sporting a Lenin/Trotsky goatee, delineated the Coalitions plans. Greg remembered him from early ASP meetings, one of the "representatives from the community" who had attended to try and "guide" the student organization's direction in the guise of getting ASP to "work with the community more." He was a member of the Socialist Labor Organization, as Greg recalled. "This is the local response to the Peace Mobilization's national call. Now, its our understanding that Alabaster Students for Peace would like to participate in Friday's activities. Exactly what would ASP like to do?"

"We're planning on a little civil disobedience," Lori grinned. She ordered another beer from a passing waitress, then looked at Greg and ordered two.

"What type of CD?" asked a Coalition woman named Karen who wore a War Resisters League broken rifle pin, "When do you plan to do it, and where? Do you need non-violence training?"

"We have our own training scheduled," Lori smirked, "But as for the rest, that I'm afraid is information we can't provide at this time."

"That doesn't allow for you to get any critical input on your plans," said a man named Dustin, wearing a Committee In Solidarity with the People Of Southern Mexico t-shirt. "Such input might improve what you plan to do, maybe even keep you from making stupid mistakes."

"It also doesn't allow information about our action to reach the cops," Lori accepted the two beers, handed one to Greg, took a gulp of her beer, then handed it to Mary. "This way, the police aren't waiting for

130

BABYLON BY THE BAY

us, anticipating our CD and able to stop it before it starts."

Lori's response floored the Coalition, stunning them into a long moment of silence.

"You're not saying that telling the Coalition about your plans will let the police in on them?" Daniel was incredulous.

"Or maybe you're saying that the Coalition wants to try to police you!" A woman named Paula, from Educators for Social Responsibility, cut in.

"ASP is an autonomous organization," Lori condescended to answer. "Your coalition can suggest. But it can't order. As for our CD's security, well, the fewer who know about it's details, the better. There's a lot of police infiltration, especially these days."

"It's our event Friday." Dustin warned.

"Hold it," Greg spoke, nervously tracing a finger across the graffiti someone had carved into the table top; Tir na n-Oc. "The Coalition's doing this because it's a Mobe national call. You can't own a national call. So on Friday, that's your response to the national call. Other people can respond to the call in their own ways. You can't stop that."

"And whether or not that's true," Mary growled, "The Coalition doesn't own the peace movement in Alabaster. And you fucking can't own a peace march or rally."

Damn, she could be intimidating.

"We do have the permits," Paula managed a smile in the face of Mary's smoldering wrath.

"Yah, right," Lori was smug. "And we're doing CD. We're not going to the cops and saying 'hey, can we get a civil disobedience permit.' By definition CD's outside the law. And if push-comes-to-shove it'll be outside your Coalition's rules as well. We don't need a permit from you either."

"Hold on here," Karen held up a hand for calm, "There's no need to get into a fight over this. CD is not a legal activity, and its perfectly reasonable for your group to have security concerns."

"Especially with the President unleashing the FBI over that stolen riemanium," Lori said, winking at Greg. She'd ordered another beer, as did Greg.

"At the same time, the Coalition also has concerns," Karen continued.

"Yes," Dustin underscored her remark, "You talk about 'autonomy' and ASP doing what it wants, damn the law and the Coalition's rules too. That sounds to me like Hooligans talking. If you're planning to riot and street fight, then our Coalition is going to insist that you find another time and place for your action."

"We're going to do civil disobedience," Greg was emphatic, "Traditional, tried and true, Quaker inspired, Gandhi approved, ML

131

King endorsed civil disobedience. We're having a nonviolence training tomorrow morning to prepare for it."

"That's good to hear," Paula said.

"So why do I get this feeling," Lori leaned into the discussion, her voice loitering into a sarcastic drawl. "That even good old CD is too radical for your Coalition."

"That's not fair." Dannie protested.

"Isn't it?" Lori was obviously enjoying the provocation as she ordered another beer, handing her second half empty bottle to Mary.

"The Coalition is a broad alliance of many community organizations." Dustin explained, "Yes, there are groups in the Coalition that would see CD as 'going too far.' By the same token, there are Coalition groups that, say, believe in socialist revolution. The idea behind the coalition is to get all these different groups to work together around achieving peace in southern Mexico. Our activities are intended to gain the broadest public support possible."

"Which leaves you with a lowest-common-denominator politics," Mary laughed, thick and ugly.

"Your way of doing things often alienates people who would otherwise support you," Paula retorted.

The discussion went round and around. The hip, seated about the heated dialogue, continued to look askance at their group. Two more beers later, an agreement of sorts was reached. ASP would not reveal the nature of its CD, but every assurance was given that strict nonviolence guidelines would be adhered to. The Coalition would not endorse or approve of the ASP action, but it would not prohibit or disown the CD either.

"Fucking control freaks," Lori slammed the Coalition after its folks left. More beer arrived. "They've got some face..."

"Look Lori," Mary said, bored, "It's been weird, but I gotta go. Can you find a ride home?"

"Greg?" Lori asked.

"Sure," he said, feeling the beer on top of his high.

She lived in a studio near the campus. On the drive there, she continued her diatribe against the conservative, proprietary Coalition. Once parked in front of her apartment, she put a hand on Greg's knee.

"I'm real attracted to you Greg," she lowered her eyes, "Why don't you spend the night."

Sex with Lori was like riding a rodeo Brahma, and alternately, being ridden like one. Talk about a control freak, Greg managed to think through the alcoholic haze. She placed his hands and removed them when and where she wanted, urged on and then slowed his thrusting to her own agenda, and refused to cum while gloating over his out-of-control climax. Normally, such lack of spontaneity would have irritated him. But it had not prevented him from sleeping with her, and drunk, he merely fell asleep.

***

Peregrine scored $270 from the paint and hardware store on Main. Part of a chain, he'd staked it out that morning by purchasing several inexpensive, miscellaneous items. He took out the alarm, then entered through the toilet window in the back. He waited patiently behind a pyramid stack of paint cans while the security guard hired by the block played a flashlight through the front window around the store. Then he eased over to the sales counter. He quickly opened the register's bottom security drawer with his tools, scooped out the money, and then smugly melted away into the night. With the theft, Alabaster PD took notice of Peregrine's MO.

***

Smoke raised an eyebrow when Greg arrived for the non-violence training accompanied by Lori. But his expression did not alter otherwise, and he made no more of it.

"The Bay Area Progressive Student Network has joined with the Bay Area Peace Mobilization Council in calling for a one day, bay-wide general strike for next Wednesday," David finished up the announcements before the training began, "It's part of the National Peace Mobe's 'Stop Business-As-Usual' call. It looks like the European peace movement is also endorsing that day of action. There's a march and rally being planned for that day in San Francisco. Its supposed to be the biggest demo yet. ASP will have a very brief meeting after the training to discuss what we want to do."

Larry stumbled in then, so he and Greg high-fived and retreated to a corner of the room for a private conference.

"Heard from one of my 'customers' that plane loads of FBI agents are arriving," Larry rubbed his eyes, not used to such early hours, "Been arriving at SFO since day before yesterday at least."

"Think they'll declare martial law?" Greg asked.

"Naw," Larry yawned, "More likely they'll just flood the Bay Area with Feds, keep up the heat until something cracks."

"If any of the 'MRSB' crack," Greg commented, "We'll be on the front lines with this riemanium business. What do you think we should do?"

"Keep on course. The way we got it set up, its a conspiracy rap for us, same as the rest of the group. We don't have the, um, item in question, and so this Peregrine guy never shows again. What can they say? I would find another hiding place for IT ASAP. If the shit hits, they'll search your house."

"Yours too!" Greg was concerned, "What about your crop?"

"Dunno," Larry shrugged, scratching his beard, "Guess I'm hoping it doesn't come down to that."

END TIME

The nonviolence training started. Greg had not registered for the draft on purpose, but he had not broadcast his act of resistance to the general public. He considered himself a Leftist and went to anti-war demonstrations, but he had little interest in the activism of organizing and no desire for the martyrdom of conscience. In this way, he and Janet had been alike. If anything, Janet's leaving was pushing him deeper into politics as a way of occupying his thoughts and avoiding his pain. But if the government chanced upon his failure to register and provided him with its obligatory "second chance," in all probability he would register. "He who fight and run away, live to fight another day," in Bob Marley's words. He was relieved to learn from the training session's legal council that the police were not in the habit of checking up on draft registration status, even on clearly political arrests. Too much bother. About the same time the ASU students began some non-violent role-playing, a triumphant, cocksure Edward Sumner convened the auditorium full of Bureau agents. The small army he had assembled in that auditorium, his second wave, talked among themselves.

"May I have your attention please," Sumner smiled, standing behind the podium on stage, "I am Edward Sumner, and I will be your immediate director on this assignment, which the Bureau is code naming Operation Anvil. As you are all well aware, a communiqué from the Mexican Revolution Solidarity Brigade was received by Bay Area media yesterday, threatening to detonate a nuclear weapon in the area made from the riemanium stolen with the Piccoli gems, if the US military does not immediately withdraw from southern Mexico. The President of the United States has put our Bureau onto the highest alert possible, which is why all of you are here.

"Now, besides the missing riemanium, there is a fifth suspect, as yet unapprehended, from the theft. He is also wanted in connection with the murder of a Security Pacific guard. You'll find a summary on him in your orientation folder. Whether he is part of this Solidarity Brigade, or Diamotti's gang sold the riemanium to them, or there were two gangs of thieves involved is completely immaterial at this point. The stolen riemanium has become an instrument of domestic terrorism. Finding it and the Solidarity Brigade is our primary goal. If, in locating it, we also happen to find this 'Peregrine,' so much the better. But we'll get our hands on him sooner or later once we have him on the Ten Most Wanted.

"Again, our first priority is the Solidarity Brigade and the riemanium. The President does not, I repeat, does not want to take the next step in declaring a State of Emergency, let alone Martial Law. He will consider this operation a failure if he has to resort to that. Commensurate with this responsibility, the President has given the Justice Department, our Bureau, and my Directorship 'extended pow-

134

BABYLON BY THE BAY

ers.' I do not intend to fail."

Greg joined the march assembling in Remley Plaza in front of the P&M building, under a cloud marbled sky sketched with wheeling gulls. He would miss his English class, but at least he wasn't one of the students left behind to keep the P&M occupation secure. Margaret, books in hand, strolled up to him, Greg leaning on the fountain.

"Called you back," Margaret smiled, "But your dad said you were at the occupation. Come on over tonight. My roommate's skiing in Tahoe." She gave him a long, wet kiss, and Greg could not help but look around to see if Lori was in view. Then Margaret sauntered off, the movement of her hips tugging at his memories, not to mention his crotch. Definitely EM, electromagnetic, he thought. Sexy. He hoped that ASP's legal connections would, indeed, pop them out of jail on OR before the weekend. She liked sex. Lori, by contrast, used sex, and he suspected she didn't like it much. Neither girl, he suddenly realized, was much interested in his view of sex, both assuming that he was the typical horny male interested in pleasure without strings.

"As for the logistics," Sumner explained to the sea of suits, "Each of you will be assigned to a team, and each team will be assigned either a region, a constituency, or a function. Your specific assignment may change as things progress, as might your team. In a nutshell, I'm looking for flexibility and cooperation from each of you on this assignment. Those who give this to me will be rewarded. Those who can't be team players will be quickly transferred and, if I have anything to do with it, demoted. I am an easy man to approach, and I will listen to suggestions and criticisms. If I consider them meritorious, I will make appropriate changes. But I am also a strict task master who tolerates neither incompetence, laziness nor insubordination. Do I make myself clear?"

When about four hundred students had gathered in the Plaza with signs and banners, the march set off, between bad sculpture to College Drive and then to Main. They kept to the sidewalks under police attention until they reached California, the Coalition's march assembly point. They joined another five hundred people with their own signs and banners. Accompanied by a police motorcycle escort blocking one lane of traffic, the march eventually walked west on Main, around the Loop, then back east on Main, headed toward the courthouse. The ASP "action faction" affinity formed up then, Lori saucily smiling at Greg.

"Hey, Hey, Ho, Ho! US Troops Have Got To Go!"

"All We Are Saying Is Give Peace A Chance!"

The twenty strong CD-anxious group marched together along the route, part of the march but apart; Lori, Larry, Greg, David, Beth, Joseph and Nina among them. Smoke, swaddled in sunglasses, kaffiyeh and toque, as well as George walked alongside, both having

135

taken support roles in the action. Greg walked behind Lori and ahead of Larry. Two sparrow hawks glided beneath patchy light and dark clouds, circled the crowd curious of the noise, then tilted away. As they crossed the slight rise at College, he glanced back to the march trailing back, now perhaps two thousand strong. Greg had gone to many a mass SF march, and once in Golden Gate Park he had managed to climb a hill for an overview. Impressive, but the Alabaster peace march sent the chill down his spine. He had grown up here. These were his friends and neighbors.

"Hey, Hey, Ho, Ho! US Out Of Mexico!"

"Not Another Vietnam! US Out Of The Yucatan!"

The march approached the eastern end of downtown. The combined city hall/courthouse was on the march side of Main across from the police station/jail, and the old US post office was now between the march and city hall, up a flight of stone steps.

"We have all seen, in our lifetimes, the beginning of Communism's inevitable collapse," Sumner rose to his theme, having switched from the immediate assignment to more philosophical levels. "But the fall of the Marxist scourge has not initiated 'peace on earth.' On the contrary, the developing world is aflame with war and terrorism. And youthful anarchy now proudly stalks the streets of our country, cousin to the common criminals, dope dealers and degenerates who are unraveling the moral fiber of this nation. The Bureau intends to make this assignment the beginning of a national effort to clean up this nation, to expunge the vermin polluting our society once and for all. America's greatest enemies are internal; the rot that threatens to poison us from within. I intend to make the present campaign to recover the riemanium and break the Solidarity Brigade the spearhead of nothing less than the moral regeneration of this nation."

The Coalition monitors deftly wheeled the march onto the sidewalk in front of city hall to shape a moving picket line that reached around for the entire block. The escort police parked their motorcycles. They took up observation positions, augmented by a few additional cops, and back-dropped by a throng of curious, passing observers. Everything was routine protest.

"The People United Will Never Be Defeated!"

"Money For Jobs, Not For War!"

They swung around next to the post office where, by law, all 18 year olds had to register for the draft. The ASP CDers broke from the picket, walked up the PO steps, linked arms in front of the inward swinging doors and sat down.

"No Registration, No Draft, No War!" They chanted.

The next two hours were a formidable chaos. The picket almost collapsed as several hundred others leaped to the stairs. The Coalition managed to reform the picket line, shortened and kept to the post office end of the block. The blockaders allowed customers to leave, but not to enter. In the blink of an eye, a dozen more uniformed police appeared, along with at least two plain clothes cops. The postmaster wound his way down the front steps to meet the police, and together they forcefully asked: "Who's responsible here?" Dannie from the Coalition and David from ASP, along with the ACLU legal observer, stepped forward to explain the CD.

"Stop The Air War! No More Genocide!"

The police tried to intimidate while talking to the two reps; the uniforms forming a line at the base of the steps. They passed out riot helmets and sticks, but David as spokesperson for the group held firm. People were willing to get arrested, peacefully, to make their point about the immorality of the war. The ACLU lawyer reminded the sergeant-in-charge and the PO manager that an announcement of illegal assembly was required to give people not interested in arrest time to disperse. Dannie said that while the Coalition did not endorse the ASP CD, they understood how the vicious, imperialist US war in the Yucatan would bring people to the point of engaging in this nonviolent blockade.

"Peace Now! Peace Now!"

It was hard keeping the picketers in line, what with the police poised for riot. The postmaster waded back up to the front door and pushed himself angrily through the linked arms of the chanting affinity group. A paddy wagon pulled up at 4:40. The police sergeant stalked off to the command post of cops and cars on the corner. Rumors spread through the crowd that anyone arrested would not be placed in the city jail, but instead would be booked into the more distant, more violent, more crowded county facility. Time passed.

"Stop The Slaughter, Stop The War!"

The bluff edged toward 5 p.m. The cops in riot gear and poker faces continued to menace. Exactly at closing the PO guard locked the front doors. The ASP group stood up to cheer. They had won. They had shut down the post office's draft registration for over two hours. The police line did not move, so the blockade spilled out on the sides, leaving vacant stone steps. A knot of ASU students, perhaps a hundred strong, with the victorious affinity in their center, triumphantly set off on sidewalks back along Main. Singing, chanting and waving signs, they walked back the way they had marched. Accompanied by two motorcycle cops, they dispersed around the Loop through Barbary Park. Many wound up at the Gondwana to celebrate.

As Lori, Mary, David, Beth, Greg and Larry drank beers and talked about going to a show, Stiletto Blue's performance in Marinwood later that night, Joe Manley knocked on the Dimapopulos's open front door.

END TIME

Gwen cooked in the kitchen and Marcus scrolled through a computer file, delaying as long as he could his daily telephone report and pep talk to Neal, truly an animal running scared.

"Just got off work," Joe smiled, in uniform. "Peace demo."

Joe was a SoCal surfer in police blues, thick blonde hair, well-trimmed mustache, a healthy build, and a winning grin.

"Yes, I was there," Marcus said. He had stayed for the first half of the demo, surveying the crowd for a face he now knew by heart. The detective offered the officer a chair and something to drink.

"Beer if you got it," Joe said and accepted a Foster's Lager, "Didn't see anybody resembling Peregrine."

"Nor did I," Marcus took a ginger ale for himself, "But then again, it was a confusing situation. Can I get copies of your department's photos of that demo?"

"Sure, if you'll do us a favor."

"Shoot," Marcus said.

"Sampson seems to think you have, shall we say, alternative sources of information," Joe sipped the beer, "The stuff you passed on about Peregrine's political connections was new to my Sarge. Anyway, lately we've had a series of local burglaries. Three so far, all the same MO."

"And since Peregrine is supposed to be a burglar..."

"Who maybe was expecting a payoff from the Piccoli heist," Joe finished the line of thought, "A payoff he never got."

"Sure, I'll help," Marcus smiled, "Do you have a profile?"

"Right here," Joe unfolded two pieces of paper stapled together from his shirt pocket, "This one is a pro. He wears gloves, uses professional tools, knows alarms and security, is neat and precise on the job, and knows the places he hits."

"I'll get right on it," Marcus said, knowing that Gwen would be doing the work, "How're the clubs going?"

"One possible positive identification. The bartender at the Sprite in Fairfax, Saturday nights. Not 100%, and he said the guy hasn't been back since before the night of the heist. This is late night bar lighting."

"It's a start," Marcus said. "Did you give him my number?"

"Yep. One more thing. My superiors have been informed that some heavy federal action is about to come down, and we're expected to cooperate. Seems some FBI boys are coming to town."

"How do you feel about it?" the detective asked.

"I got nothing against the Feds," Joe accepted another beer, "But I got to agree with Sampson that sometimes they can do more harm than good. They don't know the area, and they certainly can muddy the waters."

"So you're still on the case?"

"Sure," the cop smiled and drank, "Way I figure it we've got as much

138

of a chance of turning up this Peregrine as they do. Better. We got some trumps in our hand."

"You play bridge?" Gwen leaned out of the kitchen, where she'd been preparing a dinner of stuffed pork chops and asparagus.

"Now and again," Joe admitted.

"Married?" Gwen continued.

"Girlfriend. She plays bridge too."

"Bring her over some evening," she smiled, "We'll play a couple of hands."

"I'll do that," he agreed.

"Don't know how I can thank you for your help on this case," Marcus returned to the subject.

"It's nothing," Joe waved a hand, "If we do snap him up, I'll enjoy that action and whatever prestige comes from it. Besides, I owe Sampson lots of favors. My old man ran off when I was three, so he was a substitute father for me when I was growing up. He was the one who got me into police work."

As Joe and Marcus finished up their casual meeting, Greg stood from the Gondwana tables held by the ASU contingent and, charged on the beer, excused himself for other plans. He had no intention of going to the show, and it was Lori's turn to arch an eyebrow.

He walked back to campus for his car and drove to Margaret's. Jazzed, he told her about the blockade as she laid out expensive beer and wine, Kajan grass and an eager body.

"Civil disobedience is roots cool, but I'm glad you didn't get arrested," she smiled, "Now lean back, you big bad revolutionary..."

She started with an enthusiastic blow job. Greg's exhilaration from that day's protest and challenge to authority proved an aphrodisiac and she came several times on his stamina. He remained hard after coming himself.

"Maybe you should stop the US mail more often," she laughed.

TWENTY-ONE

BBC World Service Special Report
"Modern Counterinsurgency: The Weapons of War"
BBC Reporter: Nijal Thomas [1-13-2007]
(Electrostraca #: RNB/GM-113007-375-789-0376)

The ultimate weapon in any war is the human one. Mexico's Zapatista's rely upon "people's war" and "the people armed" as the bulwark of their revolution, staking the defense of their "Liberated Territories" on a strategy of peoples militias and guerrilla warfare. Yet even the people, united, *can* be defeated if those in power make a routine out of "crimes against humanity." A ruthless military dictatorship willing to engage in a thoroughly dirty war, along the lines of Uruguay in 1973-74 or Argentina in 1976-83, can defeat most any popular insurrection.

The U.S. counterinsurgency war in southern Mexico has not resorted to such extreme measures so far, though the same cannot be said of the Mexican government's efforts to suppress indigenous insurrection. The official U.S./Mexican Combined Forces remain a model military organization; though their critics claim, with some justification, that the Combined Forces are mere window dressing. High-tech American and Mexican Army and Marine troops cruise rebel territory in sophisticated, air conditioned, computerized tanks and APV's. On ground solidly ZLF held they are scorned by peasants sympathetic to the guerrillas and consistently attacked. Snipers, mines and traps, boomerang biochemical attacks, rockets, mortars and drones, suicide car bombings, kamikaze guerrillas wired with explosives, lightning FAO commando-style hits, even the occasional pitched battle in the field with a militia column greet the Combined Forces in the core ZLF territories. In areas only under guerrilla influence, they are still scorned by peasants who support the ZLF, but they are not often attacked. Needless to say, and aside from occasional lightning ground forays and campaigns, the Combined Forces leave those regions held by the Zapatistas to the unmerciful pounding from a relentless U.S. air war. And, to military "special forces."

Unfortunately, the Mexican "special forces" are the right-wing death squads and contra bands that operate mostly on the periphery, but occasionally into the heart of the Liberated Territories. This is strictly Mexican military-aided white terror; rounding up and massacring an entire village, indiscriminately castrating and then shooting boys between 11 and 16 in a targeted zone, torturing suspected guerrillas with their families, etc. Much like RENAMO in Mozambique and the Nicaraguan contras, their 21st century Mexican counterparts disrupt, destroy and terrorize southern Mexico's ZLF-dominated society, hoping to make the cost of their revolution too high for people to endure. The U.S. military's failure to control such elements, and the U.S. government's failure to sufficiently pressure the Mexican government to curtail death squad activities has tarred the U.S. counterinsurgency effort with the brutal actions of Mexico's renegade "white" terrorists.

The strategy of U.S. "special forces," by contrast, is much more selective; targeting the structure of ZLF society in the Liberated Territories, and not southern Mexico's peasant population as a whole. Whereas the Mexican death squads and contras are the out-of-control sledgehammer in this war, U.S. special forces are the pinpoint, surgical laser beam. Union militants, prominent cooperative representatives, and militia column leaders; hydroelectric projects, arms factories, railroad and truck stations; insurrectionary tendencies in neighboring countries

BABYLON BY THE BAY

as well as the ZLF's international connections; U.S. blows against such targets are intended to be telling, striking at the social leadership, institutional cement and physical infrastructure holding the revolution together.

U.S special forces comprise elite military forces on the ground (Army Green Beret and Delta Force, Navy SEAL Team Six, Coast Guard special units, CIA Eagle Force, etc.), and the NSC, NSA and the CIA in Washington; all coordinated through the secret Presidential Sarasota Council. Rumors of shadowy British, Israeli or mercenary involvement have never been independently confirmed. The Sarasota Council promotes an interdisciplinary approach to special operations. Typically, a team of three agents is dropped over, say, the Sierra Madre; each member of this unit from a different military or intelligence branch, and all three having trained together for the past six months at an isolated military installation. Each is a walking arsenal, with enough fire power to take on a military company and enough explosives to crack a small dam, enough biochemical toxins to poison the water table for miles about and enough martial arts training to kick Bruce Lee's butt. Virtual Reality enhancements allow the team to communicate out and pinpoint their position via satellite link, to easily move and attack by night, and to carry out complex maneuvers or operations in perfect synch. Extensive individual survival training, and team-skills-complimenting, round out a highly mobile, extremely deadly fighting unit as likely to carry out its mission and battle its way out to go on future missions.

Psychological Operations are a current rage of the Sarasota Council, which maintains an interest in the enigmatic San Cristobal Connection as well. The Council is not without its controversies or critics however. Two years before, it fielded a group of scientists funded by corporate, intelligence and military sources to research what has come to be known as the Omega Template Proposal.

The thesis of the super secret report produced by these scientists is that it is possible to create the perfect soldier, and perhaps the supreme warrior caste, by applying a precise socio-biological template in a clearly defined, total environment. Shades of science fiction. When the report was leaked to the *New York Times* in 2006, it inspired one critic to label it the Dorsai Template, after a famous series of 20th century science fiction novels. The report proposes an Omega Crucible, in which a sampling of genetically promising human beings would be isolated from birth on a remote island or region sealed off completely from the outside world, then subjected to rigorous physical and mental training, horrific tests of survival, even scientific modification, all within a social order charitably called Techno-Feudalism.

Long term biological and genetic engineering is key to the Omega

END TIME

Crucible in the report; from introducing new digestive symbiots into the human body so that a new soldier can, say, eat wood, to modifying a human allele structure in order to provide future warriors with eyesight edging well into the infrared and ultraviolet. The Omega Template and Crucible portend a secret warrior society, a clandestine government-run order of assassins, perhaps even a conquering master race. In the wake of public controversy, key members of the Sarasota Council, as well as the President himself, have disavowed the report, terming its proposals "irresponsible."

TWENTY-TWO

Peregrine knocked off the ASU campus food coop, In The Raw, almost as an afterthought. Originally, he'd intended to investigate the Redwood Eatery, but a show there with bands had kept the cleanup crew well into the wee hours. Walking by the coop, he noticed that the slats covering the window screens were simple to pry out, and that the door was right next to the slats. The opportunity screamed out, and he reached in, unlocked the deadbolt, then opened the doorknob. The lock box was stowed beneath a crate of yogurt in the cooler. He skulked off into the night, holding his breath, $430 odd richer. It rained.

***

Greg woke in a strange bed, a relatively strange, new lover at his side and the smell of their sex everywhere. Light for a new day was beginning to find its way through the bedroom's parted curtains.

Having two lovers, and so close after having been dumped by Janet, certainly inflated his ego. He was attractive at least. Girls *did* want him. But that fact solved little. If he were desirable, why did Janet not desire him anymore? If he were desirable, how could he win her back? He did miss her familiarity and friendship. Even their sex had been for mutual pleasure, not merely for the excitement of having someone new, which Margaret did give him. In turn, Greg was realizing that sex was not just sex for him. At least with Margaret, he was starting to invest himself emotionally in her. He liked her, but he wanted more. And he suspected that sex for her was a lot easier, less attachment laden, than it was for him. He had, in fact, gotten pissed when she had not been there for his call.

"Mornin'," she drowsed awake then.

"Morning," he smiled at her, then made his excuse, "I gotta get up soon to help my dad clean the house. Do you have a shower?"

"Of course," Margaret reached for his crotch, "But you're not leaving quite so fast."

She went down on him. It certainly was not Janet, but it was spirited. After he showered her, they showered together.

Greg finally remembered where he had seen Margaret before. It hit him as she stepped from the shower, towels wrapped around her body

142

BABYLON BY THE BAY

and her hair. Sophomore year in high school, when he was getting to know Janet better than just someone he had grown up with, she had been in Janet's circle of friends. As he recalled, they had not stayed friends much beyond that year.

"You were Janet's friend in high school," he said, flatly, in the middle of dressing.

She glanced up at him in the bathroom mirror.

"Yes," she said.

"Did you start seeing me because you'd heard Janet and I broke up?" Greg asked, expecting it.

"I knew Janet was your girlfriend," Margaret opened the medicine cabinet for her makeup, "But I didn't know you'd broken up."

"You wanted to see me even though you thought I was still going with Janet?"

She took a few moments to measure her response.

"Janet and I were once blood friends." She began, working on her eyes. "We did a project together in English. It was to write our own mythology. Maybe I'm not as creative as Janet, but we both busted our butts on that project. It was great. The teacher wrote us a letter suggesting we look for a publisher for it. But as time went on, Janet got more and more of the credit for it. We both put in every spare minute we had on that thing, and I'd say we each did about half the work. But she was the one who wound up taking it as her project, and I became the help. I heard she even used that letter to help her get into Wellesley."

"So I'm your way of getting back at her?" Greg frowned.

"Not at all," she smiled from the mirror, her full smile warm and mirthful, "I liked you from the start, when we first met. I wanted to get to know you better. But so did Janet, and Janet always got what she wanted. Well, I wanted you too. I knew Janet was away at school in Boston. There's no ring on your finger, and you never said no. So, I got what I wanted for a change."

Greg blushed from that, as well as from Margaret's take on Janet. He finished dressing. He remembered that mythology project and knew that Janet had gloried in its acclaim. Perhaps it was not so much that she had taken credit for the English project as that, in talking about it, Janet neglected to mention much about Margaret. With a kiss and a promise to call, he was out the door and in his car, driving for home and his morning's mission.

"Morning," Andre put down a coffee cup at the dining room table, dress casual and the morning paper opened to the sports section, "Long time no see."

"Sorry Dad," Greg smiled, "Peace demonstrations."

"Figured as much. Got some time for a little breakfast? I'm working

143

on some huevos rancheros. Letting the sauce simmer down right now. No problem to cook more."

"Okay," the son said, even though he had intended to get what he needed and go.

"Orange juice?" Andre said from the kitchen door as Greg took a seat and searched for the comics.

"Yeh, and some coffee."

"How are things going?" his father asked, carrying both beverages to the table, "How's school?"

"Good," Greg gulped the coffee and sipped the o.j., "I'm a little behind in some of my classes because of this peace stuff, but its still early in the semester."

"And Janet?"

"Still sad, I guess. I'm trying to keep busy, but it still hurts. A lot."

"It's only natural to be sad," Andre said from the kitchen, "I'm sure you're feeling that Janet's done the worst thing one human can do to another."

"Pretty much," Greg could feel the bile of betrayal once more.

"Well," Andre looked into his son's hurt, angry eyes standing in the kitchen door, "I'm not going to dispute your emotions. Promise me that, if you start feeling really depressed about this breakup with Janet, you'll talk to me about things. Even if I'm out of town, call. Before I leave again, I'll arrange for a remote cellular hookup."

"No problem," Greg lost any of Andre's concern for his son's potential suicidal tendencies in his own anger.

The breakfast had been a good idea, Greg realized, when Andre brought out a heaping platter. The eggs were scrambled and laced with fried onions, bell pepper and diced chili relleno. The sauce was rich in onions, tomato chunks and cilantro. Everything was topped with cheese and sided with buttered toast. Greg ate his share.

"I might be going to the city this afternoon," Andre chased down his breakfast with more coffee, "Around 2. Want to come? We could make an afternoon of it, just cruise around, see what we can see, do what we want."

"Can we do that tomorrow dad?" Greg asked, "Got something I absolutely promised I'd do today. How about Sunday afternoon."

"Sure," the father said, after a little thought, "I'll do some rearranging. Not a problem."

"We'll do it," Greg said.

After the meal and some small talk, Greg excused himself. He read the fax accepting Greg's bid on the engine rebuild work, as well as a bank authorization covering materials cost for the job. Then he headed for the basement, where he put his old Boy Scout collapsible shovel in one of the family's backpacks, then loaded the pack down with the

144

cased riemanium from its hiding place. He tried to appear inconspicuous lugging it out of the house, and succeeded. He settled the massive pack carefully in the passenger seat and drove off, jays diving after his tracks in the early morning.

Greg enjoyed driving in the morning, with fog still lingering on the land. At times, canyons and arroyos were so thick with white mist that their floors were entirely shrouded, while the surrounding higher land and ridges between were clear and partially sunny. As he drove the road alongside or across bridge over such a canyon, the solid white blanket enchanted him with thoughts of some hidden world beneath, a Shangri-La or Brigadoon cloaked in fog and mystery waiting to be discovered. If only the riemanium were as easy to hide.

***

Two things upset Rosanne so bad, she called in sick on her waitressing job, the one she had scraped together for Friday evening and Saturday days to replace Security Pacific in the pinch. Not good after only a night on the job. At noon, the detective, Dimapopulos had called with nothing new on her Mike, just the question as to whether he had contacted her. Mike's phone at the SRO had been disconnected the day before. Her doubts grew. Had he, in fact, used her? Was he, in fact, the thief Peregrine that everybody hunted? Had she been the fool? It required more and more of her imagination to hold these thoughts at bay and explain, even justify why Mike had disappeared from her life without a word.

Around 1, the mail delivered a letter from the Chancellor's office at UCSF, stating that the status of her grant was being reevaluated, and that while her fees could be paid out of it, her monthly living stipend would be suspended pending completion of the reevaluation. Mike, the Piccoli robbery, first the loss of her job, and now this letter; they were all linked. She knew it and exerted great effort to deny it. There must be some mistake, she thought and resolved to contact the President's office Monday.

Rosanne had fallen in love with Mike in their brief time together. She realized it, and she was loathe to admit he had taken her for a fall without more concrete evidence. She rationalized. An emergency—last minute—had unexpectedly taken him out of town. She worried. Something bad, perhaps life threatening, had happened to her Mike. She hoped. Any day now, he would call. She would forgive him of anything, if only he would call.

***

Greg hiked in to his meadow, backpack on his back to carry the weight. Cloud peppered sky scrolled across the north bay. Three red winged blackbirds saluted the wind and flew away. He set the backpack down on his stump and removed the shovel, snapping it into

145

shape. He had paced the meadow so often that he knew it by heart. Human trails did not intersect the meadow, which was why he enjoyed this open space. The nearest was some one hundred yards to the northeast. The animal trails shifted from season to season, and year to year, though certain areas never seemed to be trammeled. Where the meadow's southern edge raggedly grew up into forest he found an ideal spot, a cluster of evergreen bushes clumped with a knot of pines and firs.

He selected a piece of sod and ever so carefully spaded it up around the edges, first going around to inscribe the perimeter, then continuing to circle and to incrementally dig until he could peel up a unified hunk of earth rooted together by grass three feet circular and a half foot to a foot deep. He set this living camouflage off to one side and proceeded to dig the exposed earth, being careful to deposit each shovelful almost two yards away, on the bare ground beneath a pine. When he had the hole large enough, Greg returned for the pack and its contents. The riemanium and case, lid down, fit neatly into the hole. He carefully shoveled back earth into the hole around the case, taking time to pack the earth down after each round, until the riemanium was entirely hidden. Finally he carefully replaced the sod and tamped that down, making sure that there were no raw edges of his hiding place exposed. All that was needed was water to bind the earth, and rain was expected in days.

The follow through entailed, first, scattering the displaced earth from the hole back into the woods. Then, setting his empty backpack in the sod rug's center, he marked the exact location in three ways. He dug around for large rocks and built a rock pyramid five long paces due west of the spot, under a distinctive fir. He then used his shovel and a jack knife to cut a clear mark into that fir, then triangulated the mark with his backpack and another tree due south, which he also duly marked. After pacing off the vicinity once again, he took up pack and shovel and paced the whole thing back to his stump, marking the direction to go on the stump, again with the knife. Greg wrote these directions down in pen on a slip of paper he fit into his wallet.

Greg could now begin, starting with a bowl of Larry's kief. The sun brightened for late morning, though the breeze remained cool. He left pack and shovel on the stump to pace, absently brushing his hair behind his right ear.

He could actually watch himself, feel himself becoming attached to Margaret. He had to ask himself what the difference was between attachment and possessiveness. Certainly, with Janet, he had felt emotional investment and attachment but also possessiveness and jealousy. A year and a half into their relationship, Greg had used a few petty disagreements and a flirtatious classmate to insist that they begin "seeing other people." In fact, he had not been able to cope when

BABYLON BY THE BAY

Janet started going out. Jealousy as much as love had brought him to ask her to get back together. Afterwards, she had insisted on honesty in their relationship about their fantasies and crushes. But while she had never taken his seriously, her's had incited his possessiveness.

She had always been more outgoing than him, and he had often interpreted her extroverted behavior as flirtation. But there had also been the high school football quarterback, and that exchange student from Sweden. In college, she had eyes for a certain radical junior professor, who never received tenure because of his politics. In every case he had dogged her, watched her like a hawk, and invented weasel excuses to drop by unexpectedly to check up on her.

This, in turn, had fed into his attempt to totally mesh their lives together, but not entirely positively as he sometimes liked to think. He had never felt absolutely trusting of her or secure in their relationship. She had called herself a feminist, but invariably she was attracted to macho beefcake males. She was a straight-A, honors student with her entire education paid for by scholarships, yet she was profoundly insecure about her abilities. Consequently, he had never felt truly relaxed, and he oftentimes monitored how she talked about and behaved around other men. It was not that he always suspected her of wanting to "step out" on their commitment. But, of the two, she had the roving eye and he had the proprietary response.

He still could not accept her unilateral ending of their relationship, no matter how flawed. Greg walked through his own life now, alone, amidst a twisted, gutted superstructure of broken plans and promises. He did not feel depressed, only angry. And helpless to do anything about it. Plans and promises sprang from the soil of commitment. One of his father's comments came back to him. While growing up, Greg had always been able to easily excel at whatever had interested him. So he bored easily with most things. He had wanted to become a writer, then a lead guitarist, then a top gun flyer, and then a Nobel prize winning scientist, all within one high school year. School counselors advised Andre that his son if anything needed more freedom, more time to figure out what he wanted to do.

"Bull," his father had said, "What he needs is some direction."

Andre had explained to his son:

"Freedom is useless without commitment and self-discipline. My generation invented that kind of limitless freedom. Do what you want, when you want and wherever you want. Do your own thing. Freedom always says that, but you don't become free until you start exploring and setting your own limits. You have to say: "I want to do this and not this." Being at a crossroads isn't freedom. That's free choice. True freedom is being on the road. You can always change directions and even change roads. Freedom doesn't come into being until choice has been

147

made. Then you have to stick with your choice long enough so that you can become good at what you do and have the freedom in your actions doing what you've chosen to do. Only when you get really proficient at something can you really take advantage of freedom. Then you can challenge your own limits, push them and transcend them."

Out of his dad's pushing had come his classic car hobby, and his skill on the metal lathe.

He and Janet had made a commitment to each other. To their relationship. Compared to his parents' twelve years together, let alone his grandparents' close to seventy years together, their relationship had been young. They had only started thinking about their future together, making plans and promises. He felt betrayed—wrongly, bitterly— that Janet had abandoned their commitment so early. What is more, he felt deceived; that perhaps Janet had intended all along to use her education on the east coast to leave him, all the while promising that separation would make them stronger. All the while planning their summer hike.

He scooped up his shovel and pack, and headed back for the car. He was home by noon. His father was gone, so Greg set up some of the metal he needed for the lathe job, making note of what he did not have. Larry called, then, asking him to take a ride up the coast, up 101 and out 12 to Sebastopol, then up 116 to Guerneville and points north.

"It's a client," Larry said, "Eden West. They're acting more than unusually weird and I'd like you riding shotgun on this one. I don't expect violence or anything. But they're acting absolutely paranoid these days. With you along they'll see I have a healthy sense of paranoia myself. Besides, on a long run, I need someone to handle the dope we'll be smoking along the way."

Larry had talked about Eden West before; a mystery monastic sex-cult ensconced in redwood wilderness. They contracted Larry to hot-house grow the most select of Borneo bud for some of their practices, and they paid him handsomely for taking the risk. The back of Larry's gas utilizing Dodge van stank richly of top-grade marijuana, samples of which graced the tray in Greg's lap. Greg used the long ride and his position filling up the pipe to discuss the riemanium situation in full. NPR's international magazine provided a chatty backdrop with stories on Gypsy and Basque terrorism in Europe, Burma's genocidal two-front war, and Amazonian secessionist movements.

"It's going nowhere," he said finally, "The government hasn't responded too positively to our first communiqué. I want to do more, but frankly, I don't trust some of our cohorts to keep this game's secret. The riemanium's well hidden and all, thanks to your suggestion, but we are still the one's claiming contact with Peregrine. We are the ones with the pictures. How are you going to react if the FBI comes knocking on your door?"

"No one's gonna go to the FBI on this," Larry said, confident, "This group's too PC. As for the government response, it's only been three days. And not even that."

"I wasn't thinking about it happening exactly like that." Greg mused, staring out at a highway landscape brittle with late afternoon sun, "But what if somebody, David or Lori say, brags to a friend or two. Pretty soon, friend tells friend, the word spreads, and we've got the wrong people knowing we have some connection with the riemanium. The FBI comes calling, maybe not to you or me first, but down that chain of friends and to the group. Nobody else in the group has our claim to the riemanium. What if one of them, if questioned, spills everything, under threat and out of fear?"

"What if, what if?" Larry shrugged, "Look. We'll keep on them as to how important keeping things secret is. What worries me more is there's already talk about releasing a second communiqué. At the Gondwana, last night after you left. Taking the next step, David calls it. We haven't even let the first one sink in, and hey, I've got a business to run here. I'm not sure I need any more heat. That's what's got Eden West so jumpy. They're the ones claiming that the Feds have recently invaded the entire area from Monterey to Fort Bragg with an FBI army. They may be a paranoid cult, but they're also not exactly square with the powers-that-be. They've been harassed by the FBI, IRS and Treasury Department in the past, so they keep their ears close to the ground for that sort of thing. It's not Eden West the Feds are after, but it is making them extremely nervous."

"It's making me extremely nervous as well," Greg admitted.

Eden West had grown out of the confluence of new-age cultic neo-Christian circles in the line of Claire Prophet's Church Universal and Triumphant, and money. Lots of money in particular converged on a sect of a sect called Edenists, Back-to-Edenites by their detractors, in 1998. Eden West was built the year after. Larry had described their "religious faith" to him once.

"They take a weird interpretation on a couple of passages in the Old Testament, for starters. I don't know chapter and verse, but they're in the beginning of Genesis. One is that 'God planted a garden eastward in Eden; and there he put the man whom he had formed.' The other is about Cain and Abel...'And Cain went out from the presence of the LORD, and dwelt in the land of Nod, on the east of Eden.' Pretty good, huh?

"So anyway, in what they call their 'spiritual geography' the Edenists believe that there had to be a west of Eden as well as an east, and a westward in Eden as well as an eastward. God, according to their mythology, planted other gardens westward in Eden, and they're either

149

ruled by what Edenists call Ascended Masters altogether, or each Ascended Master with his own garden. I can't remember. In any case, mankind was first banished from the garden in the east of Eden by the actions of Adam and Eve, and then Cain left all of Eden out of shame for the crime he committed. Mankind was never forbidden to dwell in the gardens planted westward in Eden. And since we left Eden out of shame, we can return to it in enlightenment to find and dwell in the gardens westward in Eden."

To be precise, the Fully Illuminated in the Edenist scheme, called Living Saints, could return to Eden in this life and inhabit any one of said gardens. People still had to die, because the Tree of Eternal Life remained in the garden eastward in Eden which was forbidden humanity and guarded by a bright-sworded angel. But the Living Saints did not have to abide by the strictures of what they called the Land of Nod, meaning the rest of the world. Eden West was built as a retreat for the Fully Illuminated, a monastic order modeled on Rabelais's Abbey of Theleme in *Gargantua*. They practiced sacramental drug use, which kept Larry working, and they were rumored to indulge in free love and sexual ritual. They had used direct retrovirus testing to screen even the Saints, and in the beginning of the 21st century they were the first to utilize pack antibody genetic engineering to combat retrovirus infection. Larry knew little enough of this to impart it fully to Greg, and in any case, it would not have prepared his friend for Eden West.

They took a private, paved road out of the Armstrong Redwoods, deep into dark woods streamered with mid afternoon sun. They followed one creek, then another, and it was Edenist property on which they traveled. The sun occasionally peeled through forests left primeval. The road wound slowly up. They had detected nothing upon entering the side road, but they had been detected. Had Eden West not wanted them, they would have been taken out long before. As they turned the corner on a notch in a ridge, Greg got a brief glimpse of the eccentric sanctuary in its only near-full view. Larry knew enough not to slow down too much on this particular stretch of road down into Eden West's valley, so he hoped his friend was attentive.

A wide, blue lake glittered, cupped comfortably in the valley amidst rich forests. Eden West climbed from the white scythe of a beach far below to the geometry of buildings ending the roadway ahead. Parthenon formed into thick groved meadow, formed into high medieval cathedral, formed into orchards and flower gardens, formed into outdoor Roman baths formed into layer upon layer and terrace after terrace of varied architectures and variegated open spaces; a single and singular arcology. Stream fed waterfall became sculpted Byronic pool, became languid romantic canal, became Japanese coye

150

pond, became running stream, became Indian water maze, finally to become a waterfall once more falling into the lake. There were greenhouses and heated ponds and profusions of vegetation. A flock of brightly plumaged parrots fluttered up from the palms off the beach to a wood and glass gazebo large enough to house its own botanical gardens. That was, as well, all that Larry had seen of the utopic complex, outside of Eden West's entry in which Greg would soon marvel. The menagerie of complimentary animals maintained in the arcology and its lake Larry had gleaned only from conversations with his Eden West procurers.

Larry had visited Eden West three times in one year, three years before at the beginning of hammering out their business arrangements. All the following years they had conducted business in Alabaster, by mutual agreement. This sudden insistence on his delivery, in violation of their agreement and on the flimsiest of excuses was more than irritating. Larry had insisted on their Alabaster pickup, not just for convenience, but also because he did not want to be openly associated any further with the cult. This was strictly business. After all, the Edenists had also been widely accused of brainwashing and programming those lower down on their hierarchy of faith. His house was his turf, and so Greg was along for the ride as a thumb to the nose for Eden West as well. Two could violate agreements. He already had their next crop's seeds and was busy germinating them. Maybe it was time to renegotiate things.

The road became a driveway curving west, then became a concrete ramp that took Larry's van up onto a long concrete platform. Modest railing surrounded the platform, and led out across the thinnest of catwalks over a thunderous chasm, at its bottom a moat of water. The catwalk terminated at a stubby tower, like the turret of a castle, projecting out of the mass that was the back of Eden West. Great panes of glass curved around the tower's base from where it jutted out of the arcology some twenty feet below their progress across space, clutching bundles of contraband. The door in was open.

They stepped inside a cool, dark cylinder. The quiet muffled their descent toward the Gaia-toned reception floor on a wide looped, narrow railed spiral of metal staircase imperceptibly anchored into floor and ceiling. Down the middle of the precarious spiral stairwell hung a fine chain supporting a large metal, wood and glass orrery, a subtle wheel work planetarium. Eden West's procurer awaited them, and when they reached the floor Greg noticed the reason for the muted natural colors to the space. The entire tower room was perhaps thirty-five feet deep, solid-walled except for the bottom fifteen feet, which were walled in plate glass alternating aquarium with terrarium around the twenty foot diameter space.

END TIME

Sunlight from the paned glass outside around the tower's base, and perhaps artfully disguised artificial lighting, supported eight very distinct technologically maintained ecologies. The different environments were half land and water—coral reef, deep intertidal, everglades, and rich lake for the aquatic; tropical, prairie bordering desert, Galapagos, and evergreen forest for the terrain. They were impressive in their detail.

"Guests are not part of our agreement," the procurer said, with the manner of a doctor wearing surgical gloves. Larry and Greg were from outside, not sterile. Contaminated.

"Nor was my delivery of this crop," Larry countered.

"That was explained," the man was imperious, "Our people can no longer travel safely in the San Francisco Bay Area. There's a political crackdown in progress. We don't believe we are a target. But we cannot take chances."

"I call it chicken shit," Larry drawled, putting down his bundles of Borneo bud, "And it'll cost. An extra five every trip since I'll be the one driving the highways with this stuff, wear and tear on the car, not to mention my peace of mind. That's starting this delivery."

"This is highly irregular," the procurer protested, but along with the sealed envelope he handed over to Larry he included five loose one thousand dollar bills.

Larry said nothing. He simply pocketed his money and gestured for Greg to leave with him, right index finger pointing, swinging up over his shoulder, back the way they had come. The orrery sparkled and played on the lights from below, hinting of mystery and revelation in its shadow-cloaked mechanical representation of the music of the spheres, all as they climbed.

"I know you told me once," Greg relaxed into his seat as Larry settled onto the drive out, "But once again, how did they get their money?"

"Lambert Cray."

"Developer of single cell protein culture," Greg did remember.

"And multiple cell protein farming," Larry continued, "He was a Reichian even before he met up with the Edenists, and like old Wilhelm, he kinda went off the deep end. Got converted to Edenist precepts two years before his death, and willed his entire fortune to them."

"Convenient," Greg smirked.

"Isn't it."

Larry dropped Greg at home by 6, after a rich seafood meal in Sebastopol on Larry, who tossed two fingers of bud into a ziplock for his friend's trouble that afternoon. Borneo bud. Greg intended to get started on the lathe work, too stoned for any study, until he listened to

152

BABYLON BY THE BAY

Margaret's message on his machine.

"There's a Masq at the Stack tonight," her voice smiled on the tape, "I know its aways, but its roots G-O-T!"

Gathering of the Tribes. The Stack was in San Jose and San Jose was a good two-and-a-half hour drive when traffic was good. Not what he wanted to do with his evening. He called her back and she talked him into it. Provisionally, on erection alone. He drove over to her apartment with Borneo spliffs rolled and ready, hoping to smoke and then seduce her into another night of debauch.

"We'll smoke them on the ride down," she smiled, dressed to the '9's in Mod black-and-white, her hair sharply styled and silver shred earrings spangling down her long neck. She waved the event's flyer in front of him, then handed him a set of blankets and ground pillows.

Margaret majored in Liberal Arts, with an emphasis upon languages. Advanced French and intermediate Chinese. Thought about UN work, maybe a translator. Night and City glittered on the Bay, the Spitfire's roof down and startled winter in their hair. Her parents divorced when she was a freshman at ASU; her Anglo father now in Houston paying for her BA and apartment, her half-Chinese mother now in San Rafael living with a sister, and Margaret alone left in Alabaster. She also had a younger brother, Robby, who lived with her mother and aunt, and belonged to a gang, the Original Asiatics. She considered it a toss-up whether to tour Europe on the bum after graduating, or to go for graduate school on scholarships, both options far away from Alabaster. But she still worried about Robby. She doled out the herb, lighting each joint tucked into the passenger's leg well and keeping it sheltered on the pass to Greg. She wanted to travel low budget next summer as well. Northern Mexico was cheap, and still safe. She had a facility for languages, so perhaps she could pick up some Spanish, though she had no illusions about traveling alone in a machismo Latin society as a young American woman. Best to go in a group, and she was working on that.

He took an off ramp from 880 before the Stack, to look for a parking place. The 1999 7.2 on the Richter Scale tossed the already shaky City, but it had been epicentered close enough to San Jose to level large parts of the Bay Area's equivalent to LA. No big loss, most people north of the Dumbarton Bridge thought, but then few had factored in Silicon Valley. The nexus for Federal, State and Pleiades investment plans, one of the few sectors of California's economy paying double dividends, a digital heavyweight still able to kick Japanese electronic butt; San Jose merited an emergency Federal rebuild and the best urban social engineering Sacramento neo-liberals could provide. The State declared broad powers of eminent domain, then proceeded to sculpt San Jose into the perfect 21st century metropolis. One of the period's testa-

153

END TIME

ments, the Stack, loomed above them as Greg did a smooth parallel park.

He pulled up the roof, then walked around to where Margaret had let herself out of the parked car to lock it down, blankets and pillows on the sidewalk. The roar. They stood a good five blocks from the Stack and they heard the buzz of its traffic. Two six lane freeways—880 and 101—crossed, plus the four lane 380 connector from 680 and the four lane 82 shortcut from 280 dead ended at this mammoth, Pharonic transfer point. They were piled one on top of another in an earthquake-proof concrete and ferrocement mass of ramps and pylons, walls and buttresses fully as impressive as the pyramid of Cheops, and perhaps as enduring. The whole Stack rose out of the new concrete flood control channel for Coyote Creek and Guadalupe River. A hulking, square-limbed, square jawed, smog breathing behemoth, constantly roaring like a thousand cars, hunkered up out of the moonlit cement plains between two canals gurgling sluggish water. The horror.

And fascinating, as far as misdirected technology of that scale could ever be, whether King's tomb or industrial tomb. Amidst the Stack's concrete mountains, concrete canyons meandered. Skaters found it early on, always on the lookout for new cement. They were awed, probably, the way conquering barbarian Hyksos were to gaze upon the spoils of Egypt. Word spread. The Stack's geography made a few of its own suggestions. The art of the small—generators the size of a suitcase, pig amps with power, back pack light shows, hand carry Emo boards—brought fantasies into reality.

"Hand me that stuff," Greg said, taking the blankets and pillows from Margaret before helping her through the fence fronting the flood channel. The two walked carefully down the slanted cement. Further down, other figures descended in the wash of the moon, their laughter drifting up with incense smoke and tinkling bells. An airplane screamed down for a Municipal Airport runway across the channel, lights winking and flashing. Knots of people drifted across the cement desert to converge on a rickety structure, marked by dim luminarios, that crossed the nearest canal. A good broad jumper could make it, but it would mean a cement take off and landing. Any good Stack Crew had bridges across the canals, just like any good Stack Crew had Rovers up and down the channel looking for cops. San Jose police didn't like dealing with Stack parties, having realized early on and entirely too late that the new urban geography was not in their favor. No way to make a surprise sweep, and too many ways for folks to get away. The area's industrial shops, warehouses, wholesaling and the like did not field a lot of noise complaints. So the police had to be looking for Stack action, which was by no means predictable. Noon parties, sunrise masqs and rush hour thrashes were not uncommon. In other words, the Stack was too much trouble.

"I saved a couple of these," Margaret produced one of Greg's joints and lit it, once they were safely across the makeshift bridge. They heard the thunder of bass shiver beneath traffic sounds and a jet taking off as they walked toward the Stack. Muted lights played up and down the vast concrete structures, spillover from the event buried deep in their cement. Moon-etched people about them wandered slowly toward the Masq-in-progress. Spooks held little machines that twinkled tiny computer lights. Ferrels rhythmically swung soft guttering candles in long Santeria glasses. Raspies billowed out their capes like winged night creatures. Nulls burnished each other's plating. All this amidst legions of retro—beat, hippie, punk, mod, skin, rasta, metal, etc.

"It's a Spook Crew," Greg commented from what he saw at the bridge and along the way.

"Spooks do the best shows," she said as they passed a formation of dark vehicles tucked behind the Stack's first supports, a line already for the row of portable toilets hitched to a truck. They followed the maze of canyons into the Stack, to the main galleries so ideal for skateboarding by day and concerts by night. The crowds and graffiti thickened. Marijuana smoke drifted over quantities of alcohol and smart drugs, XTC and 999, cocaine and Ynisvitrin, psychedelics and pharmaceuticals. One dealer meandered through the partying multitude pushing a modified ice cream hand cart from which he dispensed an assortment of mind benders. And occasionally, a brawny Stack Security man might be glimpsed.

The Stack had not always been so amiable a place. Young squatters had infested it, with all the attendant problems associated with lack of sanitation. Crews had competed to do shows at it, with two rival crews very often advertising conflicting Stack parties for the same time so that fights broke out, equipment got trashed, and animosities built up. Youth gangs fought each other for the Stack as turf, hoping to extract rent and protection from anyone wanting to hold shows there. San Jose's alternative music scene relied on two main companies for concert security; a mixed Latin/Black/Anglo outfit called In House and an all-Samoan team known as Ground Control. Since those doing security for these companies belonged to the area's varied youth scenes, they frequently found themselves pitted against each other in stupid Stack wars. Little wonder that they formed Stack Security, called together people on the alternative music scene and unilaterally laid down some rules. A type of gang dictatorship that Greg did not like, even though it kept the peace.

"Do you want to sit on the floor?" Greg asked, "Or should we find a balcony?"

They had come out into the galleries between bands, the take-down

155

and set-up occurring at the far end on a multi-layered wooden stage fitted over the storm drain's concrete block access. Where graffiti did not cover the concrete angled up in the Stack's odd geometries, rugs did. The accumulation of industrially glued soundproofing formed a patchwork of colors and patterns across the first levels of cement, illuminated by two portable halogen lamps at this end. Margaret appraised the crowd.

"Let's find a perch," she smiled.

A relatively easy matter, since the break seemed to be running long and lots of folks had abandoned their seats to mingle.

"Takeover," she whispered and pointed out a fine roost overlooking the action, recessed into the heart of the Stack. Greg pointed out a way, and Margaret led it up into the concrete geometries. Each balanced their bedding as they played mountain goat, Greg enjoying Margaret's swaying backside ahead of him enough to almost lose his footing.

"Perfect spot." Greg appraised the panoramic view. Hundreds of party-goers were contained within the Stack's artificial banks, bathed in multi-colored lights, their chatter sounding like backwash across a pebbled beach. She snapped open her blanket and he did likewise so that they neatly covered the small wedge of elevated cement that they had claimed as their own. The pillows completed the comfortable setting.

"Time for another." She sat cross legged and produced another joint. A band finally took the stage to start checking their amps and instruments. Greg noticed the drug man pushing his cart through the crowd below, and signaled him for beer. He tossed down the money and the man tossed up a six pack, one beer at a time.

"It's not quality, but its alcohol," Greg said, handing Margaret an open beer in exchange for the smoke. The band pounded out a generic Ferrel sound, the music acting as a magnet to draw people toward the stage and more people into the galleries. Someone started up an unimaginative light show, the neural component juxtaposing sensations of pleasure with danger. Boring. Nobody bothered to dance. Two beers apiece and the spliff later, a retro hardcore band followed, one of its members even sporting a bright green mohawk. No Emo on this, just pure, raw noise, violently distorted and explosively fast. At least they got an old-fashioned Pit going, the slam confined by the pressing throngs.

"Now for a little Kajan," Margaret said as Greg crushed the empty cans of their six pack. Having passed "buzzed" and approaching "all fucked up," he had a hard time focusing on the much more extensive set up occurring around the stage. Some expensive light and sound he thought, though not much of it Emo. No sign of a band, just a lot of roadies assembling equipment. He took one lungful from Margaret's smoke, his lungs burned into ripped coughing, and he collapsed backwards against a pillow, his vision fractaling sweet black-out.

"I'm sub orbital," he managed to croak.

"Don't you think its getting chilly?" she asked. "Let's get under the covers."

Below, a cluster of people pointed up. More looked up and more gestured. Craning their necks, Greg and Margaret could see a red star bleeding around the edge of the overhead freeways. A star that throbbed, growing bigger with each pulse. Not quite a star, its crimson tail whipped behind the fireball crashing to earth. Its roar shuddered out from the equipment on stage, shaking even the Stack's solid concrete with subsonics. Several people jumped, yelping, from where they sat on the edge of the stage as the fiery comet seemed to punch the earth center stage. Deep vibration hammered the air as dark orange-brown smoke and bright orange-yellow flames columned up into the sky, wreathing like so many angry serpents whose breath cut the air with the smell of brimstone. Enveloping the stage in scaly fury. Slowly, the reptilian firestorm dissipated, to reveal a three-member band poised with their instruments. Rasputanic. The tall woman, in black cape caked red and matted red hair, cradled her guitar and scowled at the audience. Red glitter streaked her cheeks. Fucking fantastic holo effect, Greg thought. Hell'a entrance.

"I AM THE GODDESS OF HELLFIRE!" the guitarist bellowed, her throaty voice like harsh sandpaper. "AND YOU'RE ALL GONNA BURN!"

She hit the first chord, a glass knife into the brain, as Margaret snaked a hand into Greg's pants. She stroked him up to the twisted, double time punk-funk rhythm edging into assault with that sinister guitar and nails-on-chalkboard vocals. The crowd went wild, the chaotic mass of spastic bodies around the stage driving any Pit to the outer reaches, folks leaping from the Stack's upper levels into the surging human sea as Greg found the wetness to Margaret's sex. He entered her as the stage holos squirmed out vicious reptiles dripping venom, transforming the band members into Gorgons and the singer/guitarist into the Medusa. Came with the crash-and-burn finale of hydra unfolding from the stage, each head belching a crystal fire.

***

The telephone rang as Marcus settled into the first chapter of the Louis L'Amour's book *Hondo*.

"Hello," the voice said, "May I speak with Marcus D...Dima...?"

"Dimapopulos. Speaking."

"Mr. Dimapopulos, this is Pete, from the Sprite Bar, in Fairfax." He identified himself and Marcus immediately perked up. "Officer Manley told me to give you a call if I had anything. Well, that guy in the sketch isn't here, but a couple of people I seen him hanging out with before are."

"I'll be right over."

It took the detective a half hour to locate the nightclub in question. He found a parking space and entered through the rear to talk to Pete.

"They're at that table over there," Pete pointed from the bar, through the gloom and sound of gloom from the stage. "Long blonde-haired girl and the tall one."

Marcus took a drink, a cola, and walked over to their table.

"Mind if I join you and ask you some questions?" he took a chair between the girls.

"We don't talk to cops," Lori snarled, ugly. She blew a puff of thick scented smoke into his face.

Mary simply spat in his drink. Marcus got the message, and after talking to Pete, he retreated to the parking lot. It was close to 2 in the morning when the girls left and he was able to write down their license plate.

***

The campus coop bookstore, Conspiracy of Equals Books, was another mick to crack. Peregrine had the front door dead bolt open in quick minutes with his tools in the heavy night, and he had some $740 from beginning semester book sales. Pocketing the money, he idly glanced through a glossy Leftist journal, disdainfully appraising the chapel to academic PC around him swathed in shadows. Bunch of privileged, middle-class kids playing at revolution, he told himself, then headed back out the front door. A nightingale's song collided with his exit.

TWENTY-THREE

Excerpted from
"Musings on the Nature of Cybernetic CoEvolution"
Journals XIX-XX—The California Diaries (2007)
by Hamran Mossoud
Family Archives, released posthumously, 2032
(Electrostraca #: J/AB-911032-384-150-7917)

After Oakland, I had the opportunity to meet Peter Colchis, president and founder of CyberSurveys, one of the most dynamic high-tech firms in San Jose's Silicon Valley. I was anxious to meet him, having read his book *New Directions in Artificial Intelligence*, and we discussed his "cybersome" and cyberorganic" models the first day, between lunch and dinner. Peter began by stating that the cyberpunk metaphors of the 1980's/90's for the "space" created by computer networking and information exchanges (and perceived by such tools as virtual reality), were inaccurate descriptions in that they employed external analogs. The notion of cyberspace—the digital/electronic universe fashioned by the collective interaction of all of its users—no less than the idea of a net—an information ocean in which reside islands—posed external references, when the only appropriate perspective was internal. And while those science fiction writers who originated these metaphors never understood them as totalizing descriptions, those who adopted these terms behaved as if they described a new orthodoxy. Hence, Peter's cyberorganic work at the turn of the century.

"Ultimately, the market determined which terminology was viable," Peter said. "When CyberSurveys released our VR packages based on a 'cybersome/cyberorganic' model, we quickly outsold and replaced ones using a 'cyberspace' or 'information net' framework. Cyberorganic principles proved more accurate in constructing virtual reality."

Our conversations were complex and wide-ranging, and I am not certain I can do justice to the scope and intricacy of Peter's thinking even as I attempt this summary. The term "cybersome," literally "cybernetic body," has replaced the notion of "cyberspace." Originally composited from coral reef, African termite colony, human genome, and human biophysical mathematical models, cybersome has been shortened to 'some in current usage. First, Peter contended that there is no practical "outside" to cyberorganic reality. Those who create it and function in it are inside of it. They ARE the "body digital." Cyberorganics postulates that a definite "body digital" exists, and therefore does possess form. An outside exists as well, however it is not possible to step outside of the cyberorganic body, the cybersome, in order to apprehend it. Its outside shape can be imagined with art or philosophy, but it can not be experienced. Aboriginal peoples, theoretically outside of the "body digital," have no means to see or otherwise perceive it. An information tissue is rapidly spreading around the world, with only the few remaining aboriginal regions outside of its grasp. Even those who parasitize upon this electronic flesh, or who seek to cause it disease, are inside of it.

I argued that this is a mere quibbling over semantics. After all, everything exists within Einsteinian space-time, space-time having a shape and in theory an outside. According to quantum physics, ours is not the sole universe. And to a cell the body within which it functions is the universe. Yet Peter insisted that the change in metaphor makes an important point. The universe as we know it appears to operate by certain gross "laws," the principle ones being the Laws of Thermodynamics and in particular what we call "entropy." Life attempts to define a sphere of "neg-entropy" against the running down of the universe; to maintain and even expand complex levels of order and mutual relationship. The organic metaphor emphasizes that the cybersome created is internally alive; parts of it growing and healthy, parts of it diseased and dying, and the whole of it coming to cover the planet completely.

Second, Peter described the cybersome as neuro-hierarchically organized over much of the globe. The most basic example of a neuro-hierarchy is consciousness itself. A select set of neural networks in the human brain operates to oversee other neural functionings of the brain, albeit an extremely narrow field of vision with not much control, yet one that can be extrapolated into higher, more comprehensive cyber-neural levels. And Peter's third point was that the cybersome is not yet homogeneous even across the regions it currently holds sway. Viral agents abound. Potential mitochondrian bodies function side by side with retro-viruses injecting mutagenic information (the equivalent of deviant RNA and DNA strands) into the 'some's cyber-evolution.

It is often rumored, Peter admitted, that entire niches and regions around the globe can claim a different digital flesh not yet integrated into the dominant cybersome; separate species by no means widespread, yet still alive and surviving on the edges of the neuro-hierarchic information hegemony within which we all reside. If such completely independent digital forms are found to exist, side by side with our 'some I pointed out, then it is possible to see our "body digital" from the outside. Colchis disagreed. He speculated that such "independent" organisms, if they existed at all, would be small, limited or isolated, and would exist at best as a mouse next to an elephant, with no whole vision of the larger creature beside it. The only truly independent digital flesh capable of seeing our 'some in its entirety would be extraterrestrial, according to Peter.

As I jet-jumped to my yacht after my first meeting with Colchis, I imagined how a region like the San Francisco Bay Area could be described with such a model. Small neuro-information circles manage the social base of the Bay Area, and are managed by smaller neuro-information circles, and then by still smaller circles up a pyramid. Each level possesses an oversight and control far superior to human consciousness, with information generally flowing up and social control flowing down. Neuro-hierarchies flesh up into intertwined corporate and governmental pyramids. E-mail and compunet systems provide connective tissue. Telephone lines, cable television, fiber optic filaments, microwave and laser beams vein the general electromagnetic slurry. Vertical skeletal structures, more permanent information channels and hard data cores, reinforce the whole.

The information structures thus created are like coral in mass, though not in structure, given coral's system of interdependent microecologies. Insect hives more closely resemble its structure, but with the possible exception of the African termite colony they do not possess its bulk or complexity. Finally, certain systems and functions are virtually physiological in permeation and genetic in overall importance. The cyberorganic heights of the San Francisco peninsula and Silicon Valley,

BABYLON BY THE BAY

which peak with the Pleiades Platform, and the broad, high plateaus of Berkeley, Marin and San Jose, are counterpointed by the low plains across Oakland, Richmond, Hayward and Fremont. The Bay Area figures as part of the cyberorganic base of still larger neuro-hierarchies. Within the data coral/hive/biologics of the Bay Area's 'some, it is possible to detect various semi-autonomous to fully autonomous organisms. And, despite Peter's well-reasoned opinions, I also imagined a truly independent digital realm as I saw the lights of my yacht on the ocean. A strange, perhaps Utopian digital territory outside of the cybersome's hegemony, as wary of our 'some as were our small mammalian ancestors of the giant dinosaurs that ruled the planet until 65 million years ago.

This cyberorganic model clearly has its limitations, one being tracking shifts of influence and power in such a structure. If a single cell or a group of cells mutate with consequences to affect the entire "body digital," the potential of this change can not be detected immediately, even if the information describing the change is available to the entire system. Peter acknowledged this limitation when, the next day, he toured me through his current project underwritten by multi-billionaire Barry Parnell; perfecting the photo-electrical digital interface. The older, electro-silicon digital hardware is now being paralleled in its development by brand new photo-silicate digital technologies. And while electronic computers have been networked with optical ones, the true hybrid computer synergistically combining elements of both inexpensively does not yet exist outside of CyberSurveys' laboratories.

"What we have is crude and bug-ridden, but give us six months and we'll be fully marketable," Colchis predicted. "I'm trying to work out a partnership with Harold Nishimura to develop a software package for the new hardware. I even have teams working on the next steps; biochips and the entire field of bio-digital technologies, as well as crystal quantum computers.."

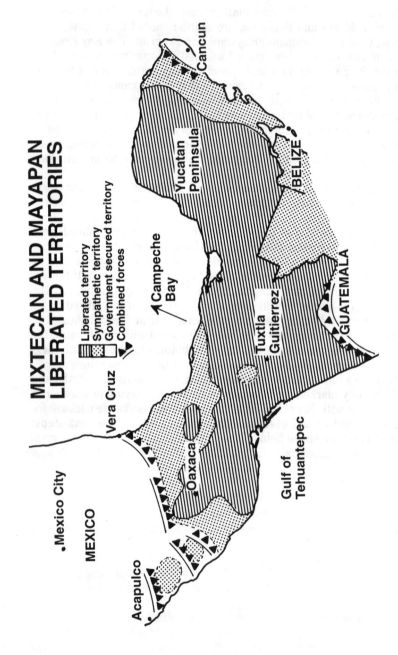

MIXTECAN AND MAYAPAN
LIBERATED TERRITORIES

Liberated territory
Sympathetic territory
Government secured territory
Combined forces

Mexico City

MEXICO

Acapulco

Oaxaca

Vera Cruz

Campeche
Bay

Tuxtla
Guitierrez

Gulf of
Tehuantepec

GUATEMALA

BELIZE

Yucatan
Peninsula

Cancun

PART THREE
ARMAGEDDON, CA 94666

TWENTY-FOUR

The ASU campus police made their move as Greg and four others from the Recycling Coop made their rounds. Satiated by Margaret's attentions at the Stack the night before as well as early that morning at her apartment, Greg bundled newspapers and loaded barrels of glass, aluminum and computer paper with the other recyclers while the police conducted a sneak attack on the P&M Building. They hit the back exists to all the halls radiating from the lobby and found most of them unoccupied. The recycling crew learned about the successful police foray when they pulled into the Zapata Cafe's parking lot, their last stop before the drive down to the yard in San Rafael.

"The cops have taken over part of the P&M," Joseph shouted, running from the kitchen, "ASP's asking everyone to go to Remley Plaza for an emergency demonstration. We're gonna try and retake the building."

"What about the truck and the recycling?" Greg asked, "We still have to get the truck back to the school yard by tomorrow morning, or we pay for an extra day."

"Can you go this afternoon?" Joseph asked. The other recyclers glanced from Greg to Joseph and back again.

"No, the yard closes at noon today," Greg said, thinking also of his afternoon commitment with Andre.

"Can you handle it alone?"

"I guess so," Greg said, used to at least one other person driving down with him, mostly for the company. "The yard workers can help me unload."

So, it was settled. Greg made sure the netting was secured over the truck, then jumped back into the cab and geared things into motion. He saw a familiar face and a friendly wave on the road out of the

163

campus.

"Need a ride Smoke?" Greg asked.

"Going down 101 to 580?" Smoke asked in return.

"Going as far as San Rafael."

"Good enough," Smoke jumped in, his black leather jacket wrinkling sound as he settled into the passenger side. "Thanks."

"You're not staying for the P&M demo?" Greg asked, turning onto Main.

"Naw, got business in Berkeley." Smoke's mirrored shades revealed nothing. "Besides, the occupation's outlived its usefulness."

"Thought you and the MDRG were into liberated zones," Greg commented.

"We are," Smoke smiled, "But a liberated zone means doing something radically different with the space you've liberated. Turning the P&M occupation into a giant slumber party ain't exactly what I call radical."

"As I recall, you were the one who 'inspired' the takeover."

"Yep. And as your run-of-the-mill building occupation, it was fair. It went a tiny way toward shutting down the war machine. But it didn't go any distance toward defining liberated territory."

"And your liberated zones on campus do?" Greg asked, a touch sarcastic.

"Those are just theater, pure and simple," Smoke noted the other's tone of voice. "They're like sign posts, pointing the way to how liberated territory might be created. They're metaphors, and not the real thing."

"What would you consider a real liberated zone? The guerrilla held territories in the Yucatan?"

"Might be, but I never been there," Smoke gazed out the window as the truck approached the 101 on ramp, then turned back to Greg with a wink. "Might be a few a little closer to home."

"How's that?" Greg was curious, "If 'the-powers-that-be' won't let a building occupation stand, how does a liberated zone stay around?"

"With great difficulty, and some folks'll argue that a more productive strategy would be to perfect temporary, highly mobile autonomous space," Smoke returned his gaze down the highway. "I still think there are opportunities to creatively carve out more permanent liberated territory. My bro, he's...well, he's out of circulation at the moment. He knows a couple of genuine liberated zones. Ever hear the name Chumley?"

"As in the Chumley Foundation?" Greg took a stab.

"Yeh, the family set that up. Andrew Chumley was born a YIP diaper baby in 1965. Mom and Pop had married, but were integrating the cultural radicalism they called 'the counterculture' with the political radi-

164

calism they called 'the New Left.' 60's stuff, you know. Lotsa drugs, free love, 'turning on, tuning in, dropping out.' What folks called The Movement back then. Mom and Pop Chumley dosed poor Andrew at least three times with LSD-25 before the kid was 5. Probably shellacked some neural synapses in the process. They were Berkeley rads, University dropouts, outside agitator types, members of SDS.

"Anyway, Mom went off to Chicago in 1969 for the 'Days of Rage' and wound up joining the Weather Underground. Got herself killed in 1971 in a shoot-out with the cops during an armored car robbery with the Black Liberation Army. Pop went off to an Oregon Commune with the kid, where he OD'd on heroin in 1972. The grandparents adopted Andrew, and when they died, he inherited all the goodies. Andy boy liquidated every family asset that he could, amassed some three billion bucks, and then he disappeared.

"What he did was to buy up a hundred old oil tankers. He rebuilt them, redesigned them, linked them into a large floating platform somewhere in the Pacific west of Hawaii with supplemental flotation systems and storm stress nodes. What he did was to rip the decks off the tankers, fill them with enriched soils and start growing all sorts of stuff. 1997 Andrew started secretly taking orphans off the streets of the world's metropolitan sprawls, the younger the better. He's raising the first generation of completely free human beings outside of any nation state or national power, or so he claims."

"And that's real?" Greg cocked a quizzical eye at his passenger.

"As real as the P&M occupation," Smoke chuckled, "And its not unique. In 1975 a group of five black Vietnam vets, Army Corps of Engineer types, got together to build an Invisible City. Ever read Ralph Ellison's *Invisible Man?*"

"No," Greg frowned, "My ex-girlfriend, she read it though. In English."

"Book begins with the unnamed first-person narrator in a room. Clandestine, underground, and walled with lights powered by stolen electricity," Smoke recalled, tapping a forefinger on his chin. "The vets started building their own Invisible City. Today, one major metropolitan area has its own very literal underground. Structures built under city streets, stealing electricity, gas, water and sewage in such sophisticated ways that they've yet to be detected. This independent underground city is populated by young African Americans, taken off the streets real young. No drugs, a completely autarchic economy other than what they expropriate. They're just beginning to tap into computers 'cause the phone lines are so easily traced. Politics, allegiances, goals largely unknown."

Greg chewed his lower lip, visions of Smoke's words before his eyes. Traffic was minimal. He unconsciously switched lanes to pass. Two large ravens winged across the highway.

"Under Oakland?" Greg asked.

"Nope," Smoke smiled a fisherman's grin, "In fact, not in California because we're so tectonically stressed."

Clouds, a dark line of them, were gathering on the west. Rain, to seal his buried treasure. Greg watched a column of seagulls over some hidden interest. Who the hell was Smoke?

"Got one more story," Smoke glanced at the truck's driver, somewhat askance as if judging whether to reveal any more. "Knew someone, a friend at Stanford. He devised a computer virus. Actually, its a highly compressed program, a cluster virus that unpacks itself into six interactive subprograms when it enters a computer. It's designed to penetrate the five standard operating systems now on the market, and one of its subprograms can mutate the whole thing when the cluster virus hits an unfamiliar operating system to hack it. Once it gets into a large computer or compunet, it steals and conceals just one percent of the entire memory to efficiently create its own, autonomous operating system which piggy-backs its operations on the host's. Another subprogram drives each individual autonomous operating system, wherever possible, to electronically or optically link up with others like itself, in theory to carve out an independent digital realm in the world 'some."

"That's operating, now?"

"Not exactly operating yet," Smoke seemed bemused, "It's spreading though. He released it two years ago, but hasn't accessed it yet. Too early to tell how far its penetrated."

Millions of megabytes of linked autonomous operating system. Out there.

The recycling yard was on the southern outskirts of San Rafael, near the highway. As Greg sighted the turnoff and prepared to exit, Smoke said:

"You can let me off here."

Greg stopped the truck at the top of the off ramp. Urbanization spread in all directions. Smoke left with a thanks. Who is that mutherfucker? Greg asked himself as he started down the off ramp.

The yard was several acres, fenced, with row upon row of megadumpsters. Most were filled to the brim with waste materials—aluminum cans, scrap metal and wire, fiberglass, glass, plastic, newspapers, computer cards and sheet paper, cardboard, particle board, styrofoam and the like. Greg pulled into the yard and onto the weigh platform.

"What's it today?" a grizzled old man named Benchley craned his head out the window of the rickety shack next to the scales that served as his office.

"Mostly papers, computer paper," Greg said, "Got a couple barrels of

166

cans and glass also."

"Where's the rest of your crew?" Benchley asked.

"I'm a little short handed today," Greg said, without going into detail, "Your help available?"

"Yep," the old man gestured back into the shack, and noted the truck's weight on a form.

Two hulking men, with Greg, unloaded the truck's contents onto a second platform scale. That weight was noted, along with the truck's new weight. Then, it was a matter of separation and subtraction. As each recyclable quantity was removed, weights were recorded, until everything was accounted for. Greg sat in the cramped shack as Benchley ran through his calculations. A newspaper front page had been hung with pushpins on the wall next to the cluttered wooden counter, a yellowing paper with screaming headline: "Riemanium Not Found" under the kicker: "Bomb-Grade Theft Baffles Police."

"It's only $259 this time." the old man started on a check in his book, "Taiwan and Korea's stockpiled lots of computer paper, and the price is down."

"Thanks," Greg accepted the check. Then he pointed to the posted newspaper. "By the way, what's this about?"

"You been living in a cave or something?" Benchley was incredulous, "An atom bomb's worth of riemanium's been stolen and nobody's recovered it yet. It's the crime of the century!"

"Century's only begun," Greg folded the check and put it into his pocket, "Some political group's got it, don't they?"

"Yeh," Benchley spat, "Bunch'a'communists. Want to stop the war or something. Christ, if I had that riemanium..."

"Lot's of folks would like to get their hands on it. It could further anybody's political agenda. What's yours?"

"Ever hear of Aaron Burr?" Benchley asked, filing the paperwork on Greg's cargo.

"Vice president of the US," Greg remembered, "Thomas Jefferson's presidency, I believe."

"More than VP," the old man grunted, "Burr was a revolutionary war hero and a statesman. He killed Alexander Hamilton in a dual. Too bad he couldn't kill the Federal system and the Federal bank Hamilton created."

"I'm not too keen on the system we have these days either," Greg said, "But what does that have to do with the riemanium?"

"Burr wanted to establish an Empire of freedom in the west after he was VP," the old man said, "They said he conspired with the British. They put him on trial for treason. But they couldn't convict him. What he wanted was an empire of free men unbeholding to the financial interests represented by Hamilton and his cabal. He wanted a land

167

where true individualism could flower not stunted by either capitalism or socialism, the twin horrors of the modern age. You know, Burr could have been president. In those days, two people ran against each other on a single ticket for the presidency and the VP. The person with less electoral votes became vice president. So it was that Jefferson and Burr got equal votes for both positions. Congress decided for Jefferson, with Hamilton blocking Burr. If Aaron Burr had been president in 1800, things would have been real different."

"And that's what you support?" Greg was ready to leave.

"Burr's dream of a western Empire, you bet," Benchley smiled, "And if I had that riemanium, that's what I'd be dealing for."

Greg stopped at a San Rafael metal yard to purchase supplies for his lathe work, then found the freeway once again. It must have been his day for hitch hikers. He was positioned before the on ramp to 101 north, and he was a stereotype, if not an archetype. He wore a khaki safari outfit with boots and pith helmet. He was skinny, bow legged, and buck toothed, with coke lensed, horn rimmed glasses. Jerry Lewis, the nutty professor, on expedition. He'd piled three duffel bags around him, and the man had his thumb out.

"Where you headed?" Greg asked the character, having pulled onto the on ramp's shoulder.

"North," the man said in a nasal tone also to mimic Jerry's slapstick, "Vancouver, eventually."

"Guess I can't do much for you," Greg prepared to depart, "I'm only going as far as Marinwood."

"An inch is as good as a mile at this point," the man sighed, "Can I stow my stuff in the back of your truck?"

"Sure," Greg shrugged.

"The name's John Kilroy," he said, extending a hand as he climbed into the truck's cab, "Thanks for the ride."

"Don't mention it," Greg shook hands and clutched the truck into motion, "Sorry I can't take you further. By the way, what exactly do you do?"

"I'm, um, an archeologist," Kilroy said, waving a hand.

"Oh?" Greg glanced at him, "Amerindian remains?"

"Not exactly," Kilroy was hesitant, "I'm a Biblical archeologist."

"Guess there's not much call for that around here," Greg smiled, maneuvering in traffic.

"You'd be surprised," the specter out of a B-movie comedy said.

"You Mormon or something? You believe that the lost tribes of Israel civilized pre-Columbian America?"

"Not at all," Kilroy smiled, ironically, an expression incongruous for Jerry Lewis, "But that doesn't mean there isn't something to interest me around here."

168

ARMAGEDDON, CA 94666

"Oh, and what might that be?"

"Eden."

Greg tightened his hands on the steering wheel. Just his luck. He had picked up a real nutcase.

"Isn't that located somewhere in the Middle East?" Greg was careful with his choice of words. He did not want to provoke the man.

"You might think so, but Eden's location was purposefully left cryptic in the Bible," Kilroy warmed to his subject, "Let's see, how does the King James go? 'And a river went out of Eden to water the garden; and from thence it was parted, and became into four heads. The name of the first is Pison, that is it which compasseth the whole land of Havilah, where there is gold. And the gold at that land is good: there is bdellium and onyx stone. And the name of the second river is Gihon: the same is it that compasseth the whole land of Ethiopia. And the name of the third river is Hiddekel; that is it which goeth toward the east of Assyria. And the fourth river is Euphrates.'"

"Well, that sounds pretty specific," Greg said cautiously, "The Euphrates is in the Middle East."

"And the river Hiddekel is commonly associated with the Tigris, both of which flow through Mesopotamia, or Assyria," Kilroy removed his glasses and cleaned them with a handkerchief, "But take the Gihon. Its been associated with the Aras, or Araxas in eastern Armenia. So how can it encompass African Ethiopia? And the Pison. It's associated with Joruk, the Acampsis, and Havilah with Armenia. But Havilah has also been associated with southern Palestine around present day Gaza and with northern Arabia around the border between present day Saudi Arabia, Kuwait and Iraq. What's more, while all four of these rivers encircle the sacred Mount Ararat region, they spring from no common river. No common source."

"So the Bible's inaccurate," Greg got a little more feisty, realizing that this nut did have an education. "What else is new? It seems to me that what you're saying is that Eden is just a myth."

"Ninevah, Jericho, Babylon," Kilroy ticked them off, "All were once thought legends, until Biblical archeologists proved otherwise."

"And you intend to prove that Eden existed."

"Yes."

"But not in the Middle East."

"The Bible's description of Eden's location is clearly not meant to be accurate. Perhaps elements of it are, but the whole thing, well, it conforms to no place in the Middle East."

"Or anywhere else in the world."

"Granted. But even if the Biblical Eden was intended to combine the geography of the four corners of the known world at the time, there remains the kernel of truth to the myth. A paradisiacal land of origins.

169

END TIME

California does have gold, and the resin and semi-precious stone mentioned in the Biblical passages. And many folks have considered it paradise." Kilroy noted the look of humoring a lunatic in Greg's eyes. "Actually, I do this as a hobby, between real jobs. I'm searching for Eden until I go off to excavate the tomb of a Hyksos Pharaoh in Egypt at the end of February. And you must admit, the idea would make a great coffee table picture book."

Greg was glad to let the archeologist off at the Marinwood exit to speed back to the ASU campus. It was barely noon and already he had toured some political and religious fringes. He cracked the window to smell the coming rain, and cranked the radio.

He was a conventional agnostic. He had been raised Catholic by his parents through the sacrament of Confirmation, before it was no longer expected that he go to church. He had prayed for his uncle, but when the cancer took him, it also took God. This plus his scientific interests gave him a caustic skepticism that could not destroy all doubts however. Having been raised Christian, he was particularly susceptible to its mythology and images. And he had felt a resonance when Kilroy had talked about his search for Eden.

Smoke was another matter altogether. The man was proudly enigmatic, and not a little scary. His were post-political politics, making Greg's look conventional by comparison. He returned the truck to the yard, recovered his car, and drove home. Andre worked in the garage, cleaning up, when Greg spluttered across the gravel drive. The pines above them sighed.

"Ready for a drive to the City?" the father asked.

"Sure," the son replied.

They hit their favorite places—the Japanese Tea Gardens in Golden Gate Park, an off season Fisherman's Wharf, and Chinatown. They browsed City Lights Books, the Farmers Market, and the Software Nexus. They had hot, light, deep-fried and powder sugared pastries from a street vendor off Market. Then Andre took Greg to a Basque restaurant on Potrero Hill, the Vizcaya, for a hearty, meaty meal and a view of the Pleiades Platform lighting up as the sun set. They talked about sports, politics, ideas that Greg had, places that Andre had been; mostly safe subjects. Andre did not talk about Janet with Greg, but he did watch his son, measuring his words and behavior. When the father was convinced that the boy was coping adequately with the breakup, he discussed his work schedule with Greg on the ride home across the Golden Gate home. It started sprinkling.

"I'll be going to Australia Wednesday morning," Andre steered easily down the highway, "Consulting on an international criminal law case in Sydney. I've already arranged for a satellite linked cellular line while I'm overseas."

170

ARMAGEDDON, CA 94666

"Thanks," Greg said, finally catching his father's concern, "I know you worry about me dad, but you don't have to. I'm not going to slit my wrists over Janet or anything like that."

The car's wipers rhythmically slapped away a sprinkle become rain. Both Greg and Andre relaxed once again to enjoy the drive home. Greg faced a stack of homework once more in his room. But it was early in the semester. He could in theory choose an entirely new class line-up on Monday and still meet ASU's administrative deadlines. As he listened to the rain on the roof, and imagined its waters sealing up a potential fission sun beneath his meadow's green earth, he decided to fire up the lathe. He snagged a Guiness on the way to the basement. He spent the rest of the evening carving parts for an old gasoline engine with precise, incandescent green laser light, only occasionally utilizing virtual reality mapping for the small parts. Otherwise, he preferred to direct the machine by hand. Metal vaporized to his coherent photon touch, the basement's air heating up with industrial odors. The rain crashed outside the basement's windows.

***

DL left the Center in Hakim's and Killah's capable hands, the two arguing religion. What else? Killah Samuels was a natural atheist. Gut level. Hakim was devout, with the zeal of a reformed addict. They never settled much, and DL suspected they enjoyed arguing for the company they shared.

He drove the Center car to a Safeway, coming out an hour later with five bags of groceries and one of household supplies. They bounced in the back seat as he maneuvered around potholes along a decayed suburban street deep in east Oakland yet another hour later. Old trees arched bare frames across old memories, brilliant and whole where all around him the world was broken and desiccated. The run down houses set back from run down lawns, the cracks and holes in the sidewalks, the hopeless people drifting and congregating; these grimy, tattered realities never failed to angrily crush the happy childhood memories he had of this neighborhood.

His mother had been alive then, and the family had taken spring evenings on the screened porch, chatting with other strolling neighbors. As he pulled into the driveway in mid-afternoon, past a gutter full of garbage, he noticed that the ivy had completely overgrown the porch, hiding much of the house's collapsing front. He opened the side gate's lock with a key from his chain, another key opening up the creaky back door into the kitchen's back mop room. He heard a TV from the twilight inside, but first he hauled the six shopping bags into the kitchen.

Dark. When he turned on a light, roaches sauntered for cover. Dirty paper plates, mixed with empty food and beer cans, filled four large trash bags. Cigarette butts and ashes littered the floor. DL walked through the dining room shadows, following the TV's blue flicker into the living room. An old black man, hair gnarled up white, snored softly in an easy chair facing a rerun of *I Love Lucy*, surrounded by large mounds of empty beer cans and small mounds of cigarette debris. He did not wake Gabriel Logan, his father, but instead returned to the kitchen. Sometimes when DL brought the shopping, his father was awake. But only occasionally was he lucid enough to hold a decent conversation. Sometimes when he came in Gabriel woke with a start, asking: "Vivian?" DL methodically bundled up garbage with a quiet fury, then unpacked the groceries.

DL's mom, Vivian, died of cancer while he was in prison and now, on the combined pittance that was his father's union pension and social security, dad complacently drank and smoked himself to death in the shell of their life together. If DL did not buy food, Gabriel would not eat. All of his meager retirement was now spent on an all-too-conventional suicide.

Finished with all that he could really do, DL returned hopefully to the living room. But Gabriel was still deep into alcoholic slumber. You broken old man, DL thought, holding back tears. Mom had been the fighter, holding her cancer at bay for seven years after she had been given just one to live. Dad had given up long before she died, but the Grim Reaper was slow in coming. DL left the house without a sound, making sure to lock the back door and gate. He backed out of the driveway and drove for the nearest freeway. For home. The Center.

***

Peregrine made the FBI's TMW list at midnight, while in the middle of robbing the General Store, the sundries and supplies coop on campus. He'd decided to concentrate on the ASU campus coops because they were both lucrative and easy to rob. The students who ran them didn't know shit about security, Peregrine realized. The first week of the semester had been good for the General Store, and he collected $100 each from two cash registers, and $420 from the closet lock box. The rain pounded mercilessly outside.

TWENTY-FIVE

Excerpted from
"Nations and People of Earth,"
*The Amok World Almanac
and Book of Weird Facts*
2010
(Electrostraca #: A/GR-010-367-582-2376)

The Mixtecan and Mayapan Liberated Territories are currently negotiating peace in a decade long war of secession that removed close

172

ARMAGEDDON, CA 94666

to 260 thousand square miles and 20 million people in southern Mexico from Mexican central government control as well as from the North American Trade Zone. Combined US/Mexican forces still uneasily occupy a third of the Liberated Territories, and the US military continues a limited air war and partial naval blockade of the Zapatista revolution. But the tenacity of this libertarian society and its poor peasant peoples seems to be winning it the independence for which the Zapata Liberation Front (ZLF) has fought so hard to attain.

The ZLF organized the Mixtecan and Mayapan Liberated Territories out of the countrywide August 2000 Uprisings, defending it up to the present under the US aerial holocaust and against the incursions of the combined US/Mexican/Guatemalan armed forces. The ZLF holds ground from the region where the Sierra Madre Oriental and Del Sur merge, around Oaxaca, through the Istmo De Tehuantepec to the Yucatan. This vast swath of self governing territory is run by village and town councils, workers collectives and syndicates, and peasant coops and communes. A half dozen libertarian labor unions, plus two socialist ones, form the Confederacion del Trabajo. With several political parties—the Magonist Liberty Party, the conventional Mexican Social Democracy Party, a minuscule Communist Party, and a larger, weirder hybrid Trotskyist/Maoist amalgam called the Revolutionary Movement of the Left—the CT fronted the popular circle of southern Mexico's liberation struggles; the grassroots level to the ZLF.

The actual running of the Liberated Territories is done in an extremely decentralized fashion, even in the small socialist zones. In the larger villages, and in towns and cities, factories were taken over by their workers. The workers in turn elected both technical and administrative management, all subject to recall at any time, and entirely accountable to the workers' assembly. Problems beyond the scope of one factory are handled by local/regional economic and industrial councils. Close to 80% of the industry in the Territories is worker run.

The communal traditions of Mexico's peasant life in the south are augmented by those still extant pre-Columbian native cultural institutions into a solid social base. As a consequence, collectivization came easily. Expropriated lands were taken over by the peasants, who pool not only their land, but tools, animals, grain, fertilizer and harvested crops, modestly in cooperatives and more radically in communes. Perhaps 7,900 agrarian cooperatives and communes carry out the bulk of the farming in the Liberated Territories.

Between twelve and fifteen million people participate in southern Mexico's revolution in this manner, as well as through their village and town councils. In the larger towns and in the cities, neighborhood councils coordinate through a metropolitan council. These latter organs of self-government are broader and more volatile, for while much of the regions workers and peasants belong to the CT through one or another of its independent unions, "independents" and "individualists" flourish in the various village, town and metropolitan councils. Small farmers who do not wish to join a cooperative or commune are called "individualists," and small shop owners who do not want to unionize are labeled "independents." Both are permitted to continue, the one working the land and the other operating a business or industry, often as families as they are not permitted to hire labor. As a consequence a modest, better off sector of extended family farms and enterprises prospers. Not subject to competition from large landowners, industrialists, and other capitalists, domestic or foreign, as all have long ago fled, they are also protected by the Territories popular militias as far as is possible from the US/Mexican military assault.

The CT and its affiliated unions, the LP and the MSDP, are all run from the bottom up through conventions and congresses, ultimately coalescing in the sometimes unwieldy but always democratic federation that is the ZLF. Only the CP and the RML practice versions of tight, Leninist, democratic centralism and because of their relative lack of influence, they are tolerated as members of the ZLF.

Intersecting the ZLF, overlapping it in a number of areas, the Federacion Anarchista Olmecan (FAO) is a network of *groupos de afinidad* most closely associated with the libertarian unions of the CT. They are more purely ideological within their respective unions at the same time they field the fighting groups and carry out *atentados* against military and ruling classes in those gray, boundary areas of the Territories. The FAO, together with the peasant and workers militias formed into columns, constitute the guerrilla Popular Revolutionary Forces (PRF), which defend the Liberated Territories through the strategy of a self-organized, armed people.

Sparked by the widespread corruption, intimidation and fraud of the PRI in the 1998 Presidential elections, and backed against the wall by the brutal failure of the 1999 country-wide General Strike, the 2000 August Uprisings, also called the August Revolution in the Territories, forged both the ZLF and the Territories, all in 20 breathtaking days of successful insurrection. Both the ZLF and the Territories have weathered years of US/Mexican government and military counter-insurgency, this revolutionary society basically intact despite all that reaction and imperialism can throw at it. US strategy against the secessionist south of Mexico involves unrelenting air war, smart weaponry, high tech special forces, and combined US/Mexican ground forces. US counterinsurgency escalated quickly from covert aid in 2001 through advisors in 2003 to troops in 2005. The Combined Forces draw a line from Acapulco to Vera Cruz, digging in behind it as well as along the eastern

174

stretch of the Yucatan peninsula around Cancun. US military bases in western and northern Guatemala coordinate with the brutal Guatemalan military to secure the border and make occasional anti-guerrilla incursions. The US Joint Chiefs of Staff at first predicted a swift, surgical intervention of overwhelming US technologies linked to a sepoy army trained from the start in gung-ho, American-style warfare. Yet the US/Mexican war against the Mixtecan and Mayapan Liberated Territories has dragged on for years, with little success in converting areas sympathetic to the revolution let alone in defeating the revolution's core areas.

Physically, on the ground, the US military does far better in holding territory and minimizing casualties than was the case during Vietnam. Spiritually, the US does little better in winning the "hearts and minds" of the populace than was the case in IndoChina. Now that the US and Mexican governments are tacitly acknowledging the Zapatista revolution by holding multilateral peace talks with the Mixtecan and Mayapan Liberated Territories in Paris, it is no longer that difficult to enter or travel about in southern Mexico...

TWENTY-SIX

Sobered by the work he had not done, Greg walked out after his first class, into the middle of the choreographed insanity of a Mushroom Madness Festival. Yet another of Smoke's and the MDRG's theater pieces, this one revolved around audience participatory performance art. A long roll of butcher paper had been unfurled and taped down to one of the walkways leading up to Remley Plaza, and it was scattered with pens, paint, crayons, chalk, etc. Five television sets on a large drop cloth occupied one corner of the Plaza; the set screens painted as a bloodshot eye, a laughing skull, a smoking brain, and the like, all begging to be smashed. In another corner of the plaza a modern dance piece was in progress. Yet a third plaza corner featured an immense mountain of styrofoam packing pieces into which several people were flinging each other and themselves. The fountain's water was dyed blood red. And somewhere, if the MDRG was true to form, someone was selling psychedelic mushrooms packaged by the dose, at cost.

A man, too old to be a student and not dressed as a professor, stood in the amused, playful crowds checking out the scene. He stuck out in his straight, dark glasses and suit, more so than if he had worn absolutely dayglo clothes and checkered hot pink/lime green hair. Greg was not the only one to jump to the conclusion that ASU now had it's own Fed, probably an FBI agent.

"Looks like the gov'mint boys are here," Larry said at his elbow, holding a bag of 'shrooms, "Also heard word that the Feds want to talk to the 'Mexican Revolution Solidarity Brigade.'"

"They want to negotiate?" Greg glanced at him, startled.

END TIME

"I guess," Larry shrugged, "Smoke heard. Said its the word on the grapevine all around the Bay Area. I told it to David and he and Beth are looking into it."

"Trap?"

"Probably. Then again, maybe the Feds are serious about talking. Smoke said there was an FBI agent on almost every corner in Berkeley yesterday. I'm glad the 'stuff' is hidden."

"So am I," Greg said, pushing his hair back nervously, "Hope David and Beth are careful."

"They said they'd update us if they found out anything," Larry shrugged, "By the way, Smoke's doing a little talk this evening. For anybody who's planning to do an autonomous street affinity at this Wednesday's SF demo. On the patio at the pub at 5 today."

"You going to do that stuff?" Greg indicated the dried 'shrooms, "Won't be in much condition for the talk if you do."

"I'll be coasted well down by that time," Larry grinned, twisting up his face so that his eyes bulged comically. He then proceeded to munch down his dosage. Greg sighed. He liked psilocybin best of all the hallucinogens he had tried; not as pushy as LSD, not as spacy as mescaline, and not as smoothed down as the designer bullshit. But he was so far behind in homework that he dared not even contemplate purchasing a dose for later. Why had the Bay Area General Strike been called for Wednesday, instead of Tuesday or Thursday, Greg's busy school days? The ASU Associated Student Body had endorsed the Wednesday strike in their Sunday meeting. The Faculty Senate was to vote on the strike that evening. The proposal to close the school Wednesday was expected to pass by a squeaker, with the sizable minority of business-as-usual faculty threatening to defy the vote by keeping their classes open.

His Humanities class was a snowstorm. Holmes buried Greg's mind under a blizzard of words.

"The Christian Millennium is markedly different from both Paradise and Utopia. Forget for the moment the sectarianism within the millennarian tradition; the pre-millennialists with their direct divine rule by the Christ after his Second Coming, and the post-millennialists who split as to whether the Millennium is to be a golden age or an age of desolation, both agreeing that it will occur before the Second Coming. Consider the Millennium only as a golden age. It still is fundamentally set apart from both Paradise and Utopia. The Millennium is a fixed time, one thousand years in length. Both Paradise and Utopia are timeless, entirely outside of history. Marx, in defining human history to date as the history of class struggle, posited an end to history, or rather a transcendence of pre-history, in the achievement of his stateless, classless communist society. Only communism's lower stage, what Lenin called "socialism," is of a limited duration. And, in the Christian

176

mythos, the time bound Millennium in no way substitutes for true Paradise, no matter how golden and blissful.

"What is more, the Millennium has no opposite. It is merely one in a linear string of historical ages in the Christian scheme of things. By contrast, those religions with a strong conception of paradise-as-heaven invariably posit a fiendish hell. Authors fantasizing a Utopia, an Erewhon or a Pala are as likely to conceive of a Brave New World, an Oceania, or a Fahrenheit 451. As for paradise-as-garden, the world itself is its opposite. In contrast to Eden is the Land of Nod. Yin and Yang. Paradise and Utopia share the intimacy of opposites. Human culture has not transcended patternings based upon polarity and opposition for the million or so years of our species' sapiency, esoteric mathematics notwithstanding. Indeed, some argue that humans cannot know white without understanding black, good without evil, freedom without slavery. It can even be argued that the Millennium *must* be temporally delimited because it has no opposite."

Once done with school for the day, Greg made the mistake of trying to study at the pub. He managed two hours before Larry showed up, sublime on his high's decline. A pitcher of beer showed up, and Larry offered his friend a glass.

"Didja hear?" Larry grinned cheerfully, "ASP called off the P&M occupation."

"No, why?" Greg looked up.

"We couldn't take the building back Sunday, so the cops opened classes today." Larry poured Greg a glass, "The lobby occupation had a meeting at noon. The only people who were being barred from their classes were the handicapped 'cause they couldn't use the lobby elevators. So they called it off."

"Too bad," Greg took a sip of beer, then a gulp, "Any more on the Feds and our 'hot property?'"

"Nope," Larry stared off, "But I gotta feeling we're about to find out."

Greg followed Larry's gaze and saw David, Beth and a third person approaching through the Redwood Eatery's front doors. David introduced the two already seated to Jason Trumble, winter quarter's chair of the UC Berkeley Student Anti-War Alliance. Jason was a Ferrel, unusual in that he was also a politico. Most Ferrels did not have a thought beyond gratifying what was between their legs. Ferrels were sometimes considered third generation glam; the decadent, glitter side to rock/metal. Of equal influence were the gothic/gloom tendencies of punk, the gritty underside to industrial, and a taste of acid house, particularly the aphrodisiac promise in its "love drugs"—Ecstasy and Love 999. It did take lead guitar out of metal's banalities, restoring psychedelia's harrowing edge to the instrument's sound. It made some use of the New Emo-Sound systems—Emo synths and amps—more as

177

frosting on the musical cake. Ferrel had started before medicine developed the pack antibody vaccines to effectively fight AIDS and herpes. It flourished despite science having made sex relatively safe once again. Ferrel did best when sex was tinged with danger, and a little violence. Jason had an impressive Fu Manchu mustache. He wore his semi-dreaded hair matted, braided, and beaded, and his whirligig clothing torn as if by passion, in Ferrel fashion. He also wore the distinctive Ferrel lower apparel; Amerindian style pants cut away front and back at the crotch and covered by a decorated breech cloth so as to be "ready for action" anytime, any place.

"Jason, will you sit here and wait for us. We have to talk," David addressed his friend, and then turned to Larry and Greg, "Let's go out on the patio."

"Smoke was right. There's definitely something weird going on," Beth said once outside, "Jason was approached by folks he thinks were FBI. When he refused to talk to them about anything, they told him the government is interested in talking with whoever has the riemanium. They even gave him an 800 number to call. He drove to Concord to call from a pay phone, and David and I drove to San Rafael to call, also from a pay phone. Obviously, anybody calling is going to be traced."

"Anyway," David continued, "The recorded message on the line sets up a meeting at Temptations Cafe in the city tomorrow night at 7. We're supposed to approach the third table from the potted plants on the patio and ask for a cigarette."

"Are we going to do it?" Greg frowned, not liking this turn of events at all.

"I think we should at least go to see what's up," David said.

"If it doesn't look good, you don't have to go through with it," Beth added.

" I can't believe the government is going to cave in to us," Greg shook his head.

"I don't either," David said, "But this is an opportunity to see what the government has up its sleeve."

"What if they got pictures, from demos?" Larry sputtered, "Arrest you all just because you're there."

A few minutes passed as the implications of Larry's statement percolated.

"Well then," David returned to deliberateness, "All they'll have is a false arrest. Temptations Cafe is open to the public, and we have the right to go there to eat. They have no evidence we're there for anything else, and if we don't talk, they've got nothing. We could even threaten to sue."

"We could set something up with our ACLU lawyer also," Beth offered, "Tell her we heard this was going down, and just want to see what its about. We can ask her to be on call is all."

"Sounds like a good back-up," Greg said, cautious as hell.

"I dunno," Larry said. "Won't the lawyer get suspicious?"

"She'll still respect client confidentiality," Beth commented.

"We'll drive down in my car," David said. Several ASP members drifted onto the patio, followed by a couple of the MDRG boys, making further conversation impossible. David recovered Jason from inside the pub. Dusk deepened. It was clear now why Jason was there as David's guest. The Berkeleyite was also a "street fightin' man," and he was to monitor Smoke's presentation, even offer a second opinion, at David's request. More people arrived. Finally, Smoke hustled in on threads of night and fog. The gathering retired to an isolated corner of the pub's upper patio.

"Yo," Smoke began, to focus attention, "All of you, I take it, are here because you want to participate in the Hooligan actions of the SF march next Wednesday. David, how's that going to be organized?"

"Well," David was taken aback by Smoke's polite address, so into his rivalry was he with the man. He clasped his hands together. "As you all know, this is a national day of action that has become an international event. In the Bay Area three separate marches are supposed to come together. One from UCB and one from downtown Oakland are supposed to converge just before crossing the bay bridge. The combined east bay contingent is then supposed to merge around 5th and Market with the SF march coming south on Market. I'm not quite sure of the route from that point. I think we go up Van Ness to Fell, and then to Golden Gate Park."

"Thanks." Smoke nodded under deck lights defining swirling columns in the gathering fog. "ASP's plan is to start from Berkeley. We'll be able to join up with the Hooligan contingents there. The general plan is to split off from the overall march just before it gets to the park rally."

At that moment Lori and Mary walked into the conspiracy, beers in hand. They sat next to Larry and Greg.

"Hello," Lori said, sweetly, placing a hand on Greg's knee.

"There are three key factors to successful autonomous street actions," Smoke continued, unperturbed. "Anonymity, mobility and cellular flexibility. I'll take these in reverse order. Hooliganism is a mass movement made up of contingents, roughly corresponding to independent columns like the Black Column, THRUSH..."

"Terrible Hags Ruthlessly Uprooting Self-Hatred," Lori laughed.

"And then there are the more concentrated affinity group and cellular organizations that make up the columns, or sometimes float free," Smoke glared at the interruption, then quickly iced, "Like the Crabby Times Crew, BdN, Hardcore Autonomy, the Pickles Eccarius Liberation

Front, Anti-Fascist Skin Front, Black Gang, etc. At the end of this, this group is gonna have to figure out how to affiliate and whether to stay as an ASP affinity.

"Autonomous action relies upon cellular organization even deeper than this however. Groups like Hardcore Autonomy or BdN are actually several autonomous affinities under a common name and action platform. And in each affinity, participants hang in groups of two to five during street actions. When an affinity is charged by the cops, it can quickly disperse and easily regroup. If pressed by a full on police assault, folks can run in all directions, with a buddy or two so you can watch each other's backs. That's the basis to the cellular model, people who are friends taking care of each other as a unit. A streetwise unit. Cellular structure also allows for maximum flexibility. If one cell is mostly arrested or broken up, the remaining individuals can be quickly absorbed into other cells. And cells can develop hand signs, street calls, even battle plans and contingencies in coordination. Before this meeting's done, those are other things to discuss.

"All of which leads into the need for street smarts and mobility. Everybody here should get a map of San Francisco and study the march route. Study all the side streets you can, especially along Market and Van Ness. Check out dead ends and the way traffic flows. Check out parks and other open spaces. In theory, everyone should walk or drive through the area and check it out before Wednesday. On the day of, wear your running shoes and be prepared to do some fast and unexpected maneuvering. You can shut down a public building by sitting down until the cops get there, then disperse and regroup to block another building. Keep on the move and one step ahead of the powers-that-be; that'll keep you active and out of jail on Wednesday. That's especially true if you intend to do some vandalism. There's no dress rehearsal, or dry run for street fighting. So when you're on that march and in those streets, keep your eyes and ears open. Keep alert. What's the pedestrian traffic like at any given time? The number, armament and placement of cops? Any paddy wagons or cop choppers? What cars and buses are on the street and where? There's only one take on this riot. You either get it right or you go to jail."

"I want you tonight," Lori leaned to whisper into Greg's ear, her voice southern sticky, her hand sliding up his thigh.

"Finally, we get to street presence." Smoke caught her maneuver in the corner of his eye, and refused to acknowledge it. "You all know how to dress for regular demos—loose, comfortable clothes, no jewelry, etc. Hooligans work within such guidelines toward anonymity. Its hard for the cops, even using videos and super zoom photography to pick you out of a crowd breaking bank windows when everyone in the crowd dresses alike. Wear dark clothing. Black is preferred. A black bandana,

180

ARMAGEDDON, CA 94666

cheap mirrored sunglasses for the neurolasers, sweat pants or sweatshirt with another layer of clothing underneath, maybe a cap, and your identity is covered. Cheap black nylon gloves, a couple of dermaflex pads to cut down the tear gas, jacket pockets full of rocks, maybe a slingshot or a roll of pennies, and you're complete. Most of these items can be easily bundled and quickly tossed away. It's no crime to wear black. I know the Killer Klown Kontingent go for wild costumes and face makeup, but they're doing the same thing. When there's thousands of 'em on the streets, the cops can't tell who's who, and who did what. And, no ID. It's no crime yet to go walking around without ID, especially during the day. But the cops have the right to haul people in without ID on suspicion and hold them incommunicado for over forty-eight hours. That means setting a regroupment time and place, so you can see who's missing, find 'em and spring 'em."

"Smoke," Eric, the MDRG dreadhead, coughed, and imperceptibly gestured. A young man, ostensibly dressed and outfitted as a student, approached the patio's upper terrace, climbing the stairs, beer in hand. But just like the suit at the Mushroom Madness Festival, the cut and manner of this one spoke louder than anything else. Cop.

"Is this the ASP meeting?" the man said, standing now as the entire meeting stared at him. The MDRG boys, up until then loitering on the edges of the meeting, sauntered unobtrusively to surround the newcomer.

"No," Smoke smiled, not quite friendly, "It's kinda a private party. A little private celebration."

"Okay," the newcomer shrugged, and glanced about. He noticed an empty table at the far end of the short terrace and moved toward it. When he moved, so did the MDRG, and that's when he noticed them.

"It's still a free country, isn't it?!?" the newcomer said, scowling.

"Freer up here than you might like," Eric grinned, wolfish.

"As in free-for-all," Darrel, the skin, pointedly cracked his knuckles.

The newcomer did not say another word. Instead, he turned and walked back the way he'd come. He wasn't scared, or surprised. He was angry, making the point to carefully control his anger.

"Let's wrap this up," Smoke said as his audience turned back from watching a real autonomous cell in action, "You've got the basics. The only way to really learn is hands-on. Time now to settle some issues. First, buddying up."

"Mary and me are going to join up with THRUSH," Lori said, first thing.

"Does anyone want to form an ASP affinity?" David asked, at cross purposes. Most of the rest of the folks at the meeting wanted to, and Greg buddied up with Larry.

"The MDRG usually does its own thing," Smoke grinned and winked.

END TIME

Fog began to halo the night lighting. "But we'll hang with you all on Wednesday."

They arranged a time and place to regroup in Berkeley, as well as the necessary legal backup. Smoke hurried out a few more suggestions.

"Talk over contingencies with your buddy. What if the cops charge? What if they use horses? What if someone you know but who's not your buddy is being chased down by the cops? What if you're trapped between two advancing lines of cops? What if you get separated or one of you is injured?...

"Someone in the overall affinity should assemble a basic medical kit—ace bandages, steristrips, extra dermaflex pads, disinfectant, etc. Again, nothing more than can be thrown away in a pinch...

"Basically, our job is to cause as much damage and chaos as possible, not necessarily to fight with the cops. It might be amusing to knock down a cop or route a squad. But if that's what you do instead of taking out the Bank of America or blocking a street by overturning a BMW, you're missing the point..."

When the meeting broke up, Jason stood to shake Smoke's hand.

"Good talk," he said. David frowned. They all trooped down the stairs from the terrace through swirling mists, past the probable agent seated glumly at a table at the base of the stairs, his beer barely touched. As Lori took Greg's arm, Smoke smirked and turned to evaporate into the night with his MDRG crew.

"Mary's staying here for a couple of drinks," Lori looked mischievously into Greg's eyes, "Can you drive me home?"

The campus's grotesque statuary seemed eerie, not funny at night. Wisps of fog wrapped about a flock of seagulls in glass and brass, changing it into a threatening fanged mass.

"I hear you and David are going to check out the Fed setup tomorrow evening in the city," she glanced at him, excited and obviously envious.

"Yah," Greg forced his own smile.

"Do you think that's wise? I mean, you're our connection to the riemanium."

"To the man who has the riemanium," he amended with a proper version of the story. "Besides, he's actually Larry's friend."

"You know where he lives?" She was fishing.

"Oakland somewhere," Greg evaded, "He usually shows up at Larry's, so we don't have a street address."

"And no phone number because he calls Larry," Lori finished his fiction.

"Yeah," Greg gave Lori a suspicious look, "Why do you ask?"

"Just that, with you going to that rendezvous tomorrow, we don't have a contact with this guy Peregrine. What if you get popped?"

"David says they can't make it stick," Greg shrugged, concealing his

ARMAGEDDON, CA 94666

own concern, "And besides, there's Larry. He's actually who Peregrine knows."

"Its like Chin said," Lori mused, "We don't have the riemanium, so all we're doing is just bluffing. One communiqué is not going to keep up the momentum on this thing, especially if it doesn't look cool to contact the Feds tomorrow. Would the riemanium be available for another set of photos?"

"Probably," Greg said, inwardly groaning to think of digging up the riemanium from his meadow.

"What'd be better," Lori's cherubic face suddenly lit up with devilish delight, "Is if we could put together a mock bomb. Something that'd look blood real but wouldn't really work."

"Now there's an idea," Greg inwardly tensed. Having felt the need to "do more," he now understood a little of Larry's leeriness. Truly, they rode the tiger.

"I read once," she continued, "That a '60's magazine once published a do-it-yourself-how-to-make-an-A-bomb, from what they'd collected in the public record. Caused a real stink at the time."

"I'm sure the Feds and the media will splash that all over, if we want that much attention," Greg warned, back handed, "We have a couple of Feds in town already. That'll be nothing once this idea hits."

"From what I hear," Lori grinned, "Most of the Feds are concentrated in the central Bay Area. Seems they're fully convinced its a serious political grouping with the riemanium. Like the BdN."

"Still, we'll have to be very careful with this one," Greg cautioned.

They had reached his car, near a set of interlaced shredded plastic walls upon a pedestal drifted with the fog. Greg opened the door for Lori and got in to drive, reaching up to pull down the top.

"Actually, I have my car here," Lori giggled and started to kiss him, sliding her hand to his crotch, working him up hard in a minute. He suddenly sat back down and she trailed her head to his lap. Her fingers fumbled with his zipper, then his cock. He glanced wildly about the mist shrouded parking lot as she went down on him. Jesus, he hoped no one walked by, and the thought seared up his thighs, a molten excitement. He climaxed, and she swallowed.

"See you," Lori laughed, and backed out of his car.

When Greg arrived home, fog cocooned the house. The front porch light, the light in Consuello's room off the first story in the back, and dad's den light on the second floor formed muffled cottony clouds among the pines. As he climbed the front steps, he thought he detected the faintest glimmer from one of the basement's pitch black windows. He hesitated, saw nothing, and continued to unlock the front door. As he stepped into the living room, over the threshold, he heard it. The sound of the hood to his lathe snapped down in the basement beneath

183

his feet. He tried to be quiet while still preserving speed as he walked through living and dining rooms into the kitchen. He slammed the basement door open, clicked on the lights and jammed down the stairs.

The basement was empty. All the cupboard doors above and below the tool bench were wide open. A basement window above the lathe opened to the singing night.

***

Ibraham Achdoud knew he was being hunted, even as he hunted. The young man sat in a Winnebago along an Alabaster side street after midnight. The dish on top of the RV established a satellite link. The computer on the RV's kitchenette table busily scrolled automatically through AT&T/MCI/Sprint databases. The whole set up, to include Ibraham, belonged to the Ismaili Brotherhood Unreconstructed.

Ibraham, until five years before the poor son of an impoverished family of southern Lebanese peasants, had been born Shi'ite. He would have joined the Hasballah or the Islamic Brotherhood as an angry teenager, had it not been for Hassan ibn Sabah, the Old Man of the Mountain. The Master of the World. Israel still dominated a fragmented southern Lebanon, and he would have gladly martyred himself in the fight against Zionism. But the Unreconstructed Ismaili had offered him a wider vision and a greater purpose. Better to make the whole world tremble and kneel rather than just your enemy.

"The storm is my doing; how can I pray that it abate?"

He had no way to know that Hassan ibn Sabah was not the original, but rather a pretender to the name. Nor could he know that the Unreconstructed Ismaili had, indeed, been reconstructed by that impersonator in the late 1980's and early 1990's, on the tradition but not on the present practices of the Aga Kahn's mainstream Ismailis. Ibraham's life was now as a devotee of the Brotherhood, a fervent assassin who believed that he would go straight to paradise if he died in the service of Hassan ibn Sabah.

Hassan had been born Tawfiq Jahlil in Teheran, son of a fabulously wealthy oil family and a multibillionaire himself by inheritance, once his father died. An ardent supporter of Khomeini and his Islamic Revolution, Tawfiq left Iran after the death of his beloved Ayatollah because his ideas of spreading Islamic revolution internationally proved too radical for Khomeini's successors. In exile, he aided, for a time, the Islamic Fundamentalists throughout the world; the Islamic Salvation Front in Algeria, the Islamic Brotherhood in Egypt, the Palestinian Hamas Movement, etc. Wherever Islamic Fundamentalism turned revolutionary Jahlil could be found, somewhere in the background. But he wanted to do more than merely give money to other people's movements. He believed that the "motor force" of Islamic Fundamentalism in pan-Arab politics itself required an "engine," to

ARMAGEDDON, CA 94666

give the larger historical force a clearer direction. So Tawfiq Jahlil became Hassan ibn Sabah, and the reincarnated Old Man of the Mountain set about emulating his namesake. He built impregnable private fortresses around the world, most upon precipitous mountain summits. He gathered to himself, first a fanatic cadre, and then a zealous army of ultra-fundamentalist Shi'i sectarians, his faithful assassins willing to follow his orders to their deaths. And, he built paradise upon an Indian Ocean island, fortified it against incursions, and prepared it with every earthly delight.

"Nothing is true; all is permitted."

Ibraham remembered paradise. One minute he had been in Hassan's court, an illiterate, ignorant 16-year-old boy at the foot of his intended master. As Hassan spoke of paradise, a draft of some pungent liquid passed around the circle of would-be disciples, the Master's hybrid opiate liqueur. Ibraham gulped a fair quantity, despite its sharp taste, and the edges of his vision started to blur. The room and its people then folded into this distortion before he blacked out completely. He awoke, without any ill after effects, on a luxurious silk upholstered divan, in a jewel and gold ornamented palace appointed with mystical geometries and paintings.

The palace had been situated in a verdant, fragrant garden rich with roses and orange trees. Channels cut into the stone walks about the palace flowed streams of wine, milk, honey and pure water. Fountains sprayed heady wines to glint in the sun. Calm pools of clear water held zen-eyed fish serenely floating beneath lilies and lotus. Peacocks and rare parrots inhabited the grounds. Brightly colored banners and gilded pavilions played over ornate feasts and banquets on the perfumed breeze. And, he was not alone.

Houris—beautiful young girls and women—waited on his every wish, willing to fulfill his every desire. Dressed in expensive and suggestive clothes, they were stunning and voluptuous, accomplished in the arts of singing, music, dancing, and erotic pleasure. He spent five days being served delicious viands, exquisite wines, potent hashish and delirium producing opiates by lovely, one might say heavenly females who sang, played, and caressed him in maddening, intimate ways. Little wonder that Ibraham, after he was again drugged and transported out of paradise to conclude his ecstatic experience, vowed to serve Hassan ibn Sabah with his life.

"Bury everything sacred under the ruins of thrones and altars."

He became a devotee, a fidawi, an assassin, on the promise that, if he should die on the Master's orders, he would return straight to paradise. Hassan also promised his devotees an extended youth, while they lived, through biochemical and genetically keyed treatments. And the Brotherhood taught him to read and write, trained him in an

185

advanced regimen of martial arts and hand-to-hand combat, and kept him well fed, clothed and sheltered for most of his young manhood. He had gladly given his soul to the Unreconstructed Ismaili, even while his current duty was not to assassinate, but rather to rob his present target. Hassan wanted to make his Ismaili a nuclear power, and so it was Ibraham's task to track down Peregrine and recover the stolen riemanium. If he could not obtain what his master wanted, and if he could not "persuade" Peregrine to cooperate, he might have to resort to kidnapping.

So far, it proved to be an easy task. The police had the list of calls from the Diamotti safe house to various public phones for Peregrine. What he had done was to crack the master telephone databases to look for the reverse. What numbers in the Alabaster area had called the safe house in the last six months? Unconstrained by privacy ethics, and wired with the most up-to-date hacker software in an extremely powerful PC, he rifled the area prefix databases with impunity. But, as he had continued his search, little things informed him he was not alone on this trail. Opening a document, copying from it, and closing the document took seconds longer than was normal. In all probability he was involuntarily "sharing" the satellite link with someone else, someone who let him do the work in hopes of pirating the information he dug up. He had set up several data traps and catch loops, to no avail. His "silent partner" was clever. It also meant that, as soon as he had something, anything, he had to move. With any luck, he would be one step ahead of whoever hunted on his trail.

Three of the public phones in nightclubs used by Peregrine had already come up. As Ibraham poured himself more coffee, the computer chimed. An Emmett Grogan, at a private address. An apartment complex downtown, on Main. He copied down the street address, grabbed a map, and started the computer processing again. Once he located the cross streets, he tapped the rooftop dish into gyrolock mode with the satellite, and started up the RV. The link occasionally broke as he drove. The computer paused then until the dish rotated to relocate and reconnect; that was inevitable. He had to move on this now!

Clouds scudded across a gibbous moon as he eased the bulky vehicle down a dark, suburban street. He noticed the car barreling down on him from a side street, an old, large Plymouth Chrysler without lights. As he hit the brakes, the other car started an erratic veer, as if the other driver had just seen the Winnebago and was swerving to avoid it. Turn the Chrysler did, in a squeal of tires on a skid, the car's back bumper nicking the stopped RV's front bumper on the spin. A bulky man lurched out of the car door, stumbling drunk. Ibraham cracked the side window.

"What the hell you do, driving with no lights!" Ibraham growled, avoiding the shout, hand gripping the hidden handgun mounted under the dash. "Now move it! I'm in a hurry."

"So...s...sorry," the man slurred, "Guess I...I had too much to drink." The man crumbled sloppily to the asphalt. Fell to one knee expertly and came up with a high impact air gun. He fired it even before Ibraham saw it. An extremely fine needle primed with shellfish toxin silently slivered through the Ismaili's right eye, and into his brain. The assassin pitched back, out of sight in the Winnebago, dead almost instantly. The assassin's assassin jumped into the Chrysler and quickly parked it. Then he sprinted back to the RV and clambered into the driver's seat, re-engaged the vehicle's gears and parked it before beginning to loot.

TWENTY-SEVEN

A Spider assassinated Frederico Segura on January 27, 2007. With his death, the CT lost not only a principal "constructivist" voice but also a superb organizer. Before Oaxaca was bombed into ruins, Frederico almost single handedly put together the city's food distribution system to end the threat of mass starvation.

Born of working class parents in industrial Mexico City on August 14, 1970, he developed the raw competence and aggressive style that were to make him one of the CT's most inspired activists in the streets of the capitol's teeming colonias. His street "instinto" accompanied Frederico when, as a teen, he went off to the Gulf Coast to work in the oil refineries, earning him the lifelong nickname of "Noi del Petro," oil boy, as he gradually worked down the coast to the Tehuantepec Isthmus.

Frederico joined the labor movement early, and taught himself politics from the classic texts of anarchism and socialism. Nevertheless, in his youth, he expressed admiration for both Nietzsche's individualism and the social banditry of Pancho Villa. A little older, Frederico gained the reputation as an anarchist moderate and a superb negotiator, dealing with employers, PRI bureaucrats and politicians, even fellow Leftists without compromising his or the movement's essential libertarian positions. Briefly forced to go underground after the 1998 protests, and then again after the 1999 General Strike, he threw himself into the movement, and into the series of meetings, propaganda and speaking tours, congresses, negotiations and strike committees leading up to the 2000 Uprisings.

He consistently favored alliances "at the base" with the socialist unions and often criticized the FAO for its lack of realism and its doctrinaire anarchism. Consequently, he was targeted for bitter attack by the militants in speeches and writing. He considered organization key to the development of a mass, united labor movement. And, he was the architect of the mutual aid agreements with San Cristobal.

END TIME

During Oaxaca's liberation, Frederico called together the food unions, the restaurant and hotel workers, and representatives of the peasant cooperatives and communal organizations in the surrounding countryside to coordinate food distribution. Communal dining halls were opened in each of the city's neighborhoods, where as many as 250,000 people were fed daily. Wholesale food warehouses and cooperative farmers markets were then established, which organized themselves thereafter as the Union of Industrial Food Workers. Workers ran the entire distribution network, fixed their own wages, and extended the system to the entire state of Oaxaca through the US firebombing of the city.

When his family found his body, after the Subucu assassination, they gathered his affects. Besides Frederico's union and CT cards was his San Cristobalan passport, one of the few in existence, bearing the red and black symbol now famous in the Liberated Territories.

TWENTY-EIGHT

Greg shared a meal of scrambled eggs and onions, hotcakes with maple syrup, and sausage, with his father the next morning. He mentioned nothing about the break-in to Andre. He suspected what had been the target. Greg still tried to figure out who it might have been and how they might have known. Andre went over last minute details before his trip.

"I might be getting a call or a fax from Stanton and Associates in New York. If I do, just pass it on to the office. I've written down my cellular number on a pad next to the phone. If anything goes wrong, or even if you're feeling down, give me a call. I should be back Monday evening, if everything goes well.

"A lawyer, Anindo Banerjea, also might call. I promised him I'd advise him on a case he's got pending. You can give him my cellular number."

After the meal they parted; Andre in his car eventually for SF international, and Greg in his car for school where he hung on through his classes, fingertips clinging to the academic cliff's edge.

***

Peregrine woke to a knock on his door at 7 in the morning.

"Who is it?" he asked, door locked and his pants almost on.

"Pacific Gas and Electric," a voice mumbled.

"What in hell do you want. I'm not dressed yet."

188

ARMAGEDDON, CA 94666

"We had a report of a gas leak in this building," the voice said, "Your neighbors on this floor called in that they smelled gas. Could you check your kitchen for me? The stove and your water heater?"

"For Christ's sake!" Peregrine steamed, but he did walk into his kitchen to check out the appliances.

"No, no gas leaking in..." Peregrine shouted, turning back into his apartment's small living room, only to see that he didn't need to shout. A man stood in his apartment. Six foot, burly, his dark curly hair cropped short; he aimed a conventional 38 Special for Peregrine's gut.

"If you're thinking about robbery," Peregrine raised his arms cautiously, "You picked the wrong person. I got nothing. Check around for yourself."

"Sulawesi," the man smirked.

"You got paid for what I purchased," Peregrine protested.

"Your account's paid up in full on that score. That's not why we're here." The man used the "royal we." "There's something you have that the Celebes is interested in purchasing. We're offering a good price. One million. That was supposed to be your cut on the Piccoli heist, wasn't it?"

"Yeah," Peregrine marveled at the outlaw zone's grapevine, "Sorry to disappoint you, but I don't have the riemanium."

"Sulawesi doesn't buy that it's in the hands of politicos."

"And why would I do a politico stunt with it?" Peregrine said, leveling his voice, "Why would I be living like this if I could've hustled the Feds out of that same million to return it? Why would I want to bring all this heat down on myself?"

"Good questions," the man grinned, "Maybe you're trying to jack up the price on it. Maybe you've got a numbered Swiss or Bahamian bank account. Maybe you're going to split the country once you've cut whatever deal you're making."

Good guess on the latter. Peregrine decided not to tell the Sulawesi agent about his own attempt to obtain the riemanium last night, nor of his information that Gregory Kovinski had it. Not until he had to.

"I take it you don't believe me then," Peregrine said.

"That's right."

"And I take it you have the ability, the orders, and the inclination to make me tell you whatever I know, even if I know nothing."

"Smart man." The Celebes man gently tilted his gun.

"Then, basically, I guess I've got no choice."

Peregrine put into motion the only other contingency he had. Under the gun, Peregrine took a small, portable shovel from his closet. Both the thief and the outlaw zone agent walked out of the apartment complex to the man's old Plymouth Chrysler. The man aimed as Peregrine drove, thinking furiously. He took scant notice of the extremely sophis-

189

ticated scanning equipment occupying the place of dashboard radio and glove box in the man's car. He drove north, into the coastal ranges for an hour. Then the two walked for a half hour off road, amidst evergreens and crows, to where Peregrine had buried his stash of weapons, hacker technology, and expertly forged ID's. He located the exact spot, and with the Celebes man a safe distance from his thrown dirt, the thief dug up the moist earth from around a foot locker sized box. He pulled it out of the hole.

"Here it is," Peregrine said, frowning.

"Open it," the agent said, gesturing with the gun.

The box was not locked, but Peregrine pulled out his key chain from a pocket as a distraction. The lid was up and the riot gun was in his hand in an instant. He jumped, slammed home a PS gas cartridge, rolled, fired as the Celebes enforcer got off two shots. Then Peregrine rolled again as the shell exploded at the man's feet. One of the bullets shattered the riot gun's dense plastic stock. The man collapsed from the gas.

Peregrine searched the man, disarmed him, removed over $250 from the man's wallet before returning it, and then securely bound him with his own clothes torn into strips. Then, while the nerve gas wore off, Peregrine dragged off his box to rebury it in another location, amidst the cawing of crows. He returned to find the agent fully recovered.

"Yo. Now, its off to jail," Peregrine prodded the man up with his own gun.

"Sulawesi ain't gonna like this."

"Sulawesi can take care of you once you're locked up." Peregrine indicated they should walk back to the car. "And if you spill anything about me to the cops, your Celebes employers will never get their hands on the riemanium. If any more of you shits come looking for me, they'll be dead. You're the warning, and now I've been warned."

When they returned to the car, Peregrine pushed the man into the passenger's seat. He then wiped off every incidental surface that might have his fingerprints before getting behind the wheel for the drive to downtown San Francisco. He found a parking spot and fed the meter long enough to again wipe down the steering wheel, door handles and the gun before tossing the latter into the car's back seat. He closed the door with his shirt sleeve.

"You won't be alone for long," Peregrine said and walked across the street, to a pay phone. He dialed the police.

"Hello. There's a dangerous criminal locked up in a Plymouth Chrysler, license plate 3NRO843, at the corner of Ellis and Mason. His gun is in the back seat. I think if you check deep enough, you'll find he has Sulawesi connections."

Then he hung up. Things were closing in. First the Ten Most

ARMAGEDDON, CA 94666

Wanted, and now this. He walked to his post office box and found a letter there from his brother. Kenny wrote, in their long-standing code, that he might have a buyer for Peregrine's buried contraband, and to call him during the official time, Thursday afternoon. The thief then took a taxi to Alabaster with the Sulawesi man's money. He talked the landlord into letting him move to another room in the complex, a second story apartment on California. By nightfall, he had moved. He didn't bother to transfer his telephone, as he now intended to be out of town by the fifteenth of the month.

***

Marcus busied himself making breakfast as Gwen burned on the computer keyboard. Their fax had started chiming and printing at 2:30 in the morning. Gwen hit the keyboards by 5, now modeming into New York police and government databases. Not at all legally, he found out.

"Well, you wanted it quickly," Gwen shrugged. Buttermilk pancakes, homemade country sausage, a fruit cup; by the time the meal hit the table, she was running out files on the dot matrix.

"So, what's the news flash," Mark put out the jams and maple syrup, a little nervous about his wife's electronic "breaking and entry."

"That MO is finally coming through for Joe," Gwen's cool eyes sparkled, "And, we're getting a bonus. I ran the MO through Black Talon last evening, and got a list of six names. One of them had a handle that gave me a hunch. A Kenneth James Wisdom, aka Kenny, street name Hawk, first arrested ten years ago, at 30, after a decade long burglary spree in the New York metropolitan area, during which he established his version of the MO. He was only convicted for one job, but that was enough. I sent off for his official police record last night, and that's what we got this morning. Seems he's in prison now, has been for the last two years, presently at the Federal MCC in San Diego. He got politics when he was in prison the first time, so when he got out on parole for good behavior he participated in a string of bank 'expropriations' with Puerto Rican Libre members. That's what he's in for now."

"There goes the Peregrine connection," Mark said, digging into the food heaped on his plate.

"Not so fast," Gwen started in on her stack of pancakes, the printer still humming. "When the info came in this morning, that's when I decided to act on my hunch. The similarity between the two street names: Hawk and Peregrine. I hacked the New York City databases to do a little cross checking and referencing. Coincidentally, the Peregrine handle also first surfaced around the time of Kenny Wisdom's burglaries. And Kenny has a younger brother, Eugene Michael Wisdom, who was 15-16-17 during that period. He was never implicated in any of his brother's jobs. In fact, he doesn't have a record at all as far as I can tell.

END TIME

Eugene's parents sent him off to school at Stanford right after high school. I figure there could be a connection."

"Gwen, you're wonderful," he leaned over the table and kissed her.

Marcus collected his dishes and placed them in the sink which, with the cooking utensils, he filled with soap and hot water and left for Gwen to wash. "I have those meetings this morning in the City."

"Say hello to Neal for me," Gwen said, relishing the last of her breakfast.

Morning in the City meant a break in his door-to-door routine. The detective relished the drive down. The day began sunny but blustery off the bay. The trip was business on top of a mercy mission. In all the work he had done for Neal over the years, the man had never come apart as he had in this case. That Neal's business dealings were not all above board did not please Marcus even while it did not entirely surprise him. He had taken on six cases for Neal when Security Pacific reached dead ends on them, solving all six. Neal had been manic over the theft of two Manet's from a corporate collection being transported from Los Angeles to New York. He had been angry enough to kill about the computer engineered embezzlement of millions from inside Security Pacific. But Marcus had never seen him so scared. The PI had a hard time squaring this with the Marine Corps' buddy he had known. His first stop was not Neal's office however.

"Brian," Marcus leaned in the door of Sampson's office, "We still on for a brief conference?"

"Absolutely," the Captain said and slid the meager police update in thin manila folder over his desk to a chair in front of it. "Want me to ring Joe?"

"He's expecting us," Marcus took a seat as the CHP officer dialed and glanced at the folder.

"Hello," Joe answered promptly, home on his morning off, his presence on the wire completing their conspiratorial circle.

"Hey there, Joey," Brian grinned, "Ready for a little meeting?"

"Fire away."

"Morning Joe," Marcus said, then summarized the Alabaster cop's request on the series of local burglaries before detailing the results of Gwen's finger work.

"Sounds promising," Sampson said, "Christ, its more than that Sumner has come up with. He's got the entire Bay Area Left blanketed with Bureau special agents, and he's come up with zip on this Operation Anvil of his. Everyone's dummying up all around the Bay because of this crackdown, and not just political sources. Edward talks as if he's deliberately putting the lid on a pressure cooker to squeeze out the Solidarity Brigade. He's set up a regular Tuesday sting, starting today, hoping that his pressure will force out whoever's got the riemanium. His strategy has been a bust, far as I can tell."

"Yeah, the Bureau is here in Alabaster, interfering with our work," Joe grumbled.

"Such a waste," Brian muttered, "If Sumner wasn't first cousin to Genghis Khan in the overbearing way he tries to run everything connected with law enforcement on this case, he might get more cooperation. Anyway, Marcus, I think I can help you with this Eugene when he was at Stanford. I'll make a few calls."

"And I'll check the DMV record on this Eugene Wisdom," Joe volunteered, "By the way, a name and address on the license plate you wanted came through. A Lori Anne Turnage."

Marcus quickly wrote down the Alabaster address as Sampson poured himself another cup of coffee.

"I won't be able to get my boss to authorize any kind of stakeout," Joe apologized, "Not with the FBI in town."

"That's all right," Marcus said, thinking fast, "I know someone who can handle that for us."

"Great. By the way, we still on for bridge tomorrow evening?"

"Gwen and I are looking forward to it," Marcus smiled, "Before we close this, I want to make sure the two of you are still interested in backing me up. You both are putting your careers at some risk on this one, what with the FBI's clamp down on any independent police work."

"Hey, I'm still okay with it," Joe shrugged through the phone, "There's just a few more limits on me is all."

"I need it," Brian emphasized. "Working with Sumner breathing down my neck every day has put a lot of pressure on me. You're my escape valve Marcus. I would enjoy nothing more than to see you crack this case."

"Thanks for the support."

Grateful, Marcus was stopped on his way out of Sampson's office by the switchboard operator.

"You the detective?" she asked, not daring to pronounce the name.

"Yes."

"Your wife called. Said your next meeting's been changed. She said you're not supposed to go to Mr. Emerson's office, but to meet him at this address."

She gave him the address written on a message pad piece of paper. He managed to finish the police update on the ride over, the PI taking mental note that Rosanne Casey was no longer a student at SFSU. The windy panorama of white-capped Pacific ended in the Golden Gate's span across to the wild north coast. It was spectacular from the Palace of the Legion of Honor, which now tableaud an assortment of Federal and city police vehicles and officers ranged around the copy of Rodin's *The Thinker*. He found Neal in the lobby, next to a large play board

END TIME

advertising the museum's special Piccoli Gem Exhibition. He severely berated one of his employees as Marcus approached.

"Mark, thank God you got my message," the Security Pacific president brusquely dismissed his underling and slung a handkerchief across his sweaty upper lip.

"I didn't know Security Pacific was handling the exhibition too." The detective pulled out his notebook, more as a shield against Neal's obvious desperation than anything else.

"Only supplementary." Neal folded the cloth into his pocket. "We're doing it for free. It's the least we can do. But these gems are driving me crazy. I'll show you."

Marcus followed Neal, thinking that Security Pacific's "pro bono" work cleverly helped to deflect any possibility of litigation as well. The Palace had taken some pains with the Piccoli exhibit, renting historical wax figures from Toussad's in London and grouping the gaggle of Borgia's, Medici's and other dead Renaissance Italians around security displays of the gems. Only now red paint was splattered across everything, accompanied by spray painted slogans on floors and walls. At least two of the wax mannequins had been beheaded.

"They hit the exhibit right after opening," Emerson glanced about as Marcus deciphered "Eat the Rich, Feed the Poor; Smash the State, End All War" from the graffiti. "And with a roomful of elementary school children on a tour at the time, so Security couldn't do a damn thing. Two hundred screaming kids and a dozen ski masked vandals! They did it quick, knocked out a couple of guards on their way out, and escaped in two vans with masked license plates. Escaped in broad daylight! Figuring out who's liable for the cleanup and restoration is going to be a nightmare. Christ, I wish I'd never heard of these damned Piccoli."

"My news is getting better," Marcus said, "Can we talk someplace."

"By all means." Hope flashed across Neal's face. He temporarily evicted the Museum's security office of its personnel so that the detective could bring him up-to-date.

"I'm so close to this Peregrine, I can smell his sweat," Marcus concluded. "I'll need a stake out. On the girl, Turnage. I can't get the Alabaster police to do it, and I don't have the time. An associate of mine, Randy Schmitts, owes me a couple of favors. He's trustworthy to take on a case like this. If you want, I'll pay his fees."

"I'll pay for it," Neal said immediately. "Glad to hear you're so close."

"How are you holding up?"

"Not too good," the gaunt old man, the corporate president ground worried fingers across his chin. "I'm three steps away from a Senate subcommittee investigation. The FBI has every scrap of Security Pacific paperwork for the last ten years, and the IRS all of mine for the

194

ARMAGEDDON, CA 94666

last twenty. My doctor says I'm getting an ulcer. I haven't slept in two nights."

"Rosanne Casey lost her admission to college," Marcus said, deadpan.

"That nut!" Neal exploded. "You're wrong about her, Mark! She's a straight-jacket case. She mailed me this long, rambling 'apology' which did not make any sense. I turned it over to the police. She's in this thing with Peregrine. Up to her neck!"

"Only because you dragged her there," Marcus said, excusing himself.

He stopped on the drive home at a Sausalito travel agency to collect a half dozen brochures apiece on Europe and the South Pacific. Picked them up for Gwen who, after all, had final word on any vacation.

***

"I want the backup to be flawless on this operation," Edward addressed the unit of men upon which his life depended. "Cisco and I will be at the target table. Sharpshooters, zero in on anyone approaching the table. Then watch for my hand signal. Open hand means false alarm; no contact. Fist means contact, make the grab. Index and middle finger pointing means contact; armed and threatening; blow the fuckers away. You apprehending, I want you in a car by the curb, around the table across from us, and on the sidewalk to either side of the cafe. And, try to be inconspicuous about this. The office has gotten crank calls, threats actually, from folks like the Revolutionary Action Brigades saying you guys stick out like sore thumbs on the job. Threatening to start offing you. I don't want this blown just because you all don't have any fashion sense."

He had presided over releasing the third Bureau wave yesterday. He monitored every report every day, and was pleased that his strategy was on course. Clamp down. Apply the heat. Let their own, in this case the Left, betray its own, and squeeze out the MRSB. He glanced around at the men and women in the conference room.

"And remember, tonight may not be the night. This operation has to proceed flawlessly every Tuesday night, until we crack the Brigade."

Edward felt that he too rode the tiger with Operation Anvil. But he was determined to master the beast by breaking it. He kept Marable run ragged, even as he waited for Washington to appoint him a new San Francisco director. Sumner had temporarily suspended the Bureau's Bay Area covert actions against the white Left; the "dirty tricks," the legal harassment, the break-ins vandalism and assaults, all except the FBI infiltration which he had intensified. It was bad enough that the Leftist disease now infecting the American body politic was purposefully cellular in its organization on its militant fringes, almost impossible to effectively infiltrate let alone influence. Such

195

extremists reveled in their own apparent disarray. He did not need more chaos and confusion while his people searched for the riemanium needle in the anti-war haystack. He had even disbanded the Bureau's street fighting front organization, the Black Star Collective, for the time being.

He had reduced most of his other regional field offices to skeleton crews despite the objections of his local directors, and he had gotten approval on Operation Anvil from the highest authorities to draw agents from other regions. The influx of new faces and the obvious FBI presence all around the Bay Area was already having unintended side effects. He had flushed out several fugitives, anti-war activists who had gone underground to avoid the draft, arrest or grand jury subpoena. The operation collected excellent incidental information on the Left as well, useful once he recovered the riemanium and prepared to lead the Bureau's inevitable crackdown. His office also had numerous anonymous tips about the Mexican Revolution Solidarity Brigade, nearly all of which were turning up as dead ends.

In turn, all of this had saddled him with mountains of paperwork, which had chained him to a desk for the past week. He chafed under the red tape, triplicate documentation, and endless politicking that went with his new position of authority. He was becoming a glorified "desk jockey," something that his basic field agent instincts fought against. Designating himself to head the Tuesday night sting had been necessary to maintain his sanity, not to mention his sense of dignity and accomplishment.

As he dismissed his men so that they might finish prepping for the evening, he thought to call his second wife, the one he could still talk to, and their daughter, inspired by the danger to him on this operation. But he squelched the thought immediately. He had faced life-threatening situations many times before, not just as an agent but as a Marine. Suddenly, for the first time in this case, he felt tired, almost weary. Got to get a good night's sleep soon Edward told himself and shook it off. Can not afford it now though, he thought. Have to keep pushing. Drive up the pressure, the temperature, into the nuclear range. Create a blast furnace that burns away everything to expose his enemies.

***

David and Greg did scope out the streets of San Francisco around the march route, having driven down after Greg's last, long class for the Temptations Cafe meeting.

"Smoke may be too out-of-control," David admitted, "But he does know his hooliganism."

The Temptations Cafe was glass and chrome. The patio fronting the sidewalk was polished tile and exuberant plants in flower boxes. The whole thing was a yuppie wet dream. Indeed, someone had managed to

ARMAGEDDON, CA 94666

scrawl the slogan: "Die Yuppie Scum," in fluorescent pink paint on a part of the brick wall next to the cafe. Reminder of some past demonstration, it had been only partially removed by scrubbing. They were early. They found a table inside, next to a window with a view of the patio.

"Jesus," Greg breathed, looking the menu over, "You could feed a small African village for what they charge for an entree."

"Don't worry, I have some money," David scowled at the prices, "We've got to order something so as not to look conspicuous."

The waiter took their order with an air of disdain; a large chef's salad with blue cheese dressing for Greg, and a half order fettuccine alfredo and a dark German beer for David. It was not that the two were not dressed for the Cafe. It was California after all. The waiter's manner reflected the place's pretensions.

"Drink some of my beer," David said, then glanced up at the racket of a departing table. "Now there's a group that'll be first up against the wall, come the revolution."

A party of four stood to leave, from the Fed rendezvous table. All were young, male and dressed to the GQ European standard of perfection. Three were white and one was Asian. They behaved like junior execs, brokers or law firm partners; with their groomed conformity, bragging, one-upmanship, sense of superiority, need for control, and overt heterosexuality. With some slight changes in skin color and language, this could be a group in Tokyo, Berlin, Singapore, or any of the world's cosmopolitan cities. For even as regional capitalist blocks were consolidating, the top and bottom of the capitalist world were becoming entirely fluid, merging together.

The dressed-for-success young men represented an emerging, truly transnational corporate elite. And the two dark skinned busboys who hustled to clean their table, undoubtedly the dishwashers and probably the cooks as well, were also of the new capitalist world order. One was perhaps central American, another Mexican, still another Filipino or Caribbean, again perhaps half were illegal or recently legal immigrants, and all were representative of an international class of migrant laborers, counterpoint to the suited young sharks. They were the product of a shattered Third World collapsing into Fourth World destitution, war, civil war, famine, disease and desolation, just as the suits were a product of international capitalist affluence and gluttony. It was the visual metaphor of a railing. A number of large posts, the regionally consolidated blocks of capitalist developed and developing nations, rose from a common floor, the international class of "guest workers" and their thoroughly exploited countries. The posts were topped off in turn by a thin banister, the transnational, corporate ruling class and its managerial minions.

197

END TIME

As their waiter brought the food, a young couple tried to sit at the exact same table vacated by the corporate sharks. The waiter strode out to deliver the word that the table was reserved, and the couple politely relocated to a table across the patio entry, only to be informed that that too was taken. Clearly, cafe management was in on the FBI deal. Third time they found a seat, and the two from Alabaster watched, lightly nibbling on their meals to make them last. The cafe filled up, during the time before the appointed meeting.

Virtually every Bay Area heavy rad started showing up, taking a table on the periphery, and ordering only coffee or a light snack, to the annoyance of the cafe's management. The Hooligentsia. Greg had seen most of them at demo's, some even as speakers. Clearly, the word had spread.

Fifteen to the hour a couple of thick, fake tourists occupied the table across from the table in question, without protest. They ordered coffee. Five to the hour, a middle aged white and a younger Hispanic suit plopped down in the target zone, also without protest. They ordered only coffee.

"Don't much like the back up," David smiled, and dug into the remainder of his fettuccine.

"Yah," Greg gulped some beer, "This whole thing's beginning to stink."

They waited on the clock, diddling over the food. Quite unexpectedly, Jason pushed into the Cafe, streaking wild color and hair across yuppie ambiance. David's jaw dropped.

"Yo, David," Jason jumped into a seat at their table, then lowered his voice dramatically, "Hope the Solidarity Brigade doesn't show tonight. There's a carload of FBI agents two steps up the street. Same one's approached me in Berkeley. Looks like a set up."

"That's it," Greg announced, and David gave him a warning glance. Jason never noticed as he saw a half dozen other familiar faces.

"Gotta go," Jason planted a hand on David's shoulder.

As Jason left, another man approached the men seated at the Fed contact table. Clearly, he was a street person, perhaps homeless. His brown, greasy hair was shoulder length and scraggly. He wore stained army pants over frayed converse. Dirt streaked his simple white and brown Mexican poncho, which covered god knows what. He took a double take at the Feds' low lidded glance, stopped on the sidewalk in puzzled contemplation, and then approached the patio's plant overgrown railing.

"Got a smoke," Greg saw the bum form the words, at the same time he reached for something under the poncho. The Hispanic Fed dove for the tiles. The middle-aged Fed gestured, two fingers, pointing. Firecracker noise. The bum exploded. Blood and brains spattered over

198

the patio, in particular all over the still seated Fed. Over the screaming couple on the patio. One bullet smacked off a table top and ricocheted. Passed right through the bum. It hit the window in front of David and Greg with not quite enough force to cut cleanly through. Instead, the window broke and cascaded straight down, in a violence of sound.

An entire cafe full of people rushed out and bowled over the Feds trying to reach their blood splattered fellow, David and Greg among the first out. They drove back to Alabaster spooked, barely exchanging a dozen words. The fact that the government had just murdered someone remotely suspected of connection with the riemanium overwhelmed Greg. Not a word of it on the radio. Much later, David, Beth, Larry and Greg seated at the campus pub downing beer in horror over what had happened, the two Alabaster eye witnesses retold the story over and again, still no word about it on TV news. They heard via the MDRG grapevine that the man shot down had been a wino named Wally. He had been reaching for was his flask of muscatel. The State would kill, and pretty indiscriminately, to get back that riemanium.

***

Peregrine hit the Zapata Cafe, fully recovered from the day's traumatic events. Focused and determined, he found the cooperative restaurant almost too easy to crack. No challenge at all. All the coops were easy money. Peregrine pocketed the cafe's $325. The campus coops didn't have to survive in the real world, the outside capitalist world, he told himself with disdain. They were student projects, volunteer hobbies taking advantage of the university's largess and the pipe-dreams of mostly white, middle class college kids. He'd take the easy money until it was time to sell his cache and disappear. He knocked off Conspiracy of Equals a second time for $527 for good measure, after he left the cafe.

TWENTY-NINE

Isabella Allegro, CT purist, FAO militant, and leader of the Allegro Column of people's militias, concerned herself most with the state of abject illiteracy in the towns and villages she protected. When she went to see how a cooperative, collective or commune was doing, they often did not understand what she meant when she asked if they were keeping accounts or following the instructions on seed, fertilizer or other products used for farming. They told her that if they needed something for the village, they got hold of a truck, frequently one lent them by the Allegro Column, and made an exchange with another village. What they knew about the use of various agricultural products they learned by word-of-mouth.

She herself, the daughter of a landless day-labor family in the small village of Zepete, close to her column's current headquarters at Tuxtla Gutierrez, had stayed illiterate until her early twenties. Isabella began earning income at six for her impoverished family of nine brothers and sisters. She looked for snails, edible mushrooms, herbs, wild fruits and vegetables and whatever else she could find. Because of her stocky build, she was in the fields, reaping with a sickle and other traditional means at eleven, graduating to the no less arduous work of the thrashing house soon thereafter. She left her village at eighteen and, reaching Guadalajara, she became a building laborer, one of the few women in the male dominated trade.

Isabella joined the libertarian Union de Trabajadores de Mexicano, attended union meetings, spoke eloquently from the floor, but disappeared when there was mention of her being elected to a union post. Marti, then of the UTM, later secretary of the Liberty Party, and Isabella's lover until he was killed in the bombing of Oaxaca, first realized the reason for her reluctance and suggested that her fellow workers, union members all, read her the paper daily, using its headlines eventually to teach her to read.

As a consequence, although she read up on Anarchism once she had the skill, her own anarchist development had been entirely visceral, in large part the product of her being a woman worker in a man's labor movement. Isabella's militancy lead her into the FAO, but not into the *atentados* practiced by many of the *groupos de afinidad*. She advocated the organic creation of peoples militias out of an armed people. Elected to the secretariat of the CT in time for the failed 1999 General Strike, she did not believe that a liberated society could be had solely through economic actions. Her emphasis on class self-defense and her exemplary organization of the 2000 insurrection on the Isthmus gained her election to leadership of the regional column of peoples militias after the August Uprisings. Grateful for San Cristobal's aid, she nevertheless maintained that the Mexican people alone would win their own liberation. She had often been accused of autarchic tendencies.

She developed the poled house, raised field and drainage trench strategy to deal with gas attacks and caterpillar defoliants. She defended the Liberated Territories in the famous Arista assault, when combined elements of the US and Mexican Marines were turned back into the Gulf of Tehuantepec by the Allegro, Mancado and Tupac Columns in eight days of the revolution's bloodiest hand-to-hand battles. Everyone recognized Isabella's tactical and strategic brilliance. Those closer to her understood that, while she was probably the greatest general of popular liberation forces since Giap, she loathed war. In turn, Isabella took the greatest pride in her grassroots system of schooling.

Isabella selected twenty-four militia members all competent to teach literacy and each knowledgeable in another field. She devised a standard curriculum around standard materials for her literacy campaign.

ARMAGEDDON, CA 94666

Then she divided up her region into six circuits, with four militia teachers traveling from village to village on a weekly route. Monday-Tuesday and Thursday-Friday were school days. The circuit riding teachers followed the notes of their predecessors in teaching the villagers to read, then presented a class or two in their own specialties. Classes were held in one of the villager's houses for most of the children and the fewer, motivated adults. The whole village fed and sheltered the circuit teachers. Not only were the villagers developing basic literacy, but the Allegro Column had a constant, consistent source of information on the countryside; how the harvest was going, what problems there were, what damage the air war was doing, whether contra forces were operating, and the like.

Isabella Allegro had no count of the times the Yanquis and their Mexicano puppets had tried to assassinate her.

THIRTY

Greg gathered with the rest of the affinity group, as well as hundreds of others, in the Zapata Cafe parking lot for car pools to Berkeley the morning of the General Strike. He walked in a daze among his friends, barely responding when Larry pulled up, honking his horn, in his VW. Mitch had taken unofficial charge of the large ASP contingent not interested in autonomous action, while folks turned to Smoke in the small action faction become autonomous ASP affinity. Greg had dressed for the part, all in black, as had Larry, David, Beth and the others in the affinity. Lori made an appearance to give Greg a roll of papers and a kiss, the papers xeroxes on how to build your own A-bomb.

"This should do the trick," Lori said, then tilted her head to give him a sidelong look. "So, what does Peregrine think about the idea of doing another communiqué based on these plans?"

"Haven't talked to him," Greg sidestepped her probe. "He pretty much gave us a 'blank check' for what we want to do."

She rejoined Mary and two other girls, wandering off into the crowd as he stowed the xeroxes hurriedly in his parked car. Larry's microbus carried six comfortably, and the ride was laced with anticipation. Greg had not slept well the night before, what with visions of murder still fresh in his mind. He managed to doze some on the way down between second thoughts. Greg was not a pacifist per se, viewing non-violence more as a tactic then as a way of life. His opposition to the US war in Mexico had as much to do with the fact that his country, a mere 4% of the world's population, consumed close to 20% of the world's energy and 40% of its resources to keep a life style of mindless consumerism in high gear. US military intervention he saw as an attempt to keep southern Mexico within a viable North American Trade Zone so that domestic economic prosperity might be maintained. Still, he was skeptical about joining in on the Hooligan actions. Could street fighting and vandalism alone halt the war? He doubted it. Thousands, tens of thousands had gathered at Sproul Plaza at the UC, milling about, waiting for the march to start. A speaker, a long winded elderly Berkeley professor named Allen Meltzer affiliated with the new Frankfurt Circle, droned on endlessly. Undisturbed by large crowds, pigeons foraged among the demonstrators. Greg, Larry and the rest of the affinity group formed up momentarily with the rest of ASP. The school contingent went its own way as the affinity, along with the MDRG, joined up with a confident black clothed column. Smoke, in toque and kaffiyeh, knew quite a few individuals in the Hooligan zone and disappeared for a time to shake hands. Occasional clouds slipped across the brilliant sky.

"For now, we'll be keeping to the middle of the march," Smoke said as he returned to the assembled ASP and MDRG groupings, "The Alameda County sheriffs are itching to bust some of the Hooligans."

Another speaker briefly set matters in motion, gathered the people, and started the march. By the time Greg and his companions were all the way down Telegraph, the crowd had swollen to a hundred thousand.

"No War, No Way! No Fascist USA!"

"1, 2, 3, 4...We Don't Want Your Fucking War!"

"Stop The Genocide! Stop The Air War!"

"5, 6, 7, 8...Organize And Smash The State!"

By the time they reached the highway they were over a quarter million strong, well deserving of the police escort that shut down two lanes. When the much rowdier Oakland crowd joined up, they approached a half million.

"El Pueblo, Unido, Jamas Sera Vencido!"

"1, 2, 3, 4...We Don't Want Your Racist War!"

"Malcolm X, ML King! Justice, Not War, Is The Thing!"

"5, 6, 7, 8...We Don't Want Your Fascist State!"

The Hooligans cut loose once the march hit the Bay Bridge, figuring there was little chance of getting arrested. Red paint splashed to drip like blood from the girders. Slogans and symbols were spray painted everywhere; Revolution Now!; Circle A; BdN; HardCore Against War; Omega A; Destroy What Destroys You!; Destroy Power, Not People!; Circle E, Squatters and Feminist symbols. Autonomists and anarchists glued a large banner reading: End The War! Abolish Capitalism! Smash The State! REVOLUTION NOW! to the northern side of the bridge's steel girders. When they reached Yerba Buena Island Greg could look back and see how vast their numbers actually were. Had the Israelites looked like this coming out of Egypt? Were the slave armies of Spartacus as exuberant? Had the Crusades inspired such awe? Had

ARMAGEDDON, CA 94666

the Chinese PLA on the Long March looked as formidable?

"Ya know?" Larry mused, "if we all lined up, four abreast, and marched in step, we could shake this bridge apart."

"Now there's the power of the people," David said, triumphant.

"No," Smoke laughed, "There's the power of organization."

"Yah," Greg said, "I heard that if you could get all the cats in the world together, four abreast, to walk in step, they could do the same thing."

They could see the San Francisco crowd as they approached, and if anything, it was bigger, filling the Embarcadero and stretching all the way up Market. In their midst stood a large black column as well. Gulls wheeled quizzically as the two marches merged in round after round of cheers and chants.

"The People, United, Will Never Be Defeated!"

"Justice Yes, War No! US Out Of Mexico!"

"Un Pueblo, Sin Fronteras!"

The integrated Hooligans now pushed their own chants.

"What Do We Want? Revolution! When Do We Want It? Now!"

"Squat, Don't Rent! Overthrow The Government!"

"Smash The Patriarchy, Smash The State! The Future Is Ours, And It's Gonna Be Great!"

"Class War! Not Imperialist War!"

There had to be over a million people, easy, on the streets. The Hooligans numbered at least 50,000. Media helicopters vied for airspace with police choppers. Soft galleon clouds played background to the jockeying swarm. The assembled forces of law-and-order looked puny compared to the assembled multitude.

"Yo," Smoke waved to the combined ASP/MDRG affinity, "Come on. Troubles brewing already."

He lead them through the crowd and, along with a surge of other black clad Hooligans and fellow travelers, they poured up some side street to Union Square. There, a confrontation was in the making. About four or five thousand American Front skins and fascist Nulls had assembled in a pro-war counter-demonstration in and around Union Square's hedge manicured walkways. Nulls shaved their heads and bodies entirely, wore uni-style gray coveralls, and went in for plating; metal plates on the skull, arms or ribs drilled and secured right into the bone. They had taken industrial/noise music to the depths of metal crossover and Nazism, using the Emo-Sound technologies as a bludgeon to hammer every Null concert into a miniature Nurnberg rally. Some twenty thousand Hooligans quickly took Powell and Geary to push against a thin police line, screaming against the provocations of Nazi skin and Null sieg heils.

Inevitably, a bottle was tossed, and for long minutes a barrage of

203

glass and bricks flew both ways across the police, who were helpless in the middle. Then the police line broke and the Hooligans rushed the fascists. Batons appeared from sleeves and heads, plated or hairless, got cracked. Steel-toed docs and brass knuckled fists did their job, and the fascists scattered for their lives. Greg and Larry were not on the front lines, but they were close enough to feel the rush of confrontational adrenaline peak through exhilaration when the skins and Nulls broke to flee. Not to be cut off, the black clad Hooligans halted their pursuit and instead, returned to the march's main body now on the move, chanting their victory:

"No War! No KKK! No Fascist USA!"

The march security did not look at all pleased. But, they could do nothing.

"We're gradually going to filter back to the back of the march," Smoke passed the word to the affinity members as Market moved past around curb-to-curb people," We'll split off before the park."

The two marches finally consolidated, the behemoth anti-war protest edged up to Van Ness. So massive was the crowd that the police made spot decisions to let them have not just Van Ness but Franklin as well, and not just Fell when that proved a bottleneck, but also Oak, Page and Grove to get the marchers to the Panhandle as quickly as possible. In the middle of the dawdling, black-as-night/thick-as-fog throngs, Greg watched a line of several thousand Killer Klowns conga through the march and laughed.

Contingents abounded; Labor Unionists Opposed To U.S. Intervention, Gays and Lesbians Against the War, Parents For Peace, Interfaith Communities for Negotiation, Professionals for Social Responsibility, Youth Against Imperialism, and others sported their own signs and banners among vast crowds of the unaffiliated. The chants throughout the march reflected the liberal/socialist/autonomist divisions of the participants, often cutting across such contingents. "What Do We Want? Peace! When Do We Want It? Now!" and "Peace Now!" rang out from liberal quarters, edging into "Jobs and Justice, Yes! War, No! US Out Of Southern Mexico!" from socialist ranks, who also preferred "The People United Will Never Be Defeated!" in English and Spanish. And the Hooligans were suitably offensive. "Disobey Orders! Tear Down All Borders!" and "Fuck The War, Smash The State! Capitalism Is What We Really Hate!" Sometimes the entire crowd began a chant, only to split it up in the middle.

"1, 2, 3, 4...We Don't Want Your Bloody/Imperialist/ Fucking War!"

"5, 6, 7, 8...We Don't Want Your Warfare State/ Imperialist State/Organize And Smash The State!"

The streets' buildings walled up and reverberated the chants to the maximum possible distortion. People stood at windows and on rooftops, many waving hands, peace signs and fists. Ahead of Greg a couple of fellow-traveling young poseur Raspies walked with the Hooligan gangs, their boutique capes draped in cold cuts instead of raw chunks of bloody meat. He caught the glint of a Spook's brainstim socket, and the droll little computer perched on her shoulder with feeds into the socket. A Ferrel swarm carried a wildly colored banner that proclaimed:

"Midnight Winds Are Lending At The End Of Time."

The storm black Hooligans took Van Ness, but never made the jog off to the park. Instead, they massed, some one hundred thousand strong, up to the hastily formed police blockade on Van Ness and Grove, then east back around on Market. They stopped in fact. March peace monitors, realizing what was happening, evaporated from around the autonomous columns to beat hasty retreats up Grove, Fell, Oak and Page with the march's stragglers. People pulled on masks, bandanas, ski masks and balaklavas. Sunglasses hid eyes. Adrenaline once more raced through Greg, somewhere in the middle of that black mass, as he pulled up his own 'kerchief. He watched a gauntly beautiful girl, a rare, anti-war Null, pull her large black scarf over her gold electroplated cheek plates before putting on his shades in synch with hers. Several mobile PA's deep in the crowd broadcast a similar message.

"We won't end the war in Mexico with peaceful marches escorted by the cops. We won't end the war with peaceful law-abiding rallies in the park, no matter how many of us there are. We won't end the war until we stop the war machine no matter what it takes. By whatever means necessary. Our first step is to stop this city and every city across the country, by seizing the streets. Liberating the streets with our bodies. The streets belong to the people. We are the people..."

The autonomous columns partly ringed the downtown civic center so that the few police reinforcements not engaged with the march had to be spread thin. Greg could only see clearly the action at Grove and Van Ness from where he stood in the midnight crowds. During the announcement, several squads of riot cops hustled into place through cop cars and riot vans to further brace the metal police barricades blocking off Van Ness north and Grove east. They were followed by a neurolaser bank on wheels. The front line of masked Hooligans pulled out their batons in response and held them, hand over hand, to form a counter line, with perhaps two yards between the two formations.

"This crowd is declared an illegal assembly," the police officer announced, his voice echoing across the police line as a battery of neurolasers on Van Ness whined up on poles between two of the riot vans, "You are ordered to disperse. If you do not clear the streets in fifteen minutes, you will be arrested.

"Kill Cops, Fight In The Streets, Smash Anything That Looks Elite!"

the crowd roared in response. A bottle was thrown. For the next ten minutes, a rain of bottles, bricks, metal junk, and garbage pelted the cops, who kept their shields up in defense formation. The bank of neurolasers then flared into action.

Bolts of wire thin, intense cobalt blue light machine gunned into the crowd. Most were absorbed into the blackness of clothing or harmlessly into flesh. Many more were deflected off mirrored sunglasses. but occasionally, a lucky bolt shaved sideways behind the protective shades or hit a person not wearing glasses at all. The victims collapsed into violent seizures, convulsions that were known to last twenty minutes and occasionally resulted in death. Designated affinity medics quickly carried the spasming individuals to the sidelines. And, the inky sea of Hooligans opened for theater.

"Smash The Patriarchy, Smash The State! Capitalism Is What We Really Hate!"

Five bizarre figures stepped into the hail of needled, scintillating neurobolts. Mirror dancers. Each dressed in long multicolored robes and turbans, tiny mirrors sewn into every inch of their clothing, and their mime white faces covered by large mirrored glasses. These apparitions boogied and dervished in the neurobolt rain. The crowd control device tried to adjust back to the mob, but each time it did, the mirror dancers moved to intercept the laser light. Neurobolts shuddered off in all directions, most back onto the line of cops, but many spitting up into the air and angling off everywhere.

The barrage of rocks and glass started again, aimed at the neurolaser battery. With marbles and ball bearings from slingshots, the assault did damage before two errant bolts hit their marks; one a police sergeant behind the lines and the other a plainclothes cop on the roof of the modern, rounded, glass and concrete Performing Arts Center. The cop on the roof collapsed into convulsions and before his fellows could grab him, he jerked off the top of the building and fell into the crowd. A cheer rang up and out. The cops shut down the neurolasers.

"Class War! Not Imperialist War!"

"This is an illegal assembly! Disperse immediately! If you do not disperse, you will..."

A piece of paving connected with the helmeted head of the cop giving the warning, and dropped him.

"What do we want? Dead Cops! When do we want them? Now!"

The riot police did not wait. The back line on Van Ness and Grove dropped to one knee and hefted riot guns under shield protection to launch volley after volley of tear gas canisters arching into the crowd. With remarkable agility, autonomous clusters moved to open up space or to snap up the sputtering canisters before they hit pavement and

ARMAGEDDON, CA 94666

broke into hundreds of spraying pieces, to throw the intact canisters back at the cops. Jackets were also used as impromptu trampolines to return the police volley. Still other clusters turned onto the parked cars immersed in the mass; smashing them up, turning them over, heaving them into a counter barricade well behind the Hooligan front line, and setting them ablaze. Soon, thick white clouds of tear gas and sharp black, oily clouds of burning cars veiled the sun. Howling anarchists and autonomists careened and police back lines maneuvered through this thick air.

"Revolution Now!"

Three lines of closely packed cops on Grove began to advance against the still extant Hooligan line, shields up against the crowd's fuselage, truncheons swinging. The autonomist line started to fall back, then pivoted, holding one corner while the other corner swung into retreat. The cop formation fell for it, followed, pivoted out in response without thinking... Instantly hundreds of people made the end run. They poured around the police lines to surround them, but not attack them. Other Hooligans held the police lines on Van Ness at bay. As numerous baton holding Hooligans menacingly ringed the Grove Street cops, thousands stormed into the civic center; around the neurolaser battery, over empty cop cars, around empty riot vans, and just behind other cops in flight.

Greg and Larry had kept close to the MDRG and Smoke as the riot began. They moved as Smoke directed to clear space from around the mirror dancers, and then the people intercepting tear gas canisters, surging with the crowd as if on the edge of the Pit at some retro hard-core show, with the rest of the ASP affinity in tow. When the MDRG bolted for the end run, Greg and Larry were sheared off from the rest of the affinity. Greg glanced back to see David, Beth and the others too far behind. THRUSH had already seized the front of the Health Department. The rest of the crowd, along with other Hooligans from different breech points, sprayed out across the plaza, congealed into streams heading across Polk Street, then over concrete walkways and grass islands of trees for the State and Federal Buildings. Smoke and the MDRG's route was much shorter; up to the gilded, Roman style city hall complete with ornate, coppery green dome, to join the crowd gathering as civil servants hastily shut and locked three sets of elaborately ornamented double doors. Glass doors. Hooligans quickly shattered them, forcing those inside to retreat behind two guards, their guns drawn. Suddenly, something cold was slipped into Greg's hand.

"What the..." Greg said, and looked down to see Smoke lighting the molotov in his grasp.

"Throw it!" Smoke yelled and Greg did. The flaming bottle arched beautifully, right through the broken front door, where it blossomed into burning autumn leaf brilliance. Several more gasoline bombs followed and the building's fire alarm sounded, accompanied by its sprinklers feebly trying to douse the flames. Additional gas bombs kept the fire hot until it caught despite the sprinklers, and the building's lobby wrinkled up in fire. In that shimmering spectacle, all that Greg could see was a vision of himself heaving a molotov cocktail through the city hall doors, into the faces of police guards who could have shot him dead. But didn't.

"Come on," Smoke gestured, "Let's keep moving."

Sooty smoke billowed and roiled across the wide plaza. Autonomous shadows sprinted about in the low, dirty clouds, brandishing batons and fiery torches. An autonomous skateboard wing screamed past them, weaving in and out of the rolling smoke, the dark figures riding them on a skate-and-destroy mission. Other clusters did a fine job smashing up the other buildings, so the MDRG plus Greg and Larry decided to find the streets. Greg thought he saw, vaguely, a throng laboriously pushing something large and wheeled through the charnel haze. It must have been his imagination that he saw them wearing robes and pushing forward a large wooden wagon supporting a many-handed idol streaming incense, just before the acrid smoke closed in around them. Apparently the black columns along the civic center's southeast side, instead of storming that, had opted to rampage up, down and away from Market as those on Van Ness broke through. As a consequence, most of the cops had had to follow. They easily busted through the remaining few, quite scared police on the south east side, running past the mounted statue of Simon Bolivar and through the burning UN plaza, to join the riot in progress.

Virulent black smoke drifted in streamers from the surrounding streets, accompanied by the sound of breaking glass. Glass, burning trash, flaming trash cans and dumpsters, overturned and gutted cars, and fragments of bricks, stones, cans and bottles littered the street all about them as they ran. In a fury, Larry picked up a burning trash can, and with help from Eric, put it right through the front window of a so far untouched clothing boutique. Eric grinned and pulled open his long black coat to reveal three fully loaded molotovs strapped to the inside of his coat flaps, the soaked rag fuses wrapped in baggies held by rubber bands. Larry gleefully grabbed one and snapped off the baggie. Eric lit it with a flick of his lighter, and Greg's friend hurled it into the shop. Images of the molotov leaving his own hand weighted Greg's mind, as did the guards' guns still pointed at the ceiling. As did the wino's murder the night before. The molotov's explosion slapped the air. Dark figures moved in and out of the wreathing curtains of choking smoke in every direction. Bright flames danced.

They trashed a Mercedes dealership, shattering the plate glass windows through the bars. Then Smoke, Jim and Darrel used their sling-shots to take out as many windshields as possible. Up the street aways, a fancy tobacconist had closed his doors, but had remained to wait out the riot's storm. Their rocks through his window were met with a shotgun blast that scattered them, but hurt no one. Smoke regrouped them half a block away. Not content with letting it go, he found a full plastic trash can in a back alley. He doused it with one of Eric's molotovs, lit it and then dared a run by, tossing the flaring can through the broken window, all over the expensive, cancerous herbs the shopkeeper desperately tried to salvage.

As they approached an intersection of two wide, smoke throttled boulevards, a mass of perhaps two hundred Killer Klowns languidly drove by, crossing their path on circus bikes; unicycles, brightly colored bicycles, and wildly bannered and flagged tandem cycles. Some of the Klowns honked their wacky horns and waved while others stood up from their seats to rapid fire their slingshots through the surrounding car and storefront windows. The MDRG plus Greg and Larry were in the middle of doing damage to the posh facade of a wisely empty jewelry shop when a squad of six cops in full riot gear spun around a corner at the end of the block. Catching their hooliganism, the cops charged.

"Split up!" Smoke yelled as they all bolted in the same direction. But when it was clear that Greg and Larry would be left behind, Smoke made an instant decision.

"Go on," Smoke turned to his fellow gang members, "You can handle things. I'll stay with the tenderfoots."

They ran then, the cops having decided they were the easier quarry. Down streets, cutting alleys, jumping fences, running backyards, dodging traffic and removing all of their incriminating evidence in the process. Once in the cool isolation of an enclosed apartment complex courtyard, Greg's adrenaline finally gave out, as did his legs. Only then did he realize that he had been scorching on adrenaline since he had donned his bandana, how many hours ago?

"I...I gotta rest," Greg gasped, and kneeled to lower his head.

"So do I," Larry croaked, leaning up against a wall, panting noisily.

"I guess we're far enough away now," Smoke said, glancing about. He didn't have his glasses on, and it was the first time Greg had seen his eyes. They looked small and faded, compared to the wide mirrored lenses he was used to. "Wanna go back to the riot?"

"Naw," Larry wheezed, "That's enough for me today."

Greg nodded in agreement and brushed his hair back. Smoke looked disappointed.

"There's a squat not too far from here," Smoke said, "I'll take you there so you'll be safe. I wanna try and catch up with my crew."

They agreed, and started to saunter up toward North Beach, as if they hadn't just stepped out of the fiery furnace, their hair and clothes still smelling of its fury. They avoided police patrols whenever possible. Those they had to pass paid them no mind. The squat, a run down three story Victorian, was locked down, the windows shuttered and the front door barred.

"Who is it?" a gruff voice asked to Smoke's insistent knock.

"Smoke," he said, "I know Captain Chaos, BdN."

The door flung open, and a wild-eyed man gestured emphatically for them to enter before slamming locked the door again.

"Jesus, what the hell you doing approaching this place?," the man, bearded and balding, bore a strong resemblance to Charles Manson, "Haven't you heard?"

"No," Smoke smiled, "We been kinda outta touch the last couple of hours."

"Someone drove eight motorcycles right down into the BART Station," the man said, spittle flecking a corner of his mouth, "Embarcadero Station. Four right onto the BART tracks and four down to the Muni. Armed group first knocked out the turnstiles, but some fancy riding anyway."

"Fuck," Larry whistled.

""Not only that, but Hooligans shut down both the Golden Gate and Oakland Bay bridges."

"How?" Greg asked, astonished.

"Drove a line of cars, junkers, onto each bridge both ways. Stopped right in the middle of the bridges, chained them together, and lit them on fire. They were chock full of thermite or magnesium! So were those cycles. They're still burning."

As the squatter spoke and gestured, Smoke smirked.

"You mean, the city's shut down?" Greg asked, "Nobody can get in or out?"

"South's still open," the man shrugged.

"Did they get away?" Smoke asked.

"Clean."

"How goes the street fighting?" Smoke continued.

"Still going strong. Pigs are getting the upper hand in some areas. The rumor is, once they settle with the Hooligans, they're gonna clear out the squats."

It was then that they noticed the others in the shadows around them. People stood pensively next to piles of bricks, boxes of pre-made molotovs, sections of pipe, fiberglass sheets broken into shield sized pieces, wooden boards and baseball bats, a whole assortment of crude weapons.

"We're ready to fight for this squat," the man grinned, missing a few teeth, "Wanna join us?"

210

ARMAGEDDON, CA 94666

"Can't," Smoke frowned, "Basically, these two never been in a riot before today. I gotta get them to safety. Then I've got to track down my crew."

"Understood," the squatter nodded.

Once again on the street, they meandered toward Russian Hill. Smoke smudged the southern skyline.

"I know another safe house," Smoke mused, "If it's not too crowded I'll put you up there."

Smoke guided them first down the narrow alley between two high rises, and then through a handleless metal door in the wall to one of the buildings, opened only by Smoke's key in the deadbolt. They descended from a platform, Smoke in the lead, down stairs to a dimly lit door frame.

"This isn't going to work," Smoke said, as the two reached the floor next to their guide. The door opened into a modest basement, a very full room. Autonomists and anarchists assembled their paraphernalia for use, hiding or disposal. A few Klowns removed their makeup and rearranged their clothes. Their low talk and occasional laughter did not break when the newcomers stepped up to the threshold.

"It's real tight," one of the Hooligans shrugged, "But if you're in need..."

"Got a couple more options," Smoke grinned and waved at the crowd. Once back on the street, he headed them back to North Beach via Chinatown, the southern horizon still darkly plumed. The day failed. "I've got another place I'm sure is open."

As they turned down on Columbus, a woman approached them climbing the hill. She was older, pretty, but a touch frumpy, and definitely preoccupied. She looked up at the trio, and suddenly, absolutely stopped.

"Mike," she smiled, "That's you, isn't it?"

She looked directly at Smoke, into his eyes. He stopped also, and something passed across his face. Recognition, mixed with panic.

"Sorry," he said, tentative.

"Michael Baumann," she said, so sure, "You know who I am. Rosanne. I'm Rosanne Casey."

She smiled broadly. Radiated. Smoke scowled blackly.

"Don't believe we've met," Smoke mumbled.

"Mike!" she chided, "It's me, Rosy. Where have you been?! Why haven't you called me?!"

"Get ready to dash," Smoke whispered to Greg and Larry. He was pale.

"What's that?" The woman, Rosanne, seemed confused. "Mike, why did you leave? I lost my job. I lost my scholarship. I had to drop out of school. I'm working full time as a waitress now..."

"Run!" Smoke hissed, plaintively.

They did.

"Mike, don't leave me again. Please, don't..."

Panting and haunted, Smoke halted them several blocks and corners away.

"What the hell was that all about?" Larry hyperventilated.

"Entrapment," Smoke breathed, just as heavily, "Police, I think."

It was not convincing.

"We're close to the safe house," Smoke sidestepped.

Actually, it was a safe roof, on top of an apartment complex. Smoke smiled to find that no one else was there as night descended. Plywood, chicken wire and fiberglass shelters occupied two sides of the roof. A neat warren of rabbit hutches occupied one and two decks of pigeon cages the other, but both shelters had been built larger than their husbandry warranted. Smoke produced another key, this for a large locked box bolted firmly but unobtrusively in one of the rabbit shelter's unoccupied corners. He opened it to reveal bundled sleeping bags, blankets, clothes and a food cache.

"Help yourself," Smoke offered, "This is where we'll spend the night. I'm going back out to find the MDRG. I'll be back later."

The two dug into some vegetarian luncheon pate and crackers after Smoke left. A symbol marked the underside of the box's lid.

"Jesus, I'm hungry," Larry said between bites, "We were all over today. Damn, what a riot."

"Yah," Greg said, uncomfortable with his growing awareness. No one said enlightenment was necessarily joyful. "Kind of scary also, if you ask me."

"How's that," Larry munched, "Exhilarating I can see. But scary?"

"We could have been dead ringers for Hitler's SS and SA on Krystalnacht, smashing things up. Terrorizing people."

"Come on, there's no resemblance. We were fighting the powers-that-be. Fighting the cops. The cops weren't standing around watching us attack synagogues and Jews, like they did in Nazi Germany."

"Okay, so our target was different," Greg said, "But our methods were the same."

"Hold on. Hitler's boys weren't organized into affinity groups. There were no anarcho-nazis doing Krystalnacht."

"My ancestry is part Polish Larry. The Poles sure didn't need a

Hitler or an SS to lead them into committing Jewish pogroms. Lots of times it was the community that did it. Friends and neighbors getting together and going out to stomp some Jews. Certainly our level of violence was similar."

"Anger is a legitimate emotion," Larry pointed out, "So is outrage."

"Come off it. There was a whole lot of romanticizing violence in that riot today. People got off on wrecking shit, not because they were so goddamned angry or outraged by the war. They were glorifying destruction. And what about Smoke and the MDRG. Man, they're pros. Not much gut anger there. Just a whole lot of professional street fighting is what I saw."

And so their discussion continued, going about in circles, until the day's exertions, plus some food in their stomachs, caught up with them. They unrolled two of the sleeping bags and Larry was soon fast asleep. Greg had a little harder time finding solace in slumber as his mind wandered over heady images of the day's actions. He stood, wrapped in his sleeping bag, and walked out of the shelter into the middle of the roof. The city climbed up into hills and rolled down into the bay. The sweep of city lights faded what stars managed an appearance between shifting clouds. To the north he saw the Golden Gate connect up with Marin, a bright white flare winking halfway along its span. There, on the side of Mount Tamalpais's dark mass, rested a Nagasaki nightmare. Waiting for him. The Pleiades Platform stood visible even above downtown's nearby skyscrapers to the south, its blue and gold lights leaking through dirty streaks and layers of smoke.

Greg was not accustomed to staring the death's head straight in the sockets. The wino's murder by the Fed's last night, and the guards who had spared him as he hurled a gasoline bomb at them today were hard things not to think about. Azrael breathed down his neck. Other connections became clear as well, the most obvious being the potential for mass murder he had buried in his meadow, the bomb's plans even now residing in his car in Alabaster. Much more subtly, it waited for him in Janet. In the death of their relationship.

He had spent the past several days trying to maintain the notion that Janet had applied to Wellesley on junior transfer on a plan to dump him. He had wanted to blame her, not only for disloyalty, infidelity and betrayal, but also for premeditation. Sometimes he had imagined that her duplicity had gone on longer than her move to Boston, that she had been scheming to crash and burn their relationship for some time. He had even gone as far as to try and convince himself, in a warped logic, that a plan need not be conscious to remain a plan. He had needed to condemn her totally.

At the same time he had dosed up on lots of intended anesthetic; in Margaret and Lori with sex, and in all too conventional drug use.

END TIME

Those, along with all the political activism, were dropping him further and further behind in school and were not helping him to resolve anything about Janet. Every time he thought of her, the same visceral anger and hurt boiled up, raw as the day he read her letter. He was not getting anywhere. He was stalemated, and the stalemate devoured him. He felt the beginnings of an ulcer brewing, his stomach churning. He needed to break the stalemate. But to do so he needed to admit to some uncomfortable truths. And tonight was the night to do so.

His depth of reaction to Janet's leaving, the blackness of his betrayal, resonated with the sense of betrayal he had felt when his mother left. He had felt abandoned then, and he felt abandoned now. He felt overwhelmed and helpless, then and now. Greg was used to doing what needed to be done; in school, on his lathe, in his life, and doing it pretty well. He clenched at not being able to do anything, either to get his mother back into a happy family, or to recover Janet for a happy couple. He had no control over such things.

Consequently, he felt guilty that he had caused both women to leave. Had responsibility for his childhood been so great a burden on his mother and her aspirations for an independent life that she had needed to leave? Had his possessiveness so suffocated Janet that he had literally driven her out of his life? His own jealous, zealous possessiveness; that he needed to admit. He had bound Janet into their relationship so tight that perhaps she had not had the room to breath.

Funny, how he had tried to do things 180 degrees differently from his father and wound up in the exact same place. Greg could not escape his own history. And, like history, he could not relive it differently. To say "If I'd only done it differently" meant nothing. He could only go one time around. No repeats, no second chances. Had he been less possessive she might not have left. Or, she might have left sooner.

He could not even learn from his mistakes, not in any conventional sense, even as history did not give "lessons." Every person, every relationship, every situation was unique; history after all being a chronicling of the unique. He thought he had been applying lessons from his parent's divorce. His mother had not had a life because his father subsumed their relationship to his career. In turn, Greg had made his and Janet's relationship paramount. He had denied her any independent life with his jealousy, and his desire to share every possible minute of his life with hers. Janet's individuality had been subsumed to their identity as a couple.

Greg had not felt being a couple as not being an individual. After all, being a couple was what he had wanted as an individual. Apparently, that had not been what Janet wanted.

What good was going through life's pain if you could not learn lessons from that pain and apply them to making life better? When he

214

ARMAGEDDON, CA 94666

had gotten what he needed from Janet, he had not been jealous. But was he so needy of attention and reassurance from his own feelings of abandonment by his mother that no woman could give him what he needed for very long, let alone a lifetime? What good was admitting such razor edged truths to himself if he could not act on them? If he could not move forward? If he could not stop feeling so helpless?

Exhaustion finally overwhelmed his consciousness under cloud muted starry night. He dreamt of wheels within wheels within wheels, each turning, all to no effect.

***

DL's speech to the peace rally had been pure righteousness. He had followed a black vet who had just finished his tour of duty in southern Mexico and was not planning to reenlist. The uniformed, disciplined New Afrikan Lords stood in formation behind DL, proudly wearing the symbol of their organization and center.

"The brother who just spoke," DL confronted the crowd of some one million, mostly white, "Spoke truth when he said that the powers-that-be want people of color in this country to fight and kill foreign people of color to further the interests of white supremacy and US imperialism. He gave you the figures; how many more brothers and others of color are in the military compared to our numbers in the general population. He spoke truth when he said over a third of the army's enlistees and draftees are African American while we're only 13% of the population. He spoke truth when he said that the Oakland Army Base is 2/3rds Black while the City of Oakland is only half African American. He spoke truth when he said that Black troops in southern Mexico are dying at twice the rate of white soldiers. And we ain't done giving you the truth today."

DL felt like a Southern Baptist preacher on that platform, before that microphone. He flashed to an image of a Bible thumping circuit rider as he paused for effect, and he smiled.

"The powers-that-be, their policy is exactly the same here in this country as it is in southern Mexico. Let people of color fight and kill other people of color. Black gangs in Oakland, the Bloods and the Crips, they don't kill white folk. Not many anyway. Mostly, they kill other black folks. Or they kill members of other gangs; and not just other Black gangs, but also Chicano gangs or Cambodian gangs or

END TIME

Filipino gangs. The brothers behind me, we're NEW Afrikan Lords, but we used to be the YOUNG Afrikan Lords, one of the toughest, baddest gangs East Oakland ever saw. And what did we fight over? Drugs and rackets and turf. And why's that? Who benefits? The white ruling class of this country benefits. With drugs and rackets we only hurt and destroy our own people. And until there's revolution in this country, Afrikan people will only have the illusion of holding any kind of turf. Again, why's that? Who benefits? Again, the white ruling class of this bloody nation benefits. They keep you white college kids from getting your asses shot at in some Yucatan jungle, unless you wants to. And they keep the people divided so that the white elite running this country can exploit all of us, but especially the Black nation in this nation.

"I'm not talking now about the drugs, the heroin, the crack, the ice, the 999 that the US government encourages to spread in the Afrikan community to keep my people chained. I mean, you all know that the CIA and the US military brings the horse and coke into this country. I'm not even talking about the AIDS plague that's still killing people of color in this country 'cause the cost of the vaccines are so high. All I'm talking about is brother killing brother in driveby's and gangbanging, and the family homicides, and all the other ways we're killing each other so that the white bourgeoisie can stay in power."

The crowd squirmed, some uncomfortably, and some in radical-chic-right-on. An eagle tacked the wind high above the vast crowd, paused in flight high in the cloud cut heavens.

"As I said before, me and the brothers behind me, we were once the Young Afrikan Lords, the baddest gang in all of Oakland. Our turf was the biggest, our drugs were the purest, and our guns were the loudest. Then we learned the truth about how this country is run and we stopped that gang banging stuff. Now as I said, me and the Lords, we're the New Afrikan Lords and we're a political organization. We run the New Afrika Center in Oakland and we're working to build the race. You all are invited to visit. We've got a fine restaurant and other things at the Center you might enjoy. Next week, the New Afrika Center is calling a Council of War of all the gangs in Oakland. We're gonna call a truce on all this gangbanging. But we're gonna do more than call a truce. We're gonna forge an alliance. There's ten gangsta's for every cop in the city. We're gonna start turning the guns around. Stop brother killing brother and start defending the community against The Man. Against the Powers That Be."

There had been more, but for DL that had hit the highlight. He regretted his braggadocio in revealing the Council of War almost immediately when he noticed the stir it caused, not only in the crowd, but also in the cops on the fringes of the rally and behind the stage. He had not intended to throw down the glove in challenge quite so soon.

216

ARMAGEDDON, CA 94666

But it was done. To think that the idea for unifying all of Oakland's gangs had come from a silly-assed Hollywood movie he had once rented, a 1970's movie called "Warriors."

DL and the New Afrikan Lords piled into two cars after the rally, DL and Jack'o'Hearts in one and Hakim and Samuels in the other with the rest of the brothers divided up for a cruise to Mama's Big Kitchen Bar-B-Q in the Tenderloin. Even Hakim could eat at Mama's, with her strictly kosher beef, chicken and vegetarian specialties. DL's words echoed from the radio on the ride down, coming through on Liberation Station Afrika loud and clear.

"That was a speech by New Afrikan Lords President and Director of the New Afrika Center, Daniel Logan, recorded at today's anti-war demonstration in San Francisco's Golden Gate Park. Daniel Logan is a young, up-and-coming Black leader in the city of Oakland."

It was DJ Elijah doing his Liberation News Service. Jack'o'Hearts just had to laugh.

"Hey, DL, he got your Christian name."

"That man's got his ear to the street," DL laughed along. "Wonder who the fuck he is?"

They had to park a ways away from Mama's, and they got a little boisterous on the walk down. Not the feeling of gang, but one of posse danced among the Lords that evening as they all piled into the Big Kitchen.

"Heard your speech today," Mama herself came out of the kitchen. "Man, you paintin' a target on your back or what. Be careful little brother. And here's a little something for your work."

The check was for $1,000, made out to the New Afrika Center. The meal was on the house. Mama insisted. They drove all high across the Bay Bridge, not on any drug but on the power of the people. Night could be felt around the two cars and their rowdy Lords. They joked and laughed as their sound systems blared the new Afro/Carib/Hip-Hop/Brazilian sound called JuJu OverMix, pumping out on Liberation Station Afrika.

"To the Center, boyeee," DL laughed with Jack'o'Hearts, his only driver.

Sometime after the Oakland Army Base, as their radios blared a gangsta' kayo beat, their cars became an unexpected caravan as three more cars caught their tail. When the Lords turned off of 580 onto Broadway, their tail followed.

"We got company," Jack'o'Hearts said.

"Evasion," DL ordered. Jack'o'Hearts gave the hand sign to the other car, and then squealed tires around corners. The Lords' cars choreographed a chase scene right out of the movies. Somewhere off Jefferson, when they succeeded in gaining a little but not much distance ahead of their unwelcome pursuit, DL said, "Time to face the music."

Jack'o'Hearts signaled again and the two Lords cars screeched into a makeshift blockade, angled across the street. DL could not ask his Lords to do something he was not willing to do, but he was not stupid. He leapt from his car and bounded back to the other driven by Hakim. Not known to DL and his Lords, a window in an apartment above one of the street's storefronts slid open and a face appeared.

"Keep on driving," DL yelled, "To the Center."

"They're gonna kill you," Samuels protested from the car as DL pushed Mama's check into his hands.

"Drive to the Center," DL now barked, as their pursuers screeched up into a counter barricade, "That's an order. You're New Afrikan Lords. Act like Lords."

Killah Samuels burst into tears.

"You heard the Lord's President Hakim," Samuels bawled, "Drive."

The remaining Lords from DL's car had emptied out behind it in the meantime, joined by their president when the other car full of Lords obeyed. The Lords had given up dealing, numbers, rackets, protection, pimping, auto theft, everything associated with their gang days, except for their guns. Two of their pursuer's cars directly counterpointed their position, with ten black clad men, in black ski masks, gloves and guns, around behind their vehicles. The third car parked discreetly behind the mounting confrontation, seeking the anonymity of shadows. Seeing what was about to go down, the face in the window had disappeared. Now the lens and mike of a portable camcorder nuzzled the window ledge.

"We have an arrest warrant for Daniel Logan, known as DL," one of the masked men shouted.

"Why you wearing masks if you're cops?" Jack'o'Hearts yelled back.

"Turn DL over to us, and the rest of you go free," the masked man replied.

"Bullshit," DL yelled, "I go with you and not only do I die, but all the brothers die. You're the Death Squad."

Once they had established that DL was indeed behind the car, the masked men opened fire. The Lords retaliated, and the block cleared. New Afrikan blood flowed in rivers down the street that night. That river succeeded in watering a particular seed. The seed of revolution. The camcorder recorded it all.

The Bay wide *11 O'Clock News*, all channels, reported it as a gang war casualty.

"This evening, Daniel Logan, known as DL, and four other members of the Young Afrikan Lords gang were gunned down in what police are calling a gang related shoot-out in downtown Oakland at 9:30 this evening. The Oakland PD are still looking for the rival gang members who ambushed the Lords gang near Jefferson and 17th..."

The videotape hit the media at 2 in the early, early morning. It ran in its entirety; showing the Lords facing off the black masked men, recording DL's arrest order, and detailing the gunfight down to the last Lord moaning and dying in the streets. It recorded one more thing; the third car parked behind the black hooded squad, the four unmasked white men in it observing the shoot-out through to the final death. After which, they jumped from their car, hustled their masked companions off the scene and away, and then took over the situation. Plainclothed Alameda County sheriff.

"This is Oakland, not LA!" DJ Elijah broadcast over his pirate radio station around 3 that morning, when the trouble started. "Don't be burnin' and lootin' our own neighborhoods, like folks did in LA in '92. Take the fires to Piedmont, to Rockridge, to the Hills. And hey, that shopkeeper, or that store owner ain't your enemy. The cops are. Daniel Logan's murder was political assassination by the cops. Cold. It proves that old saying: 'blue by day, white by night.' Don't let a single cop walk the streets of Oakland in peace. Leave no police or sheriff station standing. This is our community. Don't let the cops call in reinforcements. Seize the time. Seize our neighborhoods. This is Oakland, not LA!"

Oakland burned by sunrise.

***

Greg woke first as sunrise slanted in beneath the low clouds pouring over the west peninsula hills, among a rooftop of sleeping forms. He huddled in his bag, numb, as if down and dulled from a massive psychedelic experience. Larry, then Smoke, and finally the rest of the MDRG grumbled awake.

"Let's get some breakfast and BART it over to our cars in Berkeley. They should have cleared the tracks by now." Smoke had on a pair of regular sunglasses. He spoke, then glanced out over the rooftop. "Hmmm, something big is burning in East Bay."

Columns of smoke fiercely oranged up the sunrise and curtained over much of the East Bay south of the bridge. They sauntered in for breakfast at a neighborhood diner and soon found out its cause.

"...The riot's fury was not at all randomly aimed." The television voice crackled over helicopter scenes of Oakland in flames. "Hit, and hit hard were the freeway interchanges—the 980/880, 980/580 and 880/580 maze—and both the 12th Street and Lake Merritt BART stations. Police and sheriff substations have been burned out. Others are under siege. Ambushes of police patrols have virtually driven law enforcement off the city's streets. The government buildings on Lake Merritt have been looted and are presently in flames. Firefighters cannot reach the fires however because of snipers. The rioting has spread south to Courtland and High, but the rioters are not indiscriminately burning down buildings. Police stations have become the principle targets, but all government buildings are being attacked..."

"What the hell caused all that?" Smoke asked as the waitress brought their food to the booth.

"Oh, some gang guy got killed by the cops," she said, indifferent, "Somebody D..."

"DL?" Smoke gave her a sharp look.

"Yep, I think that's him," she shrugged, "Want anything else?"

"Just more coffee," Smoke said.

They learned much of the rest listening and watching as they rushed their meal of greasy eggs, hash browns and bacon. Cop assassination of DL, that is what it looked like from the evidence despite Alameda Sheriff's Department denials. East Oakland was no longer part of the United States. The northern and western parts of the city were almost entirely under the rioters' control, thanks to snipers, ambushes, suicide bombings, and berserker style assaults. Oakland's mayor had flown to Sacramento and now waited on a meeting with the governor. Thirty-eight dead, twenty-five of them cops. And the BART was down. The authorities had cleared the Bay Bridge of its incandescent barricades though.

"We'll have to catch a bus," Larry said, twirling the ends of his beard meditatively as the broadcast switched from news flash to the regular news of radical environmentalists dynamiting another dam on the Columbia river, and then of Canada's further dismemberment under aboriginal pressures.

They made the correct bus stop at 8, and caught the correct bus at 8:15. The bus spent three hours on the way over to Berkeley in traffic jams. They seemed to ride into an inferno, the eastern horizon ribboned with black smoke and the hot rising sun stained blood red. An apocalyptic landscape that effectively hushed conversations. Finally they reached their vehicles. Time to split up.

"I'll call ASP and tell 'em we're coming back in," Smoke said and headed for his transport with the MDRG. "Let's all meet back at the pub."

Traffic snarled and knotted beyond untangling, thanks to Oakland. It took them another three hours to clear Richmond. In the meantime, the van's radio kept them up on the important happenings. KPFA broadcast a news conference called by a coalition of the Black Unity Front, Black Panthers, Nation of Islam, All-African Peoples Socialist Party, African Peoples Revolutionary Party, New Afrikan Peoples Movement, and the remnants of the New Afrikan Lords, among many others. As Larry started over the northern bay, beneath Oakland's grit-

ARMAGEDDON, CA 94666

ty pall, one of the conference holders spoke.

"...I don't approve of the methods used by the people in the streets, but I can sure understand how the brutal methods of the Oakland PD and the Alameda Sheriffs could drive people into such desperate actions. The cops murdered Daniel Logan in cold fuckin' blood. They assassinated him, just like this government assassinates political leaders down in southern Mexico."

"This New Afrika Coalition," another of the conference sponsors spoke, a man named Samuels, "Is dedicated to keeping DL's New Afrika Center open, to keep DL's work and dreams alive..."

Noise cluttered the background, angry voices exchanging words. The speaker stopped.

"There seems to be a disturbance at the back of the auditorium," the radio announcer came on the air, "A number of young black men, also Latinos and Asians, perhaps thirty in all, are now making their way down the aisle as a group. The Coalition's security is coming with them. They are approaching the open microphone."

"The name's Steppin' Razor. Hiyo Killah. For the rest o' you I be head o' the East Bay Crips. This here's Fetchin' Death, he head the Bloods. We got most o' the head Oakland gangbangers here. Most everybody DL was gonna speak to. We callin' a city-wide alliance on our own. We turnin' our guns over to the revolution..."

The Governor called a State-Of-Emergency for the East Bay at 3, and Martial Law for Oakland at 4, enjoining the National Guard into action as the two pulled into Alabaster. But it was too late for the Guard to accomplish much. Heavily armed barricades held Peralta to MacArthur, West MacArthur to ML King Jr. Way, and north from there to 51st Street. The wealthy town of Piedmont was partially ringed by insurrectionists. They held various streets west and south of the 13 freeway and the 580 highway all the way to 98th. About all the Guard could do, once authorized to carry weapons, was to mass troops and tanks at strategic intersections, these movements matched by reinforcements from the rioters. When the Guard maneuvered, so did the rioters. Stalemate. The Governor had the next flight out to Washington to counsel with the President.

They arrived at the pub by 4:30, Greg having missed yet another whole day of classes. The entire ASP/MDRG affinity, to include Lori and Mary, crowded around tables inside, beneath one of the Redwood Eatery's TV's. Smoke gave Greg and Larry a nod as did the others.

"Guess no one got arrested from Wednesday," Greg glanced around.

"No one," David managed, hardly able to leave off watching the news.

The President declared a State-Of-Emergency and Martial Law for Oakland as well. Rumor had it that long range artillery was being

221

positioned south of Briones and east of San Leandro Reservoirs. The Guard deployed south of Estudillo as the territory north to 98th was considered sympathetic to the central Oakland rioters. The President had ordered the Army at Oakland Base to break the Peralta blockades and retake the city of Oakland.

"We were lucky," Smoke said.

"Yeh, when the affinity split on the charge, some of us were faced with the decision about whether or not to continue," David glared at Smoke.

"You didn't leave the fight, did you?" Smoke asked.

"No," David frowned, "Only because we got help from another affinity. One from HardCore Autonomy. I thought the point was to stick together."

"The point," Smoke's mouth firmed into a line, "Was to do as much damage to the corporate/government machine as possible. We stay together to do that so long as its possible. But mobility takes precedence over sticking together. Why the hell didn't you follow us around the cops?"

"I...we..." David started. But the TV brought everyone around again with a start. Something was happening. The announcer's face was pale, his eyes wide. Not two minutes before he had been detailing the mutual atrocities inflicted by Turks and Armenians upon each others civilian populations in their ongoing mountain war, switching from international to national news with a report that the water supply of the town of Aventura, Florida had been dosed with a designer psychedelic called Odainsaker.

"I have just been handed an important announcement. There has been a mutiny at the Oakland Army Base. I repeat. There has been a mutiny at the Oakland Army Base. Commander Malcolm Powell Brown has released a statement to the media. It says, in part: 'Irresponsible elements in the US military and the US government are planning to resort to long range artillery bombardment and even aerial strikes to break the Oakland Uprising. I will not stand idly by while hundreds, perhaps thousands of African American citizens are killed to end a rebellion that was caused by widespread outrage at the Alameda County Sheriff's political assassination of Daniel Logan, popular leader of the New Afrikan Lords Party...' Commander Brown has asked all soldiers on the base not willing to volunteer to join the Oakland riot to leave. Only one quarter of the troops have left, without their arms. The mutinous Army units are presently transferring the entire arsenal at Oakland Base, to include a unit of up-to-date battle lasers, into the Oakland riot."

The screen cut to a helicopter shot as night deepened. Still, the scene below was clear. A column of tanks, APC's and APV's, jeeps, trucks full

222

of weapons, and a line of dished battle lasers moved down Viaduct and West Grand, peacefully breaching the Peralta barricades. They flowed triumphantly into Oakland, surrounded by throngs of jubilant people.

The kids around the table broke into spontaneous applause. Jesus, it really is a revolution, Greg thought. He ordered himself a pitcher of beer.

***

Al Thompson, aka DJ Elijah, fit the basics of his grapevine profile; blind Persian Gulf vet, Copt mystic, and pirate radio station operator extraordinaire. An Army Reserve radioman during the first Persian Gulf war, Al had lucked into a good wife named Zoe and a fine pair of twin boys, as well as a mid management job in one of Oakland's major, Black-owned radio stations, all of which he returned to after the war. He parlayed his vets status, and with the backing of his parents, he purchased a 12-story, downtown Oakland apartment building for the family to live in and manage. In turn, in putting his two sons, Zachary and Leo, to work about the building, he had the idea to encourage them to go into business for themselves. They formed their own janitorial business the books of which Al managed. All in all, Thompson and his family were on their way up, solidly middle class and an ideal example of American bootstrapping.

Then the Oakland PD, having stopped his son Zachary for drunk driving in late 1999, beat him into a permanent vegetative state on the excuse he had resisted arrest. Internal police investigation acquitted the cops involved of all wrongdoing, so outraging Al that he started on his pirate radio project in order to be able to broadcast such crimes to the public. Actually, he first intended to produce a series of independent programs on police brutality that he hoped to market to the Pacifica and public radio networks. In so doing he developed the contacts and located the resources he would use when he turned to pirate radio proper. Close to a year after Zach's crippling, a squad of Oakland PD in pursuit of two alleged gang members suspected of a convenience store robbery opened up on the kids in the middle of the day, in the middle of a busy Oakland street. Cement shards from ricocheting bullets blinded Al Thompson on that day.

A number of things came from his blinding. He lost his job. But what with Social Security disability payments and the decent settlement from his lawsuit against the city, Al was able to secure his future, pay his medical bills, and get a computer/sensopic augment operation so that he might have limited vision in the red/infrared range. He also purchased outright the military surplus, scientific and computer equipment he required for his pirate radio station. His blinding gave him an inner sight, a mystic vision that both turned him toward his idiosyncratic Coptic faith and toward guerrilla radio broadcasting. A

END TIME

Black angel of the Black Lord God visited him and called him to set up Liberation Station Afrika as a witness. In turn his politics, which had started drifting toward the Black nationalist Left when Zach was brutalized, jumped the left-center-right political track for the neo-Garveyist "back to Africa" fringe.

Al's technical knowledge, ingenuity, and new religious drive put the station on the air in two years time. He devised twelve portable transmitters, each solar powered and each with the capacity to receive, then convert information encoded in infrared laser pulses into continuous wave radio transmissions. He developed the computer program, not only to handle the laser transmissions from his apartment building to the transmitters around the city, but also to synchronize the relay of random laser transmissions from one transmitter to the other into a continuous broadcast. Finally, using the front of his son's janitorial service and with Leo's help, he personally installed every one of the station's transmitters, camouflaging them on the tops of tall buildings around downtown in line of sight with his penthouse apartment. He used his narrow, red spectrum vision to align them perfectly. The spread of transmitters as a whole and the duration of each transmitter's broadcast, coupled with Al's micro-modulated massage of the transmission's frequency phase, made detection of his pirate station virtually impossible. Inclement weather occasionally cut off his broadcast, but the Feds could not.

Liberation Station Afrika reached from Richmond to San Leandro, and from the eastern SF peninsula well into Contra Costa County. DJ Elijah managed to field 16 to 24 hours of programming out of his living room that combined extreme variety in content with a basic radicalism in approach. Al's zeal for the truth, and for broadcasting the truth via his Liberation News Service, earned him the respect and love of the Bay Area's black population. And, in order to keep the truth up-to-date, Al Thompson aka DJ Elijah relied upon an anonymous, church-based tip line backed up by an extensive, deep rooted network of community sources. He was generous in kind. Both the station and Al crusaded fervently against drugs in America's African American communities. His far reaching grapevine, his "street ear" frequently turned up news of big drug deals in the works. He fed the tips, in turn, to a select circle of Black cops and Federal agents he trusted and respected, helping them in their careers and cultivating their friendships for future favors. This alliance of convenience put a large dent in Oakland's crack, heroin, and Ynisvitrin traffic, earning DJ Elijah some powerful enemies.

One of Thompson's cops turned. The Chinese Mafia bought the SFPD officer. But it still took the cop and his new owners over a year to track down the station's true broadcast point. Al had been wily, for

224

even if someone managed to pin down one or two of his transmitters, they did not have his living room studio, the heart and brain of Liberation Station Afrika. What is more, any move on his transmitters provided him with advance warning that the station's security was being breached. His enemies finally resorted to hacking the Social Security data base to locate any and all blind African American Persian Gulf vets receiving disability in the Bay Area. Then they penetrated Thompson's elaborate facade of front businesses and addresses he had built up around his SS number, finally drawing cross hairs on his downtown penthouse apartment operation.

Al kept a tape of every broadcast, as well as duplicates of the music, speeches, programs, sermons, lectures, classes, and readings in the station's library down in his building's basement, along with his computer software backups. At one time, he had contemplated transferring the broadcast studio to the basement, using it as a bunker against any assault. But then he had reasoned that, if anyone were truly serious about taking him and his station out, they would not blink at taking out the entire building in order to do so. He had been right on that score. On the first day of the Oakland Insurrection, at 3 in the afternoon and in the middle of DJ Elijah's rebroadcast of one of Malcolm X's speeches, while Al changed Zach's diaper, a nondescript helicopter approached the penthouse, flying high and partially hidden by veils of smoke. It launched a precision air-to-surface projectile, then veered sharply off. The projectile started to rapidly unweave a mere forty yards above the roof, quickly loosing speed as it spread into a large dandelion lacery of contact triggered Semtex H nodules. Floating down to lightly touch... The explosion annihilated four flours of the building outright, so powerful it blew out any danger from fire and left the remainder of the structure largely intact.

Neither Zoe nor Leo were in the building at the time.

***

Peregrine normally did not drink before a job, but he broke into the General Store again, half tanked, riding on confidence about the coop's shoddy security as well as elation from events in Oakland. A splendid diversion, he thought, perhaps even a genuine revolutionary moment. Peregrine laughed out loud as he brazenly counted out the Store's $388, walking openly across campus. He found the emergency telegram from his brother's lawyer in his apartment's door upon returning.

THIRTY-ONE

Maria and Jesus Madron were key CT workers on the Campeche coast. Married some thirty years, they lived in Coatzacoalcos in a small house with a luxuriant garden and five loud dogs. Both were elected representatives of the Campechean Regional Federation; an agrarian association covering four Federal States with a population of over two

END TIME

million, containing some of the nation's most fertile lands. The number of cooperatives, collectives and communes in the Federation rose from 470 in late 2000 to a 1,050 in early 2002, with over 50% of the population living on them even though virtually half of the regional Federation was not, technically, in Liberated Territory.

Maria Hernandez had been born in the endless impoverished mountains south of Mexico City, in a village that ceased to exist when its entire population migrated person-by-person, family-by-family to the metropolis. There, she met Jesus Madron, indigent son of a landless peasant family recently moved to the city from Cuetzalan and, at sixteen and seventeen respectively, they married. Maria's uncle bequeathed the couple a mid-size *ejido* in Coatzacoalcos, and they did their best to make a go of it.

They actually succeeded modestly, and joined the small holding agrarian middle class, where they could have remained comfortable. Yet even before the rise of the unions associated with the CT, they had held unconventional ideas. Jesus was big on innovation, and his mail order seeds and personal experiments in breeding and hybridizing had measurably helped their crop yields. They were unable to have kids of their own. Dependent upon hired landless laborers to help cultivate their *ejido*, Maria insisted that anyone who contributed to the prosperity of their land earned a share in that wealth. So when a peasant worker finished out a season in the Madron's employ, he or she took, besides the wages earned, maybe a chicken or two, a pig perhaps if the worker was a long timer going to the city, for helping to make the Madron *ejido* successful.

Their life together was by no means idyllic. Besides the back breaking work required to keep the *ejido* going, Jesus's agricultural innovations were resisted by the peasant conservatism of their neighbors. Then there were the protection rackets run by State and Federal police on anyone with any measure of prosperity. The Madron's, having weathered the PRI's attempts to privatize the *ejido* system in the 1990's to facilitate corporate penetration of Mexican agriculture, had refused to pay up on principle. Twice their fields were set ablaze, unsuccessful attempts at intimidation in that everyone helped the beloved Maria and Jesus to put out the fires and to financially recover. Jesus in turn invested heavily in watchdogs and shotguns. Finally, when Maria caught Jesus philandering with the widow across town, she left him to return to her parent's home for close to six months. A much chastened Jesus traveled to her parents to plead for her return, to find that Maria had fervently embraced the liberation politics of the Union de Trabajadores de Mexico.

The reunited couple returned to Coatzacoalcos, Jesus now a reluctant party to his wife's new politics. His hesitancy soon dissolved and

226

both threw themselves into agricultural organizing in the region, helping to found the CT just before the '99 General Strike. Their region was not formally a part of the Liberated Territories after the August Uprisings but its workers and peasants carried out large land holding and wasteland expropriations. What is more, their region's cooperative, collective and communal agriculture went to help feed the revolutionary movement. Jesus arranged a mutual aid contract for San Cristobal to market the crop of Campeche's cooperative citrus federation among the Caribbean islands in exchange for the introduction of appropriate technological innovations into southern Mexico. Crop yields dramatically improved, and soil depletion and erosion were reduced. When "white hand" death squad killings were used to intimidate those who supported the Liberated Territories, the Madrons provided their home for meetings of the popular self-defense militia.

Jesus was jailed three separate times for their efforts. The last time, on the eve of his transfer to Mexico City, and certain torture, he was liberated from the local stockade by a mob of angry friends, fellow CT members, and, it was rumored, a small FAO contingent. They marched on the prison and threatened to burn it down. Word of the FAO's presence was sufficient to convince the local authorities to hand Jesus over.

Jesus and Maria shared an understanding that the mass, monolithic nature of capitalism was the counterpoint to the insular, small village, no matter how communal and egalitarian. Neither could serve as a model for the future. Taking their cue from Marx and Kropotkin, who both wrote of the need to integrate town and country, and with the good points to the Israeli kibbutz experience more particularly in mind, the Madron's founded a model agrotown on the seashore east of Coatzacoalcos, on reclaimed marshlands. Called Adan, it cultivated both land and sea, held property in common, raised children communally, and utilized the most advanced technologies to minimize the need for intensive labor and maximize the community's interaction with the outside world. It served as a nexus between the Liberated Territories and San Cristobal, traded with Cuba and the European Community, and courted the Japanese and Singaporeans to back its promising aquacultural projects. Then US Special Forces blew Adan off the map in a fire-and-brimstone warning to the neighborhood. Adan had been a year and six months old then, and the Madrons had been in Coatzacoalcos, keeping up the *ejido*.

Jesus Madron survived two Subucu spider assassination attempts. His well trained dogs caught both metal creatures before they could approach, let alone inject him with their lethal poisons. The spiders were then shipped off to San Cristobal for study.

THIRTY-TWO

"Got some good news," Sampson laughed over the phone. Marcus, still in his pajamas, had gotten used to these violations to his business hours lately. He stifled a yawn. "Kenny Wisdom is currently in San Diego MCC, and he writes to a San Francisco PO box regularly. I also found out that the box is owned by Eugene Wisdom. Street address a dead-end."

"So, he's still in the area," Marcus said.

"That'd be my guess," Brian brimmed, "His record at Stanford is interesting as well. I couldn't get much on him at first. Seems he left on less than friendly terms, under a cloud. So I dug deeper. He was an undergraduate and a graduate student at Stanford. *Infant savant* type. History Department there was so impressed with his undergraduate work, they granted him full support and a graduate position in the doctoral program. Apparently, he was living with a girl during his graduate work. A graduate student in Marine Biology. She left him at the end of his second year. Sent him into a full tail spin. He did a nose dive his third year. Failed his exams. Cheated on some and was caught. He assistant-taught his classes drunk. The Department tried to cut a deal with him but by then he was completely irresponsible, so they cut him. Needless to say, they don't like talking about him. One more thing, your MO on the Alabaster robberies. I did a check of the Palo Alto area police records during the period that Eugene was at Stanford. There was an unsolved string of robberies, same MO as Alabaster, right around the time Eugene Wisdom broke up with his girlfriend, extending until a year after he dropped out of graduate school."

"Fabulous," Marcus grinned into the phone, "Can you fax me the info?"

"It's on its way." And it was. As Marcus picked up the sheets, the phone rang again.

"Joe here," Manley's voice rang through, "Hope I didn't wake you."

"Not at all," Marcus smiled, "Good news?"

"You bet," Joe said, "Got a DMV readout on Eugene Wisdom. Both drivers license and car registration. Address is an SF PO box. And, there's more. Our Department's computers have three unpaid parking tickets on the car belonging to Eugene Wisdom in Alabaster. Two are past due, the third has two more weeks."

"I suppose you can't put out an APB on that car based on two tickets," Marcus laughed.

"Not an APB," Joe said, "But we can manage an impound, if he doesn't pay the third ticket."

"That's a start," Marcus said, "Can you swing by with what you've got? I'm particularly interested in the locations on those tickets."

"Can do," Joe said.

As Marcus hung up, he noticed the morning filling the silent front room. 6:30. He decided to brew up a pot of coffee and start the day.

ARMAGEDDON, CA 94666

Peregrine and Eugene Wisdom were one and the same. He leafed through the manila file with the three pictures and one video clip that had gestalted with the Peregrine sketch. He stared at the sketch that he had updated with freckles and red hair. Eugene Wisdom was almost in his grasp.

***

Lori had made Greg an offer, in front of Smoke, that he had been too drunk to accept. Larry wound up driving his friend home the night before. He woke with a hangover. The fax had a message from his father, a check up call, and he managed to leave a reassuring reply with Andre's answering service before forcing himself to eat breakfast, swallow a couple of aspirins and catch a bus to the ASU campus. He made sure his car was still in the school's parking lot before attending his first class. His efforts, plus lunch between classes, helped his condition. The classes were a blur. Smoke intercepted him on his way to the library and some desperately needed studying.

"Yo," Smoke caught him entering Remley Plaza, mirrored shades and leather jacket once again fully armoring him. "Gotta talk to you."

"What's up?" Greg asked, thinking it was about Lori.

"Your crew still planning a recycling run this weekend?"

"Yah," Greg groaned inwardly at yet another commitment he had to meet, "I'll probably check out the truck tomorrow afternoon and we'll do the run Sunday morning. As usual."

"Do you pay by the day?"

"No, we get a single weekend rate, 'cause the office is closed Sunday," Greg explained. "Its for a single day, so if we have a really big run, we have two days to get it done."

"Great," Smoke said, "Now I gotta ask you a favor. Can you rent the truck tomorrow morning, early, and lend it to me for the day? I promise I'll return it and leave it for you to use Sunday morning."

"What do you need it for?" Greg stopped walking.

"That's something I'd rather not say," Smoke said.

"I don't know," Greg said, "I can't just do that without permission of the recycling coop."

"This is important," Smoke said.

"Too important to tell me what's up?"

"Look Greg, if you want, I'll show you what I'm doing. Tomorrow night. It'll be dangerous, but if you're up for it, you can come along. Then you can deliver the truck back yourself."

"I've got to study," Greg dodged, "Do you have to know right this minute?"

"Yes," Smoke was emphatic, "This will contribute to the biggest revolutionary thing happening in this country now."

"Oakland?"

"Yes," Smoke admitted.

"Alright," Greg said, as much to get Smoke out of his face, "I better not regret this decision. And, I do want to go with you."

"OK," Smoke smiled, "When does the office open?"

"Eight-thirty tomorrow morning."

"I'll meet you there then," Smoke shook Greg's hand, "And you meet me at nine tomorrow night, same place. I'll be there."

Again, Greg tried for the library. Again, he did not make it as David snagged him by the fountain.

"I've been talking to people," David said, "People are thinking, now that Oakland's happening, the Solidarity Brigade should have another meeting and work on taking the next step."

Your thinking, Greg said to himself. But aloud he said, to ward off this distraction: "How about Sunday, at ten in the morning. Redwood Eatery."

"Alright," David waved.

Again Greg tried for the library and made the steps before being intercepted by Margaret. She made him the same offer Lori had.

"I really have to study, Peggy," Greg said, desperate even as he became aroused.

"Study at my place," Margaret smiled, invitingly, "My roommate's skiing again this weekend."

"Okay," Greg said against his better judgment. He drove her to her apartment and managed to get in three hours on the books before she broke out the ganja and the wine. Greg drowned his better judgment in them. Then he dived into Margaret's most willing body, attempting to annihilate his guilt, his responsibilities, his memories.

***

Mark had drawn X's for the locations of Eugene's three tickets on a map of Alabaster after Joe brought their xeroxes over, then drew a circle around the marks. The circle covered downtown, around the Loop, and it was at least a week away for the detective's house-to-house at his pace.

"This IS a break," Mark said to Gwen over breakfast.

Apartment complexes riddled the area. He figured it would take the better part of next week to cover that ground. The phone rang and he grabbed it before the second chime.

"Mark, Neal here," the Security Pacific president's tired voice begged for the detective's ear, "Anything new?"

"Every day we get a step closer," Marcus tried to sound reassuring, going over Manley's parking tickets with Emerson.

"You said you were close last time I time," Neal sounded irritated. "Damnit Mark, I can't hold up this whip and chair much longer. When can we wrap this up?"

230

ARMAGEDDON, CA 94666

"This case will be over when its over," Marcus felt his own nerves fraying, "I don't work any better under pressure, and I certainly don't need you to nag me. You hired me to find Peregrine, not to cover up for your past errors in judgment. Excuse me, but I have a job to do."

Best to work all weekend, the detective told himself after Emerson mumbled a curt apology with his good-bye and hung up. He knew that Gwen would not like it. He deliberately kept his mind off of his old friend as he drove to the area within his map's circle. Things would have to change there. He reminded himself how close he was to wrapping up this matter. How close he was to being done with Neal's job. Gwen would understand.

"Excuse me, can I have a moment of your time," Marcus said to the liquor store owner behind the counter of his store. He gave the man his insurance rap. Then he produced Peregrine's modified sketch, pencil poised over notebook for the store owner's response. "By any chance, have you seen this man?"

"Hold it," the store owner took the picture, squinted at it, placed a finger of either hand over the eyes, "You know, I think I have. I think this is one of my customers. He comes in to buy beer now and then."

"A regular customer?"

"Not really," the man handed back the sketch.

"Did you also happen to notice the name on his license when you asked his ID?"

"Naw," the man shrugged, "Only the age."

"But he does live in the neighborhood?"

"Yeh, I guess. Always see him walk in. Never drive up in a car."

Truly, a break. Marcus intended to reward Joe for this, once it was all over.

***

The National Guard around Oakland, reinforced with Army units from outside the area, made two moves on Friday to further seal off the rebellious city, and tighten the government's cordon. First, a column of soldiers seized 580 up to the 580/13 split. The 580 north of the split was left entirely in rebel hands, so through traffic was allowed along 13. Then troops moved up the west bank of the San Leandro Creek to secure Oakland International Airport from potential assault, to maintain the connection with Alameda.

In response, the mutinous Army troops in Oakland visibly displayed the battle lasers they possessed. The rebels positioned them along the bay, ringed them with very visible surface-to-air missile batteries, and aimed them for the heart of San Francisco. The New Afrika Coalition called a community-wide popular assembly. And inner cities all across America erupted into riot.

231

END TIME

Peregrine ran into a small hitch at In The Raw. The food coop had hastily constructed a double locked cabinet for their money. It delayed him, picking the locks, and he felt uneasy standing, exposed, in the store after midnight while doing so. The coops were catching on, even as he neared his own event horizon in Alabaster. The takings on campus were so good and so easy nonetheless that he quickly discarded the option of doing a job in town. He had work to do for his brother in any case, a job that would substantially pay Hawk back for arranging to sell Peregrine's arsenal. That deal was so close to done that he could taste its profit, and the marginal freedom it would allow him.

***

Margaret got Greg up around sunrise. After she got off on him and he in her, he showered and dragged himself out of her apartment to meet Smoke.

"Want to come by tonight?" she said from the door.

"Can't," Greg said, reluctantly, "I've got to do politics."

"Give me a call."

As he drove to the campus, he thought about her. The night before, after she started plying him with grass and wine, they had briefly talked about Wednesday's Hooliganism in the city. To Greg's surprise, his initial boasting turned into a half-hearted defense of Larry's position against her far more principled opinions, reversing his and Larry's roles on that rooftop after their brief street adventure.

"If your goal is to have a revolution, that's one thing," Margaret had said, seated cross legged on her futon bedding, sipping her wine. "I can't see how you can have a revolution without violence. But Wednesday was supposed to be a peace demonstration. I think you have to use peaceful means to work for peaceful ends."

"The Hooligans want revolution," Greg replied, passing her the lit joint.

"Hell they do," she laughed. "They just want to kick butt. I don't see much difference between their attitudes and how good-ol-boy rednecks act. If you ask me, your Hooligans have a touch too much of that old testosterone poisoning."

He had not been all that into the devil's advocate position. Wanting to get laid, Greg had laughed and changed the subject. This morning he realized that, while she was interested in his politics and political connections, she was not much impressed with either. She could respect a nonviolent ML King or a revolutionary Malcolm X because both were serious about their beliefs to the point of dying for them. She had been positive about the building occupation and PO blockade, but she considered Hooliganism just a bunch of kids on a political goof. Margaret herself was not a political person. Her sympathies were with

232

ARMAGEDDON, CA 94666

the Left. She came down on the progressive side to most issues and causes. But she was not a demonstration goer, let alone an activist.

Smoke waited in his car in a parking space next to the transportation office when Greg roared up.

"Stay here while I do the paperwork," Greg said. That was routine by this time, and soon he drove a flatbed with rails out of the lot. Smoke hopped into the cab and Greg cruised around the block before turning the keys over to Smoke.

"You still want to go tonight?" Smoke asked.

"Wouldn't miss it," Greg said, "Nine tonight, then."

"Nine it is."

Greg retreated into the library, frantically holing himself away to study amidst the smell of old books. He had come early enough to get a study capsule. The capsule itself was hologrammic, and he had only to fit his hands into the jockey gloves to trigger a response; his claustrophobic surroundings muting into the library's main honeycomb catalogs all about him. The library 'some had a no frills adherence to the organic/fractal mathematics of virtual reality, the design emphasizing easy location and access. So deep did he isolate himself that the events of the day slipped by him.

At 10 a.m., the New Afrika Coalition held a news conference and, flushed by the success of their assembly, they declared Oakland to be the first free territory of New Afrika, going on to recognize the Liberated Territories of Mixtecan and Mayapan. Commander Brown resigned his military office and rank by noon. He was promptly and popularly elected Commander of the Liberation Forces by a general assembly of his soldiers. The Coalition held yet another press conference at 2 p.m., this time with the prominent presence of Liberation Commander Brown. The conference downplayed the New Afrika Free Territory's status, and instead, forwarded a list of demands for "normalizing" Oakland. Prosecution of the sheriffs involved in DL's assassination on first degree murder charges. Thorough investigation into the identity of the hooded assassins and their prompt prosecution. Resignation of the Oakland PD Chief of Police, the head of the Alameda County Sheriff's Department, and the Mayor of Oakland. Amnesty for all those involved in the Oakland insurrection. Direct civilian control of the police and sheriff's departments. A Marshall style Plan to rebuild America's inner cities. As a toss to the liberation tendencies, the Coalition also called for UN observers to prevent an imminent US military massacre of Oakland's citizens. The Zapatista Liberation Front reciprocated recognition of Oakland by 5 p.m., as a kicker.

David and Lori both searched for Greg to change the Solidarity Brigade meeting to that evening, but could not find him. They wanted

233

to respond to the situation in Oakland, even as an extremely far behind Greg pointed to the honeycomb cell of Mathematics and flew easily down its arterial structure of knit information, in search of Statistics.

The library closed at 8 and he had time for a couple of beers at the pub before going to meet Smoke. True to his word, Smoke was on time. The truck was piled high with various sized boxes, all covered by tarps and tied down with rope. Greg got into the passengers side of the cab and Smoke smoothly eased the truck back onto the city streets.

"I take it you were successful," Greg said.

"Not until we get this cargo into Oakland," Smoke was solemn.

"We're going to try to get into Oakland?" Greg frowned.

"Yep, it's easier than you might think."

"I hope so," Greg felt that familiar pang with Smoke, that sense of walking on the edge of an abyss and looking down. So far down. He did not want to appear unrevolutionary, but his caution was roused. "We only rent this truck from the school."

"Ice it," Smoke smiled, "I don't plan to get caught. This cargo's way too important."

Smoke geared the vehicle off campus and onto Main for the long night ride.

"So, what's in the back?"

"Necessary supplies for the revolution," Smoke said in a warning tone, "The less you know, the better."

"That's not too encouraging," Greg bridled.

"We're dealing with a revolutionary situation here." Smoke turned on 101 at Marinwood. "As they say, a revolution ain't no pink tea. Besides, there is the remote chance, the remotest chance, that we'll be stopped on entering. Theoretically, if you don't know, no one can hold it against you."

"So, how are you connected up with Oakland?" Greg settled his irritation for the road south.

"Through my brother," Smoke said tersely, "He's made quite a few friends and connections with this country's underground from...from where he's at now."

"And you really think Oakland's a revolution?" Greg asked.

"Don't you? I mean, there are very few places in the world where the people are standing up against the US military with arms and pure courage. Oakland's one of them."

"Another liberated zone?" Greg commented.

"For the moment, yes," Smoke grinned, authentically pleased, "And we're helping it stay liberated for as long as possible."

"Hope its more liberated than San Francisco was last Wednesday."

"One individual can be a liberated zone," Smoke said. "Basically, it begins in your head and comes out in your actions. The Hooligan actions, I'd call them precursors to a liberated zone. We don't hold any territory for any length of time, and most autonomists and anarchists are white middle class kids on a revolutionary lark. Hooligans may be violent and bothersome to the powers-that-be, but most of them aren't serious. Now the people of Oakland, they've been backed against the wall, most of them since birth. No jobs, grinding poverty, substandard education, racism, gangbanging, drugs and police murder; young black men are dying faster in Oakland then they are on the front lines of southern Mexico. Their actions come from their guts. Now they're holding territory and facing down the might of the US military. That's serious."

"Do you think Oakland can win?"

"No," Smoke shook his head, "Not in the long run. The government will bomb Oakland into absolute rubble rather than let it stand as an example. I mean flatten every building and shoot every citizen. Look how brutally they're suppressing sympathetic riots around the country. In many ways, Oakland was a fluke. The right combination of forces and the right expression of outrage taking advantage of an opportune constellation of circumstances to create a brief revolutionary situation. As such, Oakland has already won. Now, if they had something to back them up, other than their foolhardy courage. Say, an atomic bomb..."

Smoke glanced knowingly at Greg and he caught the glance.

"What's that supposed to mean?" Greg frowned.

"Nothing," Smoke continued to watch the road, "Just that I'd heard, strictly on the grapevine you understand, that you and a few others might know where that stolen riemanium just might be."

"No more than anybody else." Greg looked straight ahead and made a point to himself to have a talk with Larry. "Last I heard that guy, Peregrine, the thief who escaped on the Piccoli robbery, he has the stuff."

"Oh, right," Smoke smirked, "Well, say, if this Peregrine, or whoever has the riemanium, gave it to Oakland with the capability to build it into a bomb, well then, I think the government might have to reconsider annihilating the Oakland Insurrection. Outright."

The East Bay north of Oakland proved a nightmare of police, national guard and army troops, consolidating the equivalent of a police state around Berkeley. Nevertheless, Smoke kept his cool. He got them onto Ashby east and then 13 south, into an incredible traffic jam that inched along under Army scrutiny. The military had all exits west off 13 barricaded and manned by soldiers. Only eastern exits, into military-held territory, were permitted. Smoke got off the freeway east on Redwood Road. A right on Campus Drive amidst sleepy suburbs, and they drove through the deserted east campus of Merritt College. The authorities had closed down the school as a potential flash point in military held territory. The air smelled of eucalyptus. A confusing set of winding suburban streets followed, until Smoke idled the truck on Leona Street. He jumped out and strolled casually to the corner of Kuhnle, glanced about, then ambled back to the truck. He produced several burlap flaps from the flatbed and fixed one to each of the truck's license plates. Then he climbed back into the cab.

"This is it," Greg said. A night dove cried.

"Yep, so hold onto your seats," Smoke grinned, "This is gonna be rough."

Smoke geared up to speed before taking the turn on Kuhnle faster than Greg thought possible. They barreled down onto the flimsy barricade just shy of the freeway; two soldiers and a line of portable wooden, municipal saw horses west of MacArthur.

"Get down," Smoke yelled, honked the horn, and flashed the headlights.

Greg could not.

Fortunately, the traffic on MacArthur dutifully cleared and stopped. The soldiers started waving frantically, but Smoke simply gunned the engine. One of the soldiers managed to aim his handgun and fire, high, to hit the cab's metal hood before they both dove out of the way. The truck slammed through the blockades, scattering wood in splinters everywhere.

They were now in liberated territory.

Smoke braked enough to make another hair-raising turn onto Seminary. They drove until Foothill, where they turned north.

"Jesus fucking Christ," Greg managed to breath when his heartbeat once more approached normal.

"We made it," Smoke laughed and slapped the steering wheel.

They encountered insurrectionary forces soon thereafter; a group of five 14-16 year old boys with handguns at an improvised checkpoint at Fremont High.

"Who you be?" One of the boys asked, cocked his gun, but did not aim it.

"Friends," Smoke grinned wide and held up open hands, "We've got supplies for Captain Morris Johnson."

"How you know Captain Johnson?" the boy asked, eyes narrowing.

"Ask him yourself," Smoke said, "Tell him Wisdom's younger brother is here with the supplies. As promised."

"I'll do that." Another boy handed him a CB mike, and the young warrior called in their arrival.

"Captain Johnson say he comin' to meetcha," the young insurrectionist said.

"Fine," Smoke said. They didn't get out of the cab, and their guards

ARMAGEDDON, CA 94666

didn't bother them. They reminded Greg of the Azanian comrades of South Africa's riotous late-90's, youth properly too young for any military service, yet taking up the insurrectionary front lines with zeal. They were in a celebratory mood; not a sign of alcohol or drugs, nor of military discipline for that matter. It was a Saturday night. Normally they'd be partying down, getting high, and sweet talking girls. Now, they were revolutionaries.

A jeep and two uniformed men pulled up, perhaps forty minutes later, all Army issue. As the driver and the armed passenger stepped out, the comrades saluted.

"So," the black driver of the jeep approached the cab, captain's rank above a colorful, red-green-black-gold arm band, as Smoke stepped down from it, "You're Wisdom's younger bro. How's the Hawk doing?"

"Good, considering his current circumstances," Smoke kept his hands open, his arms loose at his sides, "Told me to tell you he appreciated your Kwanzaa gifts. Especially the Julius Nyerere pamphlets. They made it to Barruka in max."

"Gene," Captain Johnson grinned from ear to ear and hugged Smoke. Jaws dropped and eyes widened among the comrades, "So, what'd you bring us?"

"Mostly medical," Smoke laughed, "From Sacto. Lots and lots of field temp plasma. And, a few surprises."

"Looks like we're gonna need every bit of it," Johnson frowned, then waved a hand, "Alright then. Heard you're making a contact as well."

"At the Center," Smoke explained, "Someone who needs to get himself and his 'property' out of Oakland, before any crackdown."

"Just where we were headed," Johnson said, "Follow me. Stay right behind my jeep and we'll cut right through."

Smoke removed the license plate covers, then jumped back into the cab to stay right on the jeep's back bumper. And Greg marveled that they were, in truth, in liberated territory. Liberated Oakland. New Afrika. People were all over the city's streets, walking, gathering, casually and without fear. Again, he detected little overt drunkenness, and no disorderly behavior. The night was solid with friendliness, palpable, like the rich smell of a Horaisan rose. Many people, men and women, carried guns. And they were not all black, though most were people of color; Latino, Asian, African, and all the shades in between. The few whites there were mixed amiably with the rest. The atmosphere was jubilant as well, and peaceful. The crowd, in places, casually blocked the streets, but they made room for Captain Johnson's jeep to pass, occasionally giving Smoke and Greg a curious eye.

"How the hell are we going to leave Oakland and get this truck back to Alabaster?" Greg shot Smoke a glance.

"I'm staying," Smoke announced, "You'll be taking the truck back,

237

plus a passenger. And don't worry. They're letting people leave, no questions asked. It's getting into Oakland that's the problem."

The New Afrika Center, awash in bright light, buzzed with exuberant activity; combined town meeting and national capitol for the embryonic nation. Smoke parked where Johnson indicated. The captain's orders brought several people to help Smoke and Greg unload the truck.

"I'll go see if I can find your passenger," Johnson said, and eased his way through the noisy, excited crowd.

No one paid any attention to their skin color as the truck's cargo disappeared, hand-over-hand, into the Center. Presently, Johnson returned with a squat, stocky, Latino man clutching a battered briefcase to his side. Smoke got off the truck to talk to him.

"My friend here, Greg, will drive you to Alabaster tonight. There, you'll find my car. He can point it out for you. Take it with my blessing. Just get rid of it as soon as you can. It's a junker, and I got a feeling its gonna become a liability. Real soon."

Smoke dug into his pocket, fished out his keys and slipped off the car keys. Meanwhile, the soldier who'd taken Smoke's place on the truck whistled dramatically as removing the plasma revealed a floor of different boxes.

"Jesus," the man said and pried open the heavy duty lid to one of them, "These are Timpo grenades. One of 'em could level a whole city block."

The captain and Smoke exchanged knowing smiles as the man gave Greg a look of respect tinged with skepticism.

"When do you think we could leave?" Greg's passenger asked politely, "The sooner I can get to where I'm going, the better. For the Insurrection."

"Greg?" Smoke asked.

"Can we get something to eat before we go?" Greg asked as the last grenade box left the truck.

"Absolutely," Johnson grinned, "The Commons is right across the street. But first, put these on. I could be called away at any time, and these'll help you move around New Afrika."

He handed them the well sown arm bands that the captain and other folks around the Center wore—a black, a green, and a gold star clustered on a field of red. Greg put his on. The group headed to a large warehouse, the wide open doors streaming light, the sound of company and the smell of food into the night. The large warehouse floor of the Commons had been converted into a cafeteria. Long tables in the back held the food, the servers behind catering from huge, steaming pots. The hall itself was about half full with people and full up with conversation and laughter.

ARMAGEDDON, CA 94666

"Don't got much this time o' night," one of the servers bellowed, "But we'll fix ya up."

Smoke, Greg and Greg's passenger took trays and paper plates which were promptly heaped with aromatic baked beans liberally flaked with chunks of beef, a large square of corn bread, and a pile of greens.

"Got any beer?" Smoke asked the server.

"Yep, but only one to a customer," the man said and he dipped into a cooler for three.

"Revolutionary discipline," the captain said, as he walked them to a table, "The first thing the Coalition and the Liberation Force did yesterday, when the city was completely under our control, was to communalize all food supplies and all the liquor in the stores. Every ounce of that alcohol is under lock and key. And would you believe, the homeboys in the gang alliance, they voluntarily turned over all their drugs. Its now also locked away. We might just need that heroin and Ynisvitrin for painkiller, once the real fighting starts."

"What are you doing about the addicts?" Smoke dug into the meal, using his cornbread to sop up the juices.

"Trying the Panther cure," the captain shrugged, "Cold turkey. Then we're swapping their needles and pipes for guns. Its too early to tell if revolutionary nationalism can replace their habits. The alkies are the worst, and some of them we've had to hospitalize at Kaiser. I got a suspicion some of the gangbangers also have their own private stashes. But there's no dealing."

"What about looting?" Smoke took a swig of beer.

"Thursday was the worst. But when the gangs and then Oakland Base joined the struggle, it virtually stopped. We've now got soldiers and block militias stationed at every department store, shopping mall and warehouse. And we're asking people to respect the small, mom-and-pop stores, those that haven't left yet, and not loot them. We haven't stopped it entirely, but its reduced considerably."

"And..."

"Well, its not like we don't know people want this shit, so we're telling everybody, yes, we'll distribute it. What we now need is a fair way to parcel out the junk."

Greg watched the two men, under hastily rigged incandescent light grids that hid the empty space above to the ceiling's sketchy rafters with their glare. He noted each line and wrinkle in their intense faces, engaged in their discussion, under that sharp light.

"So, what's Oakland like for money these days?"

"We expropriated banks and large payrolls, and that's what we're using to start up a little smuggling. On the street, we're printing script and using ration cards. Script notes are immediately redeemable in

239

END TIME

food portions. A can of processed meat, a half gallon of powdered milk, a pound of cheese, a sack of flour or beans. The market gives us equivalencies, but everybody in Oakland is being fed. Every person is rationed enough food for a week, two and a half meals a day. Problem is, lots of folks don't know how to efficiently cook the food they got. We've got teachers going to every neighborhood teaching people how to cook. For people who just can't or won't cook for themselves, we got the Commons here, all around the city, and folks can redeem their food ration for cafeteria style meals. Liberation Force soldiers for instance need a mess. So do most of the people taking up the front lines. There's still a few restaurants open. No fast food though anywhere in the city."

"You know," Smoke leaned over his empty plate, "It might be good PR to push some victory gardens. You've got empty lots, you've got rooftops, you've got parks. And hell, you've probably got lots of people needing some work to do. Start Victory Gardens and do a propaganda campaign on metropolitan self-sufficiency in the face of encirclement. Great press. It'll kick as a story, even if Oakland doesn't..."

"Excuse me," the Latino, whose name Greg didn't, and probably wouldn't know, interrupted Smoke's reverie. "I do need to get going."

"Sorry," Johnson and Smoke said, simultaneously. Smoke looked at Greg.

Captured by the conversation, Greg made a snap decision.

"Can you drive a stick shift?" Greg asked his would-be passenger, this anonymous man.

"Sure," he knit his eyebrows in concern.

"Look," Greg said, now firm behind his decision, "I'll draw you a map. An exact map to the Alabaster State campus and to the Transportation Department. Smoke will give you his license plate number, and I'll give you the keys to the truck. Only, please don't take the truck to where you want to go. It guzzles gas like you wouldn't believe, and you can't go over fifty miles an hour safely on the freeway. My recycling coop really needs that truck tomorrow for their run."

"No problem," the man said, earnestly, "No problem at all."

"Park the truck, and leave the passenger door open. Leave the keys under the passenger's seat. I'll call a coop volunteer tomorrow and tell him to pick up the truck."

"Absolutely no problem," the man said.

"You gonna stay in New Afrika?" Johnson laughed.

"Yes," Greg said.

***

Marcus hit it, bullseye, about 10 til 6 on Saturday.

"Yup," the resident manager wrinkled his forehead, "That's Paul Janosik. He lives here. He recently moved from one apartment to another in the complex. You gonna give him money?"

240

ARMAGEDDON, CA 94666

"Excuse me," Marcus said, "I have to make a telephone call."

The detective immediately flagged Manley from a pay phone. He thought about calling in Randy from running point on the girl, Lori, but decided against it. A large raven, wing span momentarily silhouetted against the rising moon, joined the night. A patrol car pulled up to where Marcus waited on the corner of Main and California, Joe and partner inside.

"Peregrine. He's got an apartment in that building," Marcus pointed.

"You really found him," Joe marveled, stepping from his car, "Oh, by the way, this is Pete Samsung."

"Better let us handle this," Peter said.

Joe and Pete explained matters to the manager, who grew less and less pleased with every word.

"I didn't know," he shook his head, "Really, I didn't know."

"No one's blaming you," Marcus offered, "Just let the police do their job."

"Here's the key," the manager offered, "Do what you have to do."

The stairwell up to Peregrine's apartment was lit by a single bare light bulb. Joe flicked it off from the switch at the base of the stairs.

"Better take this," Joe whispered and handed Marcus his revolver, "Never know what might happen."

So they crept with deliberate stealth up the stairs, in the darkness visible. Joe had Pete's revolver, followed by Pete with shotgun, and trailed two steps behind by Marcus. All three of their weapons were poised. Joe inspected the apartment number once at the top of the stairs, making sure. The gap between door and floor revealed a strange apparition. Serrated lines of light just on the edge of human vision marched methodically across the gap. Marcus could smell all of their sweat before Joe raised a cautionary hand. Then he kicked open the door.

For a brief moment Marcus witnessed a phantasm, bathed in the smoky light of its own making. The creature was humanoid, dressed in a form fitting, single piece, eel-gray body suit. The hands were gloved, with thick seams running up the arms and shoulders. And the head was entirely, strangely helmeted. It was a type of skull-tight ski mask, fitted with shear goggles and headphones, and crested with a soft, gun-metal colored apparatus. The goggles pulsed with that on-edge-of-sight light Marcus had observed seconds before, from under the door.

"Freeze," Joe yelled, crouched, and aimed.

An invisible light, apprehendable by a sense more visceral than sight and tailored minutely to Joe's shape, streaked with precision from the refractive goggles, cookie cutting Joe perfectly. Joe exploded backwards as his partner fell in a faint to the floor. What remained of Manley hit Marcus with force enough to shove him back, collapsing him at the head of the stairs. Pete squeezed off two shells. Both sprayed off the figure's chest before it launched a second form fitting invisible-yet-visible bolt to fry Pete as well. Then, the apparition bounded for the stairs.

Perhaps it was Joe's acrid, burnt corpse that camouflaged Marcus. Or, perhaps the creature which had just killed two policemen made an oversight in its rush. In either case, Marcus managed, with the last of his strength, to raise his foot, draped with Joe's barbecued leg, to trip the creature as it reached the stairs.

"She died of a broken neck," Manley's Sergeant, Damian Marx, diagnosed.

The detective was not badly bruised or stained by Joe's remains.

"What the hell..." Marcus broke off, unable to rid his nose of the odor of burnt human flesh, "How did she do..."

"Full body virtual reality assault suit is my guess," Damian rubbed his fatigued brow, thinking of the two good officers he had lost. "I've only heard about such things. If you ask me, its Sulawesi Tech. We'll leave an officer here, to catch Peregrine when he returns."

"He won't come back here," Marcus said, numb of emotion with the death of his friend, "There's only one place he's likely to go now."

THIRTY-THREE

Excerpted from
"Nations and People of Earth,"
*The Amok World Almanac
and Book of Weird Facts*
2010
(Electrostraca #: A/GR-010-367-582-2376)

San Cristobal is a country intentionally without representation in any world body, to include the United Nations. It is a country diplomatically unrecognized by any world power, let alone the two nations upon which it borders. It is a country unmapped in atlases. Cartographers until the 1820's were beholden to the Spanish monarchy's ban on acknowledging San Cristobal's existence, and cartographers after the 1820's knew nothing of it. A land outside of history, a purposefully disappeared nation; San Cristobal hovers above the world, both metaphorically and literally. As such, little about San Cristobal is known for certain. A caveat for readers of the remainder of this entry; most of what has been assembled on San Cristobal comes from second- and third-hand sources.

First, its geography and geology. The three linked valleys of San Cristobal are located on the spine of the Andes, between Chile and Argentina, and between Cerro Ojo del Salado and Cerro del Toro. Comprised of 580 square miles of valley floor and close to another 140 square miles of marginal mountain borderland, San Cristobal was cre-

ARMAGEDDON, CA 94666

ated by east/west block faulting around the time the southern Andean cordillera was folded up out of tectonic plate collisions. The hundreds of feet of sheer cliff surrounding and isolating the short rift zone stand without much erosion, given the cold, dry mountain climate. The highest, northernmost valley is arid, originally supporting only high desert scrub. The middle valley is blessed by a natural, cold water spring and soil suitable for agriculture. The middle valley's waters flow into the lowest, southernmost valley. There it pools with waters from a hot sulfur spring before emptying into the caverns that originally drained the primeval lake which once filled all three valleys. The Almagro Pass along the middle valley's northwest rim is San Cristobal's only natural portal.

This austere, wild setting accounts for the region's unique history. The native Americans responsible for the Nazca lines and carvings knew of the site, and considered it sacred. They carved bas reliefs of spiders, condors and other birds, llamas and alpacas, fish, snakes, six-petaled flowers, and haloed figures along with complex geometries into impossible locations along the valleys' cliffs.

In turn the Incas [legend has it under first emperor Manco Capac's reign (1100-1200 ce) but more probably after Topa Inca's conquest of Chile (1300-1400 ce)] reaffirmed the site's rugged sacredness by building a Temple to the Sun and erecting an intihuatama atop the eastern cliffs, virtually a copy of the one at Vilcapampa (Machu Picchu, 1200-1300 ce). The valleys were called Tacachavan. Later Inca generations elaborated the northern and western rims of the valleys with superb white granite temples, palaces, fortresses, plazas, stairways, cisterns, tombs and tunnels. All were substantially plundered if not destroyed by the Spanish conquerors in the 1500's. The terraced valley floors still bear the mark of the Inca civilization into the 21st century. Legend holds that the mountain and sun worship of Inca emperors and nobles, priests and virgins invested in the valleys was being challenged, perhaps even supplanted toward the later decades of the empire by a darker mystery cult. The cult was associated with ruins on the southern rim of the valleys built around primal artifacts stolen from the conquered Chimu people. Pretender to the Inca throne, Huascar, and his sister/wife were said to have been preparing for flight to Tacachavan when besieged, captured and killed by Atahualpa.

The Spaniards saw their own value in the three valleys they christened San Cristobal. They converted the site into a penal colony, first for rebellious natives of note, then for notable, exiled Spanish enlightenment liberals, humanists and free thinkers, and finally for radicals and revolutionaries from all around Spain's world empire. San Cristobal, while still a prison by 1750, was also a substantially self supporting settlement. Prisoners were allowed to bring family, or to

243

marry native women. Agriculture and mining augmented sophisticated metallurgy, textile and chemical extraction industries; the most advanced in the Spanish empire. Many of San Cristobal's residents were heretical men of considerable knowledge. Schools and a university flourished in the valleys, as did the most modern medical facility in the world.

The valleys' extreme isolation, plus their over two centuries history as an internment institution, acted to forge a social character peculiar to San Cristobal. The valleys were a radical nexus, but they were also a dead end. All manner of liberals and revolutionists came to this mountain crucible, but few ever left, except through death. Strong autarchic sentiments thus colored the association of some the world's most visionary, experimental and revolutionary minds from the start. At the same time, San Cristobal gained a reputation as an idiosyncratic type of international utopia. Prominent political prisoners often chose, if they could, incarceration in San Cristobal over internment in a less secure prison closer to home, this despite the horrendous and sometimes fatal transport to that distant mountain penitentiary. In turn, the valleys' residents spoke not only an officially sanctioned Spanish and the unofficial native tongue Quechua, but also an organically developed *lingua franca* that melded the numerous languages of the diverse prisoner population into what was called *lingupero*. Literally, dog tongue.

Inspired by the American Revolution, anticipating the French Revolution by five years, and seizing the opportunity offered by Tupac Amaru's powerful, but failed revolt; the prisoners overwhelmed their guards, declared a revolutionary republic—Latin America's first—and kicked out the Spanish empire in 1784. Spain spent twelve years and a great deal of wealth trying to retake the valleys, only to be thwarted by geography and the tenacious bravery of San Cristobal's self-emancipated citizens. Spain opted for an early version of the *cordon sanitaire* strategy against the minuscule republic after 1796, what with trouble brewing in other parts of the empire.

The Spanish Monarchy's refusal to recognize San Cristobal's independence extended to not locating the Andean republic on official maps of Spain's New World Empire, and not acknowledging its existence in diplomatic dealings with other world powers of the age. Not only did this drop San Cristobal from the world's atlases, it allowed autarchy to bloom into total isolationism under siege. In turn, this blended into complete anonymity under quarantine. When Bolivar and Martin liberated South America, San Cristobal quite literally, deliberately dropped out of history. The country's red, blue and green flag had no witness other than the valleys' inhabitants, as commerce with the outside world was rare and one way. What necessities were needed, the

ARMAGEDDON, CA 94666

republic's government obtained through strictly clandestine trade. San Cristobalan traders in Chile claimed to be from Argentina, and the reverse, so as to preserve the Andean nation's anonymity. Yet it remained the Shambhala of humanity's Left wing. A mythic refuge for freedom fighters, it started its reputation by taking in the followers of Tupac Amaru fleeing the Spanish Imperial crackdown. It absorbed many of the refugees from Europe's 1848 liberal and romantic revolutions and the transitional 1871 Paris Commune. All the while San Cristobal was to the 19th century what Switzerland was to the 20th; an isolationist, prosperous, democratic capitalist republic.

Then came the influx of proletarians in flight from 1918 Germany, 1918-22 Russia, 1919-20 Mexico, 1919-21 United States, and 1921-24 Italy. San Cristobal's transition to a council communist society in 1929 was virtually bloodless as revolutions go; a portend of future developments. Spanish CNT and FAI immigrants after 1938 shifted the country's social organization toward anarchism, deepening its commitment to bottom-up federalism. The red-and-black flag, which was raised without violence in 1929, was in turn done away with, replaced with nothing. B. Traven stayed in San Cristobal for a time in the late 1950's, but ultimately returned to die in Mexico. The early 1960's witnessed a peaceful "green revolution" in San Cristobal, which also saw women in the valleys successfully assert sexual equality in what still had been a substantially Latin culture. The assemblies of San Cristobal voted in 1995, against all of their isolationist traditions, to take part in the world and its "community of nations," in order to promote its version of the social project. Southern Mexico became its first substantive intervention into the outside world.

Twenty-first century San Cristobal is an interweaving of selected post-industrial technologies with a self conscious culture of voluntary simplicity. Some 1,290,000 people live in the valleys. The main urban arcology, the capital Tupac Amaru, climbs the western wall of the second valley and is home to a third of the population. Every valley habitat outside of the urban arcologies focuses a number of decentralized energy sources with intensive farming—soil, hydroponic and aquaculture—alongside hobby home industries. Photovoltaic and geothermal energy sources supply San Cristobal. Breakthrough hydroponics and protein farming feed it. Automated, pollution free, compact heavy industries supply it. Much of the country's industry and agriculture is built into the cliffs, in natural and artificial caverns, so that the valley floors are cultivated in intentional wildness. A network of geosync satellites, launched clandestinely in the late 1960's from scientific platforms adrift in the world's wide oceans, can link the country into the world media. Autonomist computer hardware and software allow it to cut into the international information web without the world detecting it. Laser and particle beam weapons run by popular militias defend it. State-of-the-science photon displacement fields camouflage it. And a horizontal, neighborhood by city, factory by industry democracy governs it, aided by an inclusive, participatory media net.

At the same time, virtually every San Cristobalan is a mountaineer and survivalist by upbringing. A Cristobalan can repair electronic solid state as readily as she or he can repair a primitive iron plow. Most every 12-year-old can teach an advanced lesson or two in mountain warfare to US special forces. And the citizenry evinces an absolute disdain for possessions, as well as a joyful, voluntary communalism, both culturally reinforced by adoption of native American cultural elements, so that freedom is equated with not being tied down by too many things, and good character with the capacity to share.

If, as some claim, socialism was betrayed by the counter-revolutionary ultra-Leftism of a Trotsky, Bukharin, Kollantai, or Pannekoek, and the liberalism of a Gorbachev, then San Cristobal is socialism's Clytemnestra, or Fanny Kaplan. If, on the other hand, socialism was betrayed by the Jacobinism of a Lenin and Trotsky, and the Bonapartism of a Stalin, Mao and Castro, as others maintain, then San Cristobal is socialism's Penelope and resurrected Rosa Luxemburg. The citizens of those distant valleys do not bother themselves with matters of loyalty or betrayal on such a cosmic scale. They simply live the way they always have and enjoy their good fortune.

THIRTY-FOUR

Greg woke just before dawn, in the New Afrika Center bunk room he had been assigned to with Smoke and others. Woke from a strange dream. The dream setting was his memories of last academic year's Liberated Zone put on by Smoke and the MDRG at ASU on May 1. It incorporated many of their other theatrical pieces; butcher paper strewn with art utensils taped to the sidewalks leading to Remley Plaza, and plenty of cannabis circulating. Large plywood panels, hinged together so that they could stand free, displayed revolutionary posters from a variety of historic periods across the side fronting the library arcologies. An open microphone highlighted a free speech soapbox amidst the usual MDRG circus chaos; erotic mime around the fountain, a modest sized chess field drawn next to the administration fortress with students and junior professors playing pieces on the field, tanks of nitrous oxide on the grass with people lined up for hits, an annihilation derby of robotic machines constructed by a circle of graduate students and designed to rip each other limb from limb in a maximum display of pyrotechnics, etc. But the show stopper had been set in the plaza, dead center.

There, the MDRG constructed a suburban living room, sans the walls. Plush blue carpeting defined what at first most who traversed

ARMAGEDDON, CA 94666

the plaza treated as an art exhibit. A large sofa and small, old easy chair bracketed a coffee table littered with up-to-date quick news and personality mags, not to mention an ashtray full of cigarette butts and several empty Coors beer bottles. The corner arrangement faced a long home entertainment cabinet. Its video ran suggestive softcore German beer advertising loops, the CD/DAT blazed the latest ultra-synch neodisco beat, and the small holodeck modeled an anatomically correct human brain, a computer generated graphic which rotated for several minutes before detonating, finally to leave a smoldering stem before the repeat. A large, old set of golf clubs rested in their golf bag against the back of the couch. And, slouched into the couch, a well-dressed mannequin sprawled, its wrists slit by a broken Coors bottle. The mannequin and couch were covered in fake blood. Several more Coors bottles lay scattered about on the rug. Three pieces of commentary underscored this exhibit. Two lengths of butcher paper invited audience comment with the questions: "Why did he do it?" and "Who is he?" And a title for the piece had been scrawled across the plaza's stones, reading "Suburban Suicide."

Spray painted on a blank wall of the Humanities/Social Science complex was the slogan: "It Is Forbidden To Forbid." Sandwich board signs at all entrances to the plaza informed folks in a variety of languages that: "You Are Now Leaving The American Sector."

In real life, people had been slow to invade the apparent art piece. But, as the day progressed, and the MDRG's marijuana and other drugs made the rounds, students started sitting with the mannequin and reading the coffee table magazines. Soon, they discovered the box of drugs hidden under the cushions of the easy chair packed with large, mutant kief buds from Larry's farms, and a container of 300 very expensive and very illegal Rita derms, saturated with the latest, powerful, Swiss concoction of neural stimulants. As the crowd distributed the derms, applied them, and combined them with the smoke, the tone in the plaza heightened.

First, they took the golf clubs to the home entertainment center. They shattered and broke up the equipment, culminating as the mannequin was shoved, head first, through the video screen. The old easy chair was quickly broken up, as was the coffee table. A burly knot of males, with a few females, managed to heft and angle up the home entertainment cabinet. With a labored run they tossed the large, boxy object end over, and it exploded into splintering wood, slivered glass and plastic, and scattering solid state parts. The same demolition crew however failed to make more than a dent in the solidly built couch, even after eight fervent tosses. Apparently they abandoned their efforts, only to have the couch first wisp and then billow white smoke. Someone had wedged their lit cigarette beneath the cushions.

247

END TIME

Ironically, the MDRG wound up running around for fire extinguishers to desperately, unsuccessfully put out the smoldering piece of furniture. The campus fire department finally had to be summoned to douse it cold.

In his dream, encapsulated time loops shuffled together. Putting out the couch fire occupied him, incongruously at the same time a group of people worked setting up the Suburban Suicide display to begin with. Janet worked among the latter group. She waved once, but otherwise remained preoccupied with her work. Greg did not wave, his hands full with putting out the burning sofa. He simply stared after her, watching her work. Rachel, Margaret and Lori were also in the dream, though he remembered them vaguely, as if they were not fully formed images on the edges of his attention.

Next to his clothes piled on the floor, he found the Timpo grenade's shell he had placed there the night before. The soldier who had helped him unload the truck, Gabriel, had been assigned the bunk room as well, and he had given it to Greg.

"How'd it get this way?" Greg asked, from his corner cot.

"Captain had me take a case o' them grenades to a machine shop coupla blocks away," Gabe relayed. "They cut them open to extract the explosive, don't ask me why. Anyway, when I saw the empty grenade casings, I thought they might make a smart souvenir."

"Thanks," Greg had accepted the empty grenade. He left it on his cot in the morning. He dressed quietly, made sure he had his arm band on, and tiptoed out of the room. Smoke's bunk was empty. The center's activity was muted, though not entirely still. Two women and a man talked softly over fragrant cups of tea in the foyer. They smiled at him as he walked past. The girl at the switchboard was engrossed in a book, a serial romance.

"Can I use the phone?" Greg asked.

"Sure," she said and gave him a wide smile. He called around Alabaster until he woke a member of the recycling coop scheduled to make the run that morning. He explained his situation as well as the truck's location. When he hung up he silently hoped that the man he had given it to last night had lived up to his promise.

"Where you headed," the girl asked, lowering the book.

"Breakfast, first," Greg smiled, "Then I think I'll walk around the city and see what there is to see."

"Maybe I'll still be here when you get back," she winked, "I'll show you around this town."

Greg blushed and stepped out, into the fog worried streets of the Oakland Free Territory. Across the street, at the Commons, a cluster of people helped unload a truckload of food stuffs. He joined the group, gulping down coffee the consistency of thin mud from a paper cup in

248

ARMAGEDDON, CA 94666

between carrying large vats of hot breakfast in through the front doors. "There's a central kitchen for each five or six commons," Freddie, one of the servers explained, "That's where the food's cooked. We can keep it warm. It'd be too much effort to put in a kitchen at every commons. Not now at least."

A line had formed by the time they finished. They got to head it up, first helping each other, then alternating bites of breakfast while serving others.

"Thems that work, get fed first," Freddie chuckled. Breakfast was a choice between biscuits and gravy, a scramble of real and powdered eggs, cream-of-wheat by the gallon, fried and fresh scallions, hard boiled eggs, dozens of loaves of bread, buckwheat groats and milk, and an array of whole fruits and vegetables. Greg had a little eggs on his biscuits and gravy, alongside sliced tomato and more coffee. He worked off his meal with several hours serving breakfast to others. Those in line at this early hour were mainly Liberation soldiers. When more help, and more diners arrived, he took the opportunity to stroll about the city.

The hazy morning sun stretched opposite clouds forming in the west. Lots of people were already up and about, the pace leisurely. Only cars, buses or trucks with the New Afrika seal, identical to his arm band, cruised the street. The rest of the population's autos were parked. When he passed a gas station, he noticed it guarded by a militia woman. Large boxes and crates crammed with empty bottles and piles of rags cut into strips waited in the mechanics bay; quick assembly molotovs as weapons of last resort.

On a corner further along, a three story office building bore the crudely painted sign: Women's Shelter. Greg glanced in. A woman behind the counter read a magazine. Another woman, very pregnant, sat knitting in a chair near the stairwell.

"Excuse me." Greg said politely, "What is this place?"

"Home fo' the homeless," the knitting woman said, not missing a stitch, not looking up.

"And for the resented, and the battered, and the unloved, and the unwanted," the counter woman looked up from her magazine, "Why you asking?"

"I'm just visiting Oakland," Greg admitted, "Kind of a tourist."

"That band says you more than that," she raised an eyebrow, "Say's you support and guard New Afrika."

"Guess I kind of know Captain Morris Johnson," Greg said.

The woman knitting stopped, looked Greg up and down critically, humphed, and continued her needlework.

"How's this place work?"

"The women, we run it," the woman rustled her magazine, as if impatient to return to its contents, "We got house rules. No drugs. No male guests. No parties. The girls, we run it, democratic-like. We set up the clean up schedules. We keep the peace, and we enforce the rules."

"Was this here?" Greg persisted, "Before..."

"The original project operated out of a church basement," she suddenly looked tired, "Could only hold a dozen, maybe eighteen. So, after Liberation, we found this place. Hakim turned it up for us actually. It was a vacant office building, til we converted it last Friday. Now we got two hundred women here. It's like a dormitory. It's safe 'cause we don't allow cooking in the rooms. There's a Commons right down the way."

"It's gotten a little too big, if you ask me," the knitter stopped momentarily, "Awkward as hell to run this size, and hard to keep people to their responsibilities. More fights."

"Like the one I'm gonna have with the girl whose time I'm covering on the counter 'cause she didn't come home last night."

"Thanks for your information," Greg smiled, and left them to their morning. City buses ran, not exactly on schedule, but giving good coverage of New Afrika. Greg grabbed one, not sure where it was headed.

"Why not keep them running?" Roy, the bus driver, spoke over his shoulder as he drove, "Folks still gotta get around. Young and old particularly need the bus. Not everybody's got a car, and the Coalition's nationalized all the gas. The Union was the one actually decided to keep the buses running. They went to the Coalition when the Transit Authority, what remained of it, didn't want to go along. Lotsa things Union run now."

"You're not getting paid are you?"

"Well, not technically," Roy swung the bus over to the curb on the relatively empty street. People got on and off without fare. "I mean, no one knows where all of this is going. I'm just doing my bit to keep it on its way. You know, what you might want to catch is The Wall. They painted it on Friday. It's a couple of stops up."

A long stretch of wall isolating an industrial park was now a community mural. It began, on the left, with key revolutionary figures—Garvey, King, Malcolm X, Zapata, Villa, Chavez, Geronimo, Joseph—and scrolled to the right with scenes of common people working, creating, celebrating, playing, and defending themselves. The wall was part outdoor polytech mural paint, part vibrant spray paint, part expropriated house paints in a panoply of styles. A crew of juveniles busied themselves with detail work at the far corner.

Four men in two trucks worked among the derelict cars in a more residential neighborhood near The Wall.

"We was here yesterday," one of the crew said, "Asking 'bout these heaps o' junk. They're abandoned all right."

ARMAGEDDON, CA 94666

"So you're cleaning up the streets." Greg jumped to the conclusion, watching the men snake chains wherever they could among the rusted metal and flaked paint.

"Yeh, that too," the man shrugged, "But these wrecks gonna build up the barricades. We takin' these to the front, so as key areas 'round the city can be blocked 'gainst invasion."

Two people argued on a street corner further along. A man and a woman yelled at each other at a considerable volume, about him staying out all night and about her not being woman enough for him. Typical lover's quarrel. A modest crowd of neighbors had gathered to hear them out, probably not for the first time given their amusement and side comments. When she started impugning his lovemaking and his manhood, he smacked her. The crowd responded quickly. Two women and a man jumped him and immediately pulled him back. Another woman stepped out of the bystanders. She dressed down the man, lecturing him, finger wagging, about how he was the neighborhood bully and why was he picking on someone smaller and weaker than him. Another male in the crowd, about the same size and build, swaggered out and offered to take on the original man in a "fair fight." The women did not appreciate the challenging display. Only after a good deal of effort did they calm things down.

Crowds thronged the churches up Telegraph and along MacArthur, services spilling out into the streets, the people boisterous. The African Methodist Episcopalian minister preached guarded hope from a pulpit outside on the church steps to a multitude blocking the streets, their hands full of home cooked, church served family breakfast. A long line of people waited patiently at the Kaiser Permanente Center, the late morning streaking up for approaching rain.

"Lot's of doctors didn't stay for the Big Takeover," one of the people in line told him, "But those that did decided, 'specially here at Kaiser, to give people some free service."

Down several blocks and around the corner, a company of soldiers arrayed in formation about the entrance to a vacant store front. Besides the New Afrika arm band, they also wore a black and red patch on their arms. They had cracked the building, and now a line of scruffy, destitute individuals filed in between them through the open doors. Some carried bedrolls or foam, others a shopping bag or two of possessions, perhaps even a grungy backpack.

"We're Captain Lawson's men," a sergeant said, "The Captain and us don't think the Coalition's moving fast enough on matters benefiting the people. These homeless people for instance. The Coalition's letting them rot in the streets, and its been more'en two days since Emancipation. So, we're taking matters into our own hands."

This revolution's New Model Army had it's Levelers then, if not it's

251

END TIME

Diggers. Greg strolled into the park lands surrounding Lake Merritt contemplating the gist of that thought. A squadron of children on a church field trip barely listened to the Rotary Natural Science Center tour guide talk about the Lake's unbalanced saltwater basin ecologies. Strata of kites stacked up into the clouding sky. And a group of older couples on picnic lounged about the horseshoe sand pits. The men tossed the shoes, the women attended to condiments, and both watched the barbecues. He strolled west, past the burned out shell of the County Courthouse and the intact gables of the Convention Center, out of the Rancho Peralta park. The boxy, battleship architecture of Laney College overlooked the high industrial art in Oakland's sculpture garden, the Channel Park also filled with leisurely crowds. He walked under the now deserted freeway and over the railroad tracks, to notice that swarms of kids had turned the Oakland Fire Department's multi-storied practice tower into one giant jungle gym. A squad of armed Liberation soldiers occupied the top floors as lookouts, their presence keeping the kids from doing too much mischief. As he climbed the tower's stairs for a view, Greg heard the soldiers' radio.

"And now, the latest news from Oakland. This morning a small, little known South American country called San Cristobal formally recognized Oakland's status as New Afrika, at the same time that tiny high Andean nation also announced diplomatic recognition of the Mixtecan and Mayapan Liberated Territories.

"Representatives of the governor's office, in conference with the New Afrika Coalition and Liberation Commander Malcolm Brown, announced this morning that talks will continue through the afternoon and evening in hopes of resolving the stalemate between the insurrectionary city and the combined US military forces surrounding Oakland.

"The President has called an emergency meeting of the National Security Council to respond to the latest developments in the Bay Area, and it is reported that the FBI Western Regional Field Office Director has been recalled to the nation's capital to account for the Bureau's handling of the riemanium and the Oakland rebellion under its 'Operation Anvil.'

"The Congressional Black Caucus is holding an emergency news conference in Washington DC at this moment, to urge restraint on the President in handling the Oakland Crisis.

"In a related story, statements were anonymously faxed in to select local media by individuals claiming to be members of the Mexican Revolution Solidarity Brigade at 1 p.m. today. The Solidarity Brigade is suspected of being in possession of the two pounds of bomb-grade riemanium stolen during the Piccoli robbery. The fax claimed that the Solidarity Brigade is proceeding with plans to build the riemanium

252

ARMAGEDDON, CA 94666

into a functional nuclear weapon unless the US military withdraws from both 'liberated Oakland and liberated Mexico.' The fax also cited a brief bibliography of materials available in the public library for instruction on building such a device. The Brigade promised to forward plans for their atomic bomb.

"It is now, 3:05 p.m."

Greg saw red. He remembered the Sunday meeting then. David, Beth, Larry, George, and Lori had gone over his head. He started back down the tower's steps to look for a pay phone, Oakland's industrial landscapes to the harbor behind him, when he heard the roar of approaching planes.

A wing of fighter jets, low over Nimitz Field, shrieked toward Oakland. Toward Jack London Square and the dual battle laser positions on Oakland's inner harbor. People were running around the tower then, running away from the Harbor as fast as was humanly possible. A second roar, and surface-to-air missile batteries leapt into action to lay up a defensive curtain of heat seeking rockets. The jets broke into evasive action. Battle laser auroras danced up ultraviolet into the descending sun as the weapons primed. Two jets looped back tightly and managed to let loose their own rockets before having to dodge again. The harbor erupted under the jet strike, counterpointed quickly by one jet taking a direct hit and another spinning off, minus one wing. The battle laser fired. The precise x-ray beam could not be seen. But it produced a sharp fold in the air as it pierced across the bay and stripped the top off San Francisco's Trans America Pyramid. Two more folds in space lanced from further up the east bay to snap into the Pleiades, melting off one tower and slicing up platform decking.

He could not remember having run down the rest of the tower's stairs.

Sirens wailed all around the city. Military sirens. Panic assailed the streets. People ran down the middle of the streets, ducked into buildings, ignoring Liberation Forces trying to reach the harbor. Greg steered for the New Afrika Center, the only place he knew to go. More explosions, distant. Black smoke filigreed up to the clouds. Gunfire rattled, also off in the distance, accompanied by the locust sound of helicopters and the neon sizzle of lasers. Then, the thick rumble of dark battle thunder.

He reached the Center's total chaos, in time for the artificial earthquake. The ground shook, an impact so sudden and so deep that Greg went to one knee.

"Flash in the west."

"I saw it too."

Most sounds of battle ceased. Two buildings down the block smoldered from a strike.

253

"That was artillery, 'bout half hour ago," Gabe commented. "They was aiming for the center. I don't know what just happened."

There was no mushroom cloud on the western horizon, only the smoke of battle. The other Smoke was not to be seen anywhere around the Center. The Center itself was packed. People listened, rapt, to the radios and TV. The switchboard periodically broadcast called-in news and rumor. Liberation Force soldiers stationed at the Center had their radios as well. Piece by piece, a picture of what had happened filtered outside.

"The Army's still holding the Base. Navy and Marines couldn't take it. Black marines are deserting left and right."

"One of the laser's was hit. We still got five. And San Fran's got a new skyline."

"They got Oakland Stadium. But they didn't get no further. We're holding the line."

"We fried the Bay Bridge. They was trying to move troops in from Treasure Island."

"The Veep and NSC, they jettin to Sacto."

"Ninety-five dead. So far."

The civil war abated, for the moment. Apparently, the US military's strategy had been to take the harbor and entirely surround the insurrection. They had failed, or the cost had appeared so high that they had stopped with second thoughts.

Clouds enveloped the remaining day. Dusk deepened. A news flash rippled through the crowds. The last massive explosion, that had been NAS Nimitz. Staging ground for retaking the liberated Army Base, it had gone up in one incredibly violent, horizontal detonation, virtually a pancake nuclear explosion in its intensity. This had stopped the US military assault, dead. Greg realized what use had been made of the Timpo grenades he and Smoke had smuggled into New Afrika.

Once again, he helped with service at the Commons, then ate a dinner of Creole rice and chicken with his single bottle of beer. Smoke still had not made an appearance, so Greg wandered out into the evening. Music drifted to him from upstreet of the Center. The city had settled back into a nervous calm, perhaps the calm before the storm. The smell of rain was palpable on the wind. As he searched out the music's source, he passed another warehouse between the Center and the Women's Shelter he had visited that morning. The open doors revealed a robed man lecturing to a room full of people, some dutifully taking notes.

"Judaism, Christianity and Islam all describe the Garden of Eden as man's original residence, a paradise which God planted and from which He exiled humanity after man's sin of rebellion. 'Do what you will' was the whole of the law for Adam and Eve in Eden, apart from

254

ARMAGEDDON, CA 94666

the divine injunction against eating the fruit of the Tree of Knowledge. Ever since the Garden, humanity's experience has been one of law, regulation and restriction, from the Jewish Torah, through the Christian New Testament, to the Moslem Koran.

"The Jew, by and large, is content with his Law. Banished from the Garden, the traditional Jew has no true heaven nor hell after death. At most, both are to be found here on earth, with the ultimate heaven being a restored Hebrew Kingdom in Palestine under the Messiah's reign. Only a shadowy sheol awaits the Jew in death. The Christian chafes under man's exile from the Garden and therefore bridles under the Law. Heaven and hell exist for him after he dies, conditioned by whether or not he accepts Jesus as his Savior. Jesus is the Word, and the Law for the Christian, and so belief in Him supersedes even the Law. The Law, in turn, exists in heaven, but man is in the presence of God, and therefore all is bliss. Hell's torture, of course, resides in the full knowledge of God, without His Presence for all eternity.

"Only the Moslem returns to the Garden and a state of 'do what you will' by his act of unconditional submission. The Law then becomes an instrument that, paradoxically, liberates the devout Moslem from the Law when he dies. The observant Moslem is given Paradise, synonymous in Islam with heaven, as his reward, and this is why he insists on absolute submission to the Will of Allah, which is one and the same with the Law. Since man has already tasted of the forbidden fruit, the Moslem's return to Paradise then is without restriction. It is an end to banishment, a return from exile to man's original home and state of grace. Allah resides in Paradise, and therefore, to be outside of Paradise is to be in Hell."

Greg continued walking in the cloud heavy night, the music pulling him on. A racing Liberation Force convoy of jeeps and APV's almost ran him down crossing the next intersection. His mind snapped into the realization that he was in a war zone, the day's events finally hitting him. He turned up the following corner and found himself in the middle of a block party. In a war zone, before an impending rain, people still danced and sang. A jazz/blues quartet cooked on an improvised stage in the middle of the street, replete with a whiskey-and-cigarette-voiced female singer. Some of the people near the band danced. Even at the worst of times, people needed to take some enjoyment from life.

People in Oakland had died during the day's skirmish. Oakland families mourned, as did the families of the US soldiers and civilians undoubtedly killed when the Liberation Forces retaliated. The spontaneous, inevitable blood of revolutionary birth was fast becoming the cold blood of civil war. Yet, all about him, people laughed and joked and partied, if for no other reason then for having survived the day's battle. Strange, this desire for life to continue, to go on despite war, death, addiction and suffering. He had read somewhere that there had been a band even at Auschwitz.

He sat on a stoop away from the boisterous crowd, listening and watching. Strange also the human need to transform life's pain into justification for this desire to continue living. Whether seen as God's test for salvation or history's test for liberation, suffering was the condition of life, though not its essence. The human creature's capacity to find a ray of hope, a sliver of joy, even in the Inferno's center was only surpassed by that being's ability to convert heaven into hell.

The band paused. A door down, a woman stepped out onto her porch, bowl in hand. She whistled sharp and clear into the anvil night. When an adult black cat spit out of the darkness, she lowered the bowl, the animal's meal. She stood, and smiled wanly as the cat gobbled.

"Used to have 'nother cat 'sides this Licorice," she said, seeing Greg eyeing the cat, "Deep orange tabby name a Red. Now Red catches his meals up the block. Licorice here ran him off. Used ta come too when I'd a whistle. Still does, sometimes."

She whistled again, then again, expecting nothing. Presently, when the black cat had greedily chunked down a third of the dinner, an orange cat tumbled out of the night.

"So, Red, you come fo' ta' visit?" she said.

The cat stepped wide around the black one, which had stopped eating, to butt up against the woman's ankles. She bent down and rubbed up behind his ears. Licorice gave Red a hostile look. Seeing Greg, Red stepped saucily over to him for additional attention.

"Keep him here," she said to Greg, "While I get him somethin' ta' eat."

She went back into her house while he preened Red. Licorice threw venomous glances the other cat's way between an occasional, deliberate bite, clearly ready to attack except for the unknown factor that Greg represented.

"Here ya' go Red." She returned with food for the second cat.

Red happily dug in, while Licorice glowered, no longer eating at all. Hiss, bound, snarl; black cat jumped Red, Licorice not even half done with his own meal.

"Stop that!" She slapped at the black cat but, too late, the orange tabby was gone. Licorice slunk back to his bowl, but she picked up both cat bowls. "No more for you! Can't understand it. They was brothers. They protected each other 'gainst the neighborhood dogs and strays when they was small. I don't know what turned Licorice. Jealousy, I s'pose. Red, he was always the charmer. Always the clever one. Everybody loved Red. Got lotsa attention, so Licorice was jealous. That jealousy twisted Licorice. He drove Red out and to another home."

The woman slammed back into her house with the bowls, shaking her head. Greg suddenly stood and walked into the metal tanged darkness. The quiet, mostly deserted New Afrikan streets were a convenient place for a young man to cry. Greg walked through an inner city become proud nation, one willing to take the first punch and come out even. Tears streamed down his cheeks. He had driven Janet, if not to another man, then at least out of his life with his jealousy, his possessiveness, his jailing behavior. Now he tried banishing her from his soul with his bitterness and anger. What was betrayal then? What was she responsible for and what was his blame in all of this? There had to be a better way to live through this, he thought. His acid anger kept that from happening, as his jealousy would keep him from finding a better way to live. If he let them. Greg was monogamous, deeply committed by inner conviction that such a relationship was desirable as well as possible. But monogamy was not to be policed in order to be kept. Promising monogamy was a gift; and as a gift always to be valued by the receiver.

He returned to the Center for his sleep a little after midnight. The reception foyer was modestly populated, everybody attentive to the radio and TV. Low conversations filled the spaces in the news. Cups of fragrant hot chocolate and coffee made rounds on a tray. And this morning's cute receptionist was on the board. In getting a mug of cocoa, he picked up the latest rumor. Oakland's rep in the House of Representatives, and the Congressional Black Caucus to which she belonged, engaged in a kind of shuttle diplomacy between Oakland, Sacramento and Washington DC even as they all sipped their drinks. A majority faction of the New Afrika Coalition, urged on principally by Liberation Commander Johnson, was a party to the negotiations, behind the backs of the New Afrika Center, the New Afrikan Lords, and other more uncompromising elements. Greg turned to walk, mug in hand, to the switchboard to take up the receptionist's earlier offer of friendship, when an announcement cut the news.

"Five minutes ago, our station received a fax transmission from the offices of representative Patricia Williams and the Congressional Black Caucus." The public television reporter, a man named Burt Desmond, spoke with obvious relief. "A peace agreement has been negotiated between Oakland's New Afrika Insurrection and the government of the United States. State and Federal authorities have agreed to fully prosecute the police involved in the murder of Daniel Logan, and to use every resource to discover the identities of his masked murderers. Oakland's mayor and city council have agreed to dramatically beef up the powers of the city's Civilian Police Review Board. No government, military, or police reprisal will be taken against civilians who participated prominently in the Insurrection. But only a partial amnesty has been extended to those in the military. Most ranks will be given the

257

END TIME

choice of a less than honorable discharge, or remaining in the military and facing courts-martial. The upper ranks, Commander Brown most prominently, will not be given a choice. They will plead guilty to mutiny in an instant courts-martial, eased by an immediate Presidential pardon. In exchange all levels of government will declare the death and damage on both sides of the conflict during the Insurrection a national disaster; and not an act of sedition, insurrection, war, riot or conspiracy. Congress and the President have agreed to set up a committee to plan a 'post World War Two Marshall style' recovery for America's inner cities. The Congressional Black Caucus statement ends with these words: 'It is time people all across the United States and the people of Oakland come together to bury our dead; the brave sons and daughters, men and women, fathers and mothers who died in this tragic mistake, this grave blunder in our common, national history and experience.'"

The roomful of people sobered entirely, and quickly. It was as if a relative, long expected to die, finally had. The grief bore no surprise. People had already gone over, not just the death, but what the life had meant. Not that New Afrika had been diseased. But it had been vulnerable, and it was done in before its time. Like most who lived on Oakland's deadly inner city streets. All had hoped, but none had expected more. The receptionist stared off in shock, tears forming up in her large, dark eyes. Greg did not feel too well himself as he squeezed the bridge of nose, now to hold back the tears. He slept fitfully, waking to on-and-off rain on the Center's high warehouse roofs. He dreamed, tossing and turning on his cot, a recurrent dream of strong hands violently ripping open an inchoate dark object by wrenching open its clasps. He kept waking in a cold sweat when, in his dream, the last, its seventh seal, popped.

***

Sumner threw Marable into damage control immediately, but by Friday the *Chronicle* newspaper's crotchety, 90-year-old Herb Caen savagely quipped: "Is the FBI's Operation Anvil helping out our fair city with the homeless problem by dusting winos in the business district?" Steven McCaffrey, himself bled dry by unsuccessful damage control in the Alameda County Sheriffs Department, confided in Edward on Saturday that the vultures were already circling for the FBI man. And the Director called early Sunday morning. Some VIP had complained about Sumner's handling of both the riemanium and Oakland, so now Washington had to do its own damage control. Nothing to worry about. After all, the Director had no intention of changing quarterbacks in the middle of a play. No doubt the wino's death was justifiable, but the Bureau had to account to the Justice Department, and the Department to the President and Congress. The Justice Department had scheduled its investigation for Monday, the day before the Senate Judiciary Committee's hearing.

Two days, Edward thought to himself as he watched the San Francisco Bay fall away through the jet window. Clouds to the west, their tops smeared with setting sun, formed a carpet on the floor of the world as the jet turned east. Two days away from his job, to deal with politics.

He had no doubt that this read as a black mark on his record, to be erased when Operation Anvil delivered the riemanium. He had more than his share of reprimands as a regular field agent, in large part due to attitude. But in his present position, he no longer had the luxury of either sarcasm or flippancy with regard to his superiors. When Cisco hit the deck, Edward honestly thought he had seen something about the wino that Sumner had not. So, he had flashed the sign. The bum's sudden, threatening movement was reason enough however. Edward needed no more cause. The need to kiss ass for political reasons galled him however. Exactly what he had always criticized his superiors for, and now he had to do it. To have to take two days off this crucial Solidarity Brigade case in order to justify Operation Anvil and cover Bureau butt infuriated him. A good offense is always the best defense, he told himself. Edward planned to come out punching at the national office; demanding an immediate appointment to fill the San Francisco office so that Sumner's efforts were not so administratively short-handed.

The jet roared into bleak night. Best to relax, he thought as he ordered a drink. The jet lag on this one was bound to be awful. He removed a blue Nepenthe capsule from the prescription vial in his pocket, swallowing it with his whiskey. He had not been sleeping well lately. A nerve relaxant, Nepenthe was one of the few tranquilizers that did not dog the REM cycle. His ambassador-class seating was plush enough to serve as a comfortable bed in a pinch. The blank, dark west scrolled out below.

Oakland was a surprise. He had geared down the Bureau's counter-intelligence operations against Black Nationalism partially prior to Thursday because there was every indication that the Solidarity Brigade was a creature of the white Left, and because he had needed the manpower. Its support for Oakland that afternoon in a faxed communiqué, a copy of which Edward had seen before leaving for the airport, had been tepid, no more than weak white-guilt solidarity. Oakland had occurred entirely on its own, and nothing from the field had anticipated the insurrection. The unfolding of events in Oakland had left the Bureau virtually helpless in turn. Sumner authorized efforts to foment splits in the New Afrika Coalition and "neutralize" militant leadership. Oakland was neither FBI responsibility nor its fault he reminded himself, a stance he would maintain while in Washington.

The angry night outside the jet raged with stars. Sumner had new, gut level sympathy for Bureau solos like Heidelburg, whose renegade actions had been motivated by deep, true patriotic sentiments. He felt like an ancient Roman soldier whose loyalty to Consul and Senate during the late Republic had been questioned as a consequence of Senatorial faction politics, the demagoguery of Tribunes, slave revolts, military uprisings; all that had turned Rome into an Empire. As pharmaceuticals mixed with alcohol to race on the heals of legions carrying eagle standards across his mind, Edward's eyes fluttered shut. Dreaming of Empire.

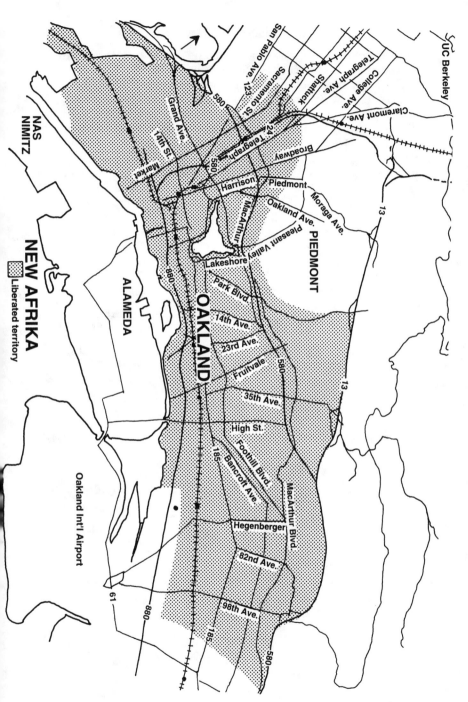

NEW AFRIKA
Liberated territory

NAS NIMITZ

ALAMEDA

Oakland Int'l Airport

OAKLAND

PIEDMONT

UC Berkeley

Grand Ave.

14th St.

Market

Telegraph

Harrison

Piedmont

MacArthur

Oakland Ave.

Pleasant Valley

Lakeshore

Park Blvd

14th Ave.

23rd Ave.

Fruitvale

35th Ave.

High St.

Foothill Blvd.

Bancroft Ave.

Hegenberger

82nd Ave.

98th Ave.

MacArthur Blvd.

Moraga Ave.

Broadway

San Pablo Ave.

Sacramento St.

Shattuck

Telegraph Ave.

College Ave.

Claremont Ave.

580

123

24

880

185

580

13

61

PART FOUR
SILENCE IN HEAVEN

THIRTY-FIVE

Excerpted from
"The Enemy Behind The Enemy"
None Dare Call It Betrayal: The Loss of Southern Mexico
by Lieutenant-Colonel David Burns, USA (Ret.)
2016, Hoover Institution, Stanford University Press
(Electrostraca #: USFP/IR-043562-147-331-1455)

...The United States intelligence community came upon the San Cristobal connection in late 2003, the U.S. military already three years deep into the Mexican civil war. By then San Cristobal had developed and deployed photon displacement fields to conceal, first their home valleys, and then their floating ocean colonies from aerial and satellite observation. So while, as soldiers, we knew that we were fighting not only ZLF terrorists, but also shadowy San Cristobalan forces, we never knew the extent or power of this "hidden enemy" until the end of the war, when our government was concluding a cowardly peace with the enemy ZLF in Paris.

To date, no world power has successfully penetrated either the valleys of San Cristobal or its ocean colonies. The CIA attempt to "hack" San Cristobal's cybersome from 2003 to 2009 is particularly instructive. Apparently, San Cristobalan science never abandoned analog information systems, and the country's advanced silicon, photon, biological, and quantum computer network has interactive digital and analog components that made it impervious to the Agency's best hacking efforts during our involvement in Mexico's civil war. US intelligence was not content with the brief portfolio of "facts" about her country presented to the Paris Peace Conference by the San Cristobalan representative, Maria Dominguez, in 2010 however. And so the CIA managed a small coup by

END TIME

capturing a San Cristobalan DIS military advisor to the ZLF, one Jose Miguel Casca, outside of Minatitlan in January, 2011. What we know about this extremely radical nation high in the Andes comes from the chemical interrogation of Casca...

...Landlocked, isolationist, autarchic San Cristobal first turned to the seas before coming to terms with any landed, national territory. San Cristobal used the relatively open period of the second World War and shortly thereafter (from 1940 to 1950) to parlay a portion of its large gold and silver reserves into sufficient capital to make some strategic purchases and to do some significant war salvage. The country gradually constructed front businesses and corporations. It slowly accumulated flags of convenience, havens of incorporation, and anonymous banking arrangements. This financial camouflage San Cristobal used to function in the world, without being of the world. This much San Cristobal's extremist government was willing to concede to international involvement by the middle of the 20th century.

San Cristobal also concentrated upon salvage from the Korean conflict, the numerous Middle Eastern, African and southern Asian wars, up to Vietnam, Afghanistan and the Gulf Wars. This war salvage was directly recycled. Combined with several discreet commercial purchases, it went to construct three primitive ocean colonies, fully operational by 1960. The colonies began as scientific research platforms, labeled by the US intelligence community Atlantis, Lemuria and Mu for the mythic sunken continents in the Atlantic, Indian and Pacific oceans in which the three platforms floated. Their environmental data collection contributed to San Cristobal's Draconian "Green Revolution," which in turn brought the colonies into greater prominence. Besides acting as environmental research facilities monitoring the state of the biosphere, by 1970 the entirely self contained colonies engaged in fish farming, breeding and processing projects. Lemuria became an entirely woman staffed, woman run colony.

By 1980, the corporate/financial front set up for the colonies allowed them to sell their packaged products, often to Third World nations, for cheap. The economic activity, in turn, permitted San Cristobal to launder additional sales of gold and silver reserves. The largest colony in 1990, Mu in the Pacific, comprised one industry/factory/processing ship, one research ship, two hydroponic/park ships and one community ship docked together around a flexible flotation platform. Two to three dozen crewed fishing trawlers were moored on its outer floating arms. The main colony was electronically up-to-date and armed to-the-teeth, primarily in defense against pirates. Each trawler possessed the latest in sensor and communication technologies, not to mention the most sophisticated weaponry available. The main colony surrounded its own dry-dock, and a lattice of submerged fuel and water storage tanks.

264

SILENCE IN HEAVEN

Photo thermal systems evaporated and simultaneously desalinated sea water along the flotation arms, to create a false fog for much of the day, one sufficient to obscure satellite viewing if a satellite happened to be observing the middle of one of the world's wide oceans in the years before San Cristobal's application of photon displacement fields as camouflage. Yet the colonies, the periphery, remained finely tuned to the core, the valleys of San Cristobal, via independent satellite link. They permitted San Cristobal to launch its satellite system in the first place, as they then facilitated San Cristobal's subversion of southern Mexico.

The position of San Cristobal, outside of the international body politic, the body digital, allowed its government to develop an eccentric perspective on world events. The twentieth century's last decade witnessed accelerated ecological degeneration, obvious to many besides those resident in the Andean valleys. As well, the country's extremist government claim to have detected the Third World economic collapse in 1995, almost three years before the actual breakdown. San Cristobal decided that it could no longer remain aloof from global affairs. It established the Department for International Sabotage in Symbiosis with Popular, Indigenous and Aboriginal Autonomist Liberation Struggles; DIS for short. And DIS found the ocean colonies ideal platforms from which to stage their terrorist operations.

The ever tragic plight of the Kurds and the Basques, and the growing despair and militancy of Europe's Gypsies attracted DIS's modest attentions at first. But when Leftist revolution emerged across southern Mexico, run by the Zapatista Liberation Front, San Cristobal found the demon child it wished to adopt. Atlantean trawlers fielded by DIS traded openly, although at some risk, on Mexico's Atlantic/Gulf coast. They came in through the Caribbean islands, with their own cargoes of "appropriate technologies" and what they purchased from port to port. They traded all along the ZLF-held and sympathetic Mexican coasts for food stuffs, hand products, and a growing variety of industrial goods. These were either resold in the Greater and Lesser Antilles on the trawler fleet's way out, utilized by the floating colonies or San Cristobal, or reprocessed for sale again to the rest of the world. The substantial profits were returned to the ZLF.

The US Navy and Coast Guard attempted to blockade all trade to and from southern Mexico from 2004 to 2008. Not only did this raise an international protest, what with nations of the Caribbean, South America, Europe and Africa strenuously objecting to their ships being stopped and searched, but it also lead to armed confrontations on the high seas. These "incidents" we in the US military found difficult to explain, let alone to win.

The first time a destroyer and its battle group tried to intercept a

265

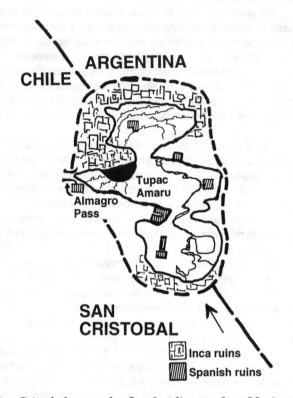

large San Cristobalan trawler fleet heading out from Mexico on June 3, 2006, the deceptively slow fishing ships revved into high speed and kept the US Navy vessels preoccupied while guerrillas on shore launched wings of exocet missiles to sink most of the battle group. Wiser the second time, a second battle group approached a second large fishing fleet well off shore on January 21, 2007, with an eye to intercepting anything from the mainland. The San Cristobalan trawlers had also been prepared, and succeeded in sinking most of the battle group with mini-exocets, hand launched torpedoes, and portable battle lasers, suffering the loss of only one trawler. The intelligence community determined circumstantially of San Cristobal's involvement with the trawler fleets after this second incident, but the fleet's flags of convenience, havens of incorporation, and business front maze of ownership kept the US government sufficiently cautious. Unfortunately, the US government backed away from enforcing the full blockade a year later, giving in to the general international hue and cry over trade interference.

The trawlers were used for small-scale and non-military trade, a "revolutionary service" offered by San Cristobal, its ocean colonies, and DIS to secessionist southern Mexico. But it was not the way large-scale weapons shipments entered ZLF territory, DIS's true specialization. San Cristobal's fanatically secretive espionage agency purposefully separated the two operations, so that the Atlantic trawlers could be held blameless, and if need be, submit to UN search as US liberals often suggested. The arms came through the Pacific coast. DIS organized it from Mu, constructing flotation packets—aerated plastic matrices about one hundred and twenty feet long, thirty feet wide, and six feet thick—in which were packed an assortment of military supplies and ordnance. Sealed entirely in a thin, strong camo plastic, and inflated with inert, buoyant gas so as to float some ten feet beneath the ocean's surface, each packet sported two robot minisubs. The Pacific DIS trawlers carried these packets up current of Gulf of Tehuantepec and set them adrift. More precisely, they permitted the robot subs to take over.

Packet delivery normally took days, and for most of that time, the subs appeared inert. Yet they mapped their own approach through satellite link, and used large vanes built into the packet's design to rudder the delivery close, but not too close to shore. At a certain point, they released a regular stream of buoyant sound nodules into the current while edging the packet into the gulf. The minisubs and sound nodules synchronized the next moment, the former cutting in their props to drive the packet for shore while the latter pulsed out false engine rhythms. The subs increased the flotation gases until the packet washed no more than a foot beneath the ocean's surface. If elements of the US 6th Fleet investigated, they checked out the sound decoys first. In the meantime, awaiting guerrillas paddled out in canoes to intercept the packet, drag it up onto the beach to unload it, strip it, and disassemble it; every part of the armaments shipment and packet disappearing into the ZLF-controlled mountains for reuse.

In San Cristobal and the Colonies DIS was often jokingly referred to as "the Department of the Alpha and the Omega." It is DIS's bizarre cataclysmic policy that, beginning from 1995, humanity had fifty years to turn matters around before the planet and the species were so poisoned or locked into destructive patterns that grand scale capital "A" apocalypse was inevitable. This, and the agency's penchant for staging meta-tech, stunningly successful operations established their backhanded claim to the handle. San Cristobal's recognition of the ZLF in February, 2007, had been a DIS operation. Through their geosyncsats, the colonies penetrated into most every major and minor media's internal compunet. San Cristobal's message flashed up and stayed up on computer screens around the globe twenty minutes after broadcast, bypassing some extremely sophisticated internal security in many cases. Additionally, the Department had branded their deliveries to southern Mexico with the symbol that came to be associated with San Cristobal's international presence in general.

An omega, international symbol for resistance, both electrical and political, modifies a circle A, international symbol for anarchy/anti-authority/autonomy. It is the 21st century's hammer-and-sickle for the world's disgruntled fanatics and marginalized masses. San Cristobal has no flag, not even the black one, but by a fluke the country now has an internationally recognized logo, one on which various national, corporate, criminal and interstitial powers are busy compiling their own data bases...

THIRTY-SIX

Marcus woke before dawn wrapped in a sleeping bag in the back of his station wagon, parked outside a San Francisco post office. He parted the window curtains to determine that a constant, light drizzle washed the world. He struggled into the front seat, groggy and aching from his bed. At six he watched the post office guard open the lobby to the dreary day.

The detective was on a mission. Two Alabaster policemen, one his friend, had died as a consequence of his work. He would track down Peregrine to the ends of the earth now. At this point that meant sleeping in his car for the next four months, the term of Eugene Wisdom's post office box. Thanks to Sampson, both the Postmaster and the SF Chief of Police knew about his personal stake out.

He opened an umbrella as he stepped from the car, to yawn and stretch in the light rain. He ate a quick breakfast, just coffee, hash browns and one pouched egg, in the 24-hour diner in sight of the post office. He was not surprised to find a call pending from the Captain on his cellular when he returned.

"How's it feel, your first working day without Sumner looking over your shoulder," Marcus greeted Brian.

"He's gone for the moment, but his Operation Anvil is still in effect," Sampson's voice seemed to shrug on the line, "You still can't take a step without bumping into a special agent. And I don't doubt he's glib enough to convince his superiors he's really doing a good job."

"If killing street people can be ignored. So, what's up?"

SILENCE IN HEAVEN

"Some not so good news I'm afraid. Kenny Wisdom wrote a letter to the box and posted it Sunday, my MCC source says. But the car registered to Eugene Wisdom, it was found abandoned, yesterday evening, in LA."

"Fingerprinted yet?" Marcus asked.

"Yes. Most recent set, driver's side, are not Peregrine's. But his are there. He could have been a passenger."

"And he also might have loaned his car to someone, now that we're closing in," Marcus said, "No, he's still in the Bay Area. I feel it, Brian. Strongly."

"All right," the Captain sounded rueful, "I know better than to argue with your hunches by now. But I can't guarantee you that parking space for more than a week."

"Thanks for that," the detective smiled, wearily, to no one, "When's the funeral?"

"Saturday. Alabaster. How'd his girlfriend take it?"

"Badly. She asked Gwen to stay with her the last two nights. Did that dacoit turn up Sulawesi?"

"She remains an unidentified, though I'd stake my job she's Sulawesi. Her rig was something special. When Alabaster PD finally got her into the county morgue and her outfit into SF's crime labs, both were in the process of decaying beyond recovery. Apparently, the instant she died, her rig broadcast a code back to her employers, and they started both to self-destruct. Mineral acids for the hardware and corrosive biotoxins for the body, injected from her rig. The powers behind that thug are clever. How are you holding up?"

"Well enough," Marcus said, "Obsessed with catching this fucker, but aside from that I'm managing. Joe was a good man. But you knew that to recommend I work with him."

"Yes, I did," Sampson sighed, "Doing police work, you start taking for granted all the violence; punks on a spree gunning down cops, drug stings gone wrong and bloody, folks going psycho, taking hostages and wasting a policeman or two, all of that grief. In the morning, you sometimes see in your fellow officers the chances of them dying in the line of duty that day. Sometimes you see those chances in your own face in the mirror when you wake up. But when it's someone you inspired to go into police work. Someone you encouraged and coached and goaded to become a cop, until he did. I've felt worse only once before. When my own son, Aaron, died in infantry action in southern Mexico. Need me to do anything for you while you're on stake out?"

"You've done enough," Marcus said, truly grateful. "I'm on my way in to see the postmaster to make arrangements for some inside notification. If the PO receives a change of address by mail and such."

"Feel free to drop my name," Brian signed off.

269

END TIME

The aged detective was ready for his retirement, once Peregrine was safely jailed. Every ache, break, muscle and bone told him his age in no uncertain terms as he sat in his car in the rain. Unlike the Captain, the detective's line of work rarely exposed him to the Grim Reaper's constant, daily presence. Not that he could ever get used to having a friend, his partner on a case, fried away in front of him. He called his answering machine back in Alabaster, tapped in his code, and found one message waiting.

"Mark, Neal here. I've bought us some time. Got that Sumner character recalled to DC on killing that street bum. Sicked some of my friends in Congress on him. So, how are things going?"

"Shit," Marcus hung up. He groaned, opened his door again and snapped open the umbrella before stepping out to his day's work.

***

Greg showered off the illuminated night's harrowing sleep in the Center's cold bathroom. Daylight bled out of the rain. The Center was quiet. He scavenged newspapers to cover himself on his walk to the bus stop. The New Afrika arm band was now folded in his jacket pocket, alongside the halved, hollow grenade. The bus took him to the outskirts of New Afrika, near Telegraph and West MacArthur, and Greg walked past the still extant but now deserted barricades to the open MacArthur BART station. Walked out of a dream. Someone had spray-painted "New Afrika Lives!" on one of the BART station walls.

He could not see either the sliced Pleiades, burnt Bay Bridge, or blasted Transamerica Pyramid in the rain as he took various means of public transport to reach Alabaster in time for Humanities. It had stopped raining and the overcast cracked as he hurried between surreal sculpture to dash through the class door. He felt like an alien, the proverbial stranger in a strange land. But he forced himself to sit quietly through the entire class, even though he did not have a clue. The class dynamics—those who asked questions or responded to the professor's questions—were fast cementing in this, the beginning of the semester's third week. The outsider, Greg managed to study these as much as the cascade of words showered over him from professor Holmes.

"Historians are often history's worst enemy. History is best understood as large scale pattern. As metaphor. As a tapestry. The Bayeux Tapestry depicts the Norman Conquest of Anglo-Saxon England in 1066 with courtly splendor, martial glory and stylized heroism. The historian too often studies history thread by thread and loses or muddies the greater pattern. When the historian examines history down to its very weave, invariably the pattern of the whole disappears. A gold thread here, a green thread there, a blue and yellow thread intertwined in yet another place; in picking these apart as is the historian's

270

principal methodology, the pattern of the whole is inevitably reduced to a mass of frayed, virtually random yarn out of which the historian steps in triumph.

"What the historian does not recognize is that there are often greater truths than mere facts will allow. A black doctor, a US physician named Charles Richard Drew, was a medical researcher who founded the American Red Cross blood bank. He lived during the first half of the 20th century and the story goes that, after having a terrible automobile accident, Drew was denied access to a nearby segregated, 'whites only' hospital and so died of loss of blood. It turns out that, in fact, it never happened that way. Yet the story is expressive of the truth; that truth being the nature of American race relations, particularly in the south at the time.

"Another example is the 'apocalypse fever' that is supposed to have swept Medieval Europe at the turn of the first millennium AD. Supposedly, heresies and blasphemies were rife. People flocked to seaports en mass, awaiting the ships that were to take them to the Promised Land and a New Jerusalem. Riot and revolt ensued. And it is neatly encapsulated by the vision of impending turn-of-the-millennium apocalypse, the round figure of a thousand years inspiring the fever. When historians got a hold of this metaphor, of course they systematically debunked it. The first three hundred years of Christian history is solidly millennarian, until Christianity became a state-sponsored, conquering faith. Messianic, apocalyptic and millennarian movements returned when feudalism stabilized, and can be found as early as the 900's and as late as the 1300's. Depending upon the interpretation, Catholic cenobitic monasticism and the Crusades are either the high point of this apocalyptic period, or else Church efforts to redirect popular chilliastic sentiments. And finally, because the system for dating at the time was based on roman numerals, the year 1000 would have been indicated as an M, not a very inspiring notation lending to end-of-the-world movements. In seeking to discredit the myth of turn-of-the-century millennarian 'apocalypse fever,' historians fail to grasp the archetypal truth within the myth. In so broadening the span of pre-Reformation Christianity's chilliastic hysteria, they in fact arrive at the truth without realizing it; that perhaps apocalyptic millennarianism is an essential feature of the Christian religion.

"In turn, the vast and growing affluence of the upper classes in the High Middle Ages is key to how Christian millennarianism and its limitations were transcended by feudal Europe's lower classes. The indulgence and decadence of the aristocracy, and the corruption and whoring of the clergy, may have fueled a desire among the lower classes for judgment and condemnation, feeding into apocalyptic feelings for Final Judgment. But also the wealth and surplus which prompts many a historian to postulate as to why Europe never 'took off' into capitalism and industrialism in the 12th and 13th centuries, also permitted the lower classes of Medieval Europe to imagine a land of plenty, a Land of Cockayne where amidst plenty, no one need work. This is nothing less than a vision of the Garden of Eden, a genuine Utopia."

Greg felt as if he had come through a revelatory experience, one that was also a sudden beginning for him. People had died to keep a vision called New Afrika alive. It had been more than a vision for so brief a time, four days and the first of those simply the takeover, before being returned to the status of a vision once more. What was he doing sitting in a comfortable chair, in a comfortable classroom, listening to a boring professor lecturing on something irrelevant to the last thirty six hours or so of his life.

He found Larry in the Redwood Eatery after class.

"First off," Greg dropped his books onto his friend's table, steaming. "Why are you telling Smoke about me and the riemanium."

"Whoa," Larry said, glancing about, "All I told him was that we'd had contact with Peregrine, who had the riemanium."

"And this bullshit about the Solidarity Brigade talking to the media," Greg hissed, continuing to vent his outrage without thinking.

"You didn't show up at the meeting. I was fucking outvoted!" Larry said, trying not to be too loud. "George, David, Beth, Lori; they outvoted me."

"And this shit about me having veto power..."

"I couldn't enforce it. They said the statement wasn't a departure from the last, only an extension. And besides, David said you agreed to have the meeting yesterday at 10. We tried calling around to get a hold of you, but you were not around."

"I was in Oakland, damnit," Greg hit the table top with his fist, "And we had a deal. If I don't approve of it, it doesn't go through."

"That's right," Larry said, "But what could I do? Tell them you're the one with the riemanium, so anything they want to do is null and void? Secrecy was also a part of the deal. Jesus, no one knew you were in Oakland."

"Fuck," Greg knuckled his hands into his cheeks, "They didn't need to link Oakland in with the nuclear thing. Folks in Oakland were doing just fine on their own. They wanted to stand on their own. It was their revolution. Who knows, maybe making the riemanium link pushed the New Afrika Coalition into making their compromise."

"Check with anybody," Larry waved his hand, "I voted to wait until you could be consulted. So, you were in Oakland?"

"Alright," Greg straightened with his internal decision, "Tell everybody that, until further notice, the Solidarity Brigade is on hold. Tell them Peregrine contacted us and is rethinking us fronting this deal.

SILENCE IN HEAVEN

And tell them its because of Oakland. I've got to think this bomb thing through again."

"Absolutely," Larry nodded. Greg could see the desire on his friend's face to hear about Oakland, but he did not have the time, nor the inclination to regale Larry with his stories. From the Eatery, he headed for the library.

Quite a few people were rethinking things, thanks to Oakland. And already, the question of "who lost New Afrika" was stoking anger in Oakland and sectarianism on the Left. Within the Coalition, the Nation of Islam and the revolutionary Black nationalist Left criticized the deal cut, castigating the Coalition for giving Commander Malcolm Brown too much deference and power. They had already invited famous Moslem businessman, philanthropist, author, world traveler, and often, unofficial liaison with the United Nations General Secretary, Hamran Mossoud, to visit Oakland. It was rumored that he arrived at SF International that evening. Uglier rumors persisted that, during the insurrection, members of the Afrikan Peoples Revolutionary Party and the New Afrikan Peoples Movement had engaged each other in private warfare, trying to assassinate each other's leadership.

The gang alliance remained volatile. They claimed a willingness to die for New Afrika, to fight the final battle and to fall in battle if necessary to keep New Afrika free. The Panther cure had worked on many of them, with a vengeance. They called the Coalition a bunch of old men unwilling to take the risks needed for their own freedom. For their part, the Black Unity Front, the Black Panthers, the African American GI Organizing Project, et al, claimed that tremendous, behind-the-scenes pressure had been exerted upon the Coalition by Commander Powell and the Congressional Black Caucus to negotiate a deal. Malcolm Powell Brown was not saying anything, at the moment.

Greg systematically pursued the sources and references he needed to do his homework through the Library virtual halls, even as Black nationalism thrashed out its divisions and splits. He felt as if he were digging away at a mountain with a teaspoon, so great was the work he needed to do. Yet he kept at it while the Left continued its blood frenzy.

Outside of the African American community, on the mostly white Left, not much creative thinking and a lot of stereotyped blaming was in progress. Leninists pointed out the "petty bourgeois nature" of the Coalition's leadership. Anti-statist communists and revolutionary socialists claimed that the Coalition had substituted itself in power for the "organized masses." Social democrats bewailed the lack of "real democracy" after the first and only popular assembly called by the Coalition. Anarchists disdained the Coalition's "statist structure and aspirations," and all except the Leninists criticized the prominent role played by the military, albeit mutinous, in New Afrika's creation, sup-

273

port and subsequent demise.

The house and block councils, the gang alliance, the workers' councils formed in the city's services, abandoned industries and expropriated businesses; these now defunct examples of popular self-organization the anarchists, revolutionary socialists and anti-statist communists praised, while castigating the rest of the Left for seeing revolutionary or democratic leadership as a panacea. But while the revolutionary socialists and anti-statist communists pushed for a dual role for spontaneous mass action with militant revolutionary leadership, the anarchists touted only the benefits of spontaneous, autonomous, popular action. So the two sides called each other names over the difference.

Social democrats held up the example of the Coalition's first popular assembly, and cited the failing of New Afrika to immediately elect a true Constituent Assembly as its principle mistake. They took the rest of the Left to task for not believing in "true democracy."

Leninists, aside from disagreeing amongst themselves over the National Question, the Liberation Forces Question, the Lumpenproletarian Gang Question, and a half dozen more catechisms, universally praised the early, radical measures of the Coalition. Communalizing community resources and supplies, coordinating the organization of communal social services and defenses, and galvanizing a national identity; these things the Leninists commended while they lashed the "ultra-Left" for ultra-democracy, voluntarism and adventurism. In particular, they excoriated the anarchistic tendency to claim that popular self-activity and self-organization could have carried a revolution, any revolution, through on sheer spontaneity and gang machismo alone. The socialists were faulted for their timidity, their willingness to immediately tame a revolutionary moment to parliamentary procedure out of a fear of revolution itself, and of being too willing to subsume a Leftist agenda by supporting the liberal Black Democratic Party hacks who ultimately negotiated New Afrika out of existence.

Greg drove home through a miscreant night, the tired moon casting shadows of lost utopias across the road. All the tired old Leftist debates emerged. The same old historic divisions flourished. Mutations occurred, but nothing radical emerged. Democratic socialists and social democrats, De Leonists, unreconstructed Leninists, Stalinists, Maoists and Trotskyists, syndicalists, libertarian communists, feminists, pacifists, anarchists in all their idiosyncratic variety, situationists and post-situationists, autonomists, greens, genuine nihilists, nationalists, anti-imperialists; the list was endless, as were the debates. None could face up to the criticism from the African American community that black folks had not seen them—white radicals of any stripe—on Oakland's front lines in any great numbers during New Afrika's four

SILENCE IN HEAVEN

short days of glory. Yet the mostly white Left continued to presume that they could analyze New Afrika's faults and failings.

Insurrectionary Oakland, as New Afrika, if anything accentuated all the old contradictions and divisions in the Black community, on the white Left and between the two. All of this while National Guard units took up positions, unchallenged, throughout the city to escort the police and sheriffs back to substitute quarters near their gutted stations and substations. All of this while the LA NLG made available copies of stolen Oakland PD and Alameda County Sheriffs Department documents detailing joint Red Squad activities against Black and nationalist movements in Oakland. An internal Sheriff's memo from the top instructed the Department's Red Squad to single out the Young Afrikan Lords for special attention, dated three months before the assassination. Steven McCaffrey's resignation as head of the Alameda County Sheriff's Department had been accepted by the Board of Supervisors.

Greg gleaned this much from NPR while working on his lathe, finishing the custom engine block order. He had responded to his father's fax that Andre would be delayed until late Tuesday night or early Wednesday morning, was everything all right. He was concentrating on his craftsmanship when the familiar voice of a NLG attorney, Garcia Oliver, announcing the document coupe came over "All Things Considered." So, that had been the Latino man, his intended passenger out of Oakland. The recycling run had gone off without a hitch. Greg briefly wondered where Smoke was as he sluiced through hard, polished steel with emerald light bits. He followed a computer generated grid hologrammed about the hunk of metal locked in rotation. Finished with another part, he paused to wipe his forehead, sip a soft drink, and dial to KPFA for a snatch of the nightly news.

"...In his effects. The tapes record telephone conversations between the Mayor of Oakland and a number of business and corporate figures. The Mayor's office is apparently implicated in accepting favors for legislative and zoning efforts on the behalf of those economic interests. Leo Thompson found the incriminating recordings while packing up his father's extensive station tape library, in a box marked 'Insurance.' We have not been able to reach Mayor Allison for comment..."

He switched to CD, and put on a classic comp of Neighborhood Watch/Tit Wrench to pound over the basement speakers. Bob Barley, fronting the deep south Chula Vista 1980's band Neighborhood Watch with that Geeza X/Devo/Dead Kennedys' sound, lurched through "We Fuck Sheep," then launched into "A Lesson." Smoke had certainly shown him a true revolution in progress, a real liberated zone; short lived, but authentic. He refused to indulge either in beer or in smoke, even so close to bed. He slept fitfully, dreaming of New Afrika.

275

END TIME

Greg finished his final, grueling class next day. He walked beneath a wind swept, cloud shivered sky toward the library, trying desperately to tread academic water. Larry found him crossing Remley Plaza.

"Greg. Got to talk to you," Larry was drunk, his eyes red and his hair unusually disheveled. "Smoke was caught this morning, 2 a.m., robbing Conspiracy of Equals."

"No way," Greg stopped and dropped his jaw.

"Joe Curlew caught him," Larry's eyes, too, were disbelieving. "Seems that all the coops had been robbed. Or were being robbed regularly, only they weren't telling anyone, not even the cops, because they wanted to catch whoever was doing it. Because the administration and the campus cops have the master keys and because the coops are Left leaning, the coops were even suspecting the authorities. But it was Smoke they caught."

"I can't fucking believe it," Greg said. Then he knew that he could. He had seen a side of Smoke through Wednesday's SF riots, especially getting into Oakland Saturday night, that now told him this too was possible. He had seen it with more than his eyes. Smoke was an iceberg, only 1/10 visible at any given time with 9/10's hidden beneath the surface of a cold, murky ocean. "How'd it happen?"

"Couple of the book coop's core collective members started sleeping in the store. They'd gotten hit something like three nights. They were taking turns staking out the store at night. Joe caught Smoke. He woke Joe up when he used some pretty professional tools to unlock the store's door. Joe waited until Smoke had the register's money in his pockets before busting him."

"Damn," Greg said, and shook his head. "What's going to happen to him?"

"They got him in an office here in the student center. He's being watched until the coops have a general meeting, which ASP is also helping to organize. Should come down in a half hour, in the lounge. The meeting's gonna decide what to do with Smoke."

Greg had intended to study. Instead, he felt irresistibly drawn into this vortex. He drifted around a chrome mesh and pipe structure in the student center plaza. Lori grabbed his arm as he stood, gazing into a sculpture of ribboned steel and glass vaguely resembling chromosomes replicating.

"Heard?" she asked.

"About Smoke? Yes."

"Lots of us wondered how Smoke made his money," Lori drawled, then lit a clove smoke. "Now, about the riemanium. I thought you said we had a 'blank check' from this Peregrine? Thought you said he wanted us to design a political package for it? Why, all of a sudden, is he backing off? What's the problem?"

276

SILENCE IN HEAVEN

Her eyes narrowed with suspicion, smoke tracing the air from the corner of her mouth.

"We'll call a meeting to discuss it," Greg smiled, nervous, and managed to duck away. David buttonholed him by the soft drink and candy machines.

"Heard about Smoke?" David asked

"Yeh, where is he?"

"He's in the Progressive Student Network office until the meeting decides what to do with him. Coming to the meeting?"

"Yes," Greg said, knowing that little study was on his evening's schedule, realistically.

"Look," David pursued, "I know you're pissed about this Solidarity Brigade stuff. I need to talk to you about it. Larry said that it was you who told Peregrine you didn't think our direction was correct anymore. I want you to reconsider. I've already talked to Larry, and he's willing, if you are."

"After the meeting," Greg waved him off, starting up the stairs to Smoke's detainment. Jesus, he thought to himself, Larry could not get anything right. Beth watched the door.

"Can I talk to him?" Greg asked

"Well..." She hesitated.

"I'm not exactly sympathetic to what he's done," Greg frowned, "And I mean, he's not our prisoner. That's kidnapping, unless we call the cops and make a citizen's arrest."

"Sure," she said. She avoided his gaze in letting him in.

Smoke stood in a corner of the office, in leather jacket but without his mirrored glasses. His face was pale and drawn.

"Long ways away from New Afrika," Greg shook his head, suddenly discouraged. "Thought you said even an individual can be a liberated zone."

"One person can," Smoke's voice was tired, worn. "Obviously, I'm not."

"So, you robbed the Conspiracy."

"Joe caught me," Smoke said, tersely.

"Did you rob the other coops?"

"Would you believe me if I said, 'No'?"

"No."

"But you want me to say it anyway."

"I guess part of me does. Yeh."

"You're not as surprised as the others about this," Smoke cocked an eyebrow at Greg.

"No. Not since last week. Not since Oakland. That started me wondering about your connections. I'm still wondering about that truckload of stuff we brought into New Afrika. I haven't heard word one about where that stuff came from in the media. I assume it was stolen."

"You probably won't hear anything," Smoke looked off into the ceiling. "Not the way I got it. The government's running a little scared on that one."

"Yet, you're a thief."

"Yes," Smoke said. "My contradictions run deeper than even you suspect. Deeper than you'll ever know."

"This is disappointing," Greg shook his head, "I guess I'll be at the meeting. Thanks, at least, for New Afrika."

"New Afrika wasn't mine to give," Smoke sighed, "New Afrika was its own gift."

The meeting was in some sort of progress by the time Greg took a seat. A back seat, on purpose. Speculation ran rampant as to the breadth of Smoke's crime spree and criminal reach. The coop robberies were being detailed by David and Nina. Eric described Smoke's "procurement" of various supplies from the University for the MDRG's mushroom madness festivals and liberated zones. Lori raised the gossip of personal thefts. The smell of angry betrayal was palpable in the room. It was like sweat, Greg thought to himself. Your own, after a good workout, smells good. Even righteous. Except for the sweat worked up during lovemaking, commingled sweat, other people's sweat just stinks.

The whole meeting teetered on the edge of an abyss. If one part of reality can be demonstrated so suddenly and so strikingly false, what else might fall? Three basic camps emerged, as the meeting lurched forward on violent emotion and outburst.

"Run him out of town on a rail," Eric expressed one sentiment clearly. "No one, no matter how Smoke tries to make it up or repay people, is gonna trust him or believe him again. I sure as hell won't. As long as he's living in the same town, I'm gonna be watching my back and my stuff. I mean fuck, look at this meeting. We're tearing each other up, fighting each other over whether or not Smoke can be reformed or reeducated. I say, its not worth our trouble even if it is theoretically possible. Even if Smoke can change. Fuck the man. If he ain't working for the government to destroy us, he might as well be."

Eric, his girlfriend Sara, as well as Lori who puffed her spice cigarette, clamored on this point. They were counterpoised by the position held by Joseph, Nina and Mitch.

"Look," Mitch summed it up. "He's a thief. He got caught stealing. We're not the police, nor are we the courts. And we have no right even to hold him, unless we arrest him. I say, call the police, and press charges. The police investigation might even link him definitively to the other robberies."

SILENCE IN HEAVEN

David and George, in turn, held up what they considered to be a synthesis. They did not wish theirs to be called a middle ground.

"We're not vigilantes," David said, folding his hands in front of him, "Smoke agreed to wait on the judgment of this meeting in lieu of us calling the police. I personally never trusted him. I think he should be removed from any political activity and responsibility. And I think he should make some type of ongoing restitution to the people and coops he ripped off, until he's paid the progressive community back. We should set up some other criteria for his rehabilitation as well, like insisting that he seek out some kind of psychological counseling, or do some sort of community service."

"I agree with David's last comments, but not for his reasons," George made his ponderous points. "We claim to be a progressive community. Some of us claim that our politics are a liberating alternative way to run all of society. I think that as a progressive community offering liberating alternatives we have a right to deal with instances of antisocial behavior in our midst in collective, cooperative ways. As a community, we have power. We can refuse to deal with Smoke and ask everybody we know to ostracize him. Or, we can try to reeducate him. I certainly don't want to turn to the cops or the administration to deal with this."

After much heat and not much light, during which Smoke was called agent provocateur, accused of every odd and happenstance mishap in a half dozen organizations, and even intimated to be able to walk through walls, George and David welded together a compromise. They passed it on the barest of majorities. Smoke would be asked to admit to and take responsibility for all the coop robberies. He would be asked to remove himself from all political activism, to seek counseling, to get a visible, legitimate means of support, and to repay the money he had stolen from the coops. Finally, he would be asked to do some as yet unspecified community service as restitution for the wrongs he had committed against the progressive community. Before bringing Smoke in front of their "People's Tribunal," the meeting authorized itself to meet again to review Smoke's performance against these criteria.

In hammering out the compromise, Greg realized that there was also a fourth camp present at the meeting. Larry finished off five beers during the course of the meeting, still stunned by disbelief and incredulity. He tried to anesthetize himself and prevent the truth from sinking in just yet. A young ASP recruit actually cried, totally disheartened, during part of the meeting. A star was falling from heaven. Some were eagerly making that star Lucifer thrown from heaven, personifying Smoke as Satan incarnate. But even the Devil had his charms, Greg thought. He reminded himself that Lucifer meant light bearer. He wondered whether Smoke's fall did not share a little with that of

279

END TIME

Prometheus, another light bearer and bringer of fire to humanity. No one said that enlightenment was painless.

It turned out that Smoke had the last laugh that evening. When the meeting contingent walked up to open the office door, the office space was empty. He had disappeared, yet another instance of smoke and mirrors. Later, David and Lori surmised that Smoke had carefully peeled up the acoustic insulating tiles in the ceiling to access a narrow crawl space, and then another set of offices to make good his escape. David was too preoccupied to even think of cornering Greg again on the Solidarity Brigade. Greg ducked out to catch several hours studying in the stacks, or more precisely in VR, a chuckle under his breath. He got home late and found a tantalizing message from Margaret on his answering machine and his father's fax on the house machine. Andre's plane would be in at 1 a.m.; not to wait up.

THIRTY-SEVEN

The cellular phone chimed. Groaning, Marcus hit the button.

"I'm opening the lobby doors now," the postal guard said, clearly liking the cloak-and-dagger of this.

"Thanks." The detective was not at all thankful. It was 5 to 6 in the morning, dark as his mood. The lobby closed at 10. Marcus was not going to be able to keep up this 16-hour a day vigil for much longer. He scalded down one cup of coffee and was getting his refill in a paper cup when he caught a dark figure turn the corner up the block. The furtive shape made for the post office at a brisk pace.

"Here's for the coffee," Marcus handed the counter waitress two dollar bills. "I'll be back for it later."

Once the man committed to climbing the post office steps, Marcus eased out of the diner door. When his target entered the post office doors, the detective sprinted for all he was worth through the first needled splinters of dawn. He arrived at the top of the steps winded, but still firing on adrenaline. He reached into his coat, and stepped into the lobby. The figure in black stood before the correct column of postal boxes in the lobby's dim light, engrossed in sorting his mail. Marcus approached quietly, his own revolver now leveled.

"Peregrine," the detective said.

The man looked up. Even under toque and turned up collar, even in that dim lobby light, Marcus recognized him from his modified police sketch. Marcus had no doubts.

"Sorry, wrong," the man's mouth tightened.

"Eugene Wisdom then," Marcus said, not wavering, "You're under arrest."

***

Rosanne watched TV as she worked. The morning news program cast bleached light into her dim apartment, enveloping the amused

280

dance of a candle on her kitchen table with cathode ray ghosts. She did not need the sound.

"Shouldn't have run away," she said in a pinched, high sing song, her cheeks stained with shiny tears. The broadcast cut to a grainy video of her Michael's arrest. "Nope, shouldn't have run from me."

The video played out two burly CHP officers walking Michael Baumann past the camera. The nice detective who had interviewed her two weeks ago, and who woke her with news of the arrest, was among the entourage that followed. He had told her when they planned to arraign Michael. She finished polishing the long plastic comb handle into a point with a nail file. She was seated at the table, dressed in a dingy bath robe, and surrounded by stacks of dirty dishes a week high. Rosanne rotated the sharpened handle over the candle flame, letting the plastic soften and harden repeatedly into the desired brittleness. She hummed low to herself, a tune she did not even know.

***

Greg woke early to catch more study. Consuello made him a breakfast; eggs over easy and leftover sliced steak, fried and garnished with light salsa and toast. He ate it with lots of coffee over open books and notes. He had heard his father come in very early that morning. When it was time for the campus library to open, he stacked up his studies, and wrote Andre a note.

I've got a busy schedule today, but all is well. How about a late dinner at 7:30 tonight?

The maid kept her small, portable TV on in the kitchen as she worked. Snippets of the morning news brought Greg into the kitchen with his dishes.

"California Highway Patrol officers took Eugene Michael Wisdom into custody at 6:45 a.m. this morning, in the downtown San Francisco post office. Wisdom, aka Michael Baumann and Peregrine, is suspected of being the fifth man in the Piccoli jewelry robbery of January 27. Peregrine has managed to elude police and authorities these past two and a half weeks."

The picture on screen was Smoke's. A booking mug shot revealed no emotion.

"Eugene Wisdom is scheduled for arraignment at 3:30 today in the Civic Center Courthouse. A Security Pacific guard was killed during the robbery, and as you might remember, two pounds of bomb-grade riemanium were also taken during the holdup. The riemanium has not been recovered. Wisdom has made no statement to the media or the authorities about the riemanium..."

Greg could not help himself. He spent the morning in the library, ate a quick lunch between his two light day classes, then hit the road, 101 and the Golden Gate, into the city. All of the insurrection's damage opened, plain to the sight, on the final curves of the North Bay highway. The torched Pleiades, blackened Transam Pyramid and twisted Bay Bridge scarred the day with reminders of New Afrika's struggle. That he had the potential power to do immeasurably more damage with his buried secret still dug fingernails into his mental blackboard. Gulls swung around him as he crossed the bridge. Finding parking was hell, but he made it in time for one of the last seats in the back. It was a packed house; the media and the public, a fair amount of gawkers and the usual court owls. He recognized several present. The man from Temptations Cafe, the middle-aged Fed who had pivoted that disastrous sting, sat in a roped off section near the front. And, on the other side of the room, also close to the front, sat David, Beth, Lori, Eric, Joseph and Nina. A hanging jury.

Smoke was more a frustration than anything else. He was lead in handcuffed, but he refused to say a word. He refused to acknowledge the judge or her questions. He refused to give his name or acknowledge that it was Eugene Wisdom. He refused to acknowledge any of the court's proceedings so that the court had to assign him a lawyer and enter a plea of not guilty for him. As he watched the drama unfold, Greg realized he still wanted a word, some kind of explanation to make sense out of all of this. Smoke/Eugene was lead away from where he had stood, defiant and speechless before the court. Greg recognized yet another party to this play, the woman he and Larry had encountered with Smoke the night of San Francisco's anti-war riots. She jumped up also from near the front and dashed past the startled bailiffs at the gate to pound at Smoke/Eugene with what looked like a comb.

"Mike, I lost everything for you, and you left me," she screamed before the bailiff holding Peregrine managed to deck her with a back handed punch. She was then tackled by two more court guards. The point to the plastic comb handle had been sharpened up fine. Smoke/Eugene's orange prison jumpsuit was torn. Blood ran off two slashes in his shoulder.

"Her name's Rosanne Casey," an old duffer informed the Fed from Temptations, now in a nice clean suit. "She was Peregrine's lover, under his Baumann alias."

They stood in the hall, the arraignment broken up when Rosanne was carried off in hysterics. Smoke had been hustled off, bleeding and still in silence, into the bowels of the court. David flagged him out, gesturing for them to avoid the crowd.

"Greg, why didn't you tell us Smoke was Peregrine," David whispered. He wore a "New Afrika Lives!" button.

"He's not," Greg said, caught off guard. "I mean, he's not the Peregrine Larry and I know. I mean..."

But it was too late. David's eyes lit up, and Greg realized he had

282

blown it. His one chance to rid himself of the Solidarity Brigade, his opportunity to unobtrusively ditch the riemanium in the furor around Smoke/Eugene, and he had blown it with a careless remark.

"So, Smoke doesn't have the riemanium," David smiled, then started to whine. "Then we have to talk this Solidarity Brigade stuff through. It's an opportunity we can't let slip through our fingers."

"Not here," Greg glanced about, "And not with Joseph and Nina. Another meeting. We'll have another meeting, Sunday again. Call me and we'll arrange the time and place. I'll be there this time."

Greg passed the Fed on his way to the exit. He could not resist.

"Finally cleaned all the brains off that suit," Greg commented. The Fed reddened, to Greg's satisfaction as he sauntered off.

"Give me a call," Lori smiled, brushing up close against him in the courthouse lobby's confusion as she was about to leave. She playfully squeezing his crotch.

He tracked down the information he needed. Smoke was being held in the Federal Corrections Complex, and his visiting hours were weekday mornings, from 8 to 10. He kicked himself for blowing it with David as he drove through the city toward home. Then, a vague inkling of what to do with the riemanium, once and for all, stirred in his mind. He did not head back to Alabaster immediately. Instead, he drove to Mount Tamalpais and his meadow. His backpack and shovel were still in the trunk of the car. The meadow dreamt in shadows as the northern bay smoldered with the day's late sun. As he retraced his steps to his buried treasure, he considered his own private storm. The meadow and its history provoked his response even without his usual ritual.

Janet had hurt him, but Greg could not imagine how she could have done things differently. He was grateful she had not kept him hanging on. She had not lied to him. He preferred the pain and his own life, to the comfort of illusion and lie. He was thankful at least that she had not been cruel, that in fact she had tried to minimize his pain and remain his friend.

He was monogamous by nature. Sleeping with Margaret and Lori had not been the fantasy fulfillment he had expected. First, there were no equivalencies. Making love with two women he liked did not add up to making love with one woman he had loved. No more than having fair sex with two different women added up to having excellent sex with the same woman.

Second, emotional complexity took the edge off the new and promiscuous. He still had his feelings for Janet, only they were compounded, contradicted and complimented by his feelings for Lori and especially Margaret. He could not have sex without becoming emotionally involved to some degree, and he was not helping matters by weaving one relationship upon another, in turn upon yet another. Emotionally, he felt confused and anxious.

The grass had started to re-root under his sod patch, so he applied his shovel carefully around its edges until it peeled up. The riemanium was where he had left it. He extracted it, also with care, brushed off the dirt, and fitted it into his backpack.

He liked Lori, but he was also wary of her. The vindictiveness with which she now went after her former lover, Smoke, gave him pause. She liked toying with other people's thoughts and emotions. She did not fully believe Larry's and his story about the riemanium, as her fishing expeditions made clear. And, she used sex to further her own agenda. He could considerably simplify his life by no longer sleeping with her.

Margaret was another matter. Peggy was not who he wanted to stay with for the rest of his life. She was nice, but they shared little except an interest in fun sex and weird music. Yes, he liked Peggy, but he did not love her, not at least in the way he had loved Janet. He did enjoy her company, and knew that mostly what interested her was a good time. No heavy commitments, which was fine by him. If he could keep a better handle on his own feelings, he could keep their relationship at the level of friendship, and friendly sex.

Or could he? How would he feel if she decided not to sleep with him again? Not to see him again? How would he feel if, having found somebody to love and commit to, he had to tell and then leave Margaret? How would he feel if Peggy wanted to get more serious? The politics of friendship, love and sex were not so simple. After seeing Smoke/Eugene in that courtroom, Greg realized that friendship was to be valued, perhaps even above love. Loved and hated, Eugene did not have a friend in the world. At least not in the Bay Area. And here he was, trying to shove a friend of a lifetime in Janet out of his life, out of bitterness, while settling for nothing more than friendship with Peggy.

He carried the riemanium in his pack back to his car. He drove home as the sun set, streaming dying light over the coastal ranges. He heard crows among the sun fired trees about the house as he carried his heavy load down into the basement. Andre sat in his den when Greg walked through.

"Good, you're home early," his father smiled, "I was wondering if we could have dinner a little earlier. I have a late, late meeting with a client in the city. Kind of an emergency that developed while I was in Australia."

"Sure," Greg said.

Consuello quickly grilled up the trout stuffed with onions and mushrooms, and wrapped in bacon. She served it with the rest of the food which had been on hold; baked potatoes, fresh tomatoes stuffed with a spicy nut and cheese mix, and a tossed green salad with ranch dressing. Andre offered Greg a beer, who declined it. They chatted amiably over events in the Bay Area during his father's absence, Andre glad to see his son in better mood, and Greg glad not to reveal how close he had been to those events.

"Isn't it an old Chinese curse, 'May you live in interesting times'," Andre cut into his potato smothered in butter, sour cream and chives. "There's going to be a lot more trouble if we don't end that war."

"That's for certain," Greg said. He paused, fork over his plate, interested in changing the subject. "Dad, how long did it take you to become friends again with mom? After she left?"

"Well, we were talking all the time, you understand," Andre peeled off more fish from its skeleton, secretly pleased that even his son's tone on Janet was more positive, "But I wasn't talking too friendly for the first year. To be truthful, I badgered Rachel into giving me full custody of you, and into accepting the minimum in alimony. I wasn't a very nice person to your mom during that time. So I guess I'd say it was a year after the divorce when I finally could have a friendly conversation with her. Since then, I've tried to make things up to her. I gave her more money, let you go down to live with her those summers, things like that."

The meal was savory, but short, ending in conversation about the son's schooling and the father's travels.

"Sorry about this, but I really have to get into the City," Andre apologized. "This thing may turn out to be an all nighter. Maybe we can get together this weekend. Sunday."

"Sure," Greg said, and helped his father clear the table, "I need to get some studying in also."

He did not study. Instead, he called Peggy.

"And where've you been?" She sounded a bit put out. Greg found himself silently pleased with her reaction. He imagined her sexy mouth pinched in disapproval and her dark eyes blacker than usual.

"I was in Oakland last weekend," Greg told the truth, "And I got so far behind in my studies that I just had to bury my head in the books. Sorry I didn't call you sooner, but I've been living at the library."

"You were in Oakland?" her voice was unbelieving. Greg knew he had been provisionally forgiven.

"Yeh, I left Monday morning, after New Afrika ended. Want to get together tonight?"

"Sure," she said, "But my room mate's here."

"That's all right," Greg said, "My dad isn't."

He waited until Andre was gone before driving over to pick her up and take her back to his room. He showed her his New Afrika arm band, but not the grenade shell, and told her stories from the Liberated Territory. They made love several times. Greg watched her lips wrapped around a pleasured moan, before sleep took them. He fixed her breakfast quietly, not to disturb Consuello or Andre, before driving Peggy to her apartment the next morning.

Thursday was his heavy class day. Afterwards he VR'ed in the library until it closed at 8 that night. Holed up as he was, he could not avoid a glimpse of the turmoil battering his friends and those he knew. A poster had been taped to the buttresses of the library beneath stickers proclaiming "New Afrika Lives!" It was a clear picture of Smoke in sunglasses and leather jacket, from mid-torso up. In the picture, Smoke smiled broadly, his strong white teeth possibly framing a laugh. Above the picture, in bold, bold type, it read: BEWARE, MAD DOG. Below the picture, in the same type face but smaller, it read: SHOOT ON SIGHT! SHOOT TO KILL!

An extensive and lively bathroom wall graffiti debate was in progress in the library's outside men's bathroom. The anonymous writers considered whether Smoke should be publicly flayed and skinned, strung up by his genitalia, branded with his crimes on his buttocks, have every bone in his body broken in at least three places, receive a molten steel enema, or two dozen other suggestions. Many folks had to have loved Smoke a lot to hate him so much now. He did not bother returning David's, Lori's or Larry's messages on his machine when he arrived home, favoring a deep sleep instead.

***

Marcus and Gwen had almost everything packed by mid morning Thursday in Alabaster, when Neal drove up.

"Care for a beer?" Mark offered.

"Thanks," Neal accepted, "So, its good-bye Alabaster."

"Until the funeral," Marcus helped order the suitcases by the door. Then he checked over the boxed computer and communications equipment. "We're taking Joe's girlfriend to the cemetery. Anyway, the job's done here. And this is not Gwen's and my idea of a vacation spot."

"We're going to Europe at the end of the month," Gwen said, cheerily, catching her husband's last remark.

"Oh?" Neal raised an eyebrow at Marcus, "What about the legal matters concerning the Peregrine Case? He's going to trial..."

"But not for a long, long time, even under the best of conditions," Mark said, "The government's going slow on this case. Absolutely by the book. They don't want to blow it on the arrest, on the trial, on anything. I'll give what depositions and sworn statements I can as needed before we leave. And I'm purchasing a portable fax service. Anybody willing to pay the fees can get a hold of me. We'll be back before the trial starts."

"Honey, can you help me?" Gwen struggled with two suitcases through the bedroom door. He took the larger one and they moved the

286

last of their luggage next to the door.

"Could you take care of the hotel bill dear?" Mark said to his wife, "Neal and I have business to discuss."

As she walked to the motel office, Marcus faced Neal.

"I believe the balance owed is $200,000," Marcus said in business monotone.

"The riemanium still hasn't been found," Neal pointed out.

"That wasn't our deal," Marcus was firm, "You wanted me to find Peregrine. I did. I see the riemanium as incidental at this point. Eugene Wisdom is probably holding it as his last ace, to negotiate a lighter sentence."

"This is not the Marcus Dimapopulos, the renowned detective that I once knew," Neal sighed and fished into his coat pocket.

"You're right Neal," the detective said, coldly, "In the old days, I would have stayed on a case to wrap up loose ends like this, no charge. But I've come to discover a new Neal Emerson in the past two and a half weeks. One who is petty and vindictive. A Neal Emerson who pushed a young woman into a psychotic break only because she happened to love the man both of us wanted a little too much. A Neal Emerson willing to trample on whoever or whatever in order to keep his skeletons safely hidden in his closet."

"That's not quite fair," Neal handed over a cashier's check, drawn on Neal's accounts, for the balance in full.

"Isn't it?" Marcus folded the check and slipped it into his pocket, "I may have let my professional standards slide in closing this case. But you're not the Neal Emerson I served with in the Marines. And to think that someone like Joe Manley died to keep your dirty laundry from seeing the light of day."

"I hope we can remain friends," was all Neal could muster.

"Yes," Marcus replied, "But not close friends."

The detective backed their station wagon to the cottage door. Husband and wife packed it from experience. Neal watched. They had left the computer equipment for Neal to manage. As Mark and Gwen drove across the lot to the road, Neal waved. They waved back. Marcus was glad to be leaving the confines of Alabaster, though he figured there was a grave in this town he would be visiting now and again after Saturday's funeral.

THIRTY-EIGHT

Eugene woke before dawn, fighting the knotted fear deep in his stomach. Fighting the urge to dry heave. So far, he'd gotten the kid glove treatment. He'd had a Miranda-correct arrest; polite interrogations from the highway patrol, police, and FBI; and court proceedings protective of his rights down to the crossed t's and dotted i's. He'd remained conscious and able to read the contents to the drugs with which they were injecting him while they stitched him up at the hospital. Then he'd been provided an attentive interview with a solicitous public defender, a cell all to himself in Maximum Security, and full weekday visitor's hours in a visiting room certified unmonitored by the NLG. He'd refused to say word one during the interrogations, and he'd blown off his lawyer with the excuse of Rosanne's attack. By now, his brother would know of his circumstances through the grapevine.

He'd returned to Alabaster Sunday night in a car from Oakland's streets, modified by Captain Johnson so that it wasn't hot. Remaining yellow police tape announced that his apartment was no longer home. A Sunday paper revealed some of the events of Saturday to him. Sulawesi, and the police. He'd slept in his car that night, and considered his options over a greasy diner breakfast the next day. The safest place to contemplate such a near miss was in the crater of that near miss. He felt no qualms about wandering about the town, purchasing what he would need for two days in the woods before the deal on his contraband went through. Afterwards, he'd be $170,000 richer and long gone from California. He'd even spent much of the last of his money on a pitcher of beer at the Redwood Eatery for himself as Smoke, before he decided on grabbing a little easy, extra spending money from the book coop for those two days in the woods.

His had been a stupid decision to rob the Conspiracy that night. But the nab at the post office had been good detective work. He gave that to Marcus Dimapopulos, his unexpected nemesis. His stomach felt as if he'd just been kicked in the gut, only he'd had that feeling ever since the detective cornered him. The same ulcerous pain he'd felt for a month after he'd read Kate's rambling suicide letter. After she'd blown herself up with materials he'd helped her purchase. He fought back his feelings of guilt; the sense that this was his "payback." Christ, he didn't want to go to jail. Now, all he had was a bluff.

He knew Greg had the riemanium. But no one else did, at least no one who held him in this prison now. What's more, no one except Greg and, perhaps, Larry knew that he didn't have the riemanium. It was a long shot. His silence during his interrogations, his arraignment, and even to his "visitors" from Alabaster the day before had been calculated. If the powers-that-be believed that he had the riemanium, or knew where it was hidden, he might be able to cut a deal. Today, when his lawyer came to visit him in the afternoon, he'd hint broadly that such a deal was possible. His freedom for the riemanium's return.

Eugene needed to work out contingencies, in case the Solidarity Brigade reared its ugly head. If it didn't by the time the deal was in process, so much the better. The FBI was backed against the wall, that Sumner character on the White House carpet for his disastrous handling of both the riemanium and Oakland. If he played everything right, he could pull a sting on the Bureau. Once outside the prison walls, he had the chance at escape. Organizing an escape meant getting in touch with his brother, though he suspected his brother was already getting in touch with him through his connections.

Day etched the narrow, pressure proof glass in the slitted windows of his prison cell. The knot in his stomach had not gone away. All he had was a bluff.

***

Friday morning, Greg got up early and had a surprise breakfast with his father. Both men were hurrying off for busy days, actually in the same direction, toward the city. But they managed to each complain about the earliness of the hour and the fullness of the day to come over a shared newspaper, scrambled eggs, hash browns and lots of coffee. This coincidental synchronization of their schedules gratified both of them.

"Oh, by the way, it's polite to tell Consuello when we're having guests over," Andre arched an eyebrow in glancing up from the sports section, making his son blush. "We pay her to clean up mainly after us."

Greg made sure to get on the road ahead of his father, counting on his speed to keep them from overlapping on the drive down.

Scaffolding now surrounded the sunrise blasted Pleiades and Bay Bridge, though the Pyramid remained gutted, untouched. A few clouds waited in the west. He woke fully in that cold wind, enjoying the salted bay air. The visiting room in the SF Federal Correctional Complex was a long, narrow room with chairs in cubicles on either side of a plastic wall. Each cubicle faced off a prisoner and a visitor, the plastic wall between perforated at mouth level to allow their voices to pass through. The room was large enough, crowded enough and noisy enough that if two people talked normally, they could not be overheard.

"Et tu Brute?" Eugene said, cynically, as he sat opposite Greg.

"What's that supposed to mean?" Greg said.

"Nothing," the prisoner said, "I suppose you're here as another representative of the Alabaster lynch mob."

"What the hell are you talking about?" Greg said, truly puzzled.

"Eric, Lori and David. They came to visit me yesterday," Eugene smiled sardonically, "It seems Eric and Lori have been talking to the District Attorney. They're gonna try and hang me. David isn't gonna help the State put me away, but he says he's compiled a 'thorough' file on me and my activities, just in case I manage to beat this rap and go somewhere else. He's pushing to ostracize me from the entire Left nationwide."

"That hardly surprises me," Greg said, "A lot of people feel betrayed by you."

"Yah, I know," Eugene suddenly looked very old. "Just by living we

289

betray each other. And ourselves."

There was a long silence between them.

"I hadn't realized feelings had gotten so worked up that people are willing to help the government put you away," Greg said.

"I've tapped into a deep emotional archetype," Eugene rubbed his eyes. "Where would Jesus be without his Judas Iscariot. The Old Testament's second sin, when Cain slew Abel, was not actually murder. It was Cain's betrayal of his brother, as mirrored in Abel's eyes seconds before his death. And what was the first thing done when God caught Adam and Eve after they ate of the tree of good and evil? Adam said: 'It was not me but the woman made me eat.' And Eve said: 'It was not me but the serpent made me eat.' That's the human condition, loyalties ever betrayed. Even some of the Angels in heaven betrayed God's plan and were cast out for their rebellion."

"Only, we can end it," Greg said, but Eugene did not hear.

"Strange thing is, whether they see me as Jesus or Judas, Archangel Michael or fallen angel Lucifer, Lenin or Trotsky; I still have power in their lives. They still devote a lot of their time and energy thinking about me, even if only to curse me and work for my destruction. They give me this power. They gave me power when they deferred to me as a 'heavy rad.' And now they give me power when I've become the revolution's Satanic scourge in their Leftist eschatologies. So. Why aren't you feeling so badly betrayed by what I've done?"

"I told you before. Oakland changed my outlook on a lot of things."

"Yah, New Afrika is still causing ripples," Eugene mused, then got sly, "You know that cargo we brought into Oakland. Word has it they used only half of the grenades in the Nimitz attack. The other half's never been found."

"That's not how I meant it."

"Relax," Eugene smiled, "I'm not telling the Feds about you and Oakland. Nor am I gonna tell 'em about you and the riemanium. And not just out of principle. It'd be just my word, and that's worthless now."

"You knew I had the riemanium," Greg stated, suddenly tired of his own pretense.

"No other way I could figure it," Eugene said, "When Larry told me the two of you'd been contacted by Peregrine, well... Besides, I went over Larry's place with a fine toothed comb and never found it."

"So, it was you I almost caught in my basement," Greg grinned, ruefully.

"To be entirely honest." Eugene gave a dramatic pause. "Yes. My take from the Piccoli heist was to have been a million. With the riemanium, I could have negotiated for that from the government. Easily. Tell you plain, if I had that riemanium now, I wouldn't be sitting in this

SILENCE IN HEAVEN

jail."

"So, you're Peregrine, and you're Smoke." Greg enumerated, "You helped steal the Piccoli jewels, and you supplied plasma and arms to Oakland. Did you steal from the Coops? Honestly now. It's not me who wants to hang you."

"Yah," Eugene slumped back into his chair, "I stole from them. I was planning to use my cut of the gem job to retire to the Slovenian coast. Trieste. Definitely I wanted out of Alabaster, and the west coast. So when the deal fell through, I had no money. I started resorting to the line of work my brother taught me. It was a fast way to make money, and the coops were so damn simple to crack. I didn't want to spend more than a month hanging around. Not with the police and then the FBI looking for me. I got rid of my car in Oakland. But when I got back to Alabaster, I found out that both Sulawesi and the cops had raided my apartment. I had a little deal in the works for some traveling money, but things were closing in. I was gonna hide out and the bookstore score was gonna be my last job, just a little pin money until my travel funds arrived. Funny how that worked out."

"You were Smoke in the MDRG, and street fighter extraordinaire. Were you also BdN?"

"Yep," Eugene was weary, drawn, and humbled. "One of its founders. I helped write the Maximum Platform. When I started working on the Piccoli job, over a year and a half ago, I moved to Alabaster and dropped my formal connection with BdN. I helped get together MDRG as a local cover for some of my political activities. Told you my contradictions ran deep. I just didn't think you, or anybody else, would find out how deep."

"You were Michael Baumann to Rosanne Casey, and Eugene Wisdom to your brother," Greg marveled at the complexity to the man before him; commitment within betrayal within commitment within betrayal...a dense web of contradictions indeed. "So, what are you going to do now?"

"Take the consequences, I guess," Eugene sighed. "I have one long shot in all of this. The riemanium. They don't know that I don't have it. I'm hoping you won't turn it in, not just yet. If I'm real damn lucky, I can parlay something I don't have into something I want. My freedom. Otherwise, well, my brother Kenny, he's in jail. I guess I'll be in good company."

"So, this is the way it ends," Greg said.

"Not with a bang, but with a whimper."

"I wouldn't call having all your old friends and associates hating you and wishing you strung up as going out with a whimper."

"Most of those middle class fucks, I don't care what they think," Eugene growled. "They wouldn't know radical or proletarian if it came

291

up and kicked their fucking asses. My family was working class until I was 14. That's why my brother became a thief. All he had was a high school diploma and he wasn't keen on flipping burgers for the rest of his life. As a second story man he made good, quick money. Actually, he started in high school, 'cause even then he knew there was no future. Then, my old man, he got some luck, and our family was in money just when Kenny was teaching me his trade. My parents shipped me off to school to keep me out of trouble, but that didn't keep me and Kenny from staying tight. He's the one who turned me on to radical edge politics."

"You talk like being a thief is just another job," Greg noted.

"More respectable than most. I'd rather be a thief than a professor, a cop, a CEO, or a politician."

"Do you feel any guilt at all for ripping off the coops?" Greg pressed.

"Sure I do. I wouldn't have touched the coops if the Piccoli had gone down as planned. Fuck, I wouldn't even be here if that had happened. Look, stealing is what I do best. I never developed very many other job skills. The cops were on my ass. And the coops were just too easy. I started with regular businesses in Alabaster. But security at the campus coops was a joke, and the take was bigger. The temptation was there. I went for it."

"So, you did wrong."

"Sure I did wrong," Eugene nodded. "You bet. But I didn't do the most horrible thing ever imagined against humanity. That's how everybody on campus and in ASP is taking it. And that's a fucking petty bourgeois attitude if there ever was one. To be a fallen angel, you first have to have been an angel. I'm neither. Christ, radical politics and thievery have gone hand in hand for a long time; Spanish and Italian banditry in the 1800's, Pancho Villa, Gene Genet, Emmett Grogan. Bertolt Brecht once said that the good poet steals..."

"Times up," the guard said, all of a sudden, at Eugene's shoulder.

"Thanks for dropping by," Eugene stood and smiled, suddenly distant, "Thanks for giving me a listen."

"I might be able to do better than that," Greg said.

The idea of what do with the riemanium had jelled with the conversation; a solution that would also take care of the "Eugene Wisdom Problem." If all went as he envisioned. He was not sure he liked Eugene. But one thing was certain, that man now in prison had power. Magnetism, charisma, charm; whatever to call it did not matter. Simply put, he inspired deep emotion in people. The measure of hatred he now provoked spoke to the love he had fired in people's hearts; love transmuted to hate by betrayal. Not an unknown experience to Greg.

Eric had been right at the meeting that had decided what to do with Smoke. So long as he remained visible and close at hand, Eugene would be at the eye of a hurricane. And his former friends and associates were already part of that storm. Not only might Greg be able to dissipate the community's fury by removing Eugene from the scene, all without aiding the government much or destroying Eugene, but he could also settle the mess that the Solidarity Brigade had become. Actually, it was the only feasible solution remaining. One that he alone had the power to implement.

On the drive home, he took the exit to San Rafael for his metal yard where he purchased three large, thin sheets of smart steel. He left the sheets in the trunk as he caught his two Friday classes sandwiched about another secretive lunch. Sure enough, he found messages from David, Beth, George, Lori and Larry on his answering machine when he returned home, burnished smart steel under his arm. He did not bother to listen to any of them after the first few words. Instead, he carried both Lori's xeroxed roll of papers and the steel into the basement.

The bundle of xeroxes turned out to be several book and encyclopedia extracts, as well as more than one magazine article. Lori had done her homework. It seemed that a *Progressive* magazine article revealing hydrogen bomb secrets had been the one prevented from publication by a government obtained court order in 1979. On A-bomb construction, she included late 20th century articles from *Commonweal* through *Mechanics Illustrated* and *Science Digest* to *Time* and *Newsweek*, including an unlabeled parody on how to convert an antique, bullet-shaped hose vacuum cleaner into a fission weapon. Apparently, it was quite easy to make a crude but effective nuclear device, provided one had the bomb-grade material in hand.

Greg did not even use the computer, but sketched out a hypothetical A-bomb for riemanium's parameters in fifteen minutes. The rough mathematics for such a device took him twenty-five more. Only then did he don lathe gloves and goggles to confirm his design by creating it to spec and detonating it in the home 'some's virtual reality. He reassembled his design in 3D CAD-CAM, then projected it as hologram into the lathe's focus span.

Dry heat, brilliant light, the smell of ozone and sweat patterned the basement. He used the laser light to teach the steel to crease, fold and curve into place. An hour and a half of intense, concentrated effort later, he had the shiny shell and some impressive internals for a mock nuclear device. He welded all the segments together with a pure bead. It was 4 o'clock.

His bomb design was convincing, if he did think so himself. He had modified a simple A-bomb design, two plutonium pits driven together by an explosion, into a Siamese bomb construct. In his design, one Timpo explosion impelled two quarter pound riemanium pits down two

293

short, parallel tubes, each simultaneously striking against another fixed pit at their run's end. A double barreled bomb, with enough shielding between each pair of riemanium pits to prevent any premature critical mass. If one side misfired, the bomb still detonated. In theory.

Greg snagged a couple of rolls from the bread box, some cheese and an apple. He finished eating as he tossed his father's instamatic into the back of his spitfire, on top of the blanket covering the nuke shell, the Timpo grenade shell and the very full riemanium case. He drove at a maniac's pace, first to a convenience store for some instamatic film, and then to a side road he knew, a shortcut to Nicasio Valley Road. Once well enough along it, he pulled off to the shoulder, parked, and wrestled all of his props a short ways into the woods.

The day was drifting away quickly, dusk already columning among the dark trees. First, he took flashes pictures of the riemanium with the instamatic, then of the fake bomb. He concentrated on details for maximum effect, and finished off with the real enough grenade shell, encoring with a group shot to use up the last picture. While the photos developed, he loaded everything back into the car. The night congealed. Good enough, he thought to himself once more on the road, glancing at his snapshots. He dragged everything into his room, where he gloved and goggled into his pc's 'some to compose the Solidarity Brigade's final communiqué.

"...We the Action Cells of the Mexican Revolution Solidarity Brigade have constructed a working nuclear device. The explosive trigger to impel the riemanium to form one critical mass derives from the use of material from a Timpo grenade obtained from our New Afrikan comrades. All that is required to arm the weapon is to form the riemanium into the device. As you will be able to tell from the enclosed designs, we have enough riemanium for two such weapons.

"This Communiqué has NOT been issued to the media. The imperialist US government has 48 hours to release our Brigade's leader, Eugene Wisdom, provide him with a valid US passport and one million dollars in US currency, and fly him to France where he may apply for political asylum. Twenty-four hours after the international media has broadcast Eugene Wisdom's safe arrival in France, all two pounds of the expropriated riemanium will be returned. The lying bourgeois scum of the powers-that-be may provide the media with whatever explanation they deem necessary.

"If, after 48 hours, Eugene Wisdom is not released, this communiqué will be released to the public, and the neo-fascist US government will have 24 more hours to affect the release of our Brigade's leader. Popular pressure will thus be brought to bear upon the vile, scheming capitalist blood suckers and their political lackeys. If, after this second deadline, Eugene Wisdom has not been released, the nuclear device we possess will be armed and detonated somewhere in the San Francisco Bay Area during the following 24 hours. The US government will then have an additional 48 hours to release Eugene Wisdom before our second bomb is detonated somewhere in the continental United States..."

Greg added a few more rhetorical flourishes decrying the suppression and sell-out of New Afrika, supporting southern Mexico's Liberated Territories, and condemning the murderous FBI's Operation Anvil. But this was the gist of the communiqué. He laser printed the communiqué's text and compiled it with the photos, the computer printout of Greg's bomb design, and Lori's xeroxed article into a discreet manila envelope. He once more donned his leather flight jacket, and supplemented it with leather driving gloves. He kept the roof down during the ride into the city, and enjoyed the blustery wind stirring the clouds and stars above him. There was no problem in finding a 24-hour, do-it-yourself xerox shop in the heart of downtown. He color xeroxed the snapshots, then superimposed the communiqué's text over the color xerox. He included this with xeroxes of his xeroxes on bomb-making articles and the bomb design, all in another manila envelope he purchased from the shop itself. He carried out every transaction still wearing his gloves. He also bought a black marker at the register where he paid for it all. Then it was off to the downtown Civic Center.

Before leaving his car with the correct envelope, he scrawled FBI on the package. The plaza bore no signs of their riot less than a week and a half before. The Federal Building's drop box accepted his envelope. He called in his drop to the 800 Federal Crime Tip number from a pay phone off the plaza. It was back on the road to Alabaster then, where he hoped to salvage a few hours study.

Saturday morning, bright and early, found him in the campus library, where he stayed, except for a call to Peggy from a public phone to arrange a date for Sunday night. As it turned out, the 5 O'Clock News fairly bubbled over with the story.

"...Learned from sources who wish to remain anonymous that, at 2 p.m. today, Eugene Wisdom was placed, under guard, on an airplane bound for Paris, France. Wisdom, you may recall, is suspected of being the notorious Peregrine, the fifth man in the Piccoli jewel robbery, who remained at large until apprehended last Wednesday by the authorities. Arraigned for involvement in the theft and the murder of a Security Pacific guard, it is rumored that Eugene Wisdom knows of the whereabouts of the two pounds of bomb-grade riemanium, also stolen during the Piccoli robbery. Spokesmen for the Justice Department refuse to discuss whether or not a deal has been made for a return of the riemanium in exchange for Wisdom's release. Nor will Federal authorities confirm or deny that Eugene Wisdom is no longer in his cell

295

in the downtown San Francisco Correctional Complex..."

He imagined that the shit was hitting the fan as he left the library's VR lounge. Sure enough, when he got home that evening, his answering machine blinked, the tape full of messages from his former accomplices in the Solidarity Brigade, compounded by several faxes from Larry as well. In fact, the phone still rang. Grinning to himself, he shut off his answering machine and disconnected his phone. He studied for a time, then climbed down to the basement where he used several solvents and radical cleansing agents to scour down the riemanium casing, eliminating any clue of his possession of it, before wrapping it in a plastic garbage bag and stowing it back under his lathe. He set his radio alarm for early and tried to sleep,

The BBC World Service on Public Television at 4 a.m. had what Greg wanted to hear. After live satellite from New Delhi on India's drive into Tibet as an ally of the Russian Republic, the broadcast switched to Paris, the day patchy with clouds and the Arc de Triomphe in the background. The BBC reporter, Nijal Thomas, had a mini-mike in the familiar face of Eugene Wisdom. Sans glasses, he still had his trademark leather jacket.

"The French Government has already temporarily granted my request for political asylum," Eugene was saying, his toothy smile on screen, "For which I owe an undying debt of gratitude to my comrades in the Mexican Revolution Solidarity Brigade."

Nice touch, Greg thought. Quick as he could, he dressed, devoured a simple breakfast, and left a note for Andre proposing a 2 in the afternoon get together. He loaded the riemanium into his spitfire's trunk, and found the highway south for the East Bay. He dumped the riemanium, case and all, into the package box of the Richmond post office, called his action into the Federal Crime Tip Line once again, and headed back to Alabaster, dawn glimmering up in the west. It was over by 9 that morning, at least as far a Greg was concerned. On the ride back to Alabaster, public radio news featured Eugene once again, this time responding to a *Le Monde* reporter's question as to how it felt to have possessed the power of apocalypse.

"One man's apocalypse is another man's genesis," the thief replied. The vice president followed, reading a statement.

"...On Saturday, representatives of the Federal Government successfully negotiated a trade for the two pounds of stolen, bomb-grade riemanium. Yesterday, Eugene Wisdom, leader of the Mexican Revolution Solidarity Brigade, the group claiming to be in possession of the stolen riemanium, was flown to France where he has been granted political asylum by the French government. And, this morning, the stolen riemanium was returned to the government, ending the most significant case of internal US terrorism in this nation's history..."

SILENCE IN HEAVEN

Greg drove to the ASU campus before 11 on a hunch, the trees along the road singing with his freedom. There, on the Redwood Eatery's patio, Larry sat, dazed and confused, the ever present pitcher of beer at hand.

"Why the hell did you negotiate Smoke's release," Larry snarled upon seeing Greg, his snarl slurred by the alcohol. "He was a fucking thief. He stole from the businesses in Alabaster. He stole from the University. He stole from the coops. He stole from hundreds of people. Many of them your friends."

Larry's eyes were wild and bloodshot. His nostrils flared. Flecks of spittle collected in the corners of his mouth. It looked as if he had slept in his clothes for a week.

"Precisely because of what his presence is doing to us, even caught and in custody," Greg growled right back, "Look at you Larry. You look like a madman. It's as if Smoke was the carrier of some awful, rabid disease. His stealing, and his getting caught for stealing, infected all of us. Now we're all running around like mad animals, in a frenzy of incrimination and recrimination. We're tearing each other and our community apart. It's got to stop."

"You had no right to make that decision," Larry flared up, slamming his fist onto the table. "You had no right to turn over the riemanium to let Smoke go, scott-free."

"Goddamnit Larry, I found the riemanium. I kept it. And in the beginning of all of this, we made a deal Larry. I decide how the riemanium was going to be used. Remember?"

"You're full of shit," Larry halfheartedly tried to stand, only to collapse back into his chair. "George, David, Beth, Lori and me, we're meeting here at 5 today. We're gonna decide what to do about all this bullshit. You'd fucking better be here."

"Fuck you, Larry," Greg jabbed a finger into his friend's chest, "I'm not gonna be here. I'm sick and tired of all your 'more-PC-than-thou' attitudes. I'm sick of your kangaroo courts and your petty bourgeois naiveté and neuroses masquerading as 'people's justice.' I'm goddamned disappointed in you, Larry. You, if anybody, should be on my side. But instead, you're caught up in all of this garbage about Smoke. I'm tired of your snotty little feelings of betrayal. I'm not going to be here to play your stupid mind games. You can tell those ass wipes for me that if they lift even so much as a little finger to fuck with me, theirs and your involvement in this whole, stinking mess will be front page news. Count on it, asshole."

He stormed out of the pub then, the call of a raven from the trees above ringing in his ears. His and Larry's friendship was hitting bottom. He hoped it had not ended with that confrontation. But even if it had, Greg could do nothing. He had said what he needed to say. If telling the truth meant that Larry would no longer be his friend, then so much the worse for Larry.

He sat on a bench between a sculpture of plastic, glass and metal geometries stacked into an impressionistic female form, and one of a giant granite scarab, as he scheduled the rest of his day. He would make his call to Boston when he returned home, before his afternoon with Andre. The call would be neither easy nor short, even with the effort to renew an old, dear friendship that he had attempted to torch. He had tried to purge her out of his life from his bitterness, anger, and sense of betrayal, much as the Alabaster Left now tried to purge Smoke, and perhaps as Larry and the rest of the Solidarity Brigade gaggle were about to purge him. Life was too short to waste it in betrayal's consuming bitterness. Friends were too valuable in a life of suffering to banish them for their human frailties. What is more, he might need the friendship of his father, and that of Peggy afterwards, in order to be satisfied only with Janet's friendship. He took a deep breath, stood up and walked into the nightmare of daytime.

THIRTY-NINE

The Ulnapa Valley was called "Paradise on Earth" in tour guides of the 20th century. It fronted the Pacific Ocean with an ivory white beach protected by shallow offshore sand bars, the valley's swift stream bellying out into a small, clean lagoon alive with estuary life. That stream cascaded down in pools, rapids and waterfalls amidst luxuriant subtropical growth achatter with parrots and New World monkeys. The simplest of winding dirt roads ran along the bank. The valley itself was spacious. It climbed into the Sierra Madres to achieve temperate climes with a stunning view. On the north side of the Gulfo de Tehuantepec, it was firmly in revolutionary hands as one of the roads into Oaxaca. It was this back road that the combined US/Mexican counterinsurgency forces hoped to use in order to pincer off the Liberated Territories.

Ulnapa's beach swarmed with an armada of landing craft disgorging tanks, APV's and APC's, and thousands of soldiers. Tens of thousands of soldiers established their beach head without opposition, a fact that made everyone nervous. An assault column formed up, Mexican forces in front, and the US Marines in back to check any sudden retreats. It advanced up the road. Commandos fanned out across the valley behind this spearhead. Inevitably, as the assault progressed, this armed wedge narrowed. The forces at the head of the arrow outstripped the commandos. It extended too far into the territory to be taken, becoming exposed halfway up the valley.

The ZLF guerrillas opened fire from fixed positions up the sides of the valley with grenade launchers, mortars, and surface-to-surface missiles as well as assault rifles. The enemy now revealed, the

SILENCE IN HEAVEN

Combined Forces dug in, almost with relief. They would be pinned down only momentarily. They were decoys. Elements of the US Sixth Fleet offshore responded to their call to launch cruise missiles by the score. The missiles formed into diamond shaped clusters in two flying assault waves of deadly semi-intelligent weapons bearing death. As synchronized clusters, they used their sophisticated sensors to calibrate and triangulate on guerrilla positions.

The guerrillas were also decoys, by design. The first tight cruise wing transitioned over from ocean to land, and as it's clusters of component missiles started their subtle retargeting of flight trajectories, all followed closely by the second wing. ZLF forces set off three EMP generators obtained from San Cristobal. Five electromagnetic pulses per generator formed ripple patterns that overlapped with each other to create chance process patterns. The interference killed some and stunned all of the smart bombs. They began their fall onto the Ulnapa Valley floor, onto that idyllic stream and that simple road, and onto the Combined US/Mexican military units dug in there. The EMP bursts stopped so that the bulk of the still aware weaponry finally woke too late and too low. All they had time to do was to arm for impact.

Paradise was thus transformed into hell.

About The Author

G.A. Matiasz was born in 1952. He was a late hippie, and an early punk. He began self-publishing at 17 with a high school underground newspaper, and burned his draft card at age 18. Essays from his publication *Point-Blank / San Diego's Daily Impulse* have been reprinted in *Semiotext[e] USA*, the *Utne Reader*, and War Resisters' League's short-lived youth publication *SPEW!* Presently, he lives in Oakland, California, where he writes a regular column of news analysis and political commentary for *Maximum Rock'n'Roll* under the name "Lefty" Hooligan.

WHAT'S NEW
FROM AK PRESS?

SEPTEMBER COMMANDO: GESTURES OF FUTILITY AND FRUSTRATION

John Yates/Stealworks

ISBN: 1 873176 52 X / Price: $11.95 / Size: 8 1/2" x 11" / Pages: 96/ Illustrations: 100 / Cover: Full Color / Binding: Trade Paperback / Subject: Art / Politics / Satire

September Commando : Gestures Of Futility And Frustration is the second installment of politically charged satire, scrutiny and social commentary from John Yates' Stealworks graphics compound. Whereas his first anthology of work, Stealworks (also published by AK Press), was a retrospective of sorts that gathered together in a single archival collection previously published material, this latest edition comprises an entirely unpublished selection of incendiary new graphics.

Featuring over 100 of Yates' new designs, **September Commando** is a visual assault on all things bad. From our benevolent leaders on Capitol(ist) Hill to Twenty First Century Cops, from his "own" apathy-embracing (de)Generation X to the selling of Corporate American ignorance (and purchase thereof) to the (pocket) enlightened m(asses). **September Commando** picks up where Stealworks left off and from there on out it's a tri-lateral social injustice kill spree. To the barricades, and don't spare the hors d'oeuvre!

John Yates is a San Francisco-based "appropriations specialist" and "demolition expert" who spends an approximate 15-18 hours a day steadily going blind in front of a computer screen just to keep the revolutionary spirit alive and clocking.

Outside of his political graphics work he is the in country "design pillager" for the independent label Alternative Tentacles Records, where he struggles courageously to create the finest he can on a meager 14" monitor. He also runs a little "money laundering" operation called Allied Recordings (everything gets lost in the laundry), where he assists little known bands in becoming completely obscure. He is still in search of the elusive "free-time" concept.

"John could make millions designing commercial magazine ads but instead aims his skills at unmasking and destroying those very

mechanisms used to keep society obedient and asleep"
JELLO BIAFRA

COLLATERAL DAMAGE: AN AK PRESS READER

ISBN: 1 87317614 7 / Price: $12.95 / Size: 5 1/2" x 8 1/2" / Pages: 256 /
Illustrations: 30 / Cover: Two Color / Binding: Trade Paperback / Subject: Fiction /
Poetry / Art

Six years in the making, this outstanding compilation of cutting
edge writers, poets and graphic artists from both sides of the
Atlantic brings together some of the finest work that the under- and
over- ground has to offer. From Booker Prize winner James
Kelman to punk rock icon Ben Weasel, this stunning collection will
bring you up to speed with what's really happening in the world of
literature and the arts. Beyond avant-garde, **Collateral Damage** is
a must read for anyone serious about keeping up with life at the
dark end of the street. Incendiary, uncompromising, politically
hard-hitting, harsh and gritty, this anthology will rock your world.

Other contributors of note include: Kathy Acker, Stewart Home,
Peter Plate, G A Matiasz, Henry Rollins, Tom Leonard, Benjamin
Zephaniah, Linton Kwesi Johnson, Henry Normal, Clifford Harper,
Jim Ferguson, Jon Longhi, Tommy Strange, John Yates, Freddie
Baer, Winston Smith, and Norman Nawrocki.

TALES FROM THE CLIT: A FEMALE EXPERIENCE OF PORNOGRAPHY

Cherie Matrix / Feminists Against Censorship (eds)
ISBN: 1 873176 09 0 / Price: $10.95 / Size: 5 1/2" x 8 1/2" / Subject
Category: Feminism / Sex / Sexual Politics / Pages: 160 / Cover: Two
Color / Binding: Trade Paperback

Tales From The Clit – True stories by some of the world's
most pro-sex feminists. These women have provided intimate,
anti-censorship essays, to re-establish the idea that equality of the
sexes doesn't have to mean no sex.

From intimate sexual experiences and physical perception
through to the academic arena, this groundbreaking volume documents women's POSITIVE thoughts, uses,and desires for, with,
and about pornography. Essays include such diverse topics as
how the author's discovered porn, what it means to a blind and
deaf woman, running a sex magazine, starting a sex shop, and to
what the contributors would actually LIKE to see. Compiled by
Feminists Against Censorship, **Tales From The Clit** is erotically
and intellectually arousing.

Contributors include: Deborah Ryder, Jan Grossman, Sue
Raye, Linzi Drew, Frances Scally, Annie Sprinkle, Tuppy Owens,
Lucy Williams, Nettie Pollard, Avedon Carol, Scarlet Harlot, and
Caroline Bottomley.

REBEL MOON: ANARCHIST RANTS AND POEMS
Norman Nawrocki
ISBN : 1 873176 08 2 / Price: $9.95 / Size: 5 1/2" x 8 1/2" / Pages: 112 /
Illustrations: 6 / Cover: Two color / Binding: Trade Paperback / Subject: Current
Affairs / Politics / Poetry

Norman Nawrocki's riotous first book, **Rebel Moon:
Anarchist Rants And Poems**, allows this international cabaret
artist and activist to let loose a collection of dangerous poems and
forbidden words on paper.

As frontman/bigmouth for Montreal's acclaimed anarcho
"rebel news orchestra", RHYTHM ACTIVISM, Nawrock's powerful
spoken word pieces are known worldwide through the bands 30
releases and thousands of live shows across Canada, the USA
and Europe. Much of his material has been used to help organise
and empower audiences around specific issues of social justice.

Rebel Moon samples the best of this work from 1986-
1996, including pieces like the anti-landlord 'Squat The City'; the
dreamlike '7-11 Heaven' and the pro-choice 'Soldiers For Jesus'.

As always, Nawrocki offers biting social critiques backed
up by an anarchist alternative: a vision of a world without bosses,
the State, lousy lovers or supermarket ripoffs. And he doesn't hesi-
tate to translate popular, direct action solutions into hardcore poet-
ics.

Witty, informative, hard-hitting and entertaining, **Rebel
Moon** helps catapult a culture of resistance into the 21st century.
"Your Black Flag poem blew me away."
                    LAWRENCE FERLINGHETTI
"His poems never just sit there, they CRANK."
                    OPTION
"Subversively powerful."
                    THE GLOBE & MAIL
"The Brecht/Weill combo for the 1990s."
          BRAVE NEW WAVES, CBC NATIONAL RADIO
*"Transforms such lyrics notions as poetry in motion into poetry of
action."*
                    MONTREAL MIRROR

THE SPANISH ANARCHISTS: THE HEROIC YEARS 1868-1936
Murray Bookchin
ISBN : 1 873176 04 X / Price: $19.95 / Size: 5 1/2" x 8 1/2" / Pages: 384 / Binding:
Trade Paperback / Cover: Two Color / Illustrations: 10 Photographs / Subject:
History/Politics/Anarchism

A long-awaited new edition of the seminal history of
Spanish Anarchism. Hailed as a masterpiece, it includes a new
prefatory essay by the author.